# PRINCESS DECOMPOSIA and COUNT SPATULA

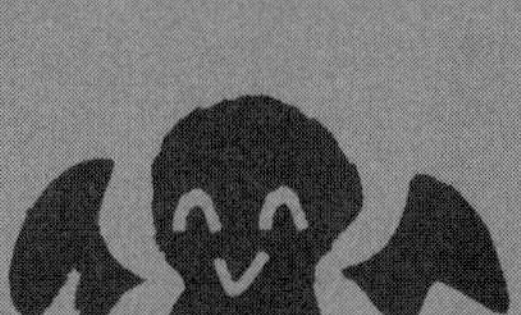

# PRINCESS DECOMPOSIA and COUNT SPATULA

## ~ANDI WATSON~

:01

First Second
New York

**First Second**

Copyright © 2015 by Andi Watson
Published by First Second
First Second is an imprint of Roaring Brook Press,
a division of Holtzbrinck Publishing Holdings Limited Partnership
175 Fifth Avenue, New York, New York 10010
All rights reserved

Cataloging-in-Publication Data is on file at the Library of Congress

Paperback ISBN: 978-1-62672-149-4
Hardcover ISBN: 978-1-62672-275-0

First Second books may be purchased for business or promotional use.
For information on bulk purchases please contact Macmillan Corporate
and Premium Sales Department at (800) 221-7945 x5442 or by email at
specialmarkets@macmillan.com.

First edition 2015

Book design by Colleen AF Venable
Printed in the United States of America

Paperback: 10 9 8 7 6 5 4 3 2 1
Hardcover: 10 9 8 7 6 5 4 3 2 1

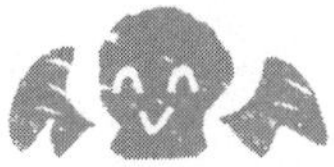

For P,
Princess Decomposia
to my
Count Spatula

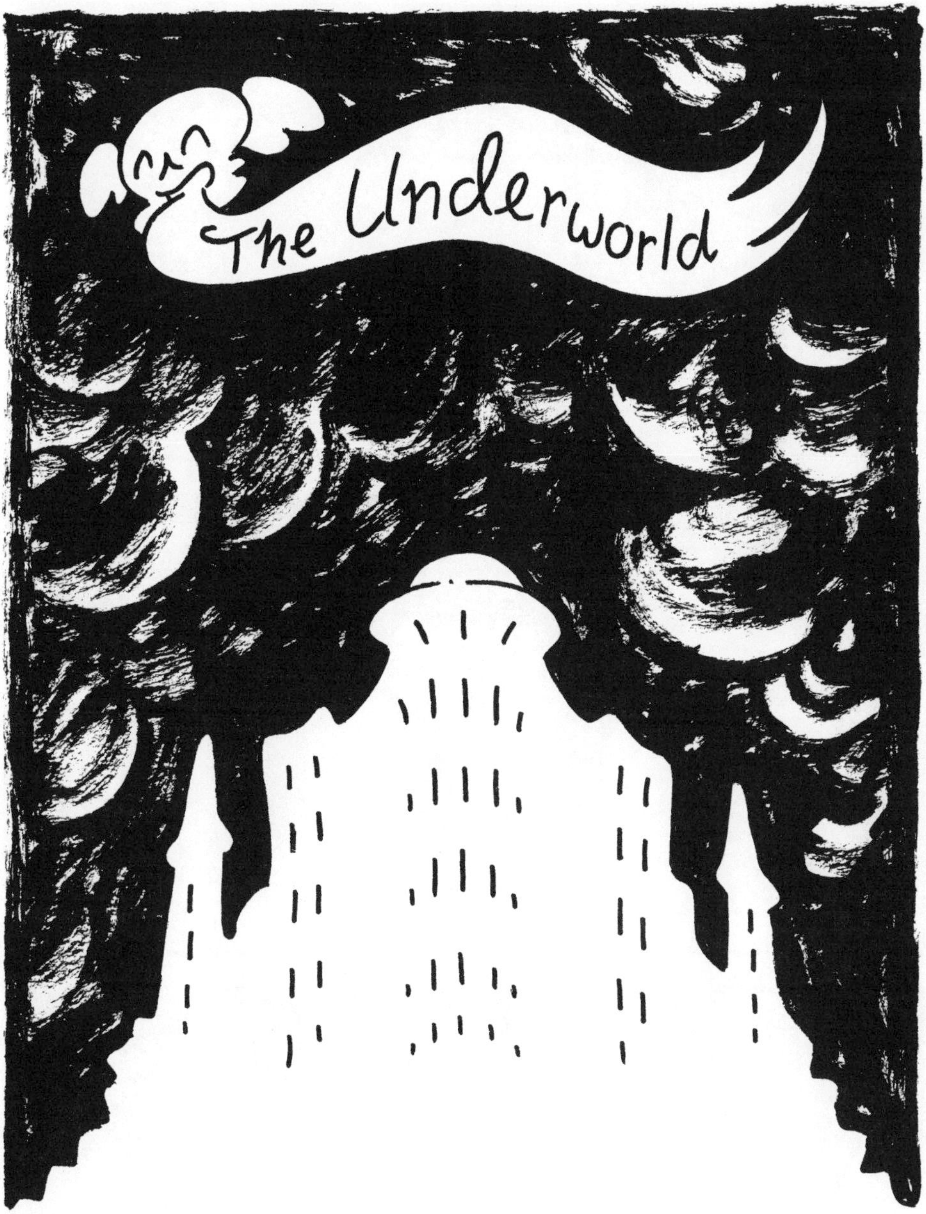
The Underworld

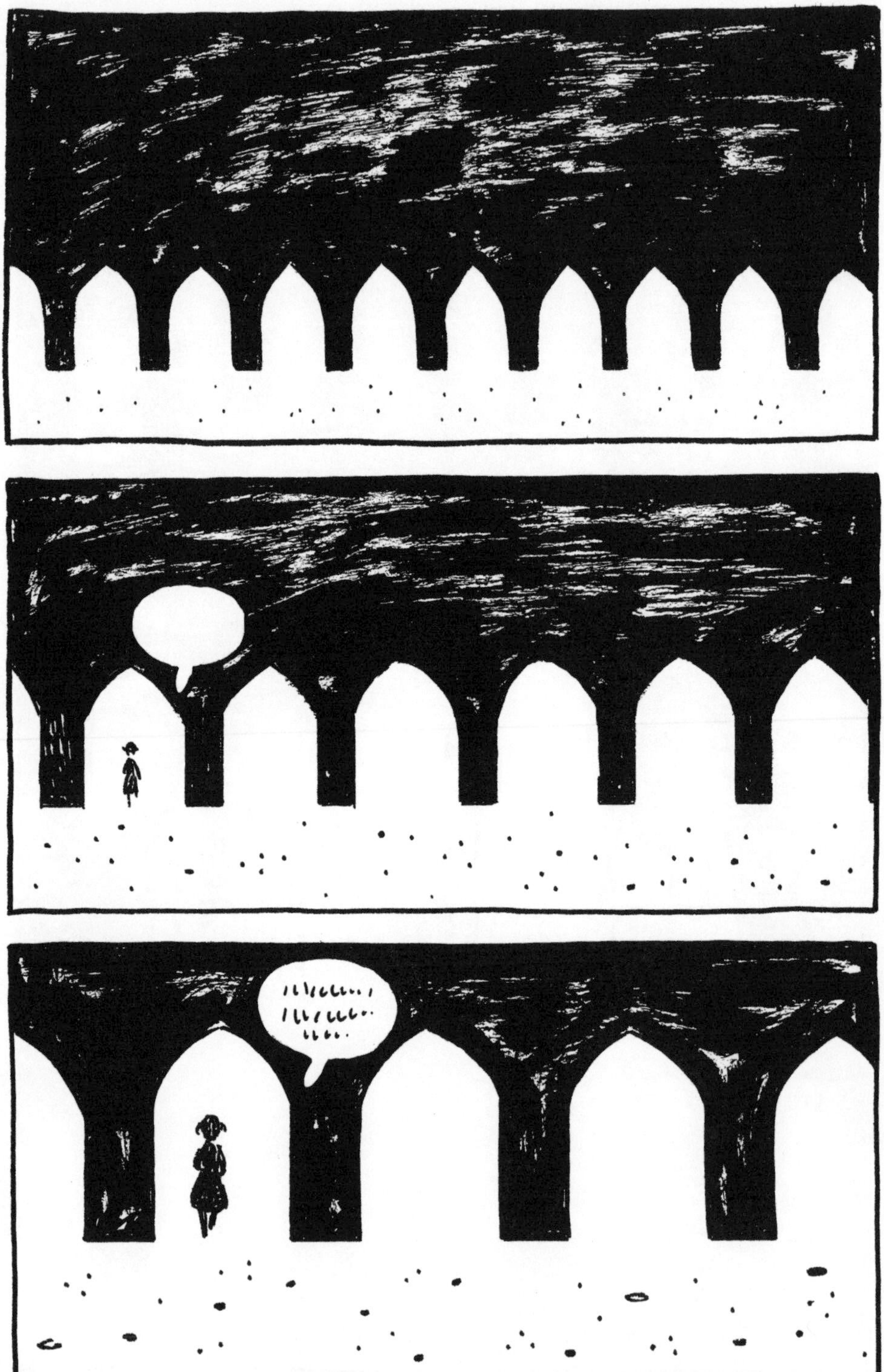

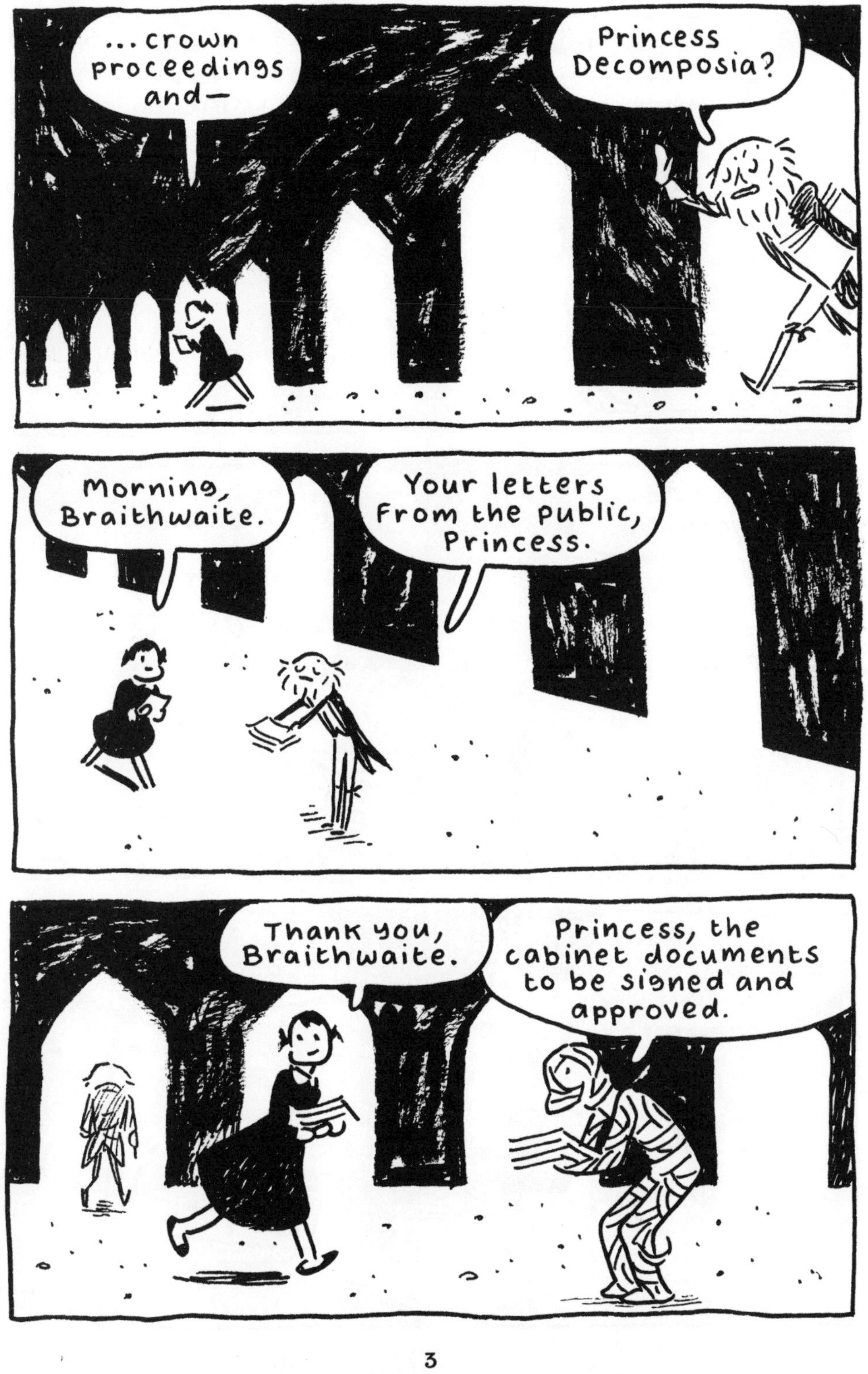
...crown proceedings and—
Princess Decomposia?
Morning, Braithwaite.
Your letters from the public, Princess.
Thank you, Braithwaite.
Princess, the cabinet documents to be signed and approved.

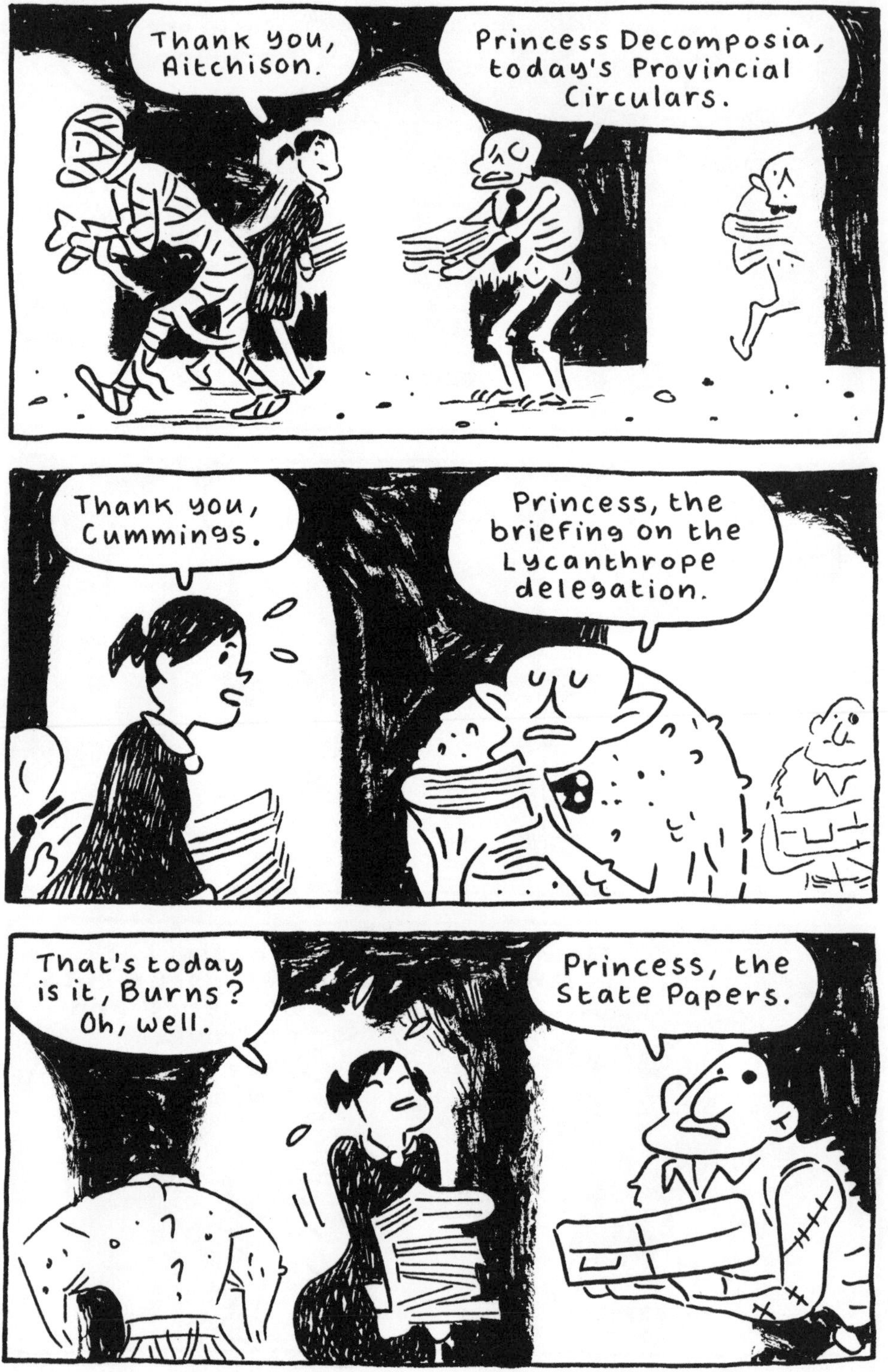
Thank you, Aitchison.
Princess Decomposia, today's Provincial Circulars.
Thank you, Cummings.
Princess, the briefing on the Lycanthrope delegation.
That's today is it, Burns? Oh, well.
Princess, the State Papers.

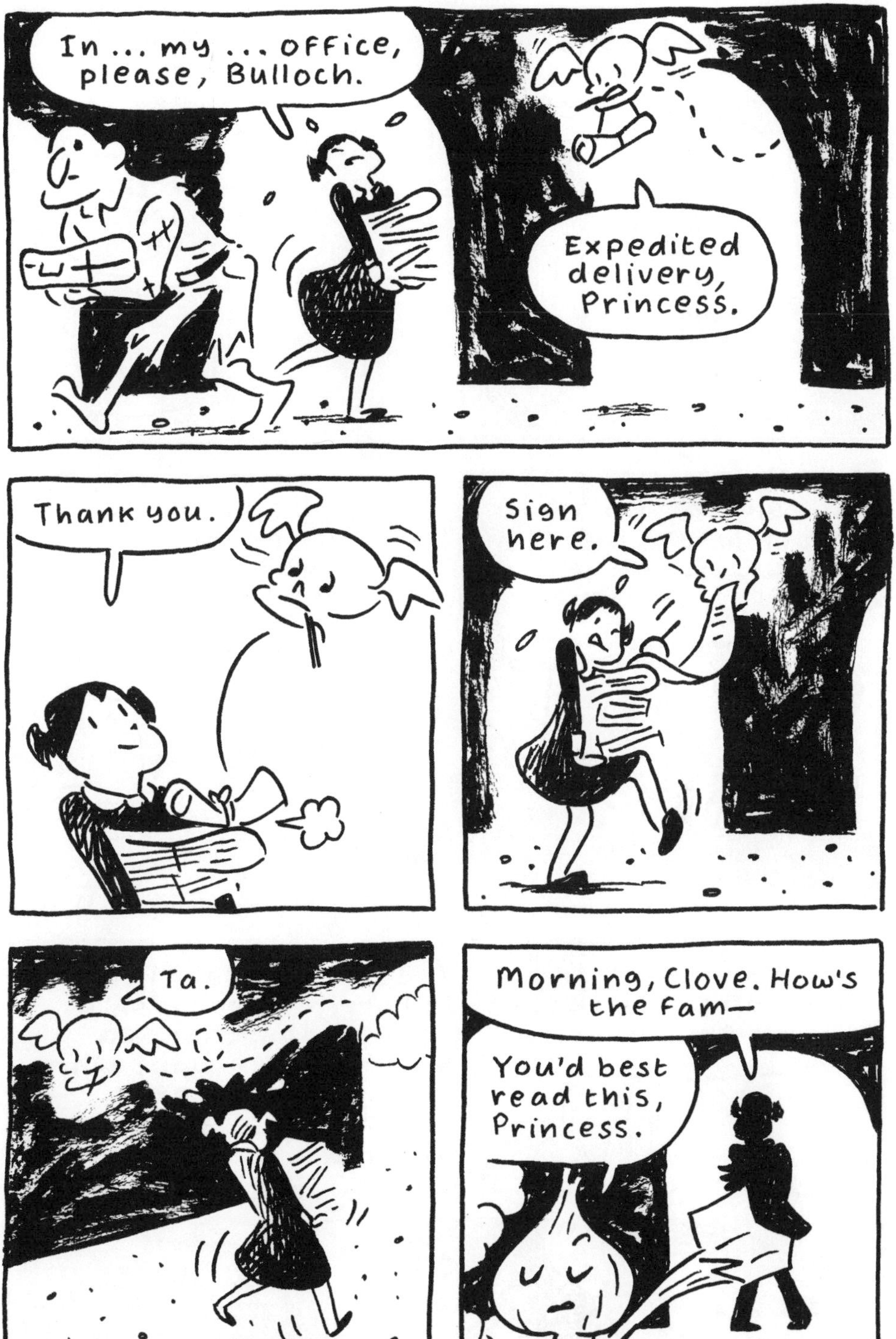
In ... my ... office, please, Bulloch.
Expedited delivery, Princess.
Thank you.
Sign here.
Ta.
Morning, Clove. How's the fam—
You'd best read this, Princess.

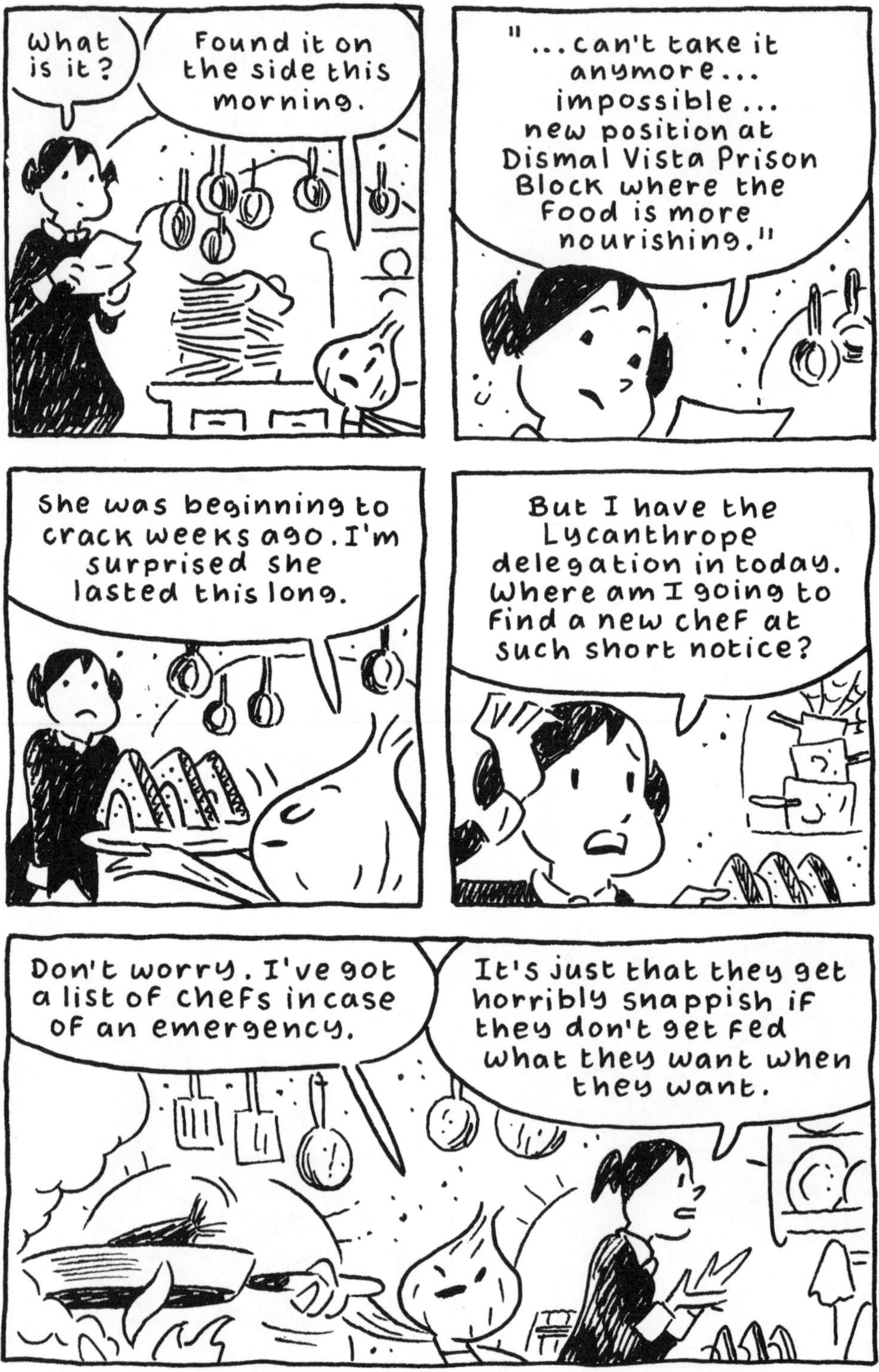
What is it?
Found it on the side this morning.
"...can't take it anymore... impossible... new position at Dismal Vista Prison Block where the food is more nourishing."
She was beginning to crack weeks ago. I'm surprised she lasted this long.
But I have the Lycanthrope delegation in today. Where am I going to find a new chef at such short notice?
Don't worry. I've got a list of chefs in case of an emergency.
It's just that they get horribly snappish if they don't get fed what they want when they want.

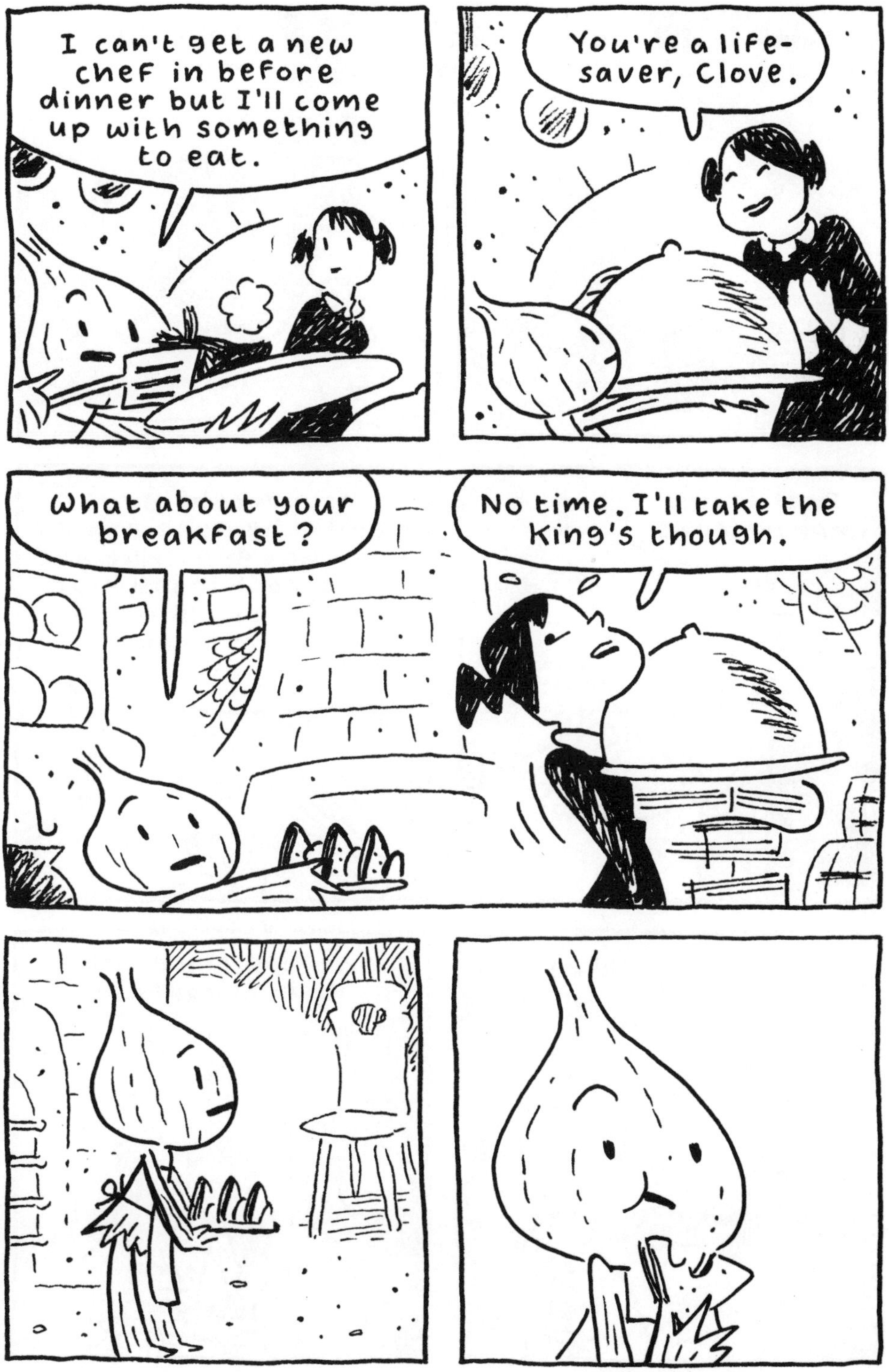
I can't get a new chef in before dinner but I'll come up with something to eat.
You're a life-saver, Clove.
What about your breakfast?
No time. I'll take the King's though.

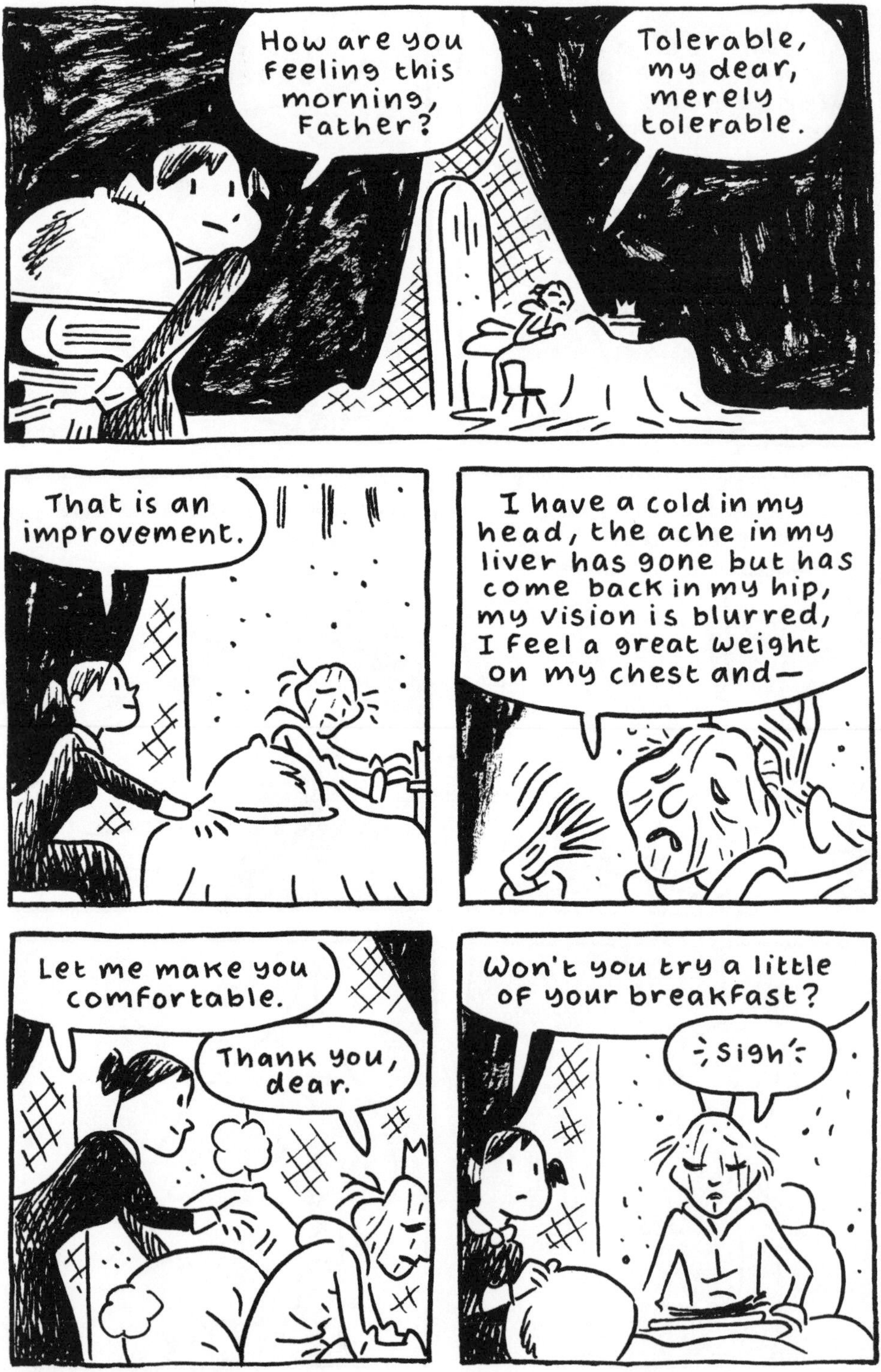
How are you feeling this morning, Father?
Tolerable, my dear, merely tolerable.
That is an improvement.
I have a cold in my head, the ache in my liver has gone but has come back in my hip, my vision is blurred, I feel a great weight on my chest and—
Let me make you comfortable.
Thank you, dear.
Won't you try a little of your breakfast?
Sigh

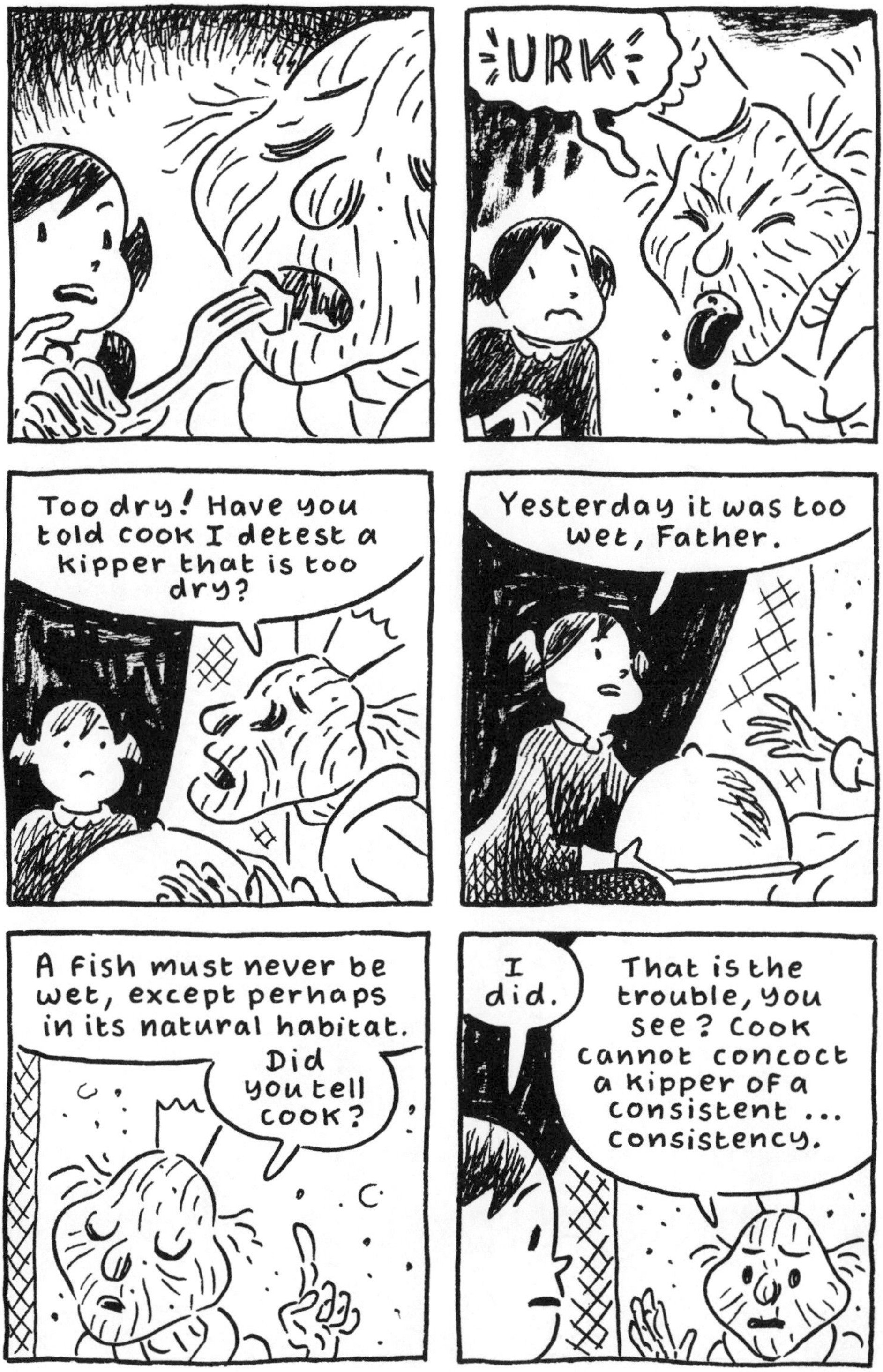
URK
Too dry! Have you told cook I detest a kipper that is too dry?
Yesterday it was too wet, Father.
A fish must never be wet, except perhaps in its natural habitat.
Did you tell cook?
I did.
That is the trouble, you see? Cook cannot concoct a kipper of a consistent ... consistency.

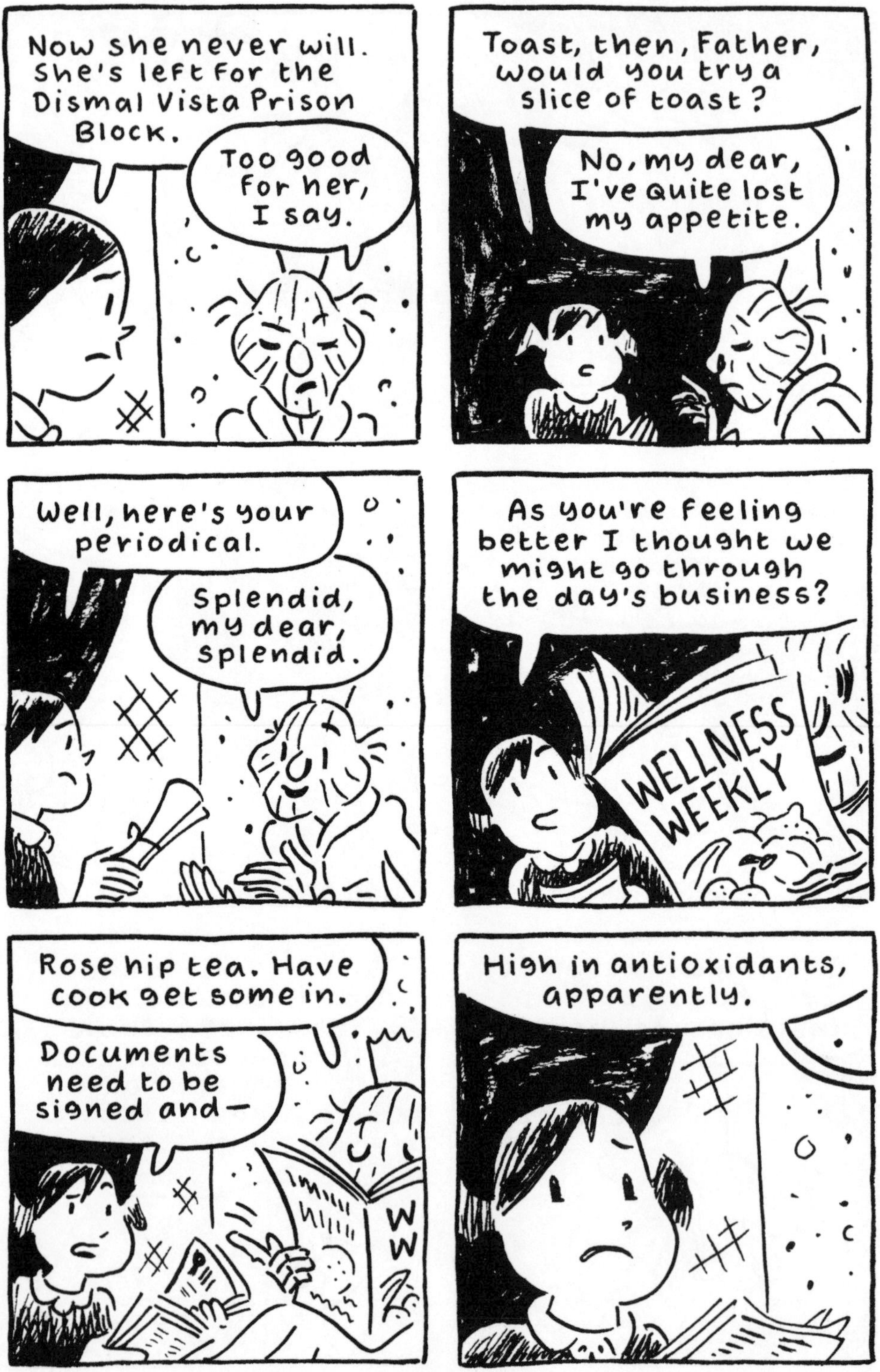
Now she never will. She's left for the Dismal Vista Prison Block.
Too good for her, I say.
Toast, then, Father, would you try a slice of toast?
No, my dear, I've quite lost my appetite.
Well, here's your periodical.
Splendid, my dear, splendid.
As you're feeling better I thought we might go through the day's business?
WELLNESS WEEKLY
Rose hip tea. Have cook get some in.
Documents need to be signed and—
WW
High in antioxidants, apparently.

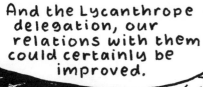
And the Lycanthrope delegation, our relations with them could certainly be improved.

I'm really quite exhausted, my dear. It's been a demanding morning.

Dead Thursday's coming up and we'll need to make arrangements if you're to—

I'm feeling rather chill and my hip... oooh.

might a walk around the—

No, my dear. I had a terribly disturbed night and my head is pounding.

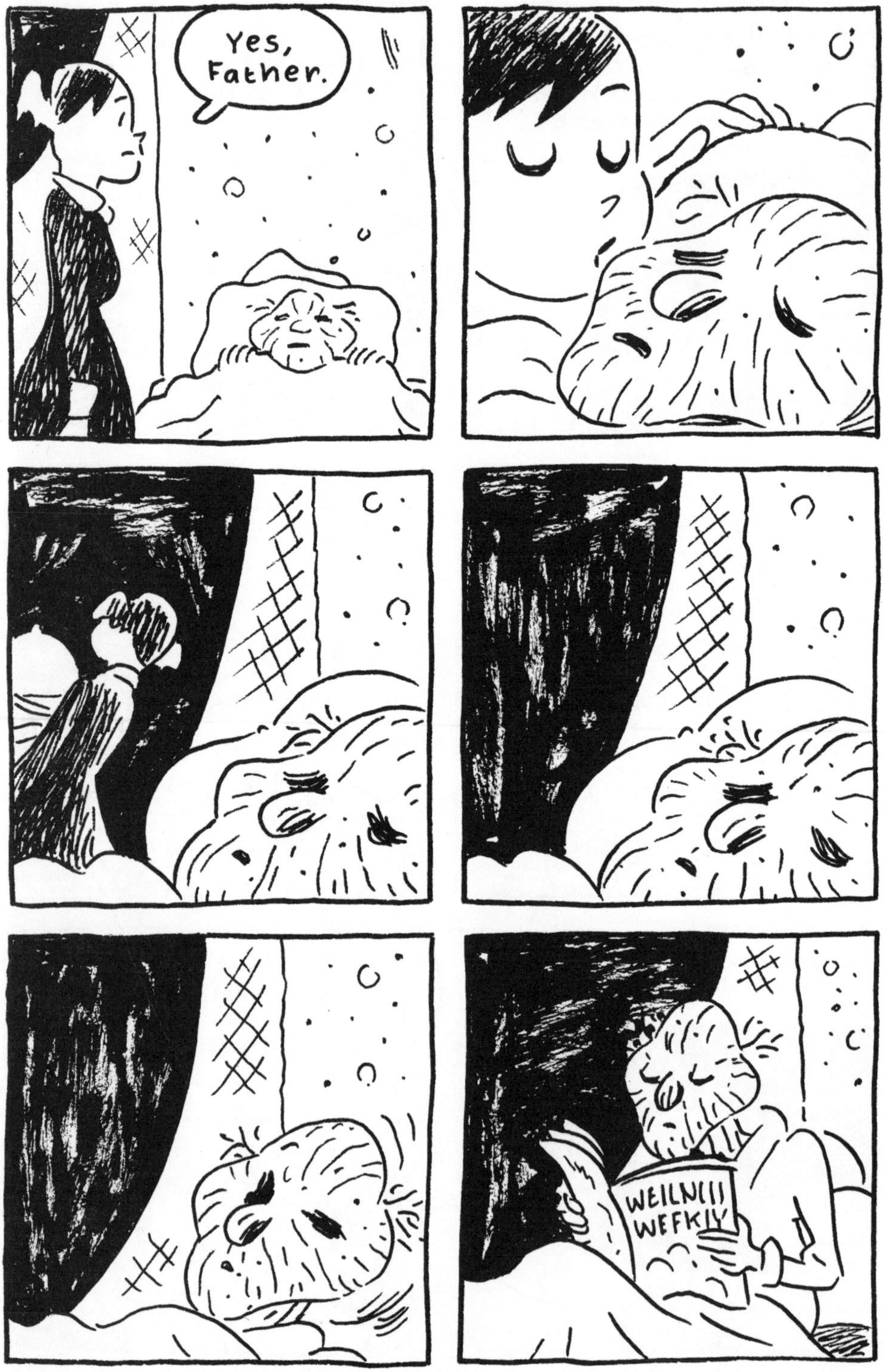
Yes, Father.

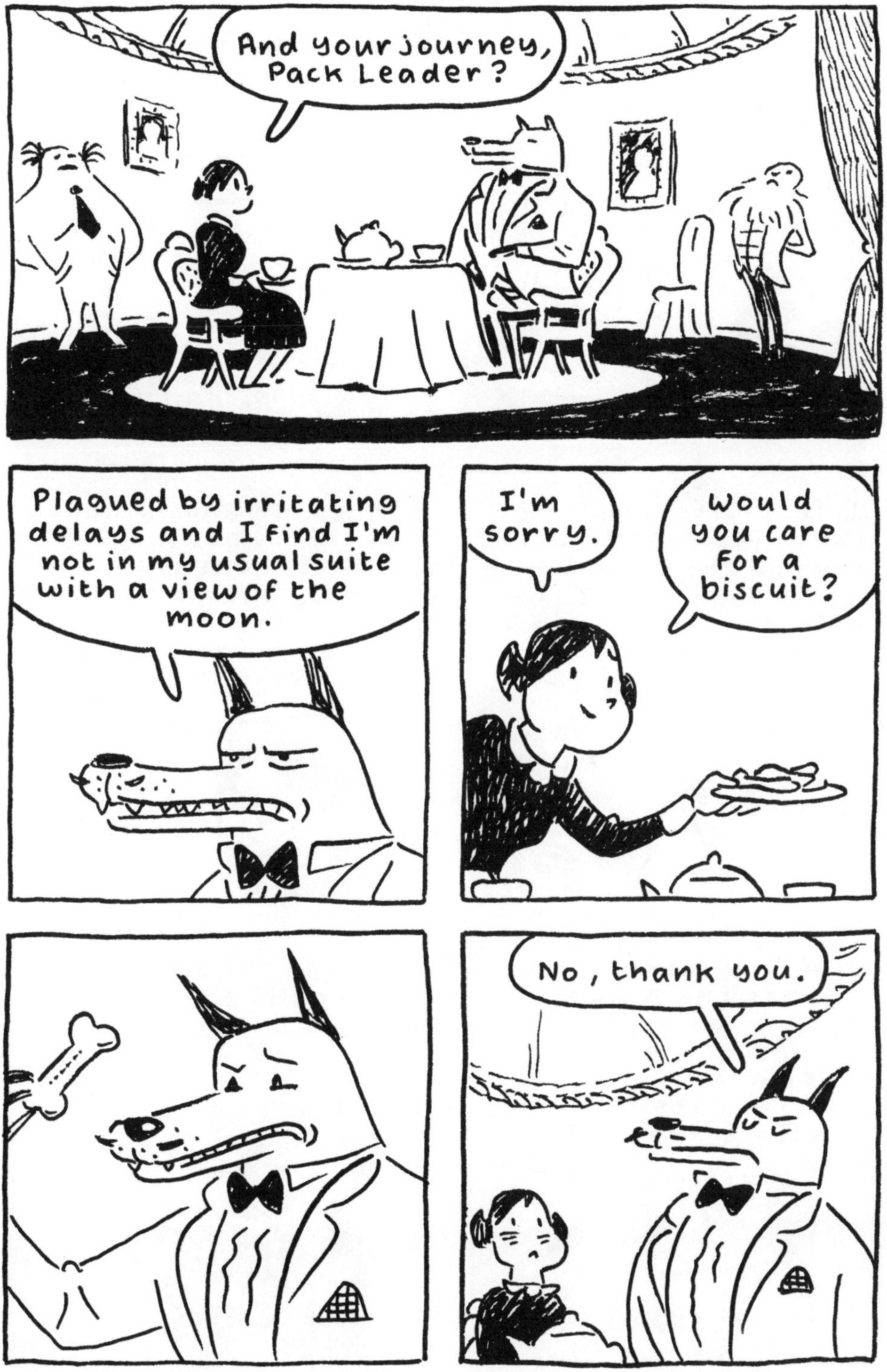
And your journey, Pack Leader?
Plagued by irritating delays and I find I'm not in my usual suite with a view of the moon.
I'm sorry.
Would you care for a biscuit?
No, thank you.

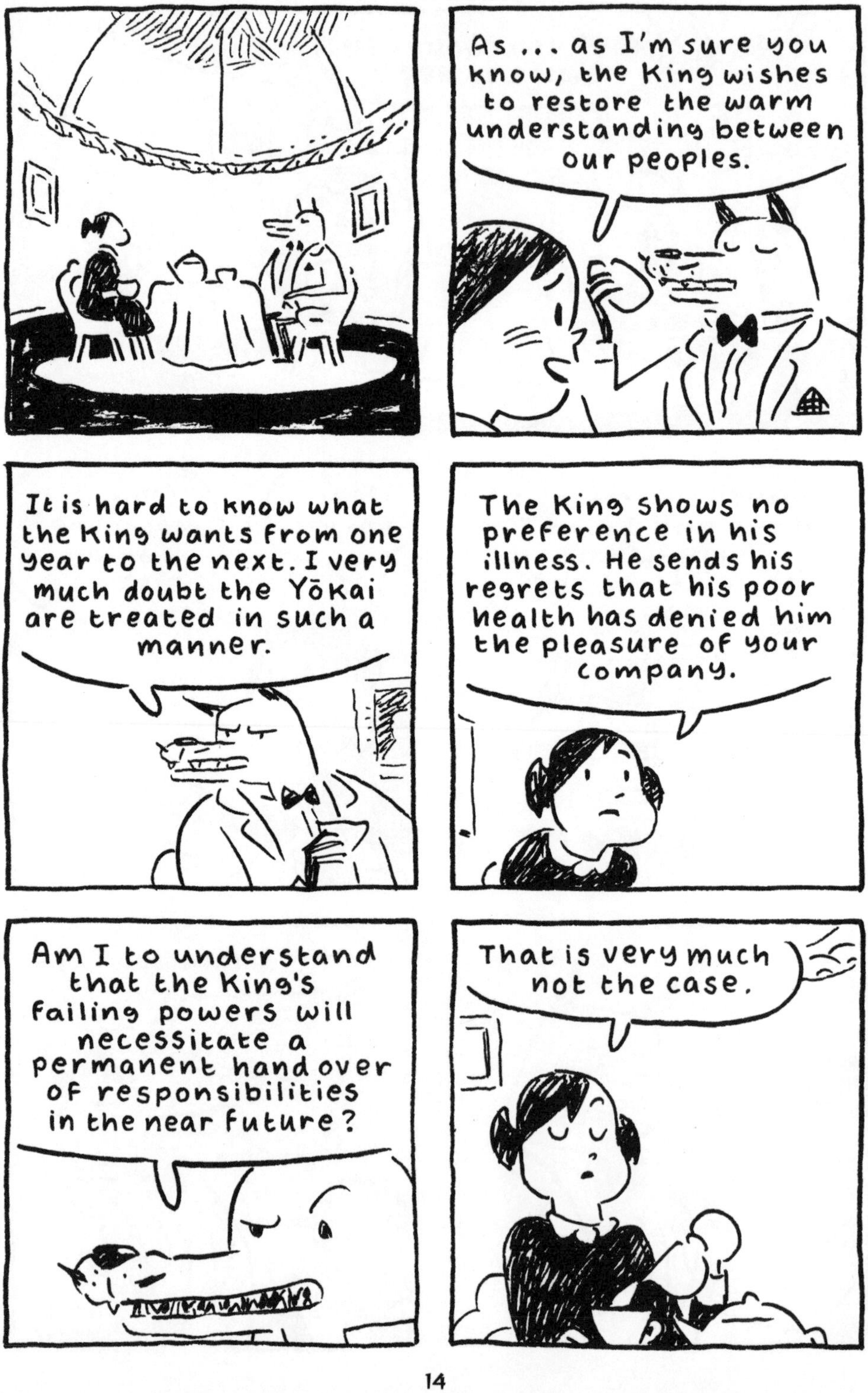
As ... as I'm sure you know, the King wishes to restore the warm understanding between our peoples.
It is hard to know what the King wants from one year to the next. I very much doubt the Yōkai are treated in such a manner.
The King shows no preference in his illness. He sends his regrets that his poor health has denied him the pleasure of your company.
Am I to understand that the King's failing powers will necessitate a permanent hand over of responsibilities in the near future?
That is very much not the case.

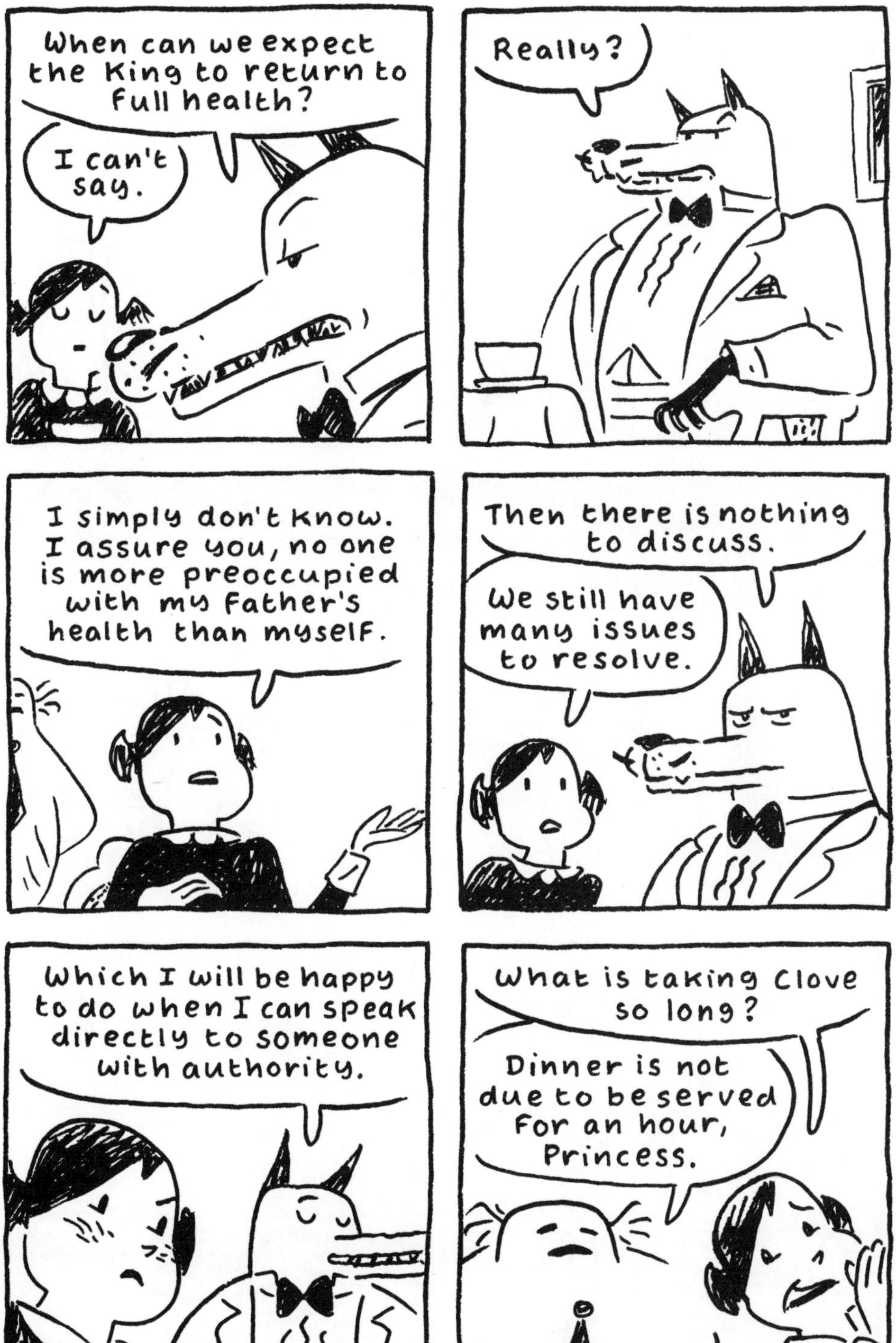
When can we expect the King to return to full health?
I can't say.
Really?
I simply don't know. I assure you, no one is more preoccupied with my father's health than myself.
Then there is nothing to discuss.
We still have many issues to resolve.
Which I will be happy to do when I can speak directly to someone with authority.
What is taking Clove so long?
Dinner is not due to be served for an hour, Princess.

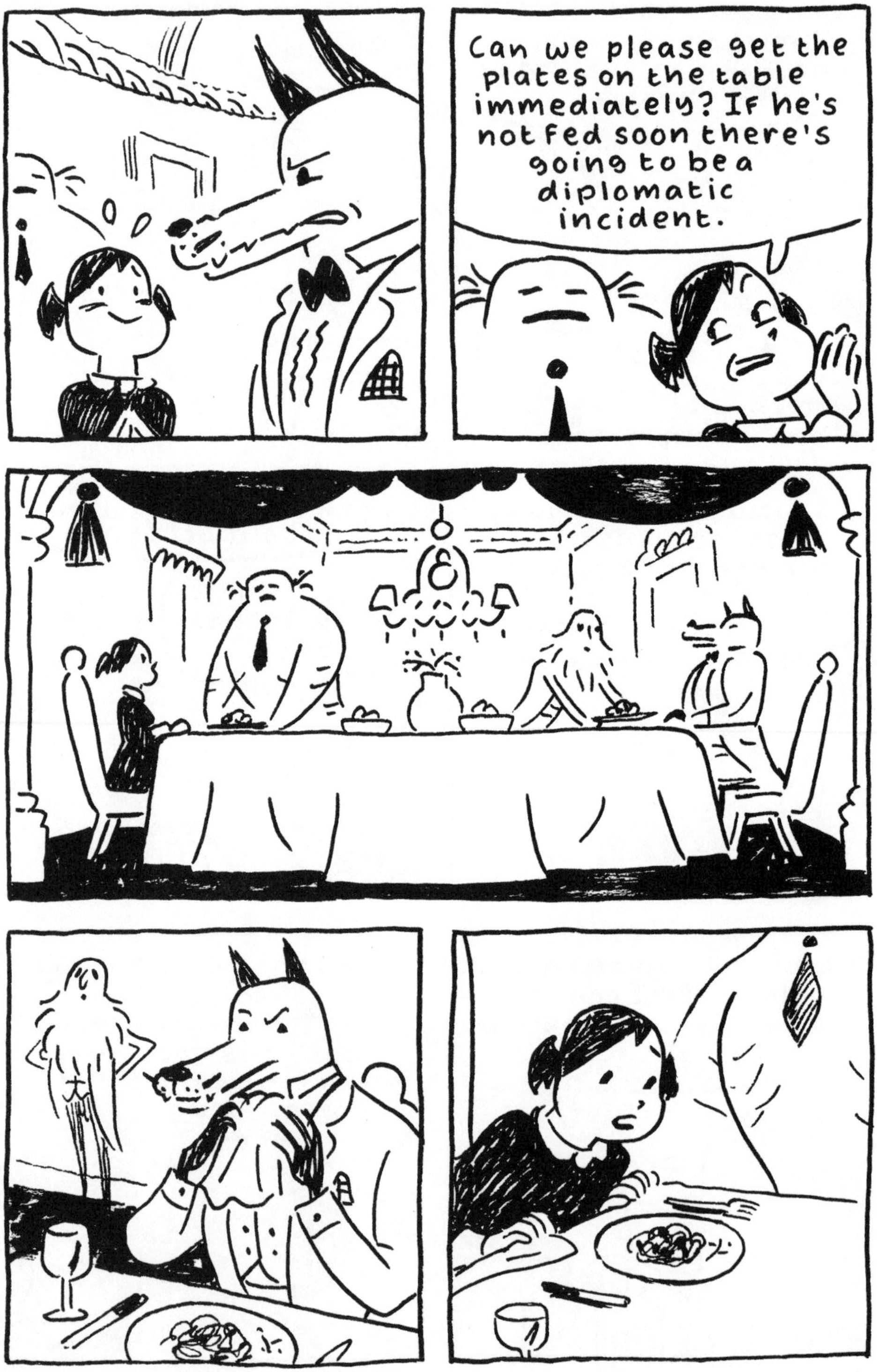
Can we please get the plates on the table immediately? If he's not fed soon there's going to be a diplomatic incident.

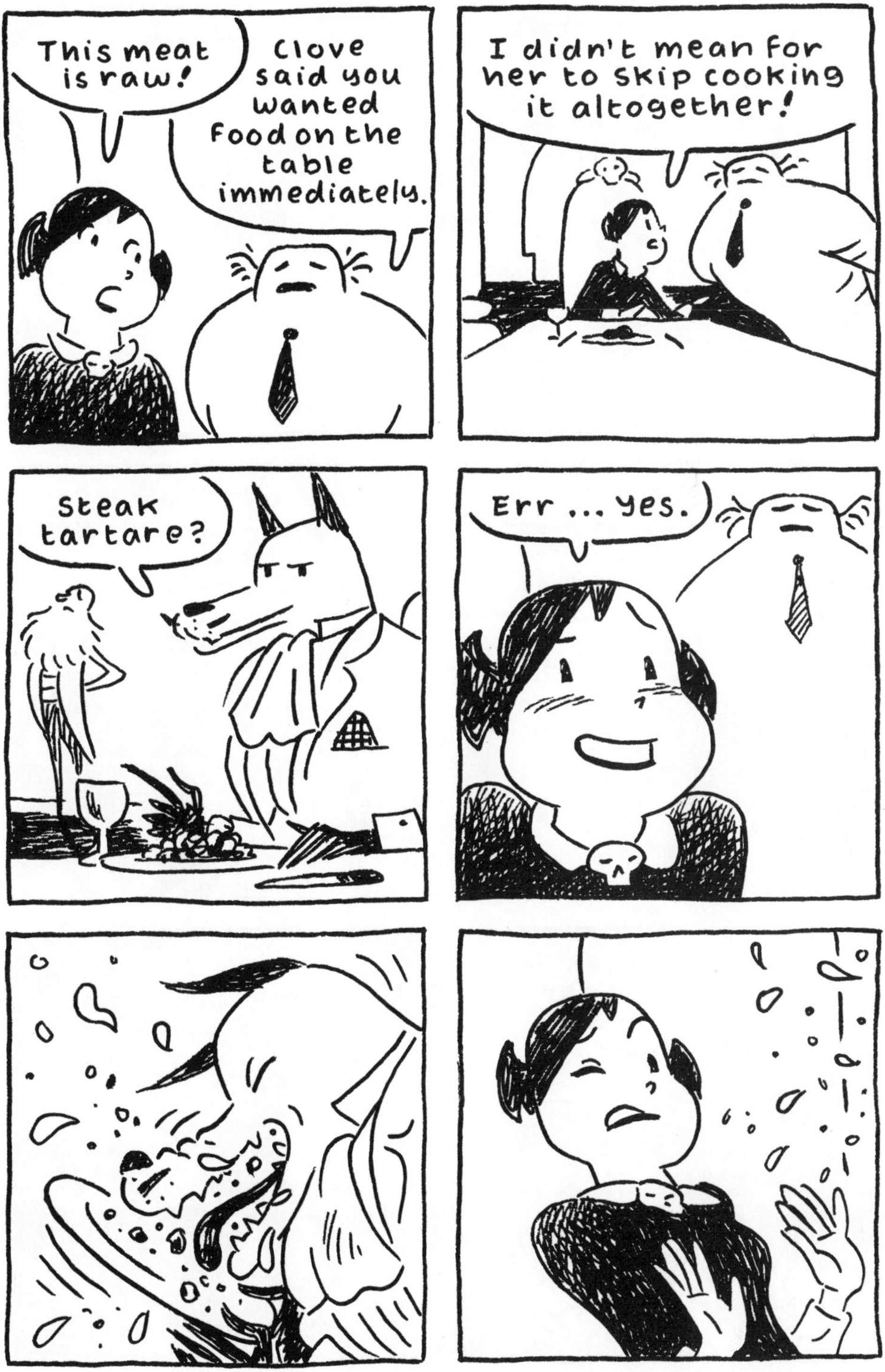
This meat is raw!
Clove said you wanted food on the table immediately.
I didn't mean for her to skip cooking it altogether!
Steak tartare?
Err ... yes.

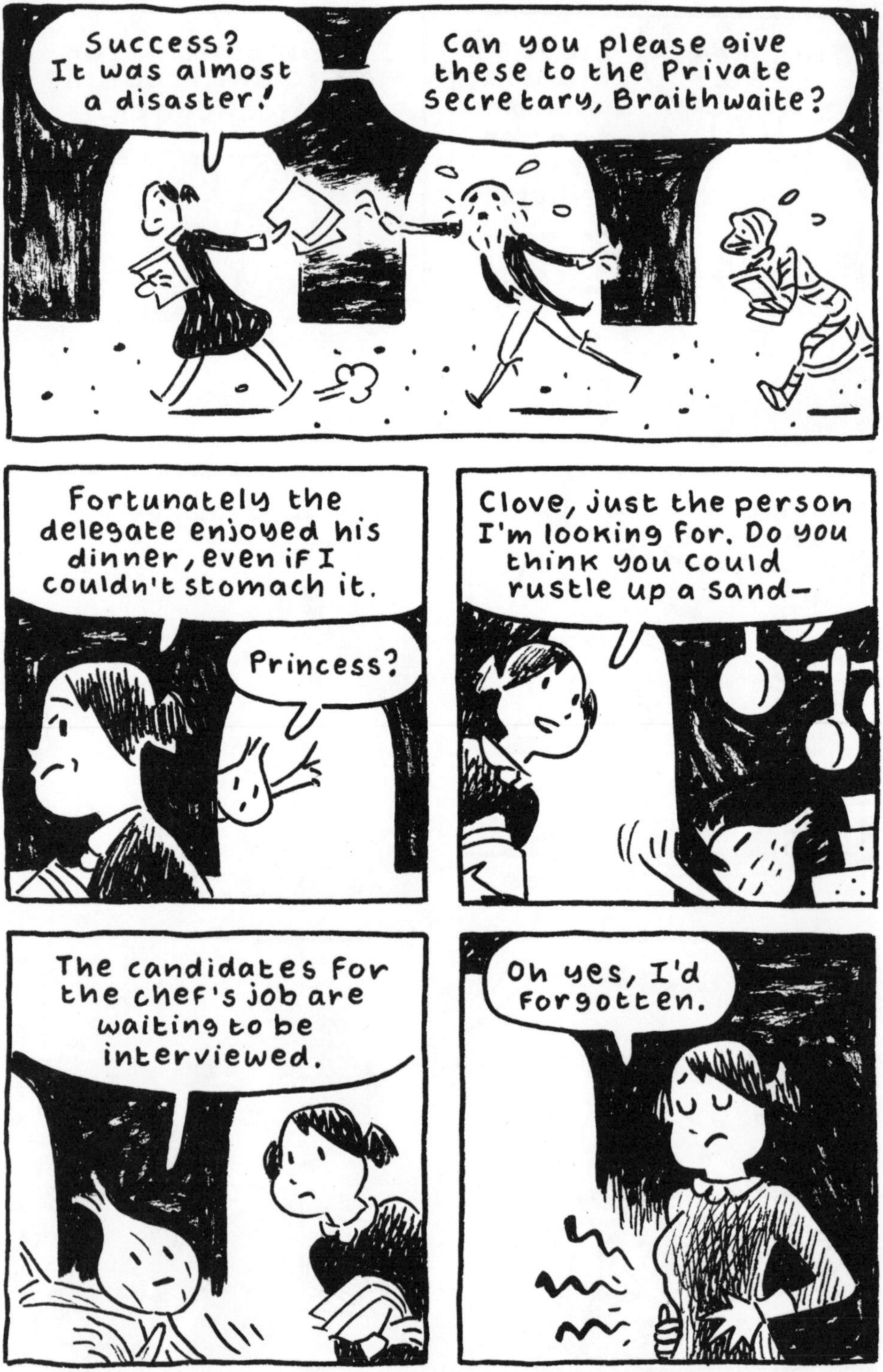
Success? It was almost a disaster!
Can you please give these to the Private Secretary, Braithwaite?
Fortunately the delegate enjoyed his dinner, even if I couldn't stomach it.
Princess?
Clove, just the person I'm looking for. Do you think you could rustle up a sand—
The candidates for the chef's job are waiting to be interviewed.
Oh yes, I'd forgotten.

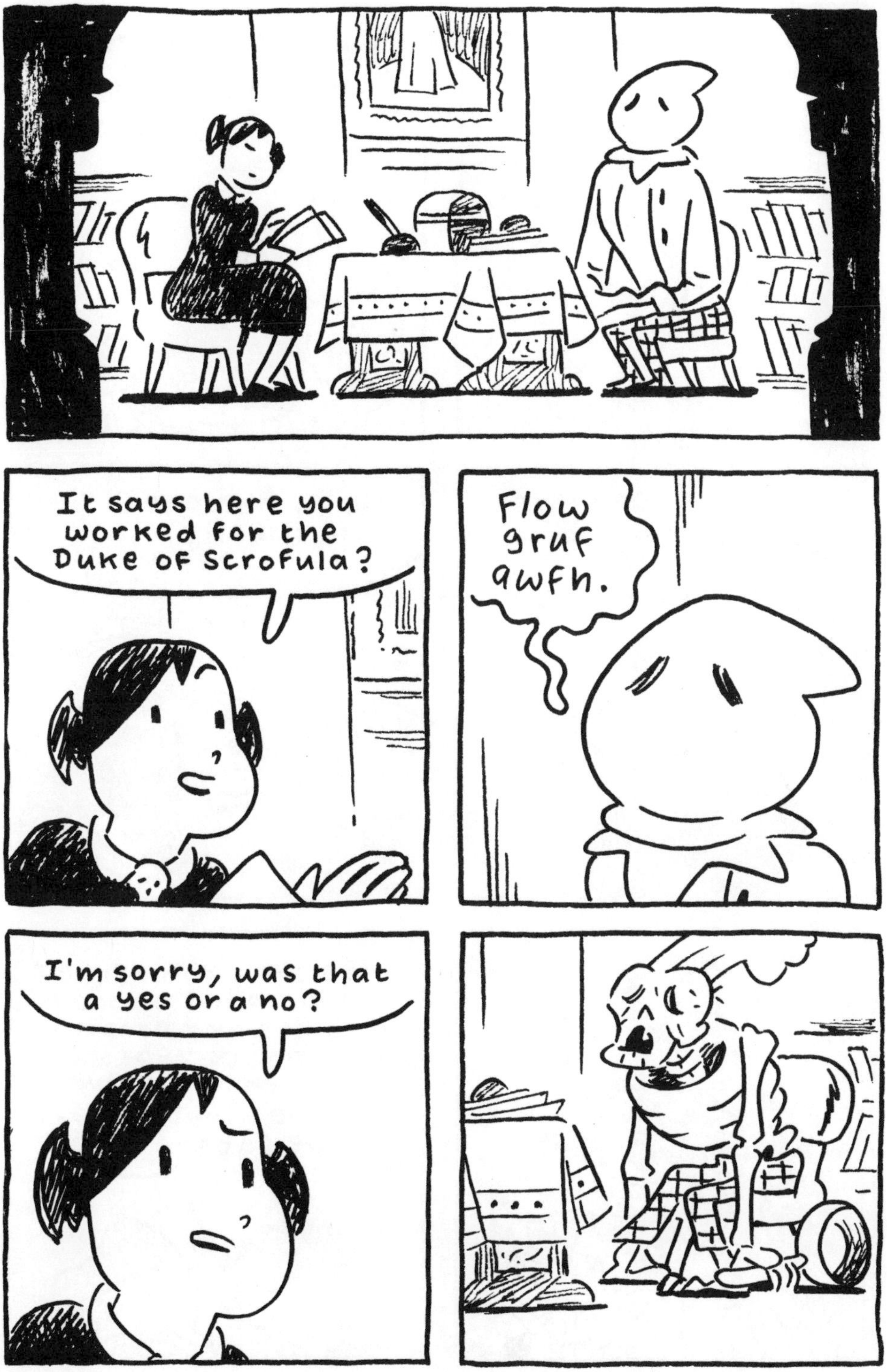
It says here you worked for the Duke of Scrofula?
Flow gruf awfn.
I'm sorry, was that a yes or a no?

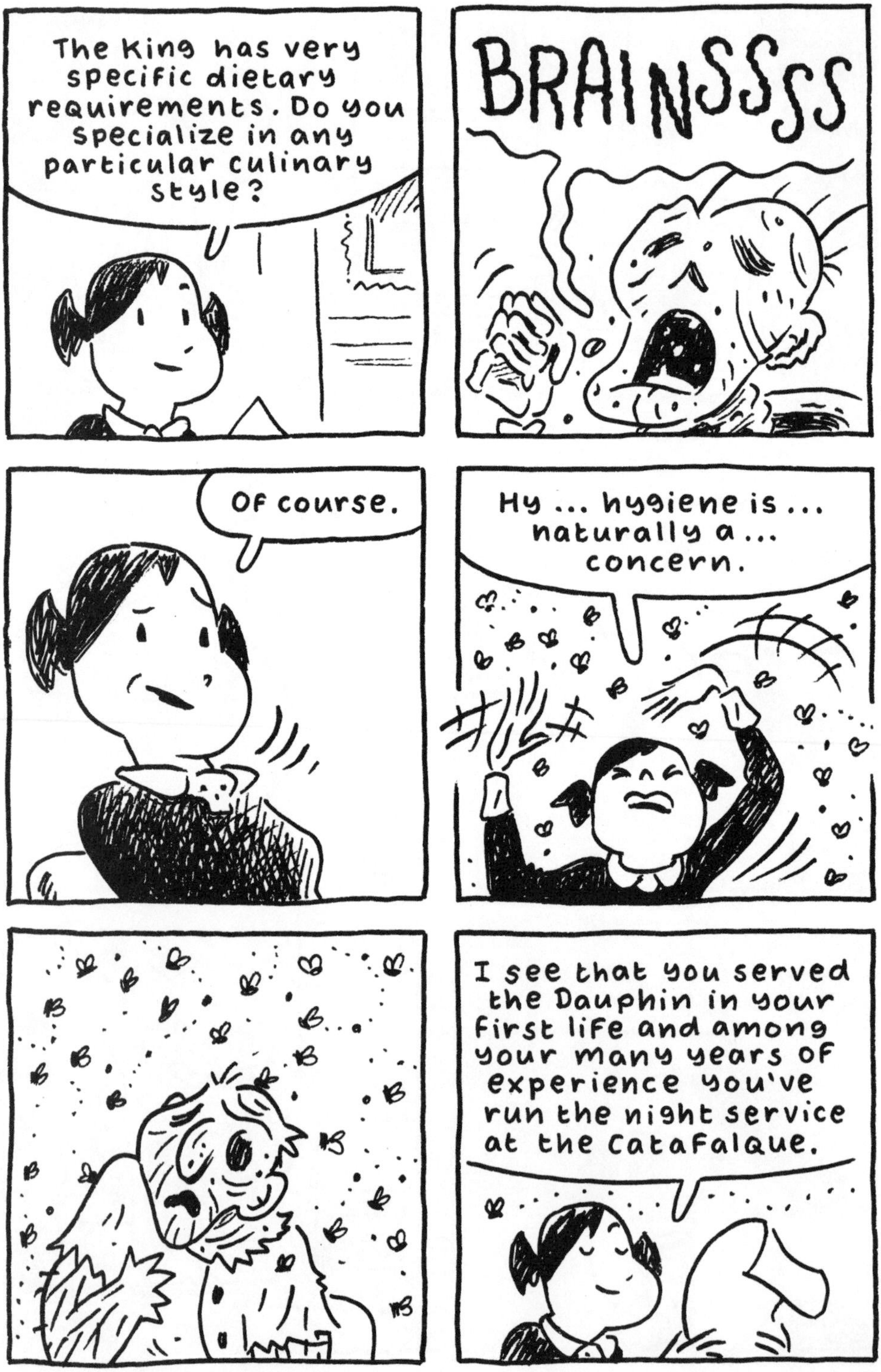
The King has very specific dietary requirements. Do you specialize in any particular culinary style?
BRAINSSSS
Of course.
Hy ... hygiene is ... naturally a ... concern.
I see that you served the Dauphin in your first life and among your many years of experience you've run the night service at the Catafalque.

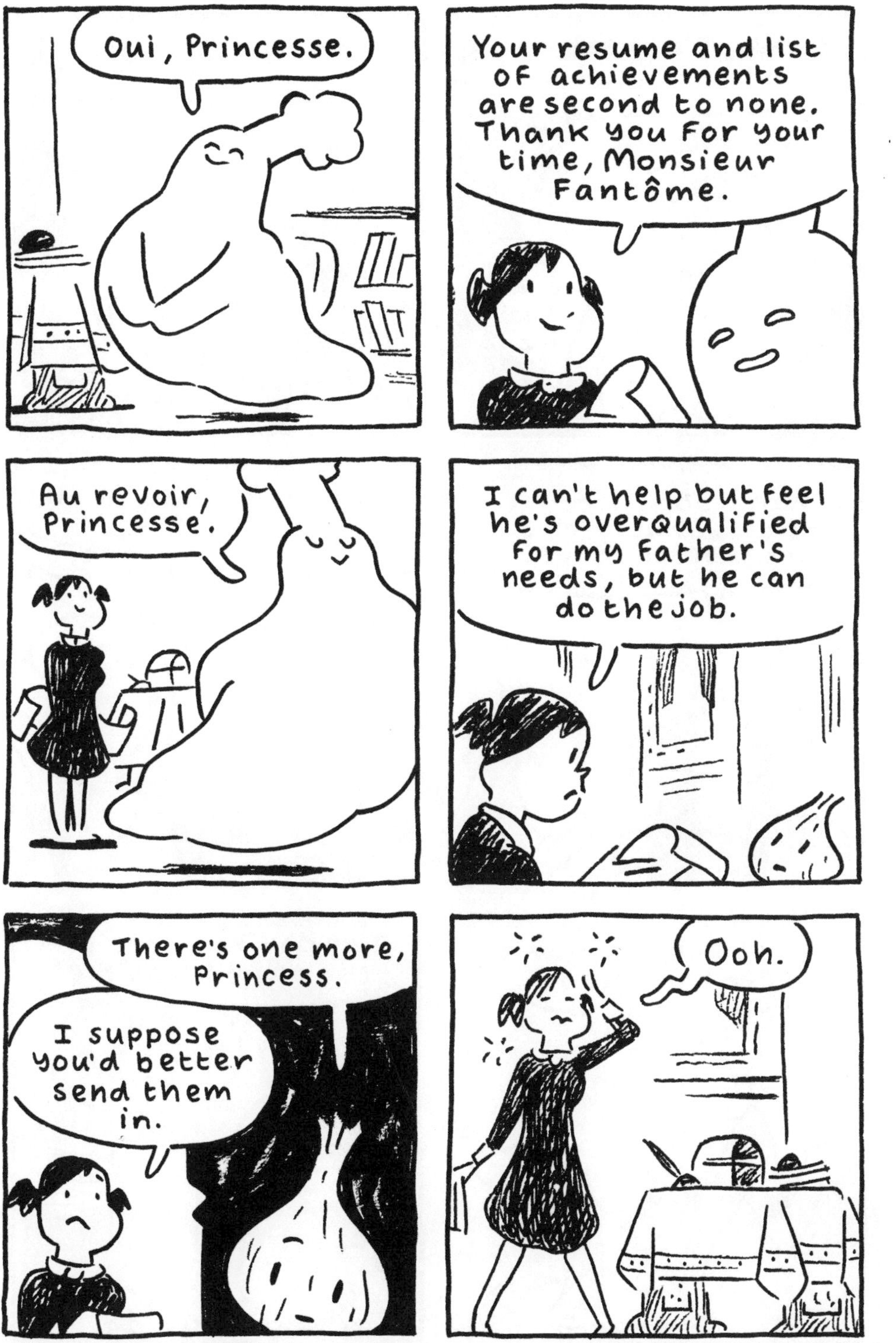
Oui, Princesse.
Your resume and list of achievements are second to none. Thank you for your time, Monsieur Fantôme.
Au revoir, Princesse.
I can't help but feel he's overqualified for my father's needs, but he can do the job.
There's one more, Princess.
I suppose you'd better send them in.
Ooh.

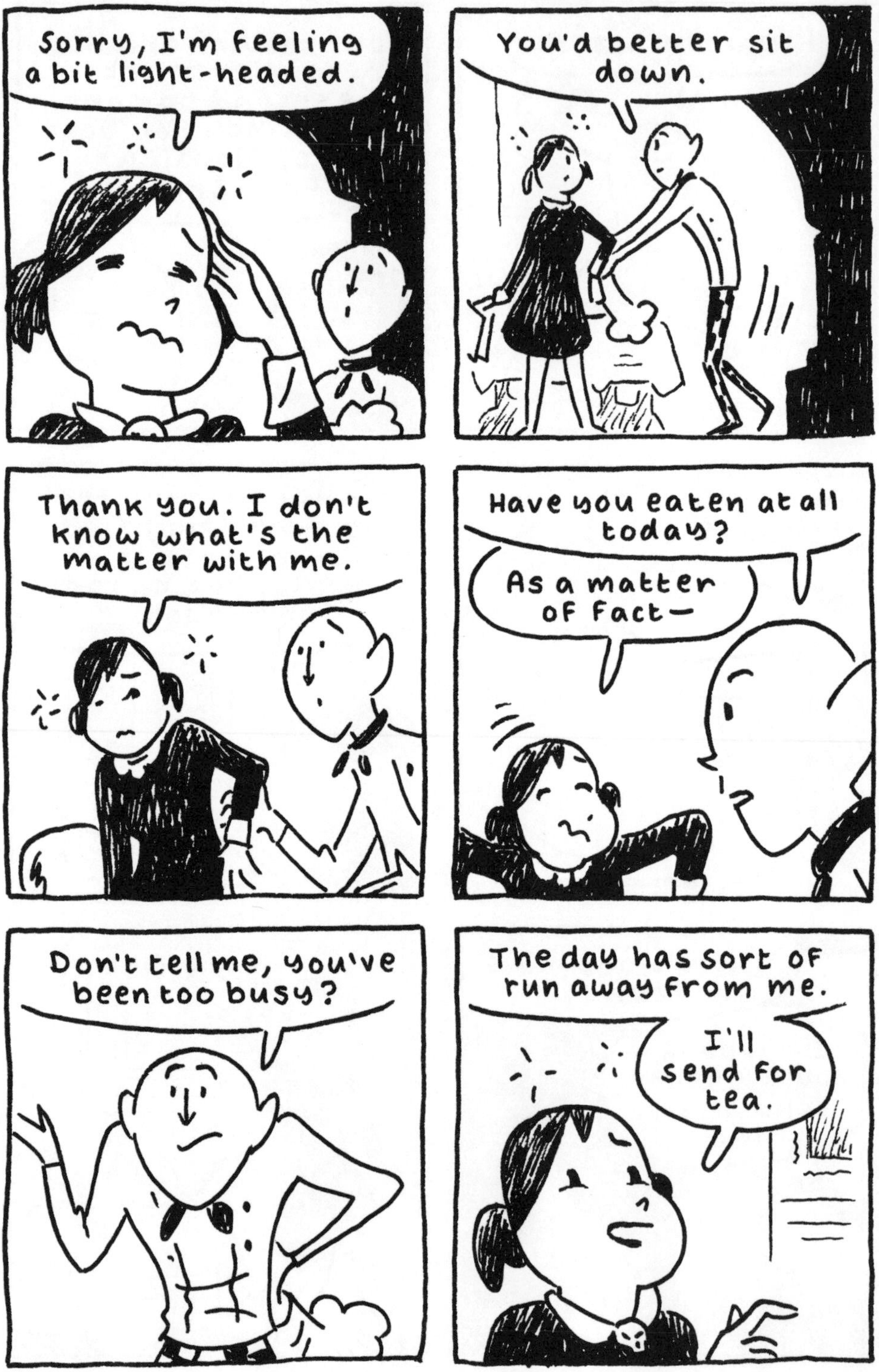
Sorry, I'm feeling a bit light-headed.
You'd better sit down.
Thank you. I don't know what's the matter with me.
Have you eaten at all today?
As a matter of fact—
Don't tell me, you've been too busy?
The day has sort of run away from me.
I'll send for tea.

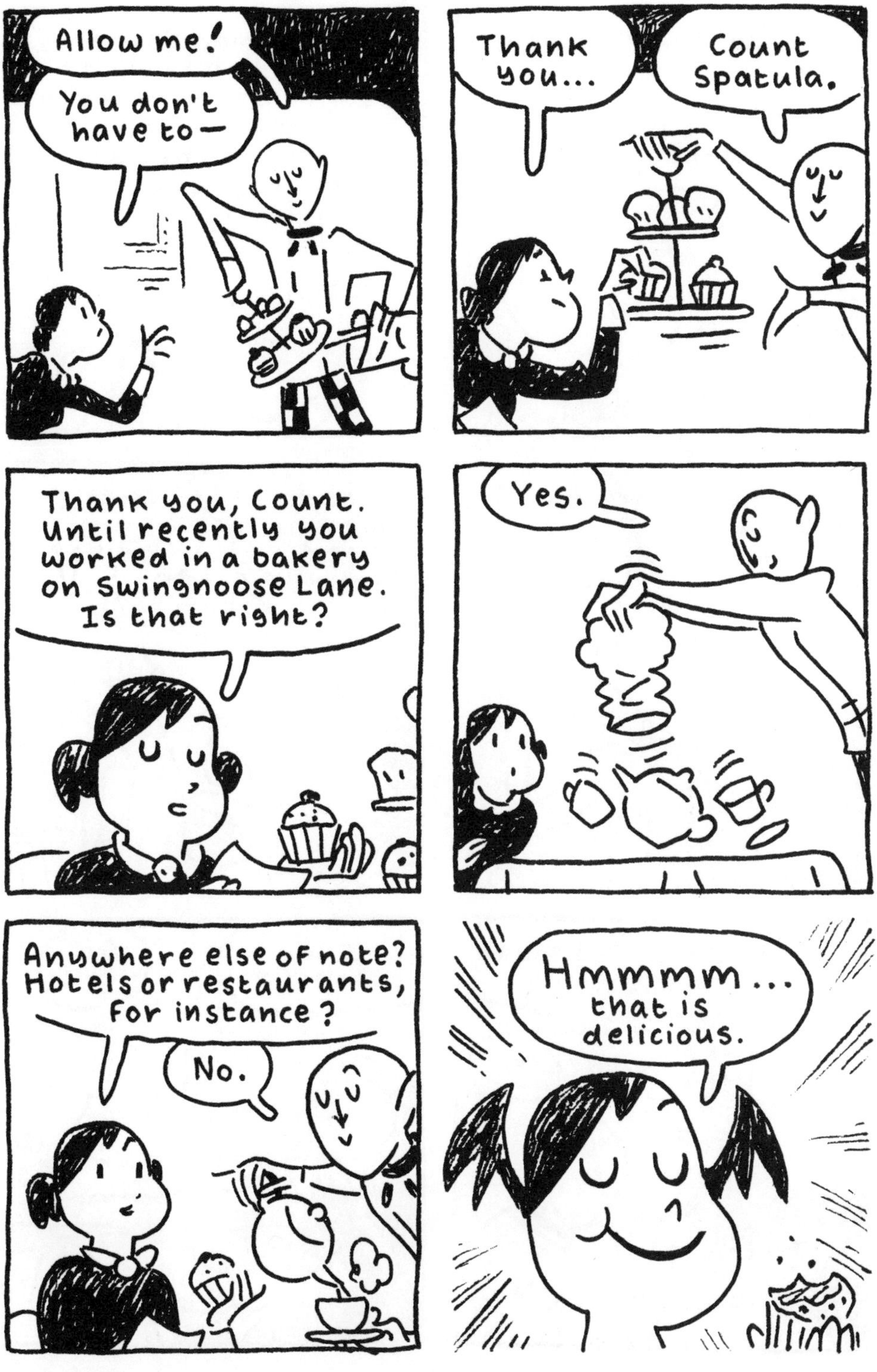
Allow me!
You don't have to—
Thank you...
Count Spatula.
Thank you, Count. Until recently you worked in a bakery on Swingnoose Lane. Is that right?
Yes.
Anywhere else of note? Hotels or restaurants, for instance?
No.
Hmmmm... that is delicious.

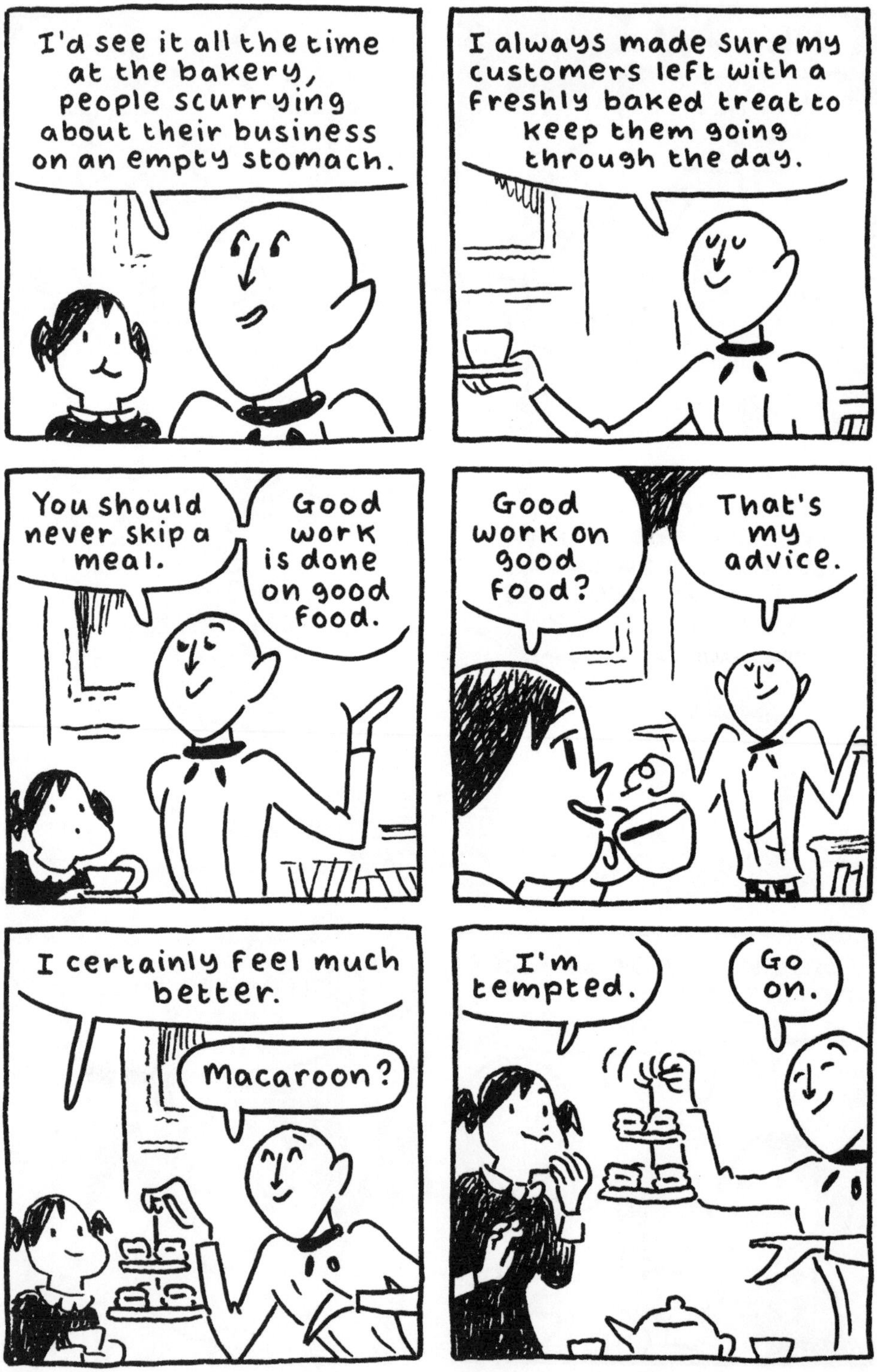
I'd see it all the time at the bakery, people scurrying about their business on an empty stomach.
I always made sure my customers left with a freshly baked treat to keep them going through the day.
You should never skip a meal.
Good work is done on good food.
Good work on good food?
That's my advice.
I certainly feel much better.
Macaroon?
I'm tempted.
Go on.

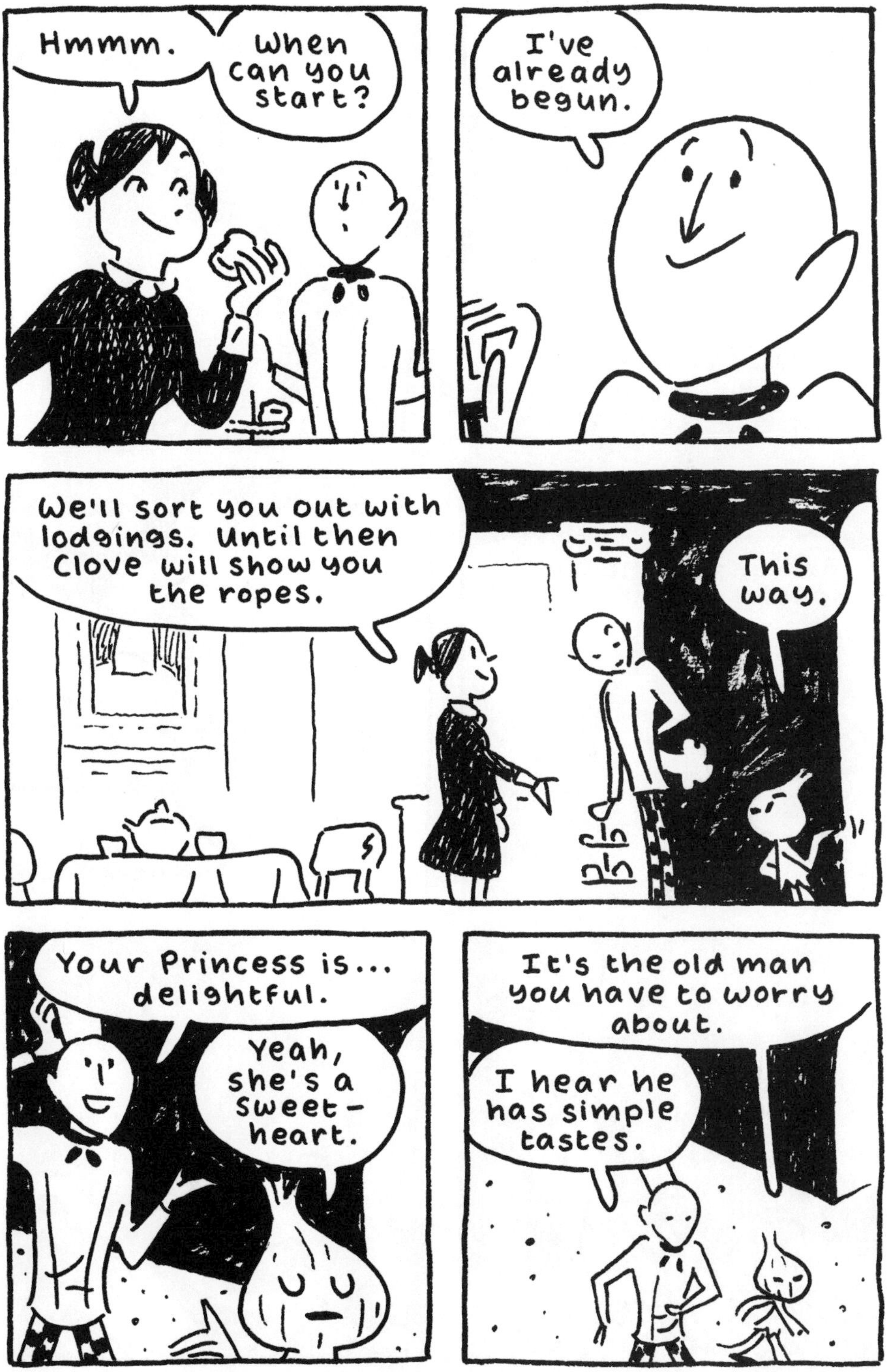
Hmmm.
When can you start?
I've already begun.
We'll sort you out with lodgings. Until then Clove will show you the ropes.
This way.
Your Princess is... delightful.
Yeah, she's a sweet-heart.
It's the old man you have to worry about.
I hear he has simple tastes.

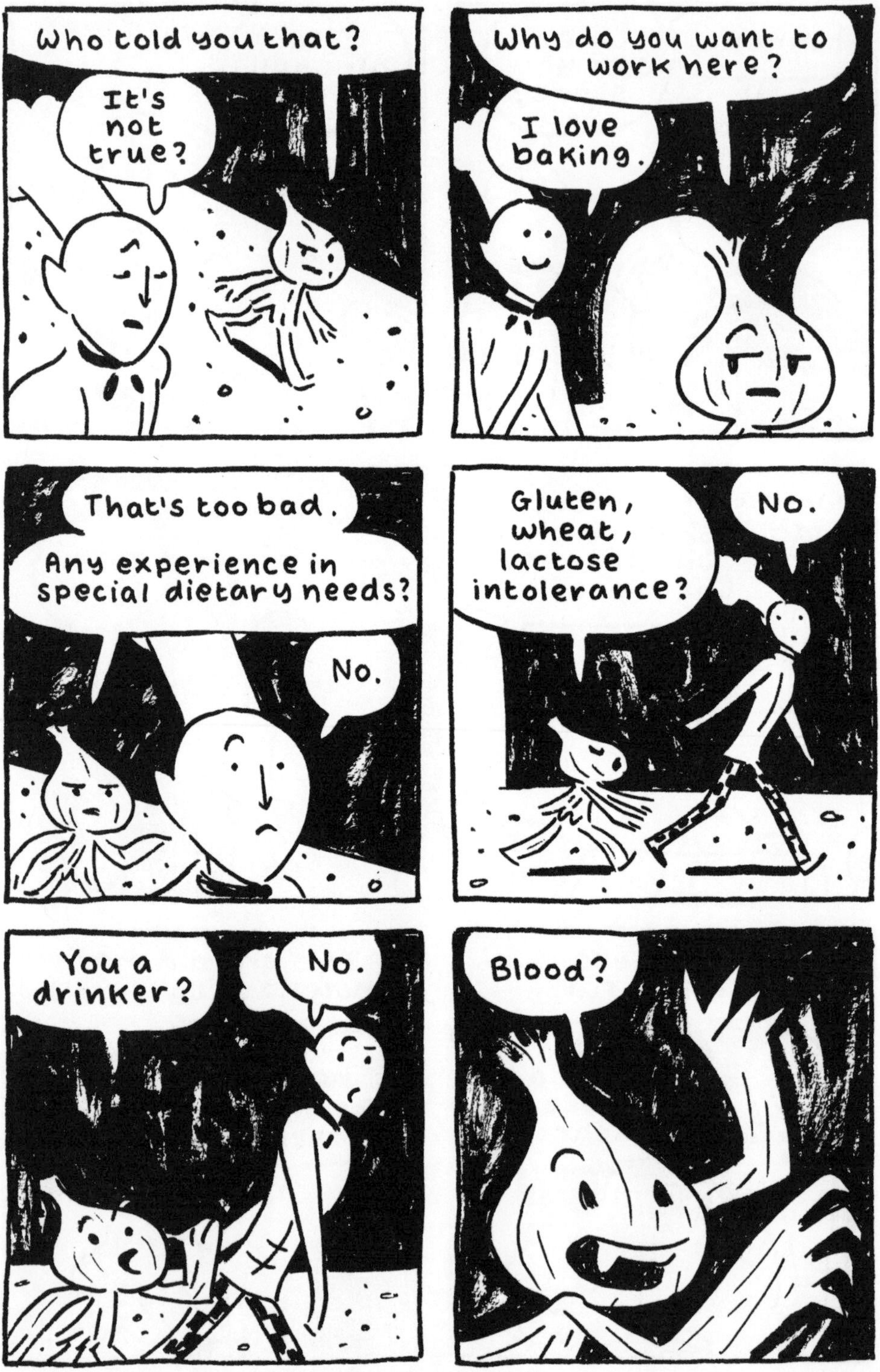
Who told you that?
It's not true?
Why do you want to work here?
I love baking.
That's too bad.
Any experience in special dietary needs?
No.
Gluten, wheat, lactose intolerance?
No.
You a drinker?
No.
Blood?

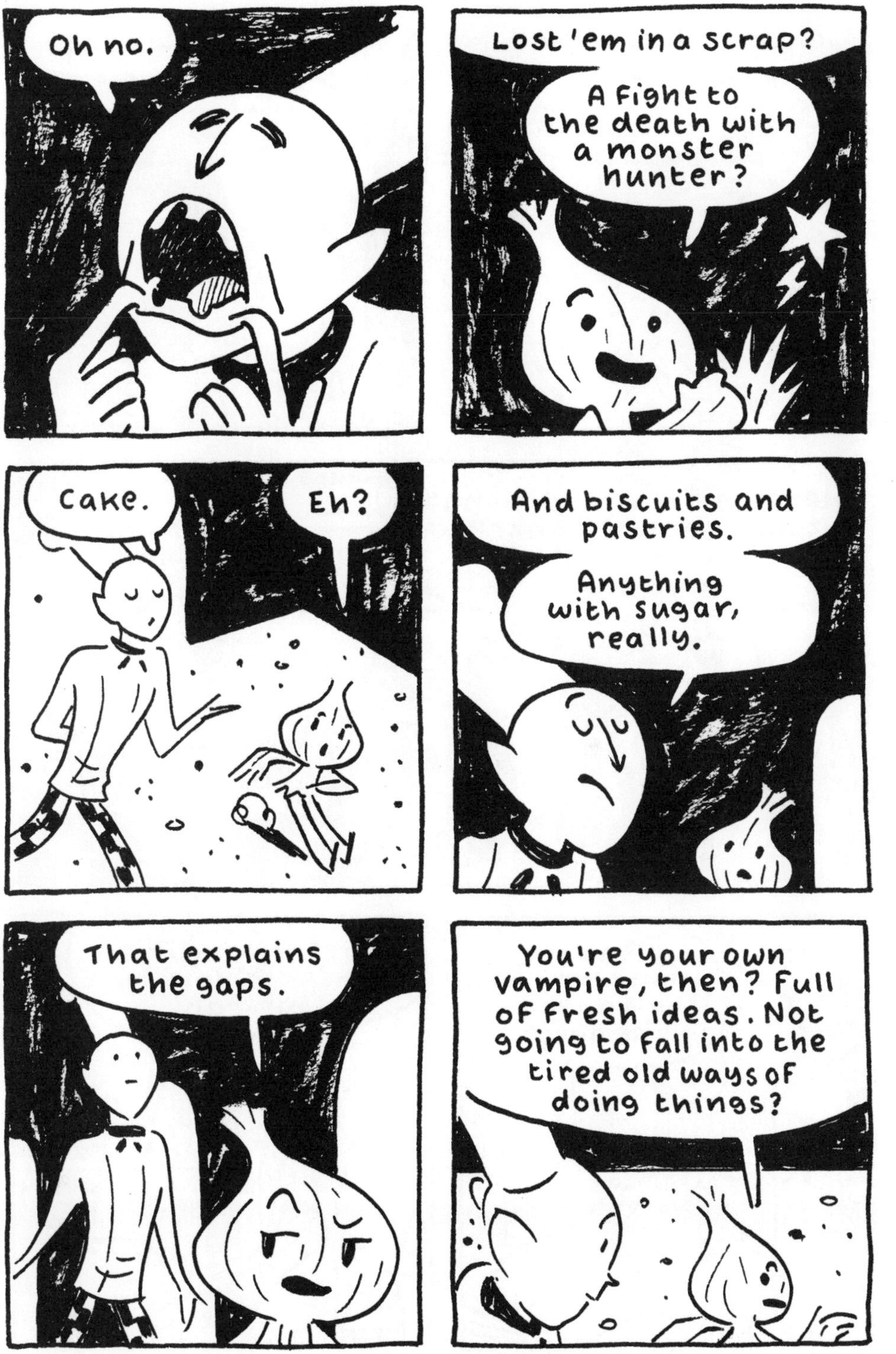
Oh no.
Lost 'em in a scrap?
A fight to the death with a monster hunter?
Cake.
Eh?
And biscuits and pastries.
Anything with sugar, really.
That explains the gaps.
You're your own vampire, then? Full of fresh ideas. Not going to fall into the tired old ways of doing things?

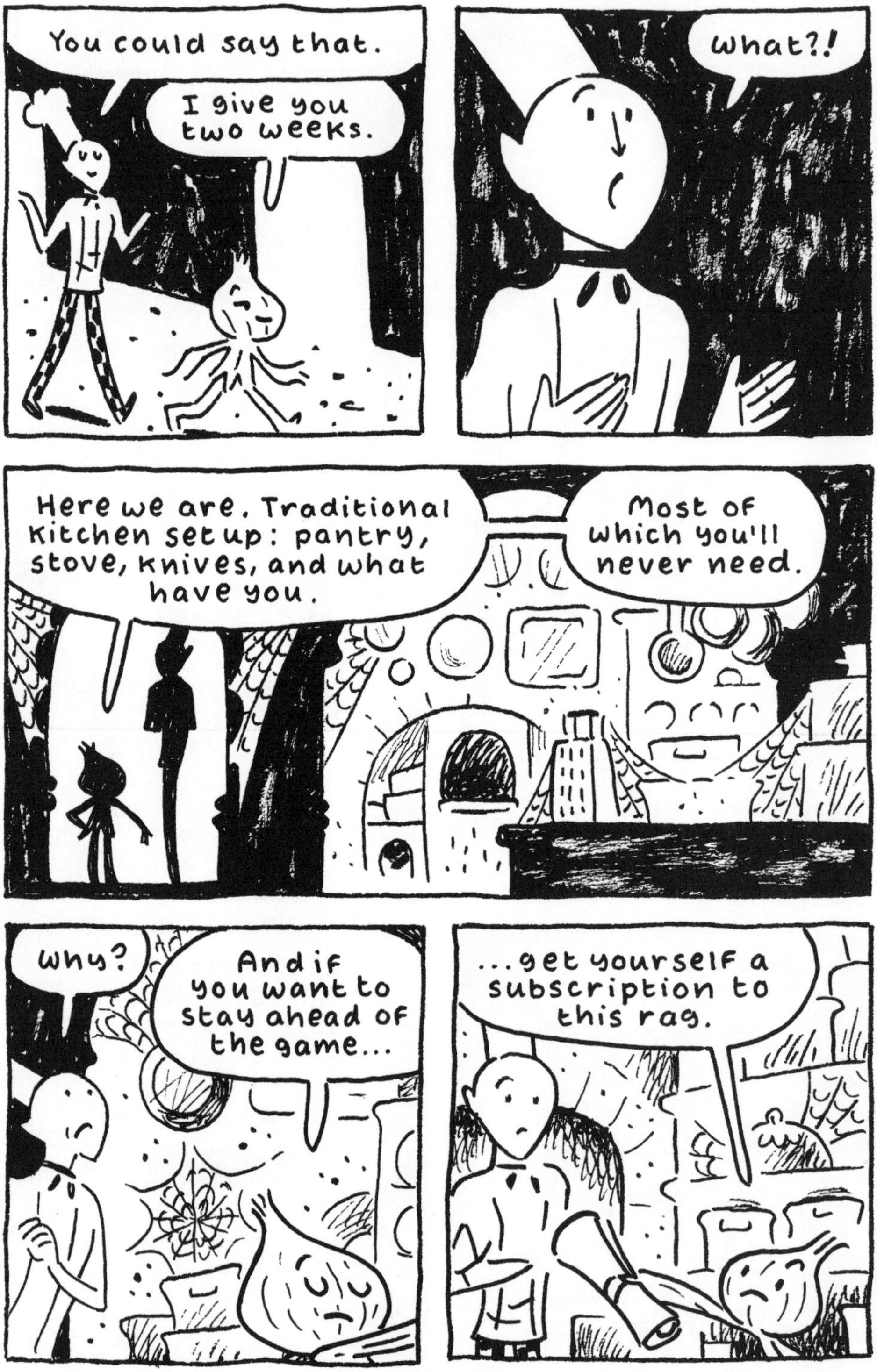

You could say that.
I give you two weeks.
What?!
Here we are. Traditional kitchen setup: pantry, stove, knives, and what have you.
Most of which you'll never need.
Why?
And if you want to stay ahead of the game...
...get yourself a subscription to this rag.

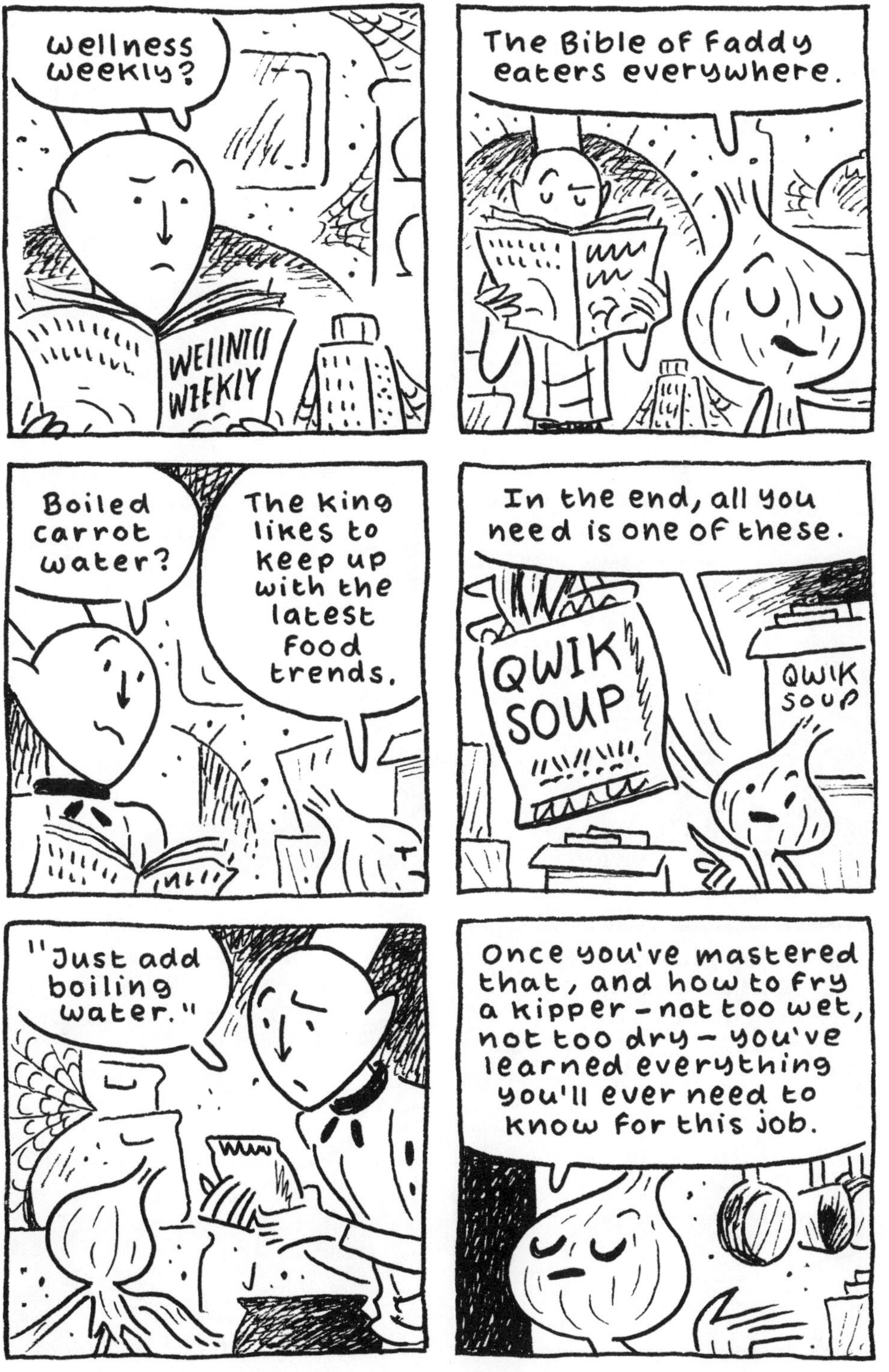
Wellness weekly?
WELLNESS WEEKLY
The Bible of faddy eaters everywhere.
Boiled carrot water?
The king likes to keep up with the latest food trends.
In the end, all you need is one of these.
QWIK SOUP
QWIK SOUP
"Just add boiling water."
Once you've mastered that, and how to fry a kipper - not too wet, not too dry - you've learned everything you'll ever need to know for this job.

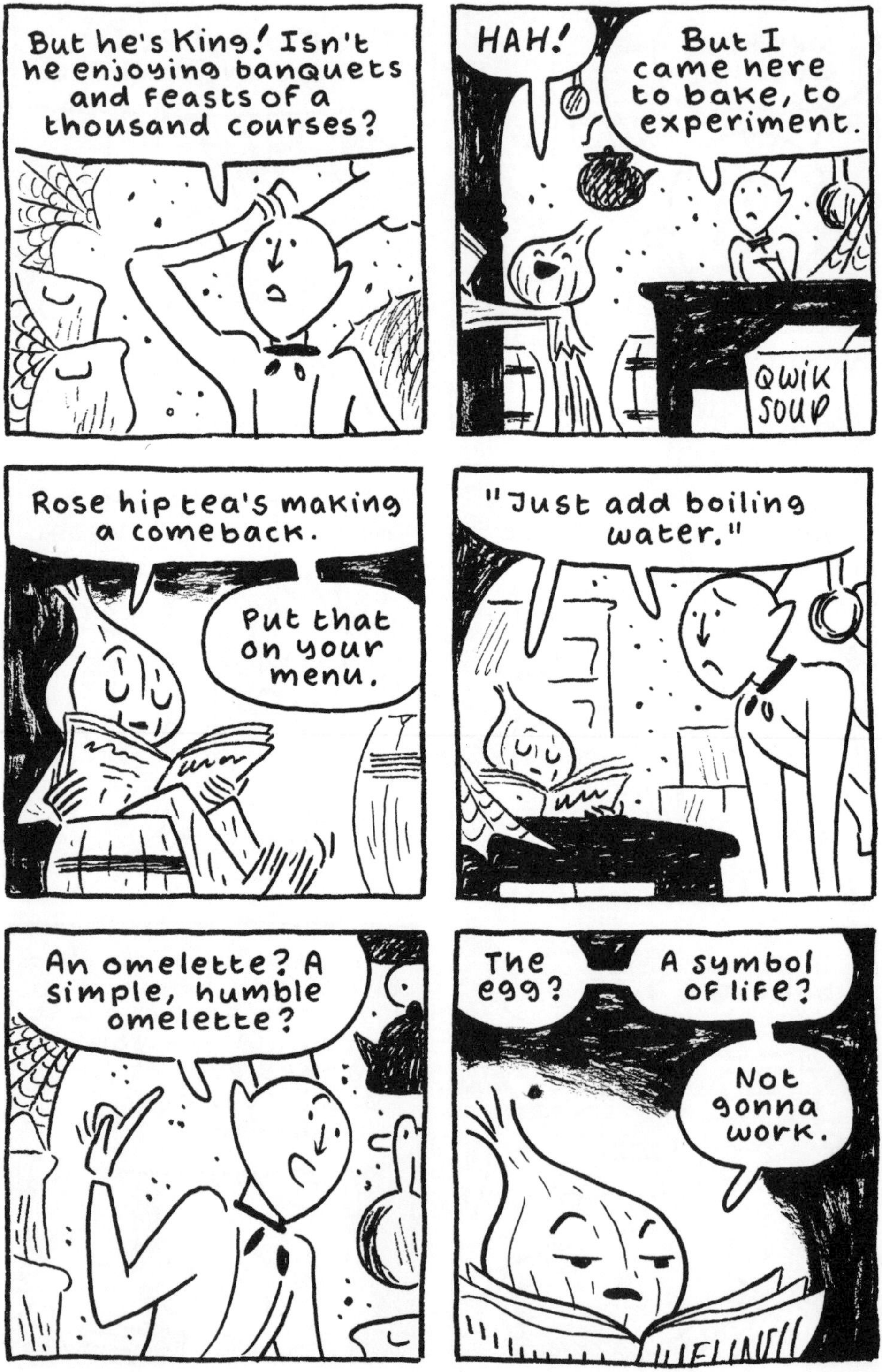
But he's King! Isn't he enjoying banquets and feasts of a thousand courses?
HAH!
But I came here to bake, to experiment.
QWIK SOUP
Rose hip tea's making a comeback.
Put that on your menu.
"Just add boiling water."
An omelette? A simple, humble omelette?
The egg?
A symbol of life?
Not gonna work.

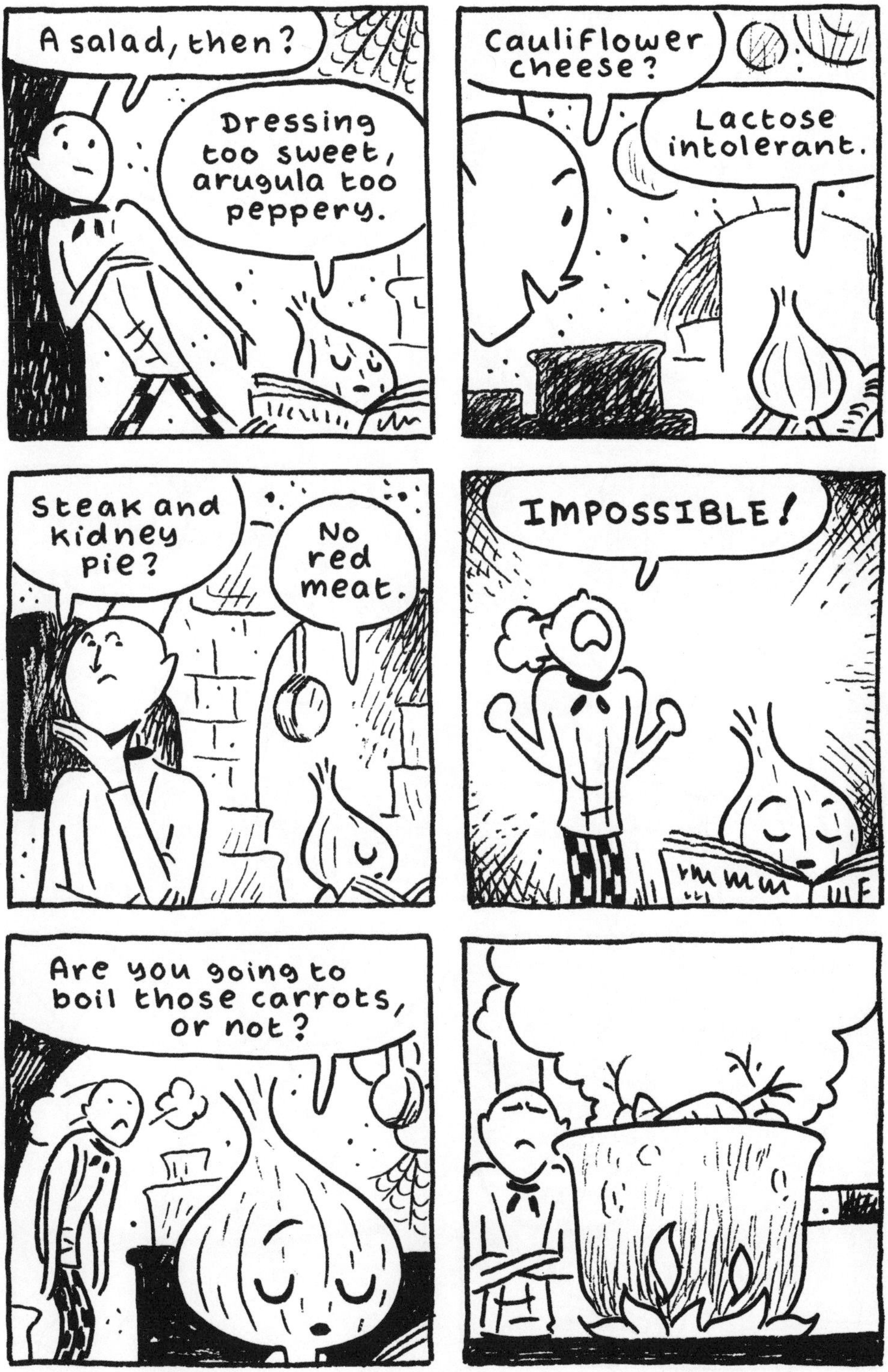
A salad, then?
Dressing too sweet, arugula too peppery.
Cauliflower cheese?
Lactose intolerant.
Steak and kidney pie?
No red meat.
IMPOSSIBLE!
Are you going to boil those carrots, or not?

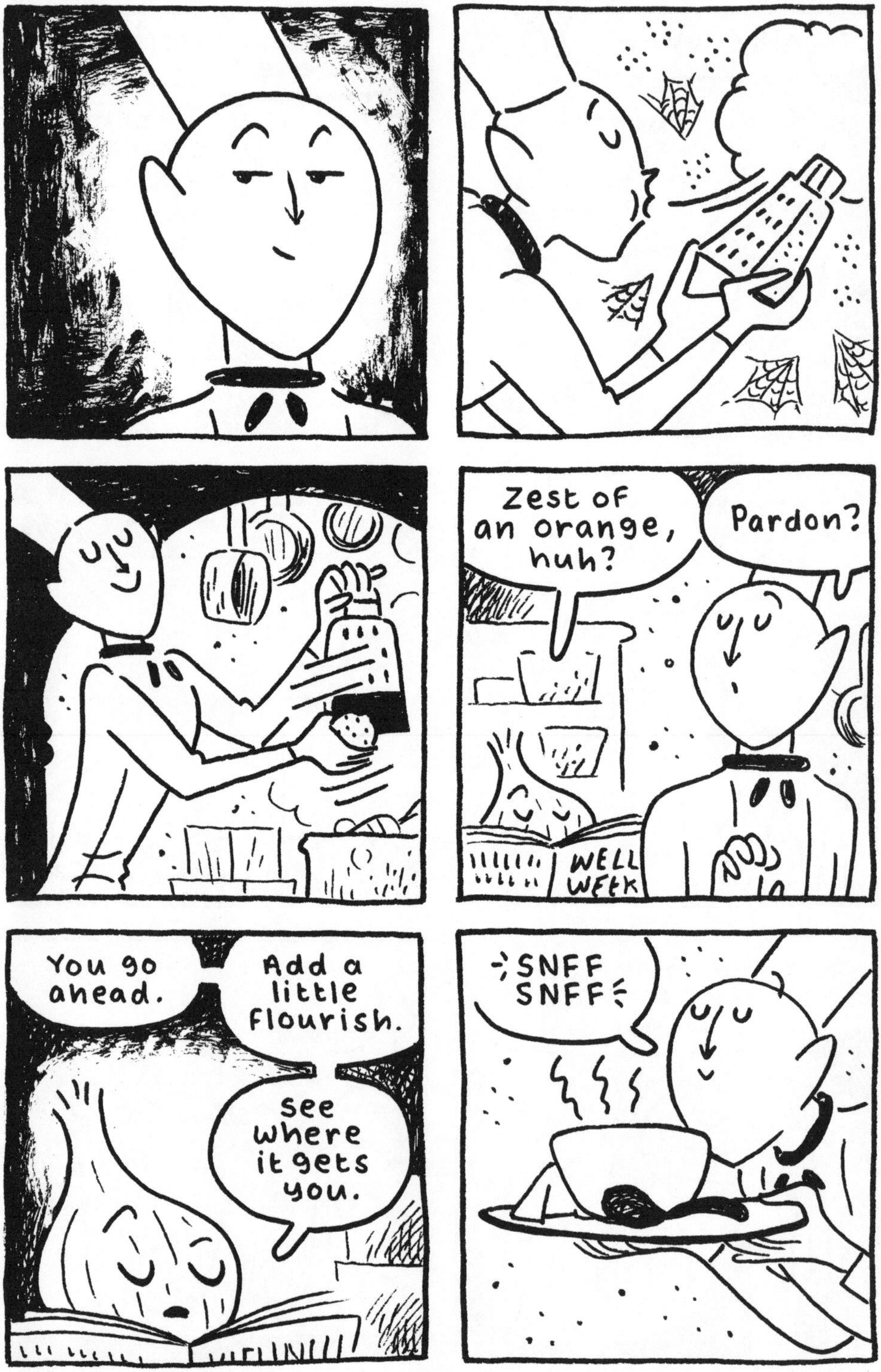
Zest of an orange, huh?
Pardon?
WELL WEEK
You go ahead.
Add a little flourish.
see where it gets you.
SNFF SNFF

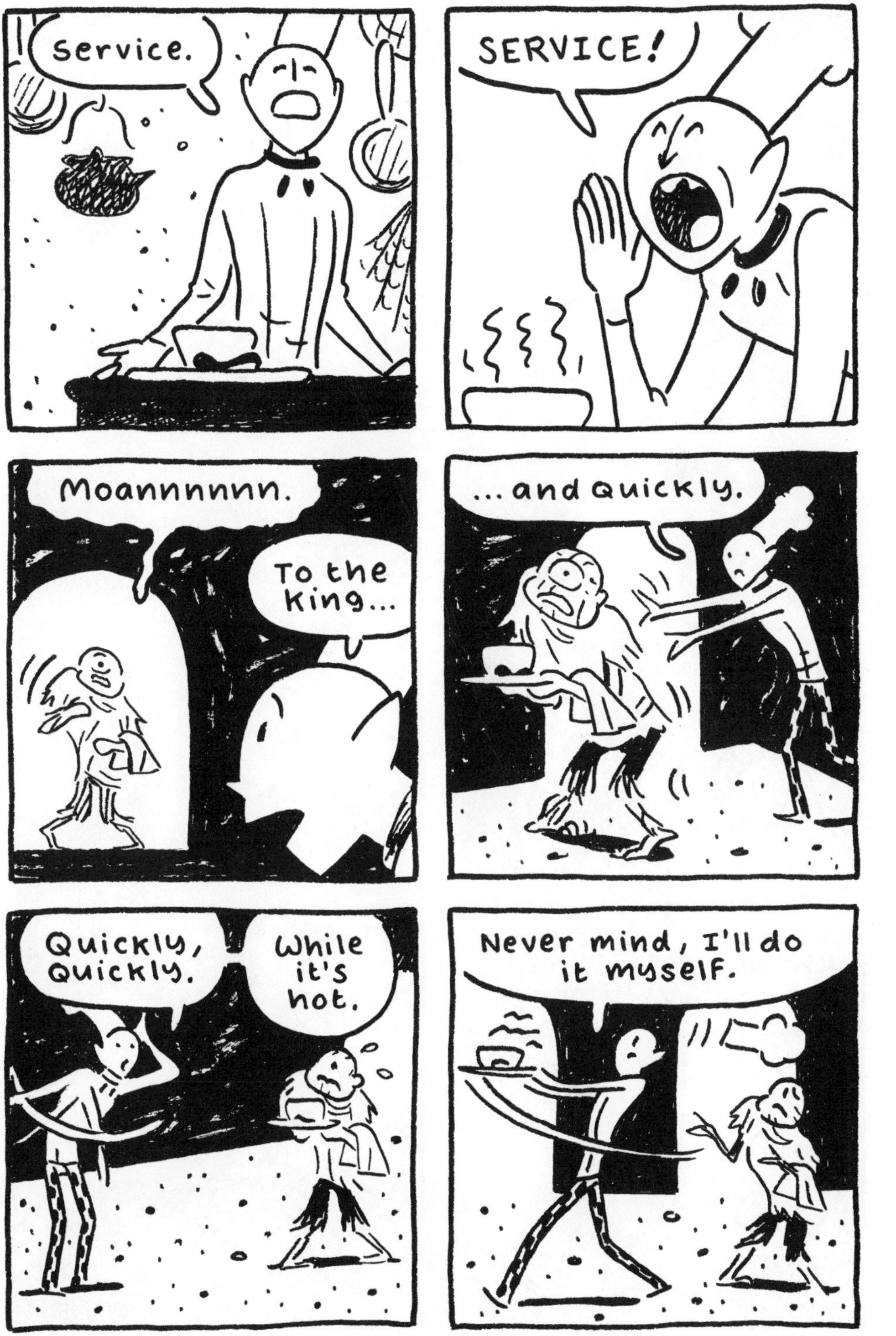
Service.
SERVICE!
Moannnnnn.
To the King...
...and quickly.
Quickly, Quickly.
While it's hot.
Never mind, I'll do it myself.

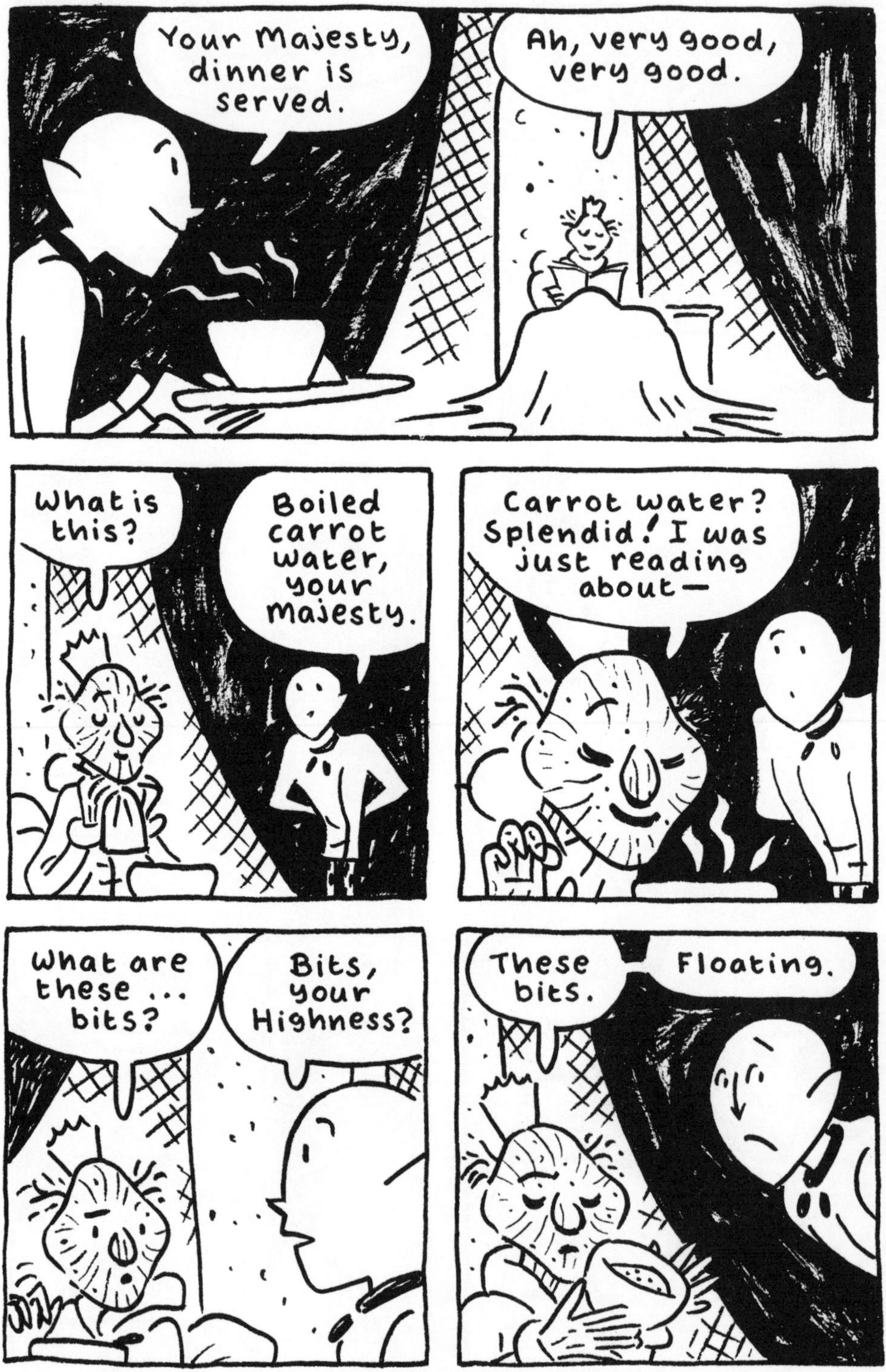
Your Majesty, dinner is served.
Ah, very good, very good.
What is this?
Boiled carrot water, your Majesty.
Carrot water? Splendid! I was just reading about—
What are these ... bits?
Bits, your Highness?
These bits.
Floating.

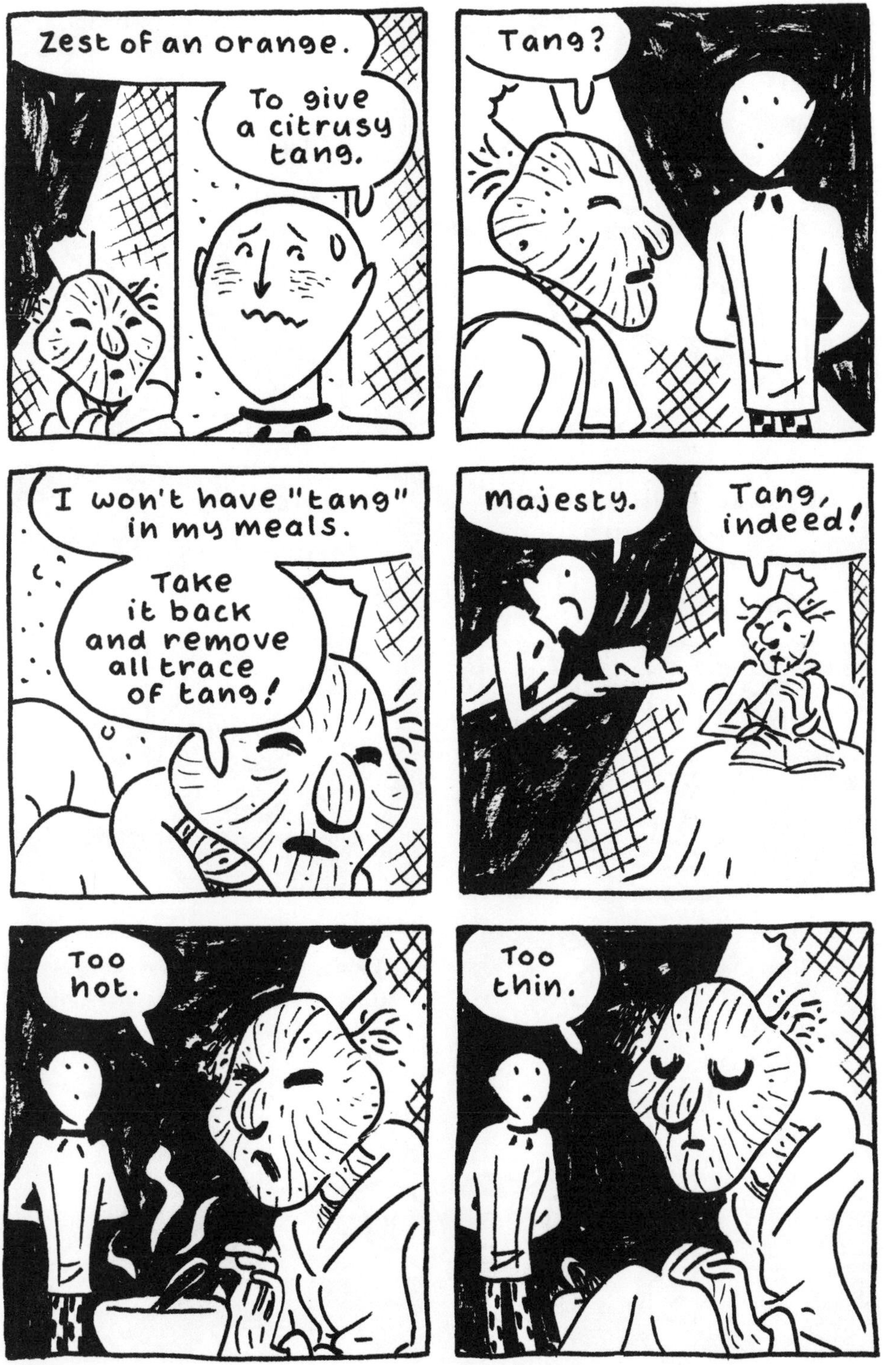
Zest of an orange.
To give a citrusy tang.
Tang?
I won't have "tang" in my meals.
Take it back and remove all trace of tang!
Majesty.
Tang, indeed!
Too hot.
Too thin.

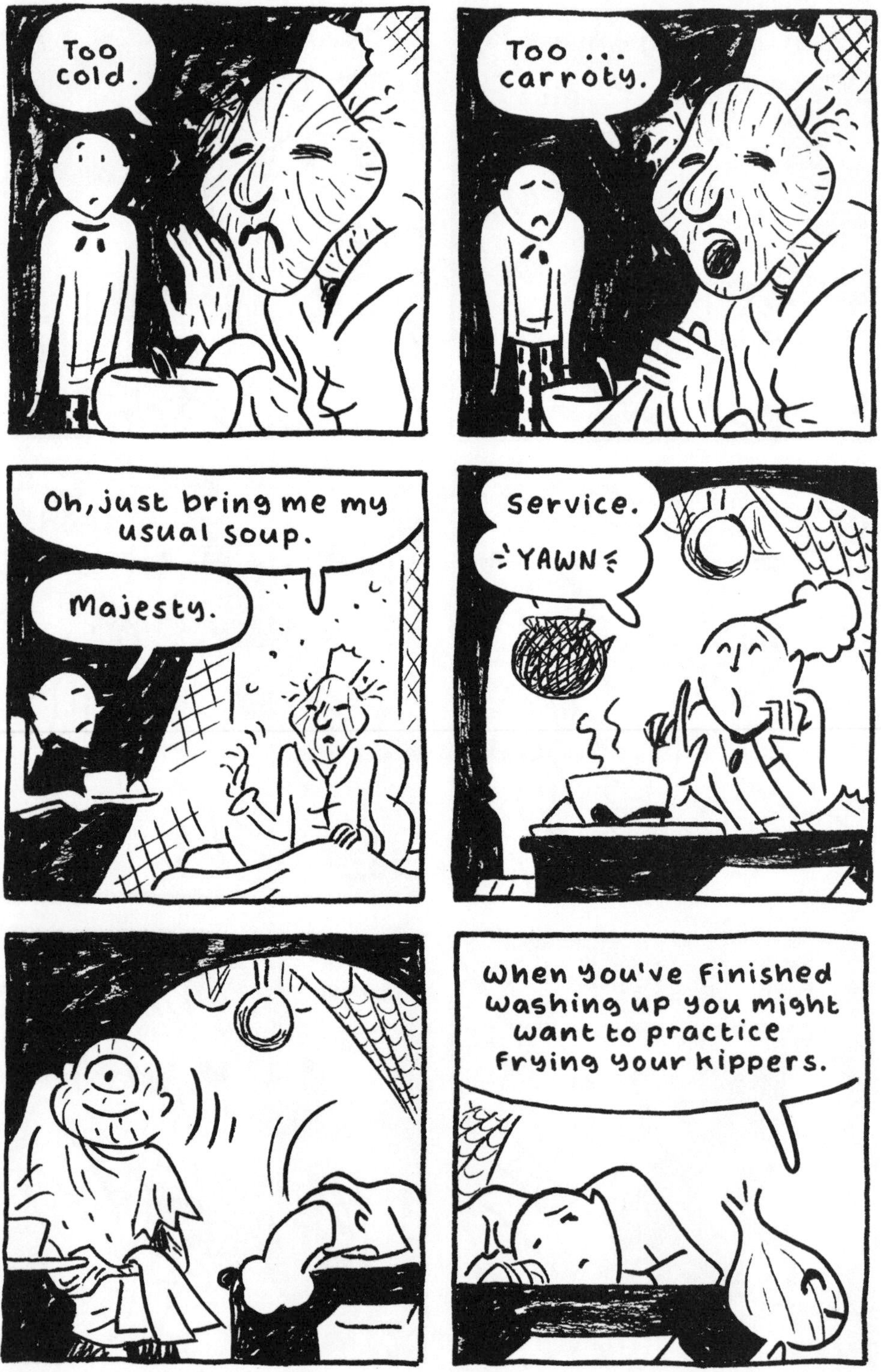
Too cold.
Too ... carroty.
Oh, just bring me my usual soup.
Majesty.
Service.
YAWN
When you've finished washing up you might want to practice frying your kippers.

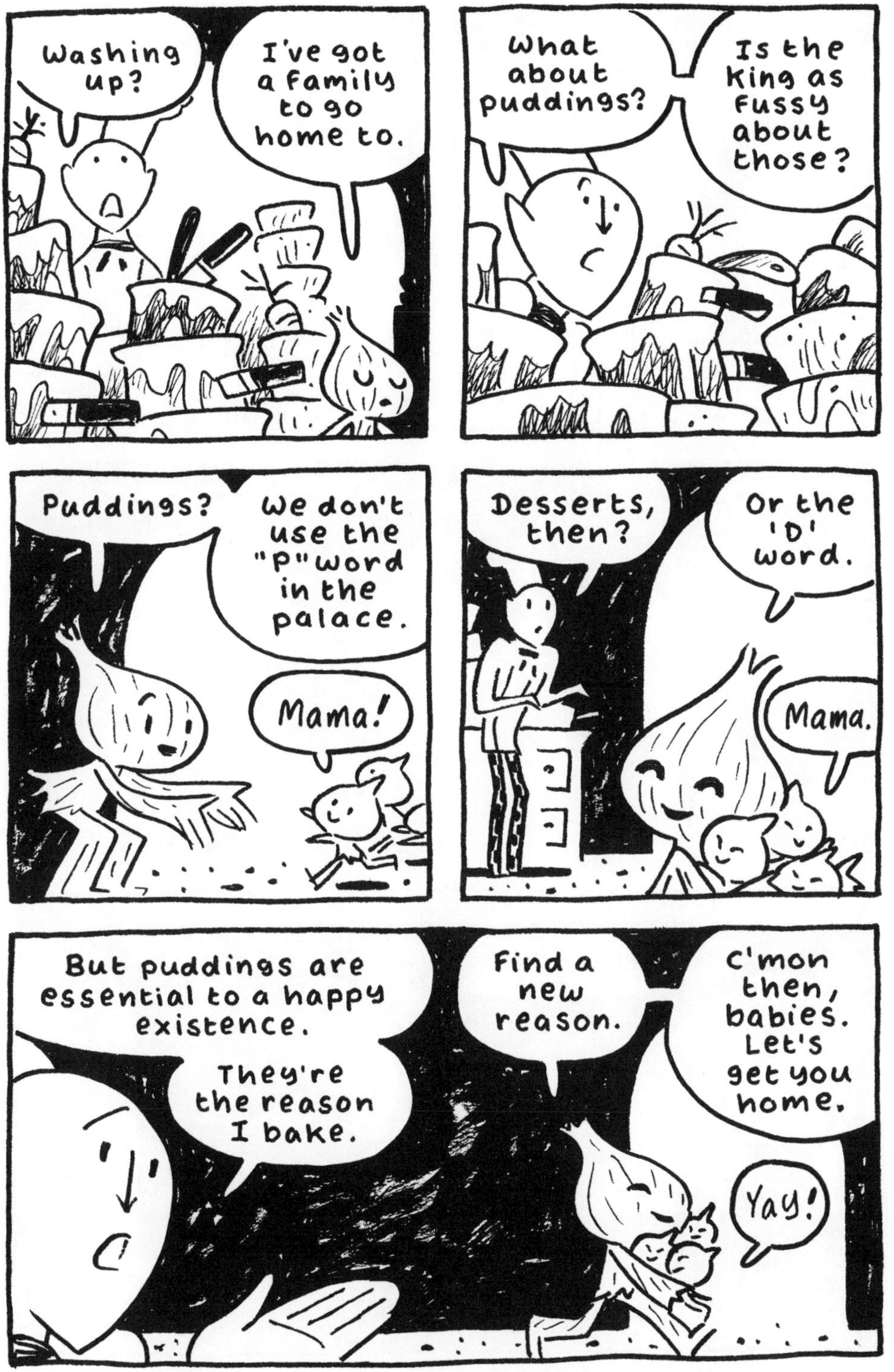
Washing up?
I've got a family to go home to.
What about puddings?
Is the King as fussy about those?
Puddings?
We don't use the "P" word in the palace.
Mama!
Desserts, then?
Or the 'D' word.
Mama.
But puddings are essential to a happy existence.
They're the reason I bake.
Find a new reason.
C'mon then, babies. Let's get you home.
Yay!

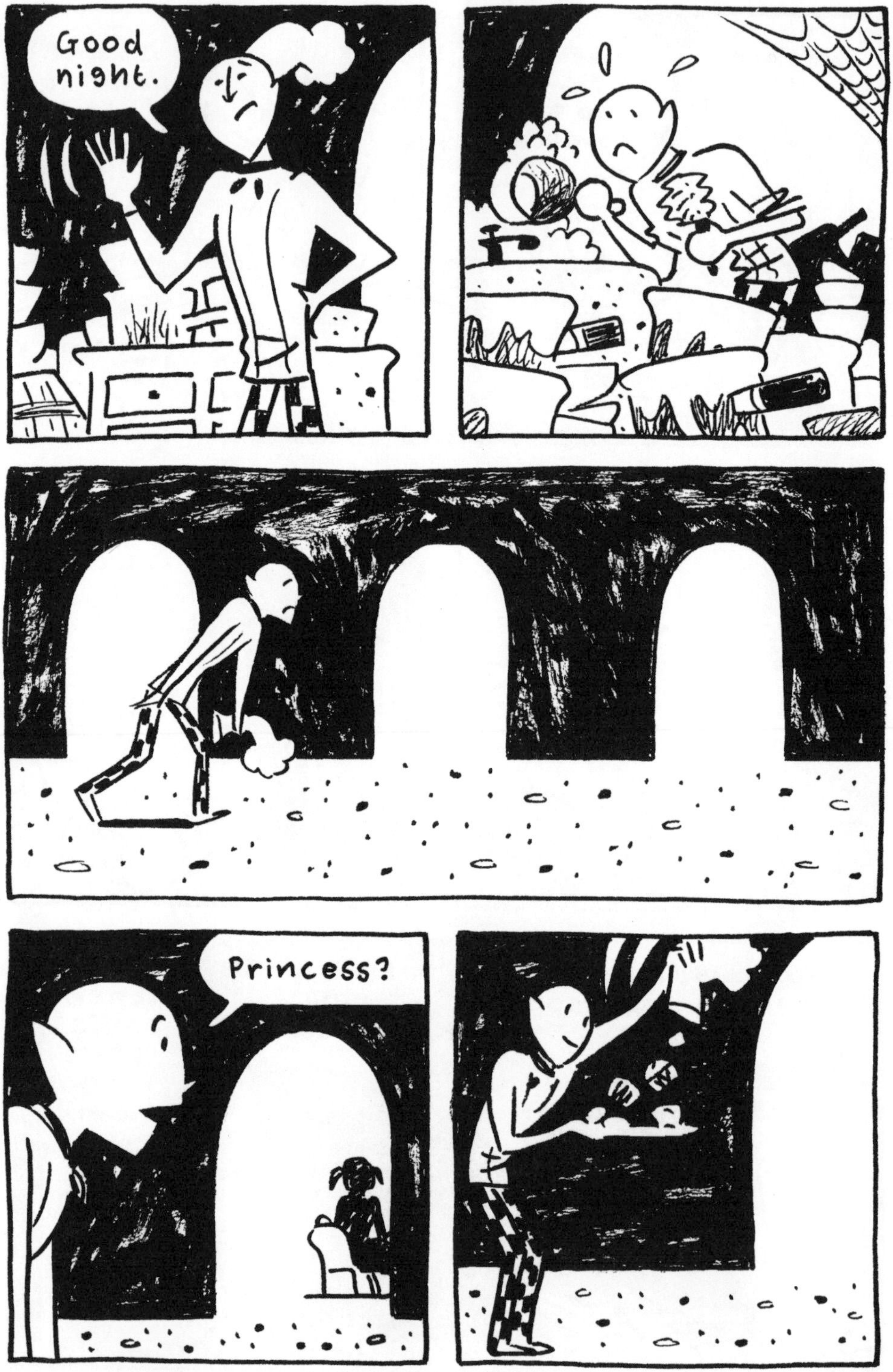
Good night.
Princess?

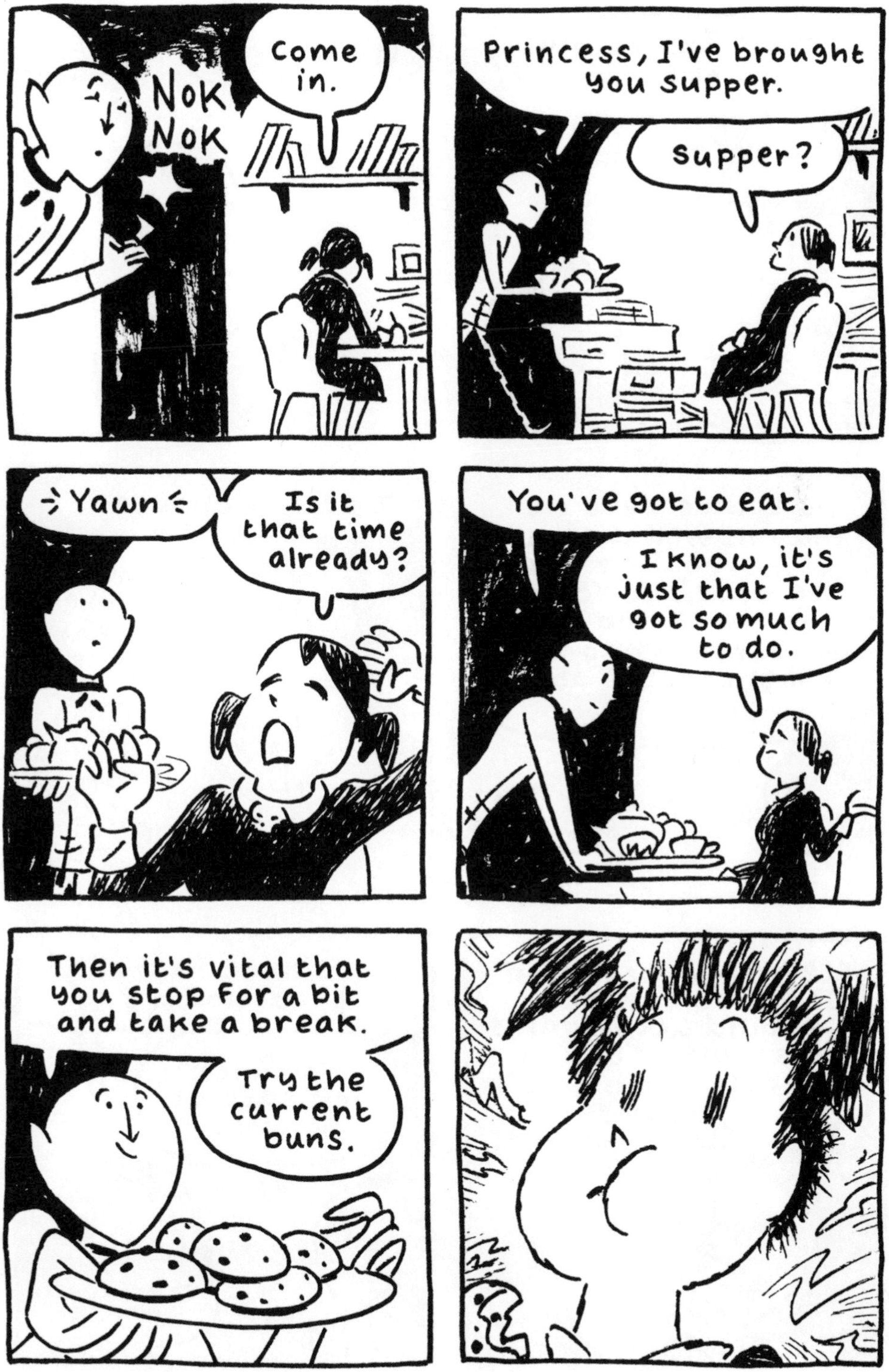
NOK
NOK
Come in.
Princess, I've brought you supper.
Supper?
Yawn
Is it that time already?
You've got to eat.
I know, it's just that I've got so much to do.
Then it's vital that you stop for a bit and take a break.
Try the current buns.

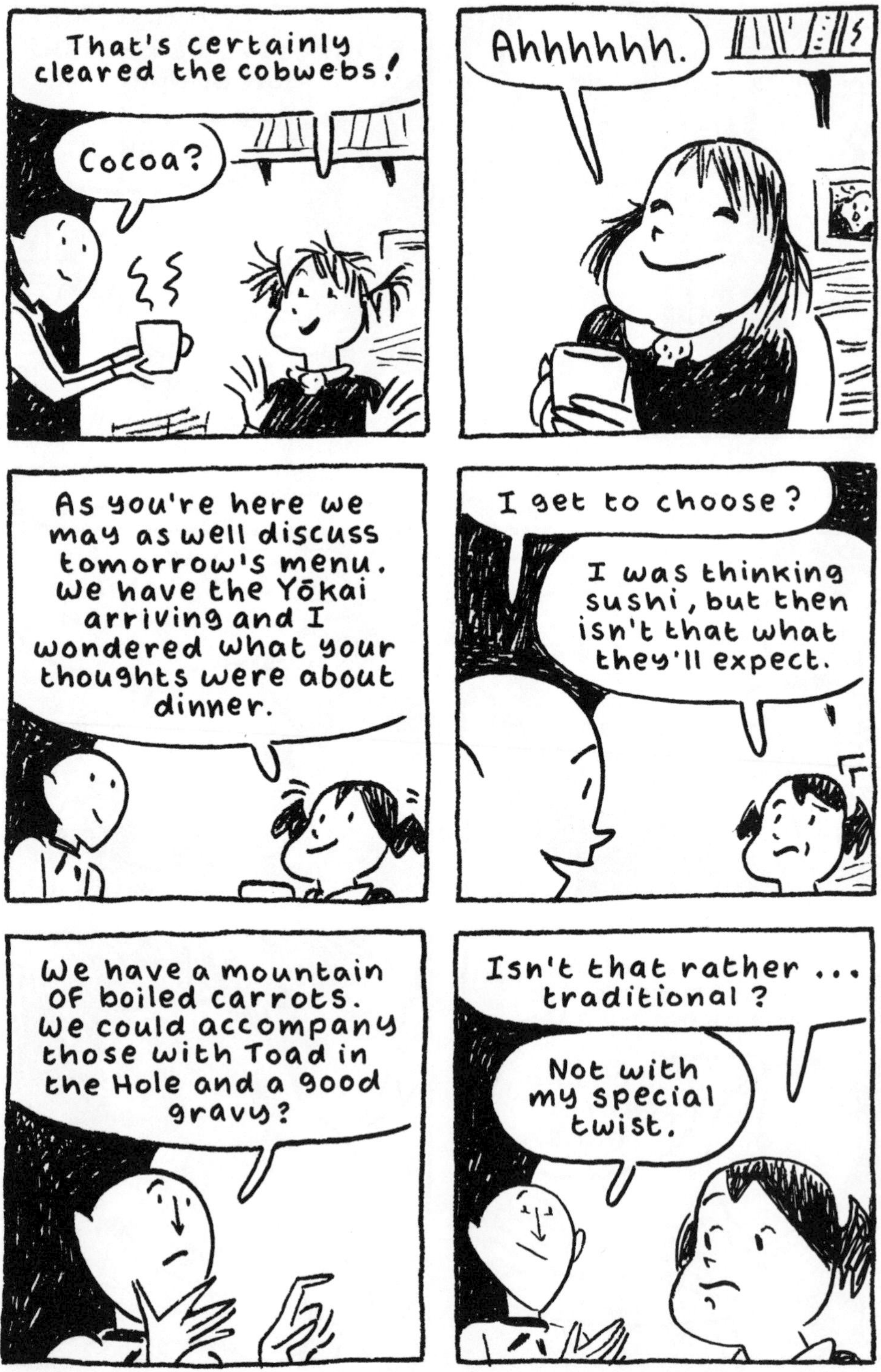
That's certainly cleared the cobwebs!
Cocoa?
Ahhhhhh.
As you're here we may as well discuss tomorrow's menu. We have the Yōkai arriving and I wondered what your thoughts were about dinner.
I get to choose?
I was thinking sushi, but then isn't that what they'll expect.
We have a mountain of boiled carrots. We could accompany those with Toad in the Hole and a good gravy?
Isn't that rather ... traditional?
Not with my special twist.

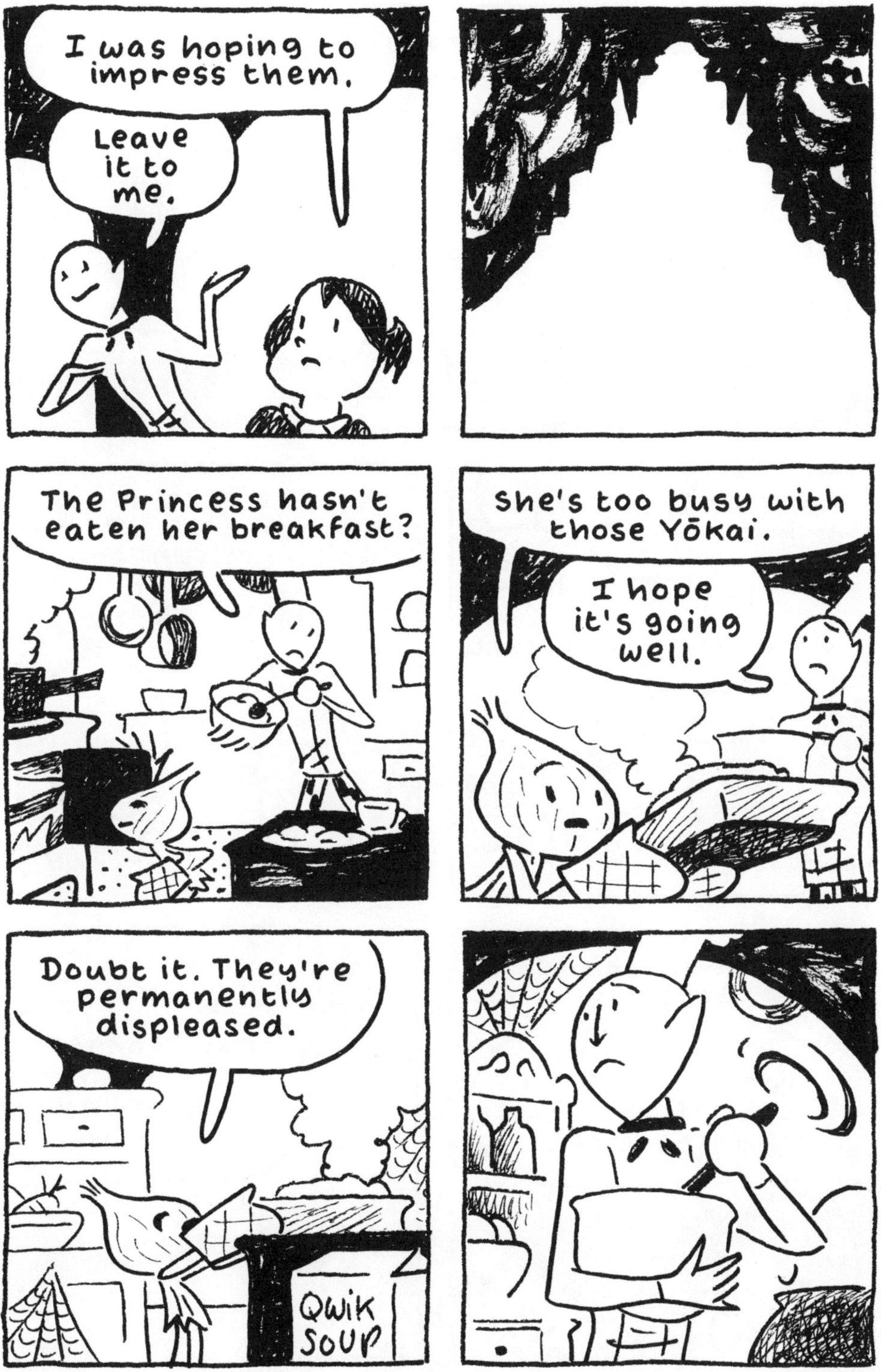

I was hoping to impress them.
Leave it to me.
The Princess hasn't eaten her breakfast?
She's too busy with those Yōkai.
I hope it's going well.
Doubt it. They're permanently displeased.
QWIK SOUP

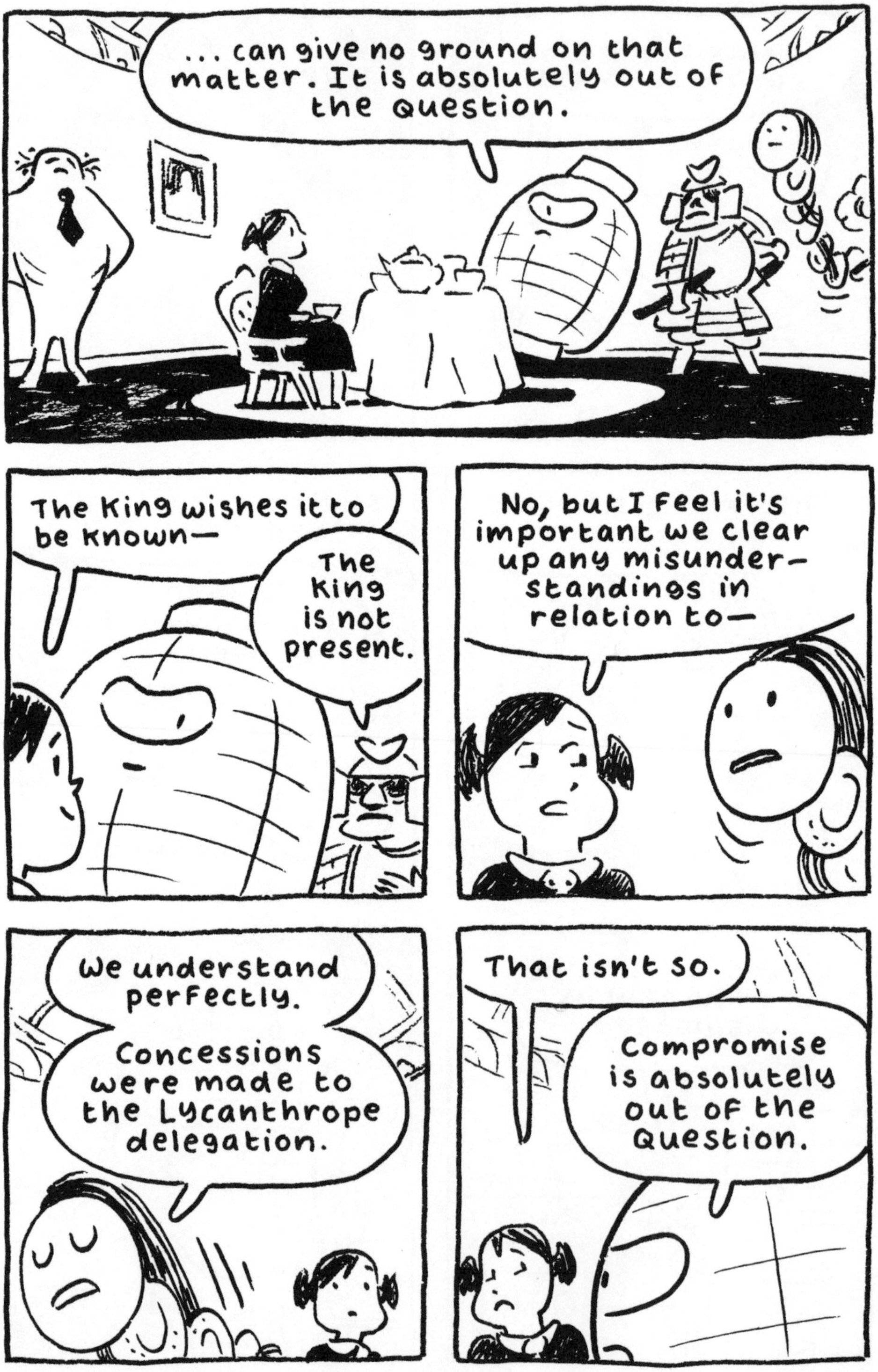
... can give no ground on that matter. It is absolutely out of the question.
The King wishes it to be known—
The King is not present.
No, but I feel it's important we clear up any misunderstandings in relation to—
We understand perfectly.
Concessions were made to the Lycanthrope delegation.
That isn't so.
Compromise is absolutely out of the question.

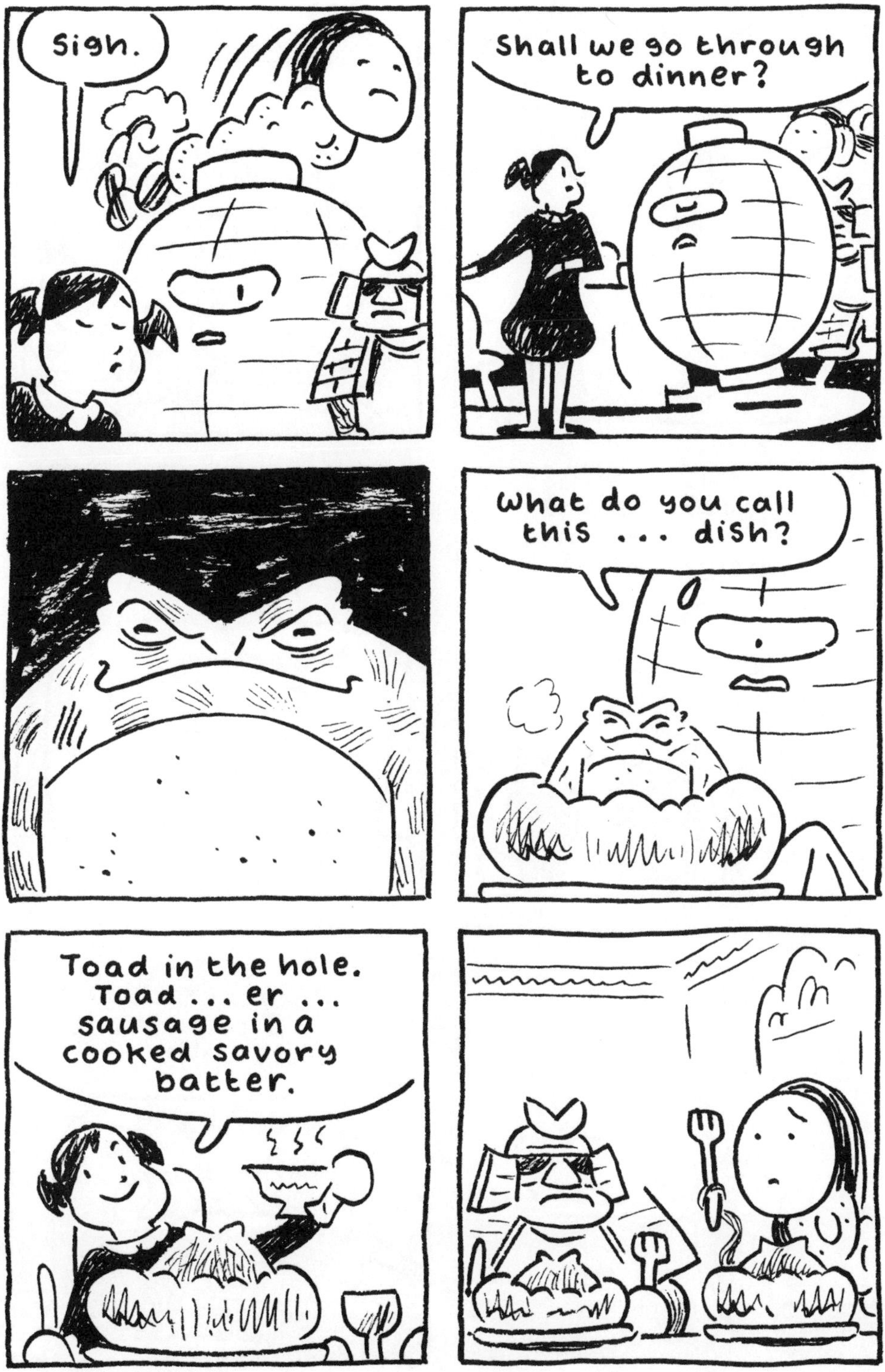
Sigh.
Shall we go through to dinner?
What do you call this ... dish?
Toad in the hole. Toad ... er ... sausage in a cooked savory batter.

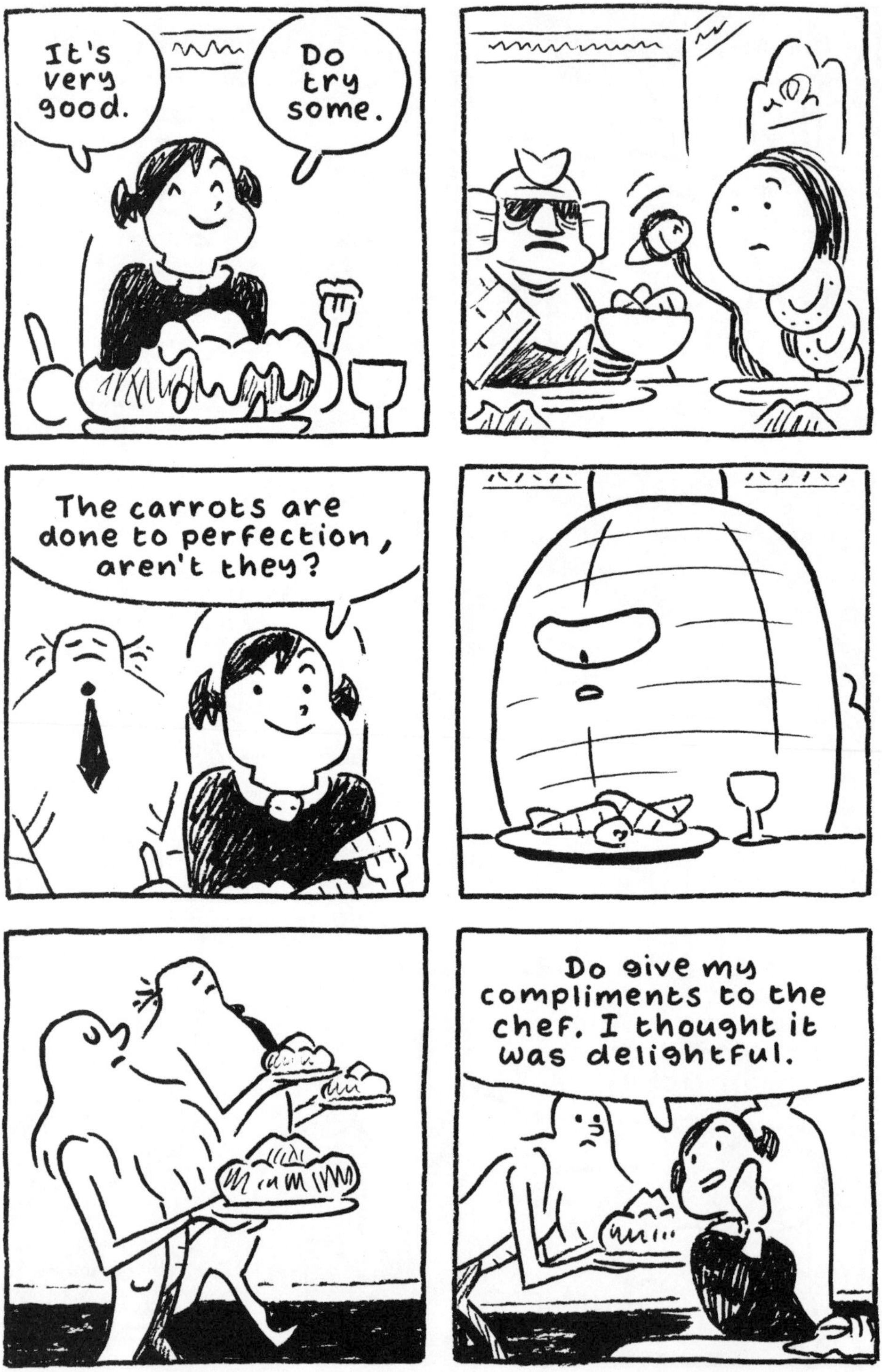
It's very good.
Do try some.
The carrots are done to perfection, aren't they?
Do give my compliments to the chef. I thought it was delightful.

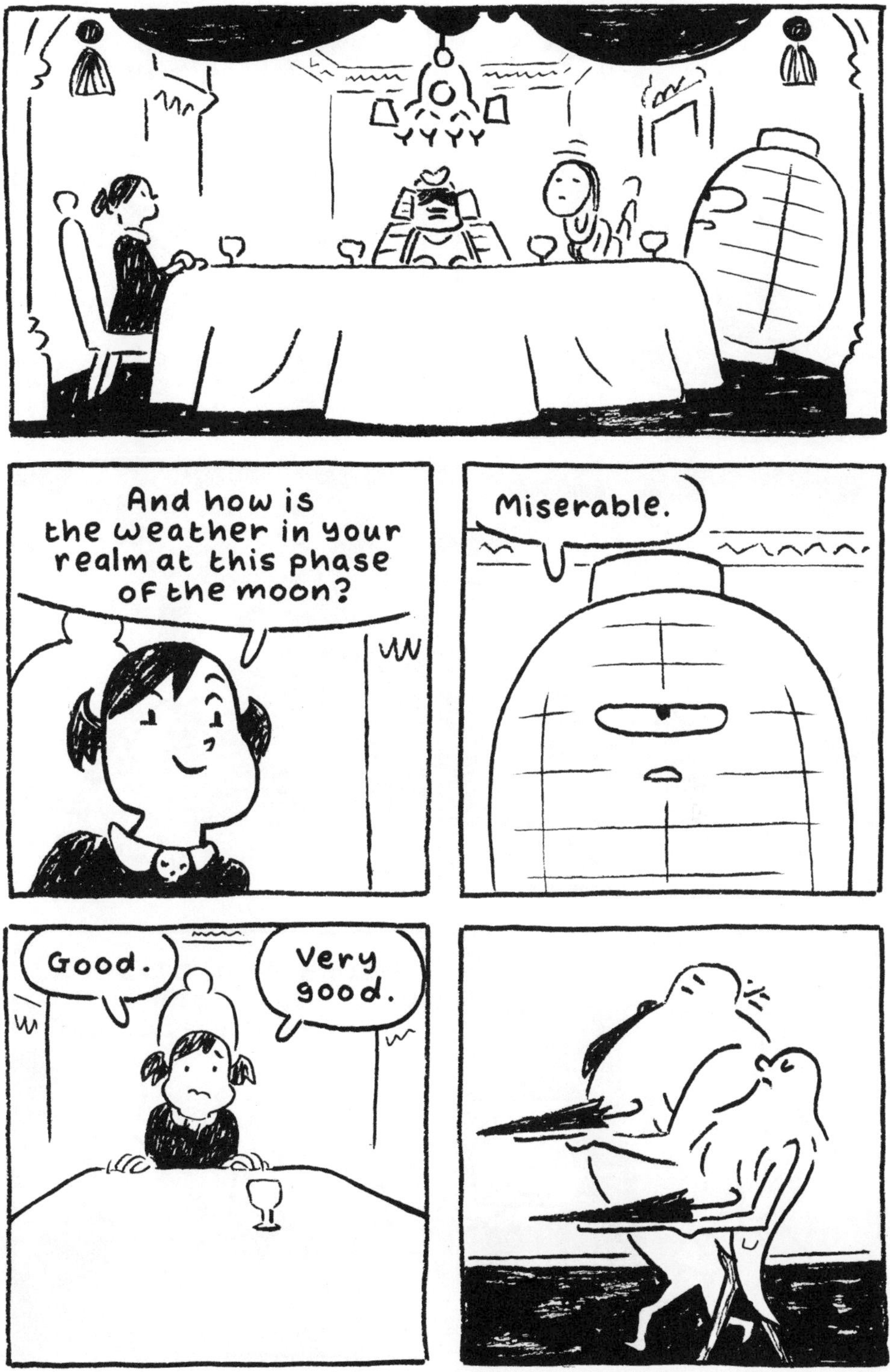
And how is the weather in your realm at this phase of the moon?
Miserable.
Good.
Very good.

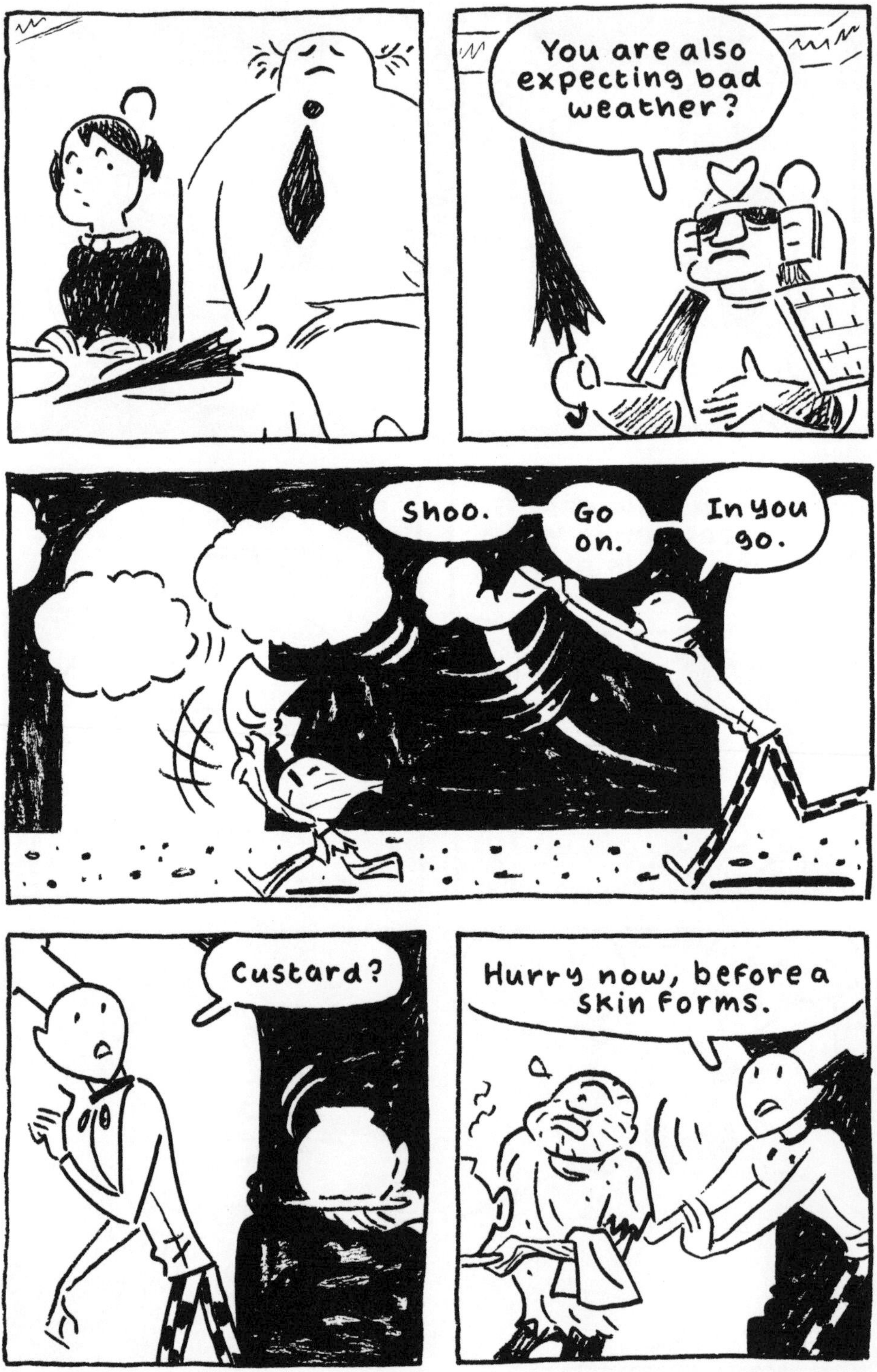
You are also expecting bad weather?
Shoo.
Go on.
In you go.
Custard?
Hurry now, before a skin forms.

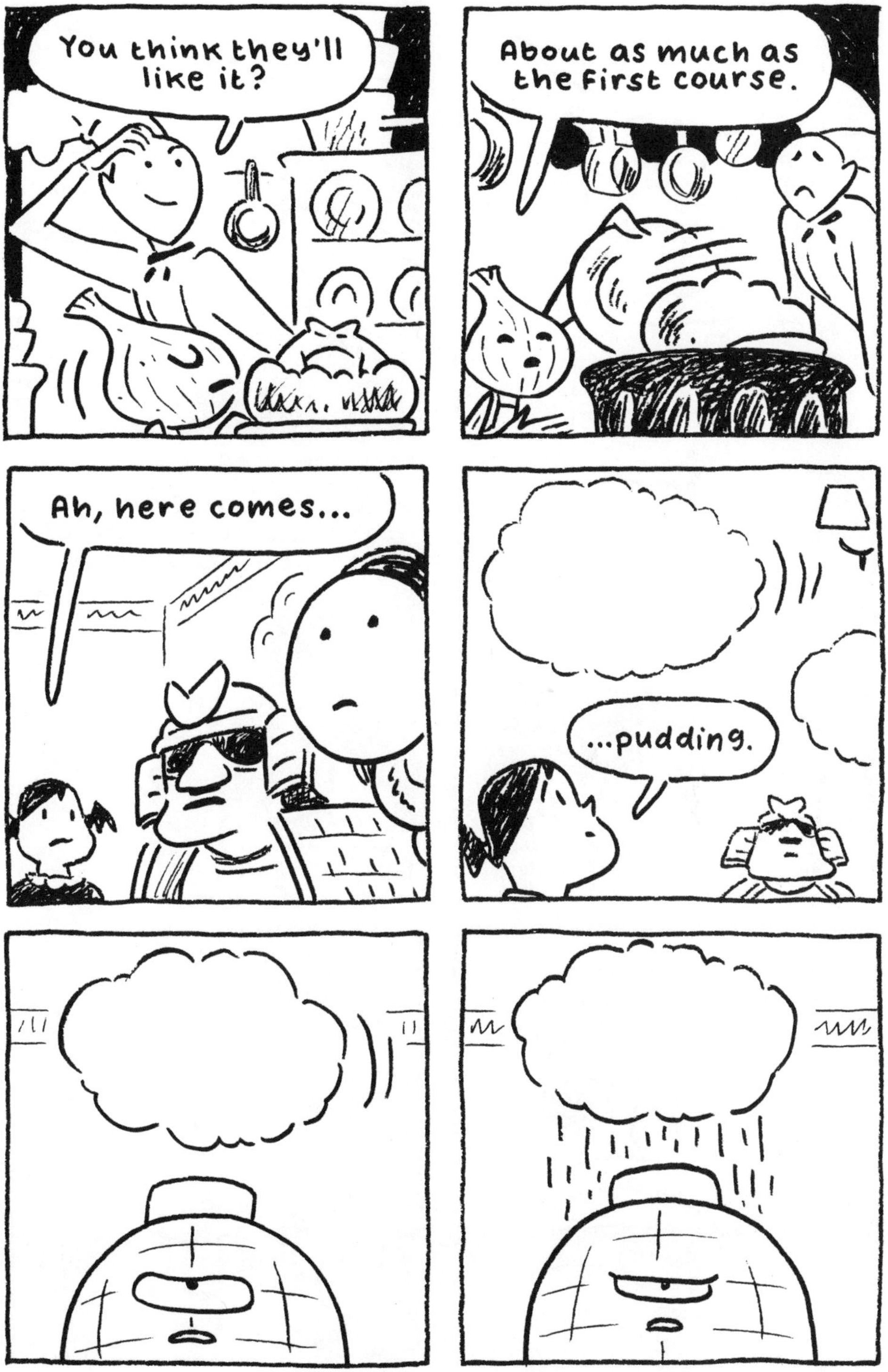
You think they'll like it?
About as much as the first course.
Ah, here comes...
...pudding.

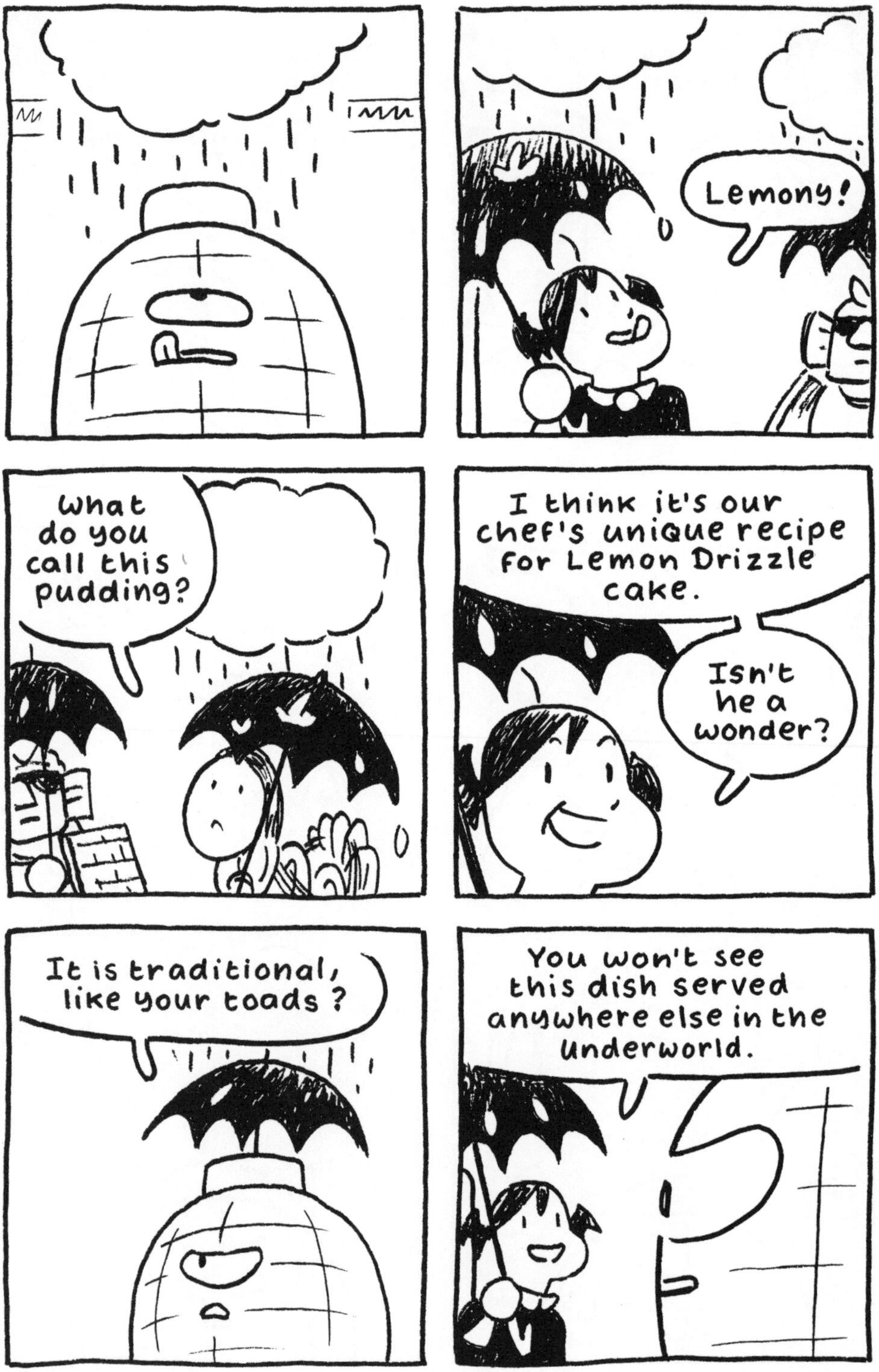
Lemony!
What do you call this pudding?
I think it's our chef's unique recipe for Lemon Drizzle cake.
Isn't he a wonder?
It is traditional, like your toads?
You won't see this dish served anywhere else in the Underworld.

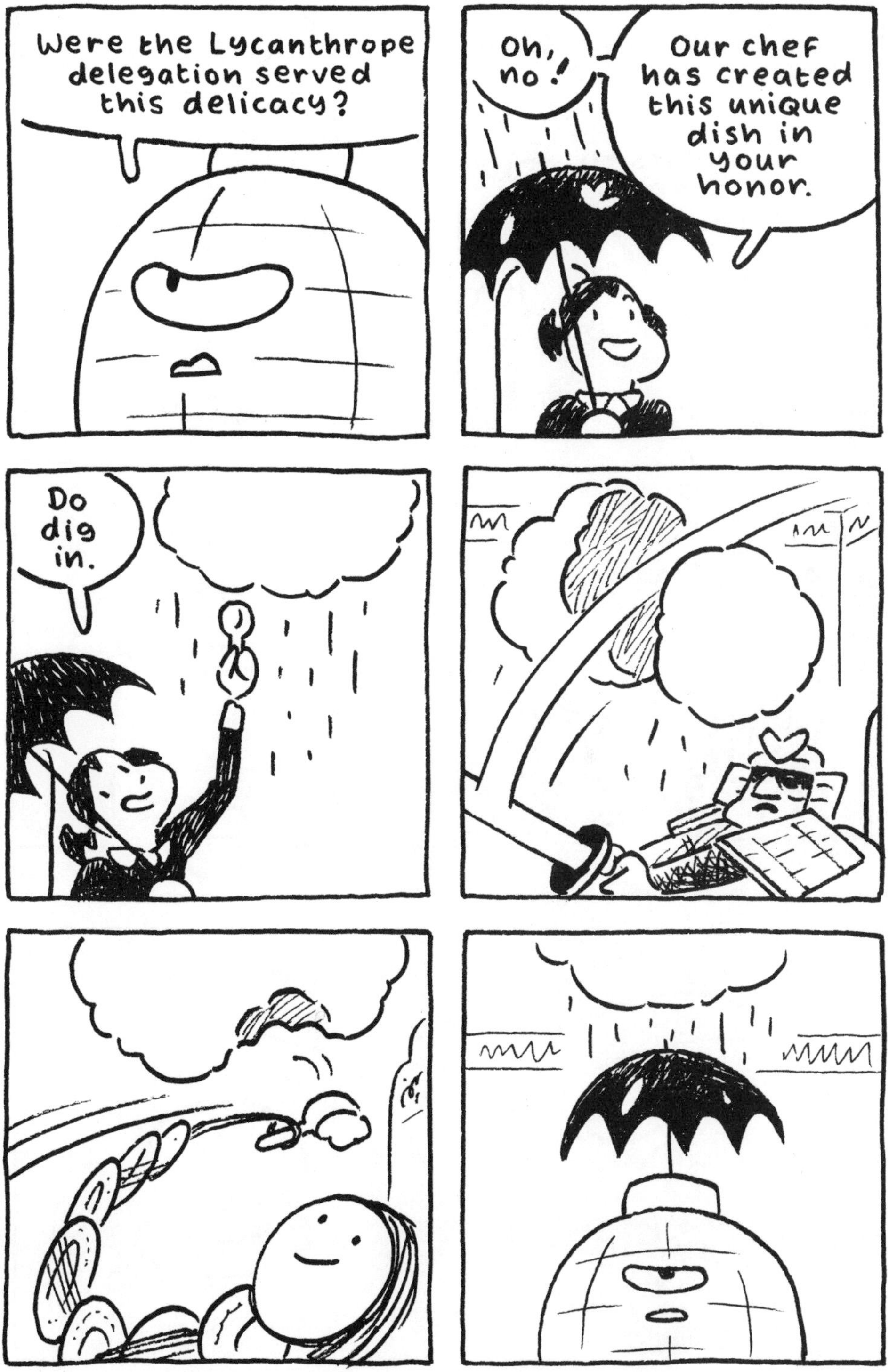

Were the Lycanthrope delegation served this delicacy?
Oh, no!
Our chef has created this unique dish in your honor.
Do dig in.

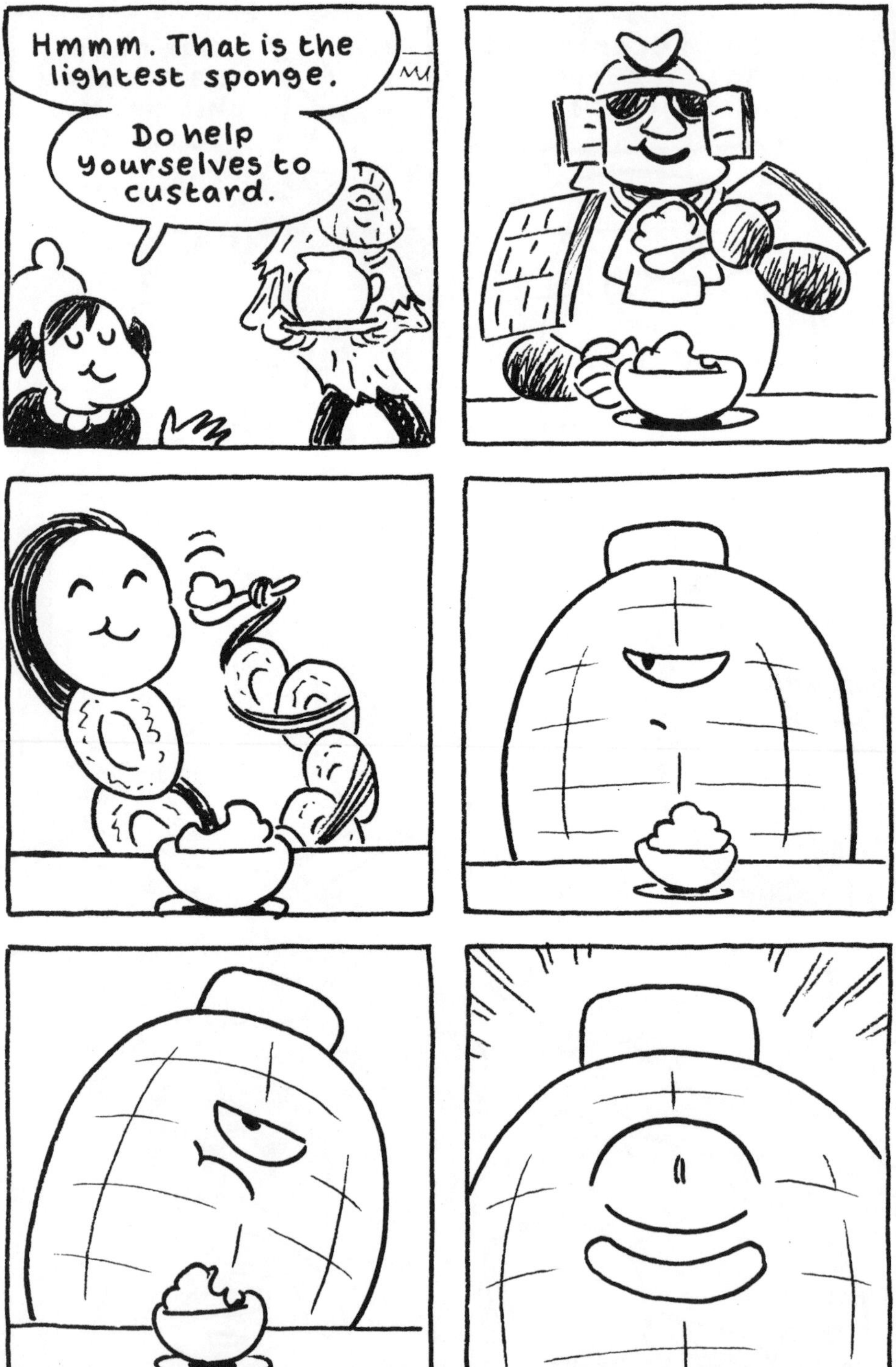
Hmmm. That is the lightest sponge.
Do help yourselves to custard.

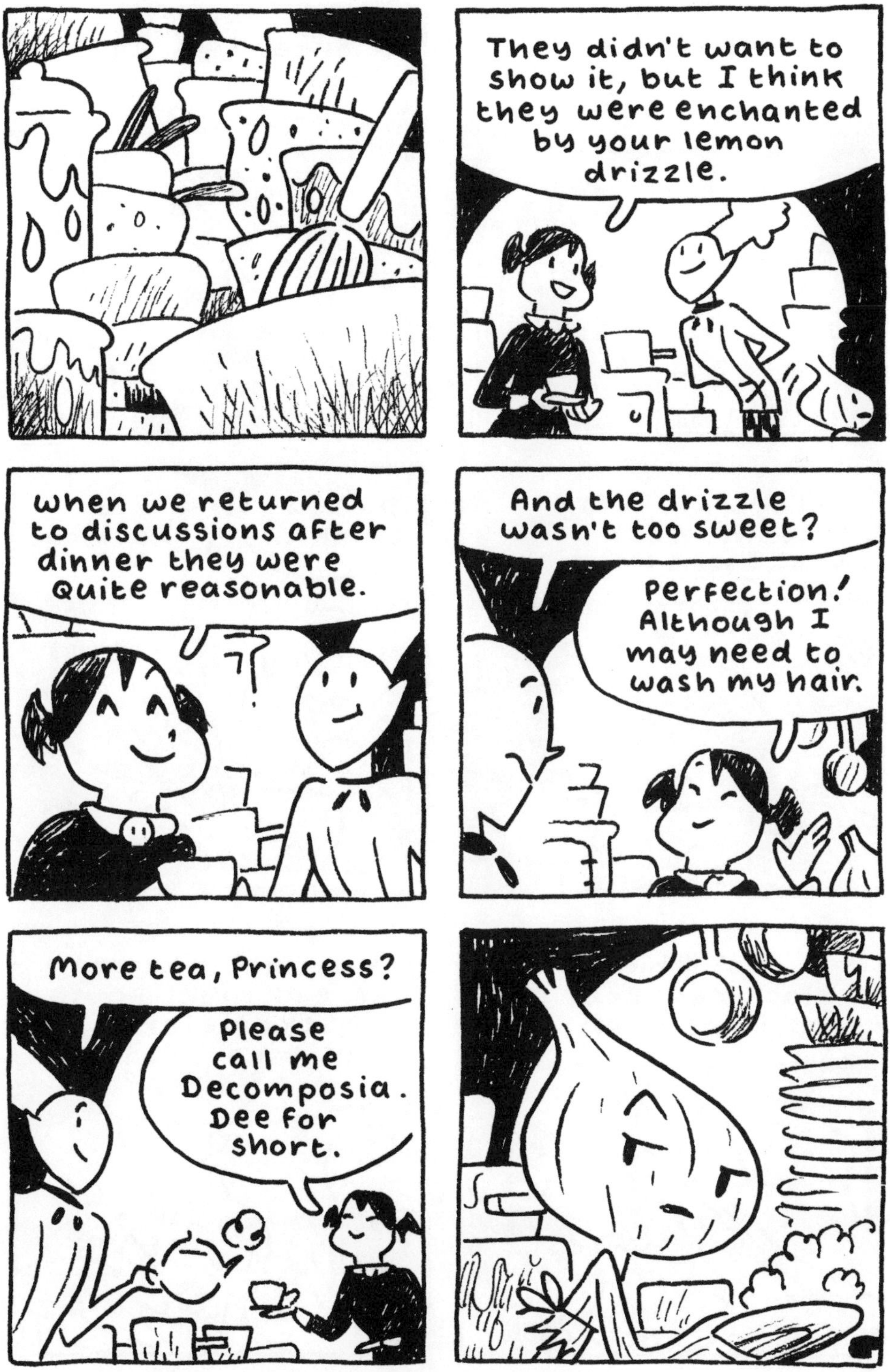
They didn't want to show it, but I think they were enchanted by your lemon drizzle.
When we returned to discussions after dinner they were quite reasonable.
And the drizzle wasn't too sweet?
Perfection! Although I may need to wash my hair.
More tea, Princess?
Please call me Decomposia. Dee for short.

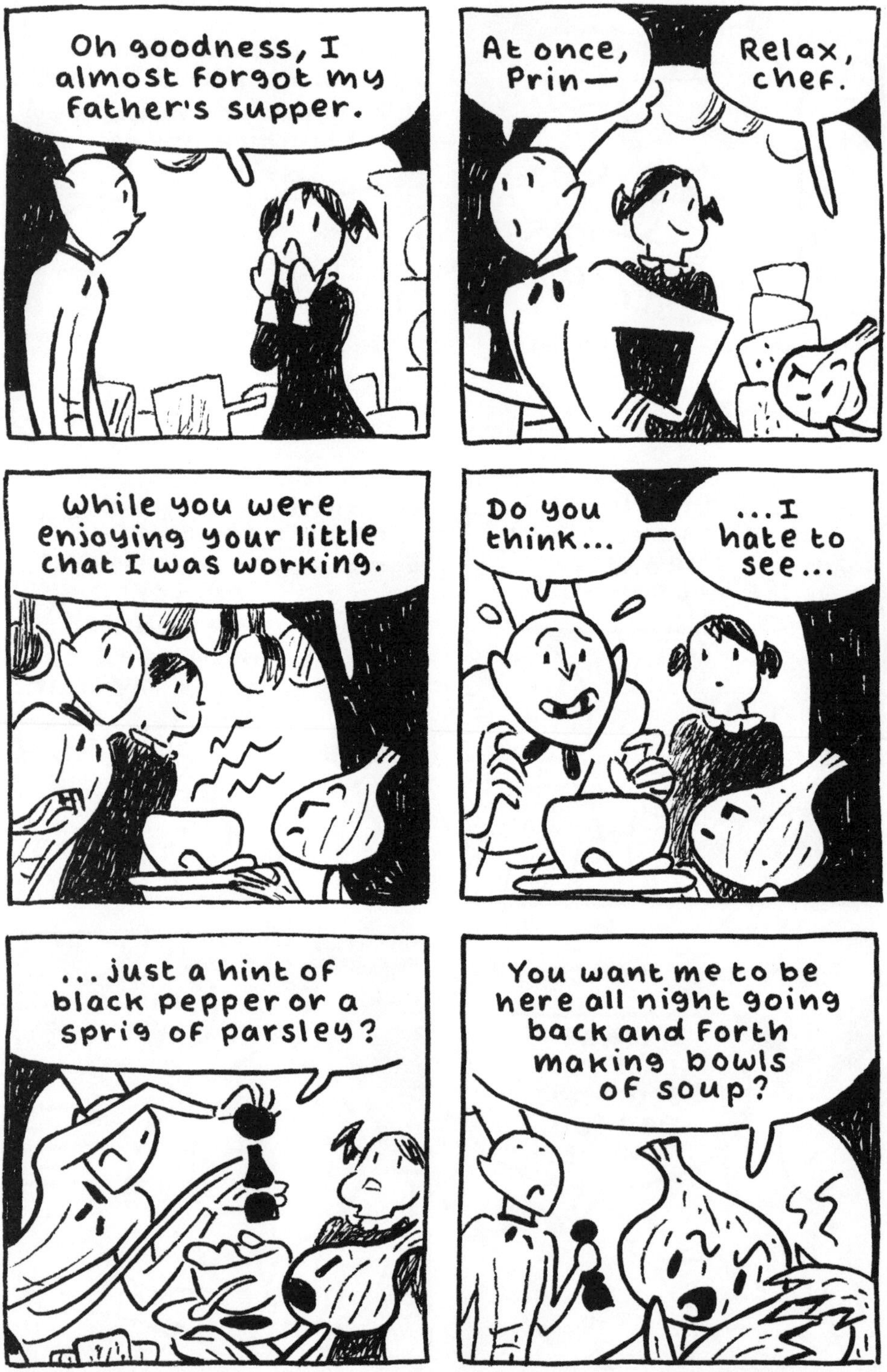
Oh goodness, I almost forgot my father's supper.
At once, Prin—
Relax, chef.
While you were enjoying your little chat I was working.
Do you think...
...I hate to see...
...just a hint of black pepper or a sprig of parsley?
You want me to be here all night going back and forth making bowls of soup?

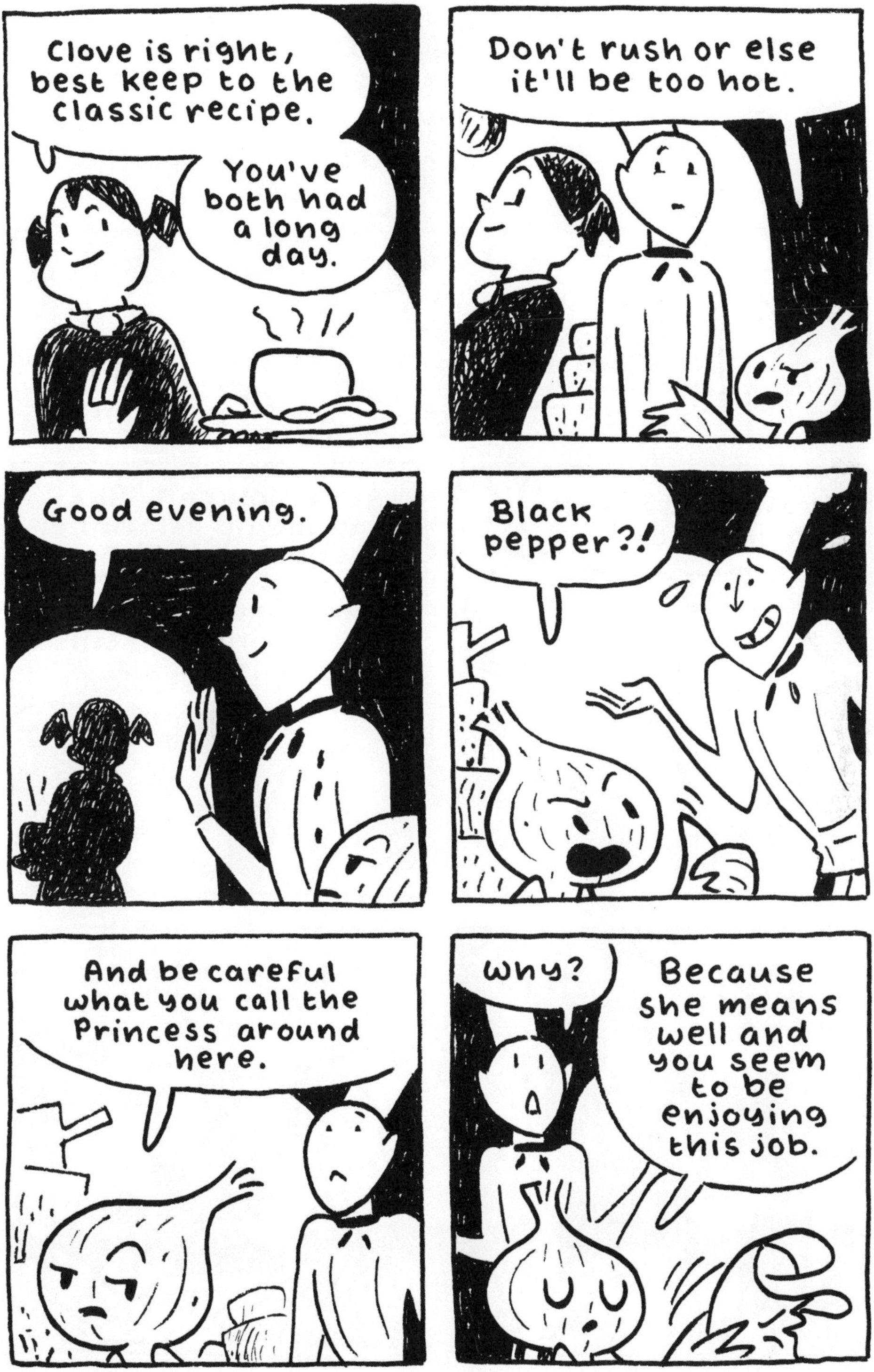
Clove is right, best keep to the classic recipe.
You've both had a long day.
Don't rush or else it'll be too hot.
Good evening.
Black pepper?!
And be careful what you call the Princess around here.
Why?
Because she means well and you seem to be enjoying this job.

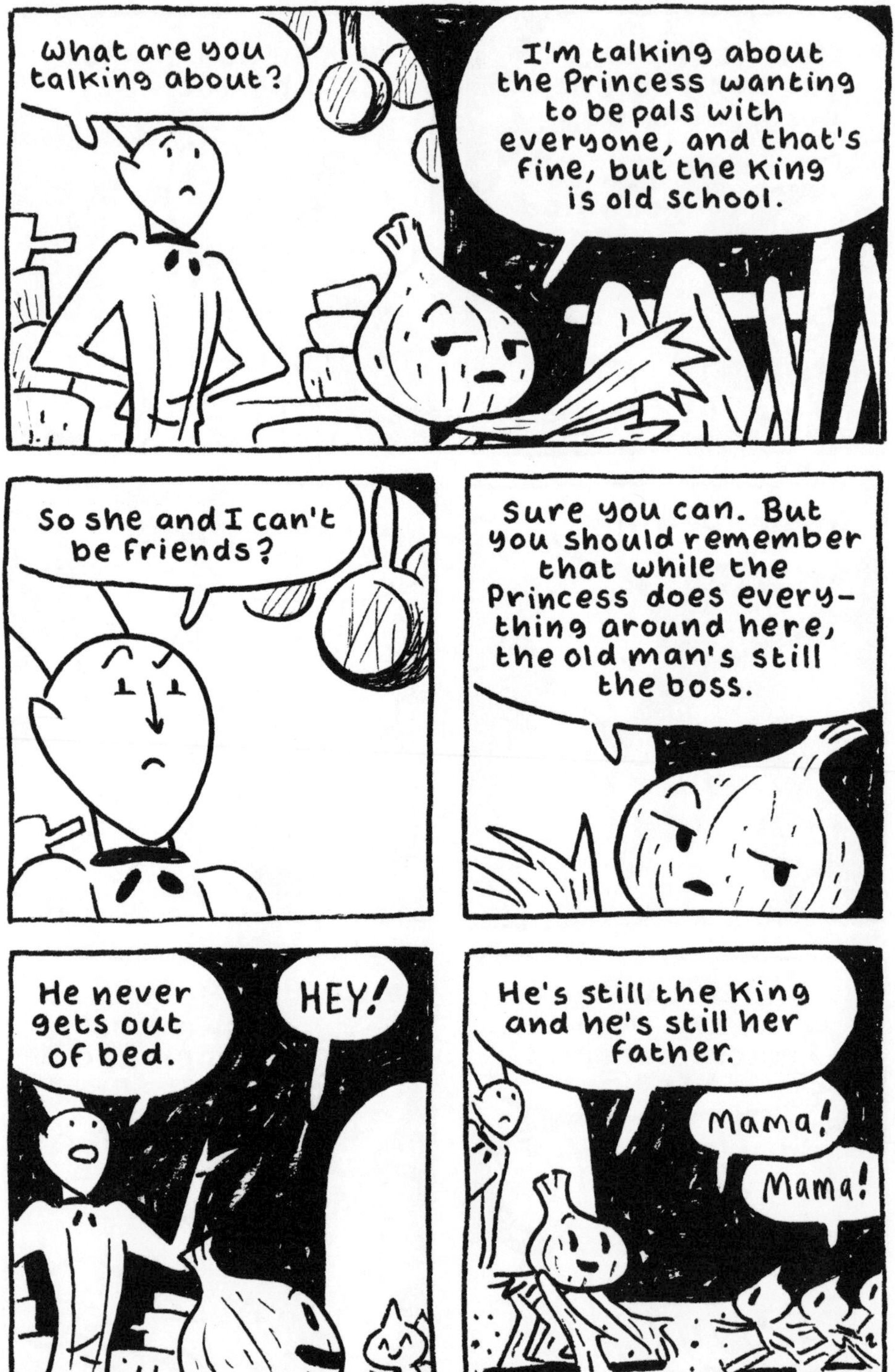
What are you talking about?
I'm talking about the Princess wanting to be pals with everyone, and that's fine, but the King is old school.
So she and I can't be friends?
Sure you can. But you should remember that while the Princess does every-thing around here, the old man's still the boss.
He never gets out of bed.
HEY!
He's still the King and he's still her father.
Mama!
Mama!

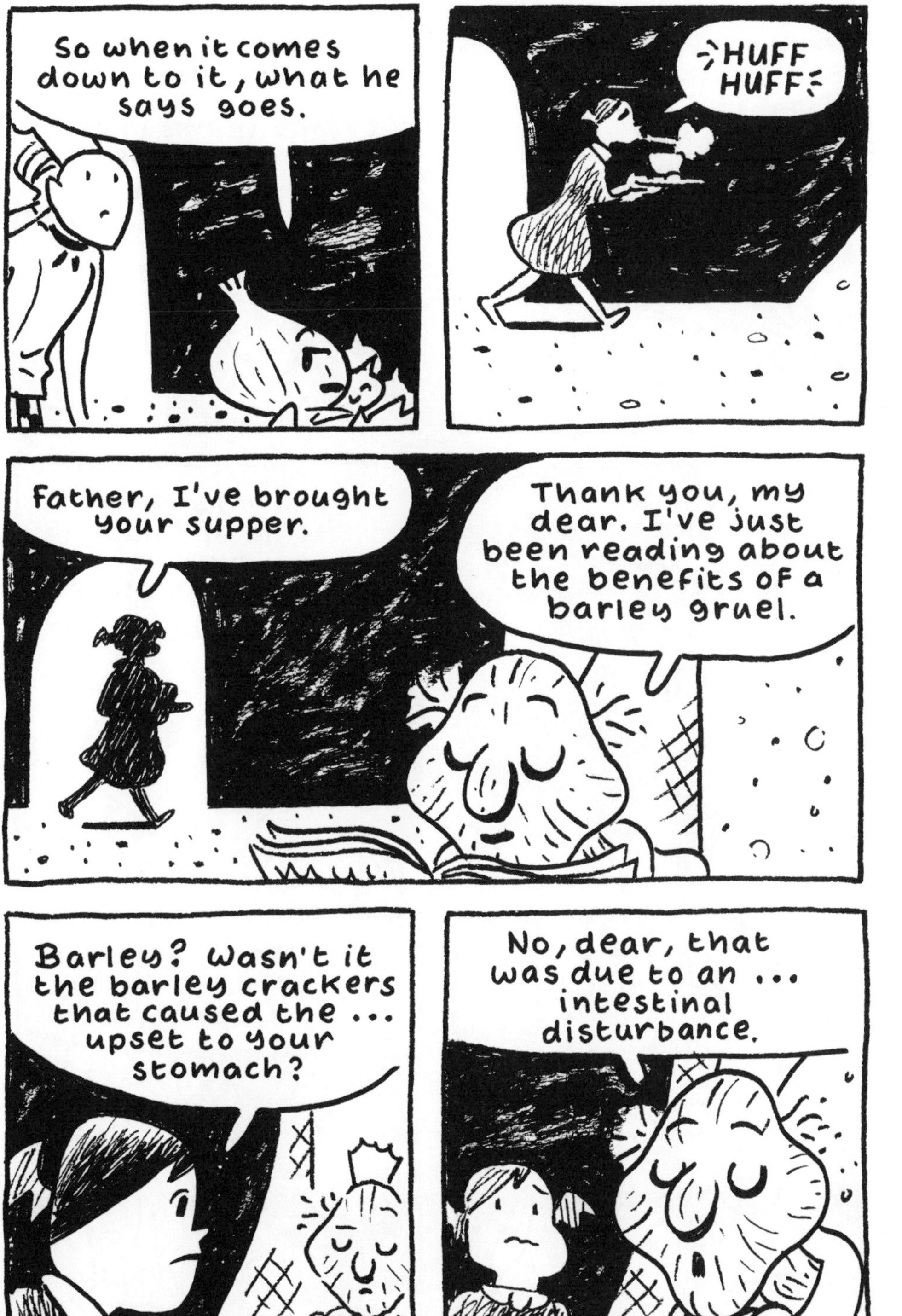
So when it comes down to it, what he says goes.
HUFF HUFF
Father, I've brought your supper.
Thank you, my dear. I've just been reading about the benefits of a barley gruel.
Barley? Wasn't it the barley crackers that caused the ... upset to your stomach?
No, dear, that was due to an ... intestinal disturbance.

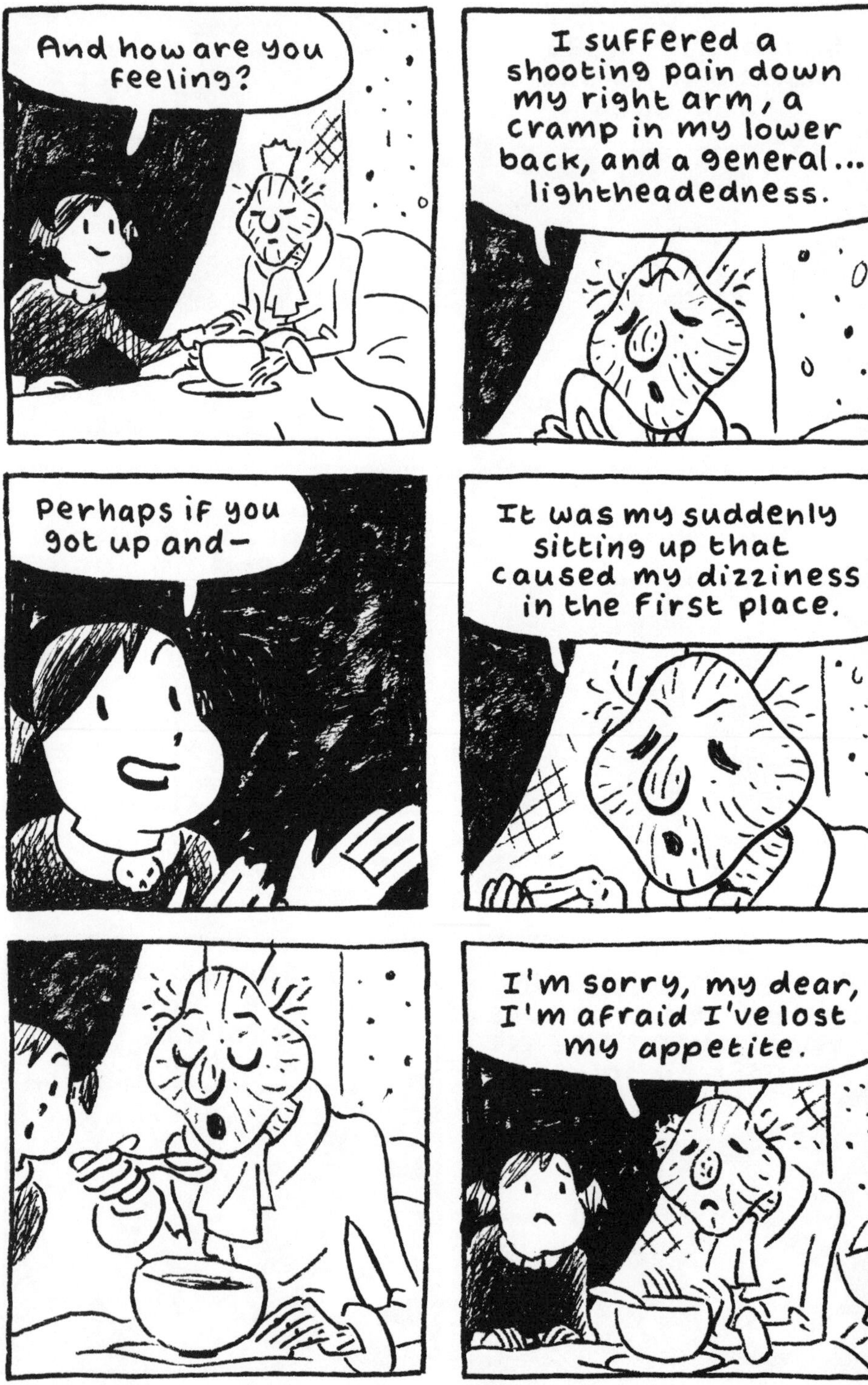
And how are you feeling?
I suffered a shooting pain down my right arm, a cramp in my lower back, and a general... lightheadedness.
Perhaps if you got up and-
It was my suddenly sitting up that caused my dizziness in the first place.
I'm sorry, my dear, I'm afraid I've lost my appetite.

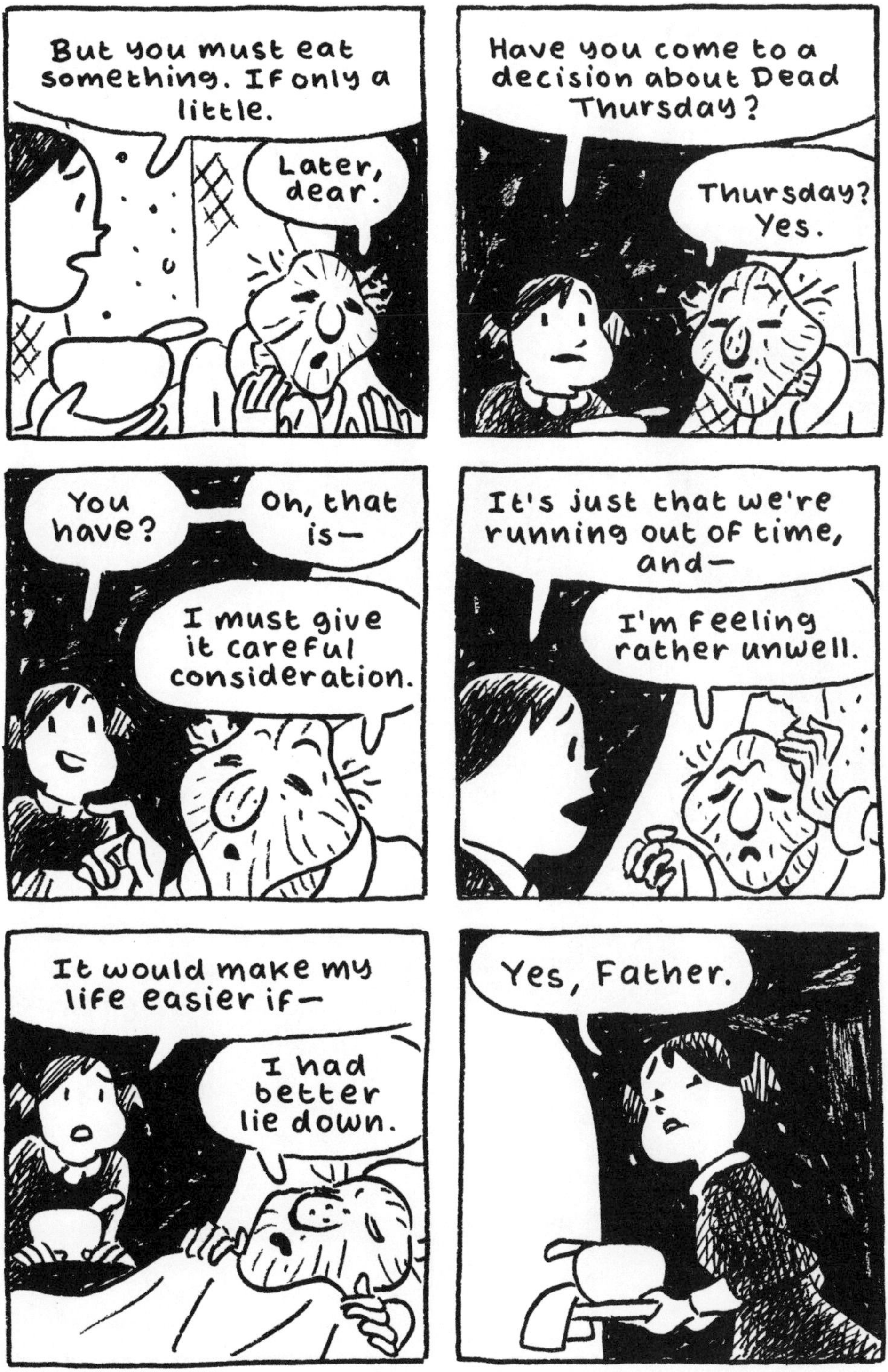
But you must eat something. If only a little.
Later, dear.
Have you come to a decision about Dead Thursday?
Thursday? Yes.
You have?
Oh, that is—
I must give it careful consideration.
It's just that we're running out of time, and—
I'm feeling rather unwell.
It would make my life easier if—
I had better lie down.
Yes, Father.

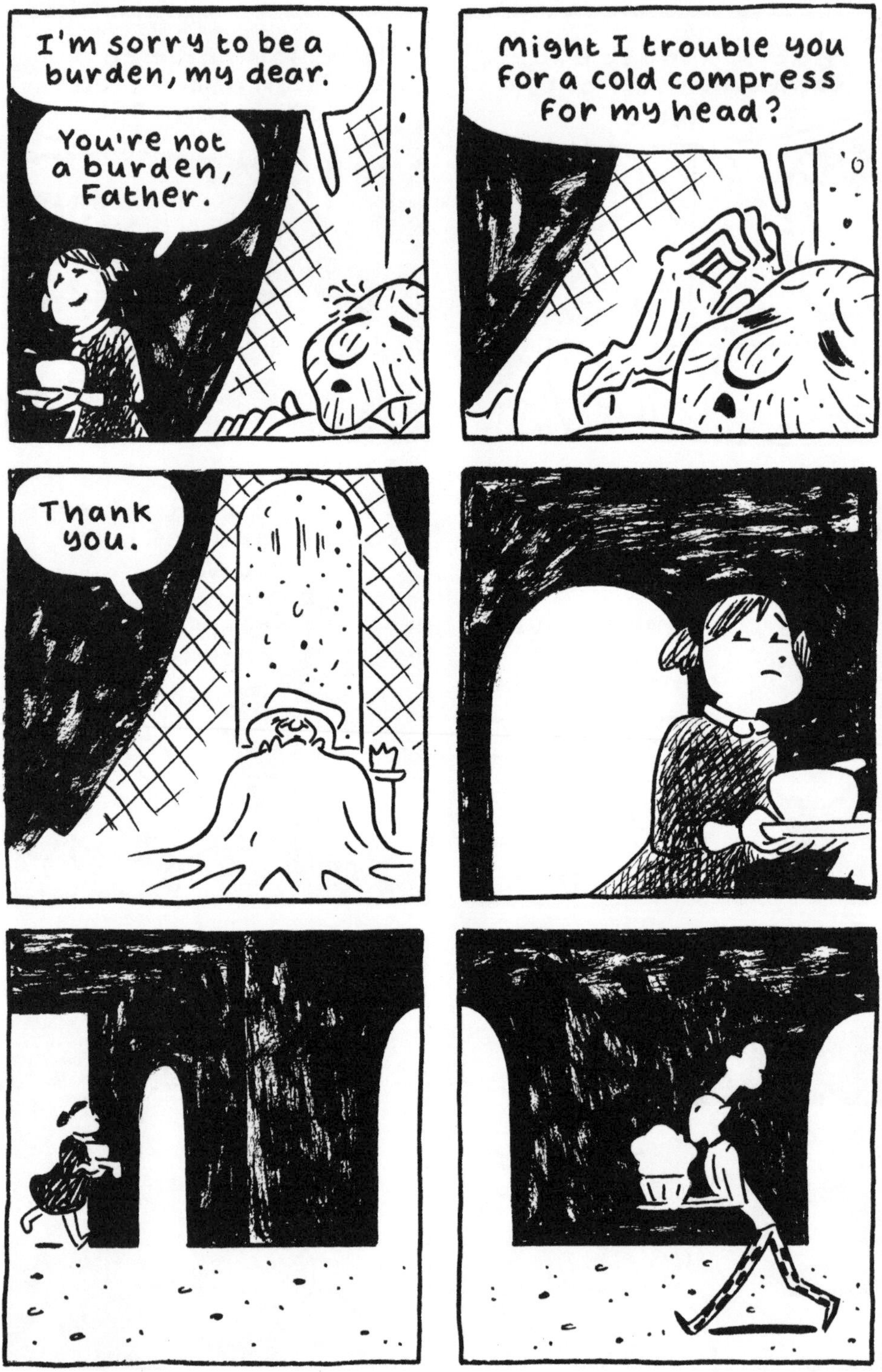
I'm sorry to be a burden, my dear.
You're not a burden, Father.
Might I trouble you for a cold compress for my head?
Thank you.

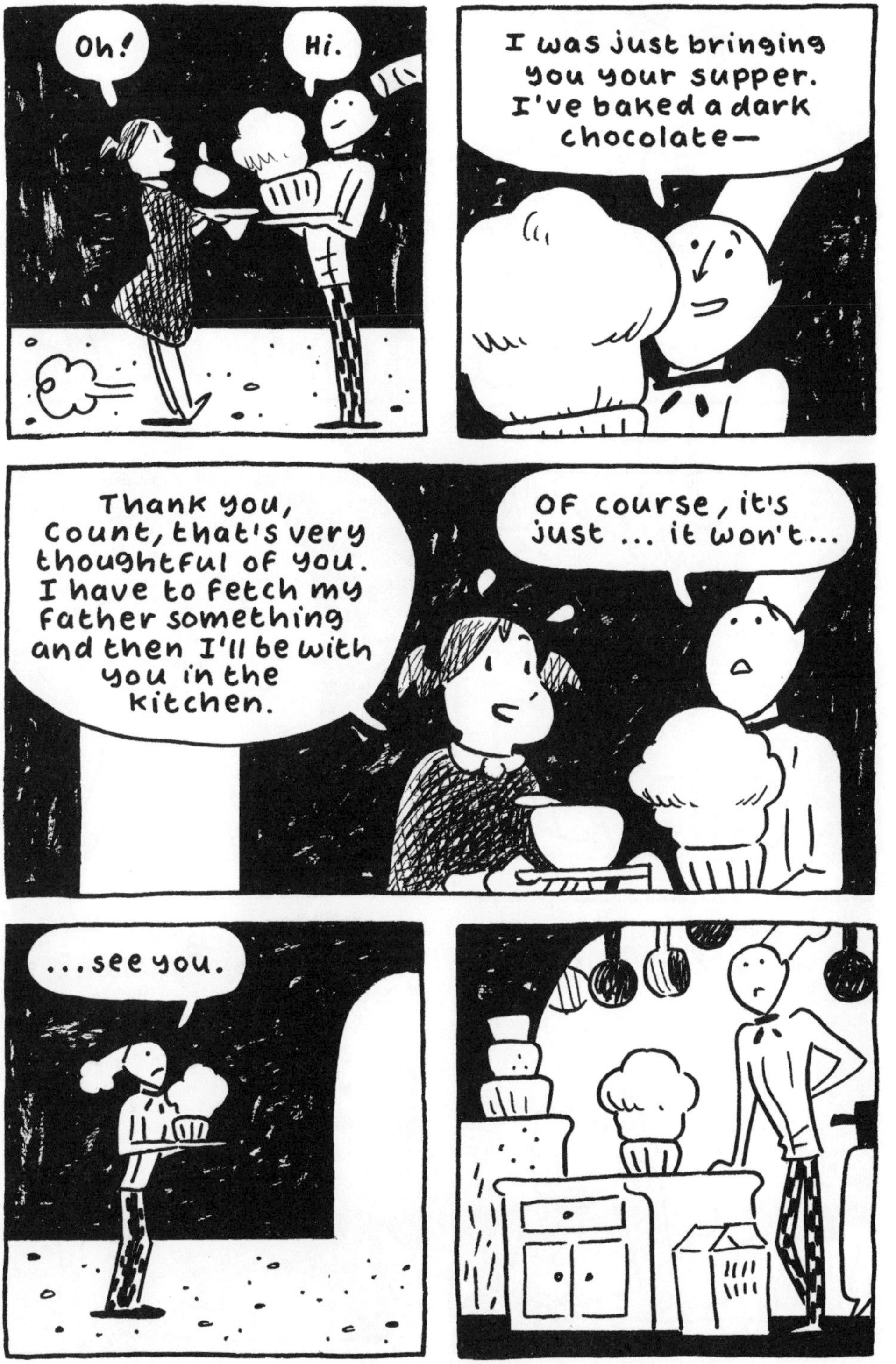
Oh!
Hi.
I was just bringing you your supper. I've baked a dark chocolate—
Thank you, Count, that's very thoughtful of you. I have to fetch my father something and then I'll be with you in the kitchen.
Of course, it's just ... it won't...
...see you.

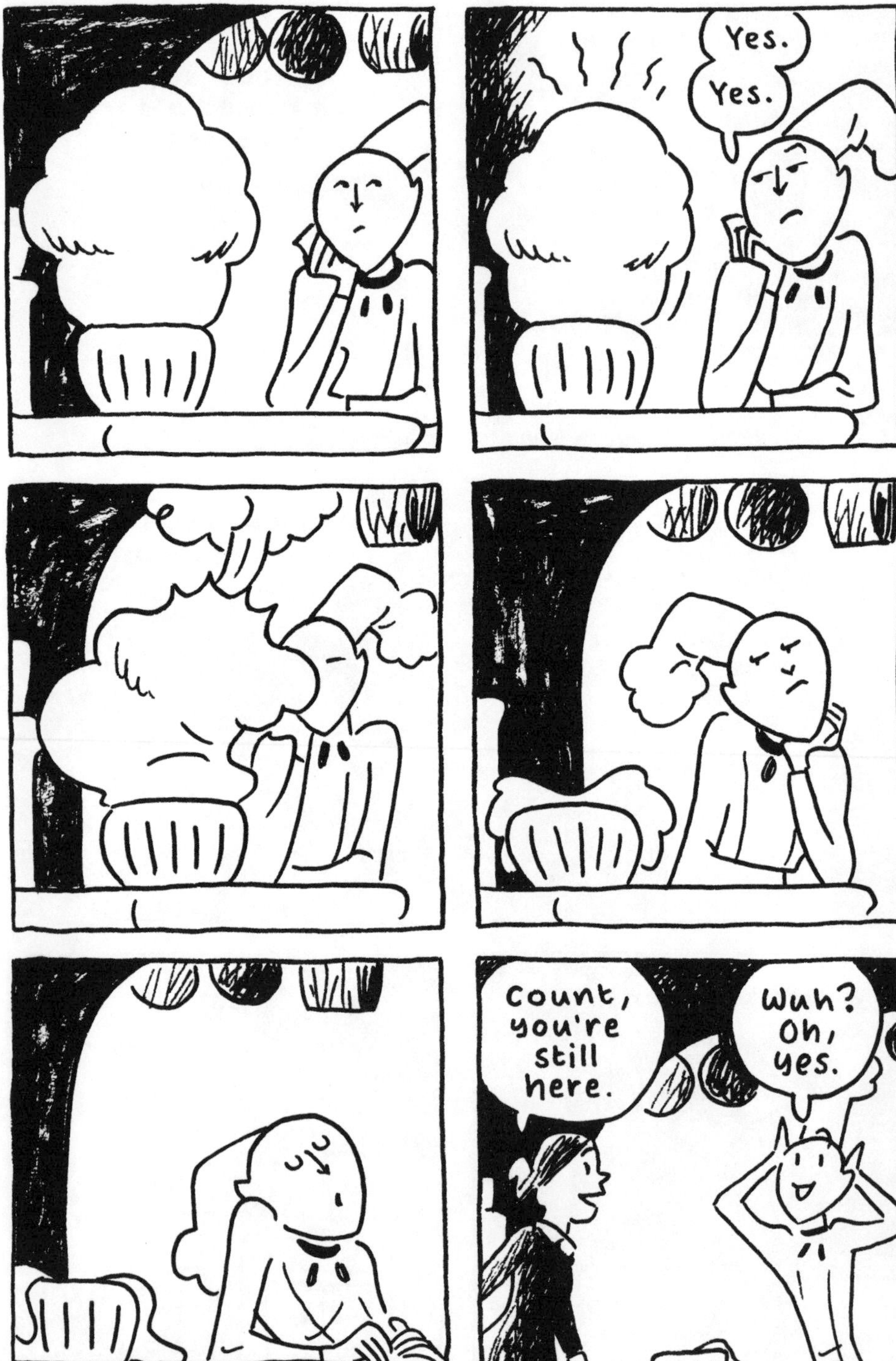
Yes.
Yes.
Count, you're still here.
Wuh? Oh, yes.

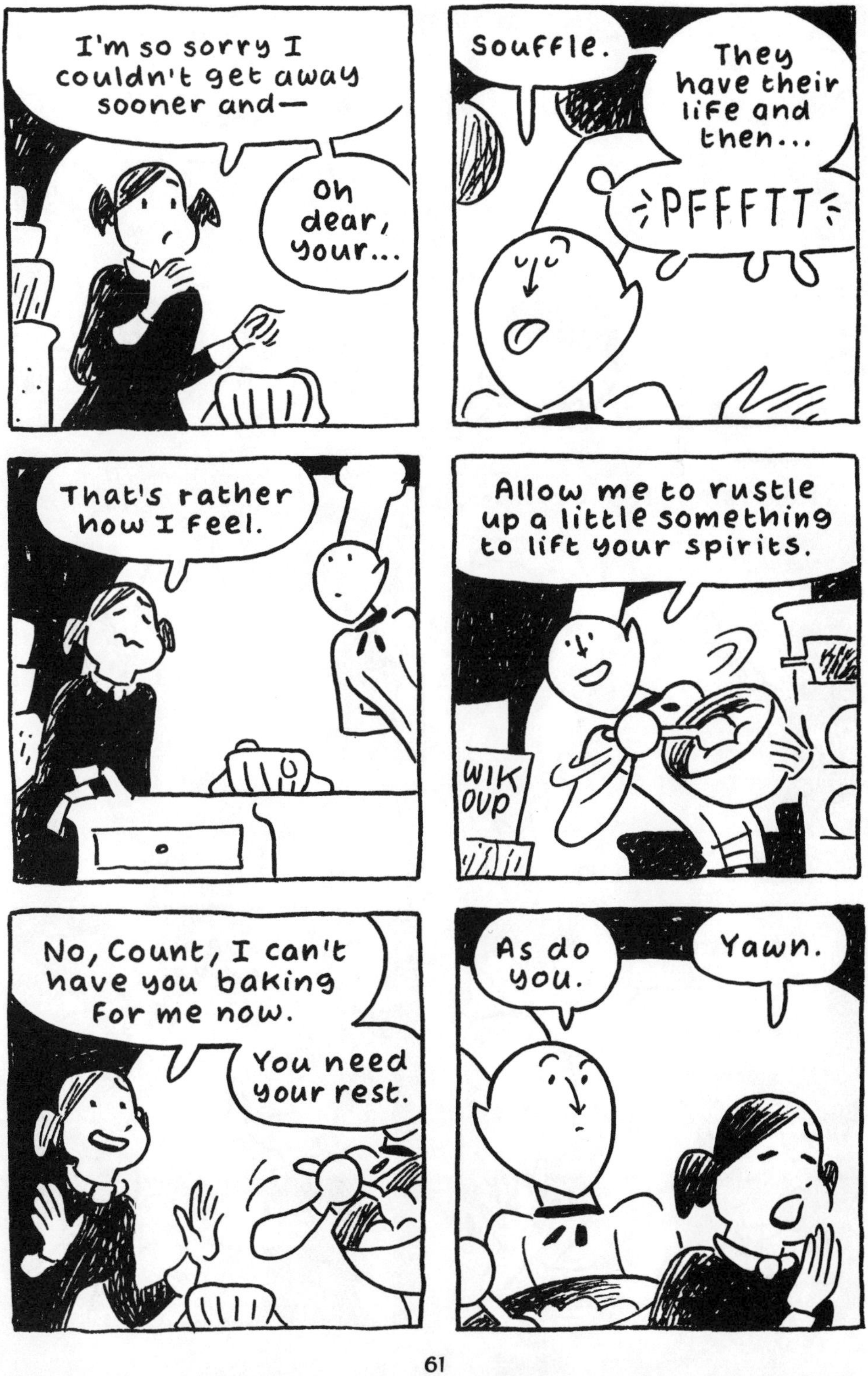
I'm so sorry I couldn't get away sooner and—
Oh dear, your...
Souffle.
They have their life and then...
PFFFTT
That's rather how I feel.
Allow me to rustle up a little something to lift your spirits.
WIK
OUP
No, Count, I can't have you baking for me now.
You need your rest.
As do you.
Yawn.

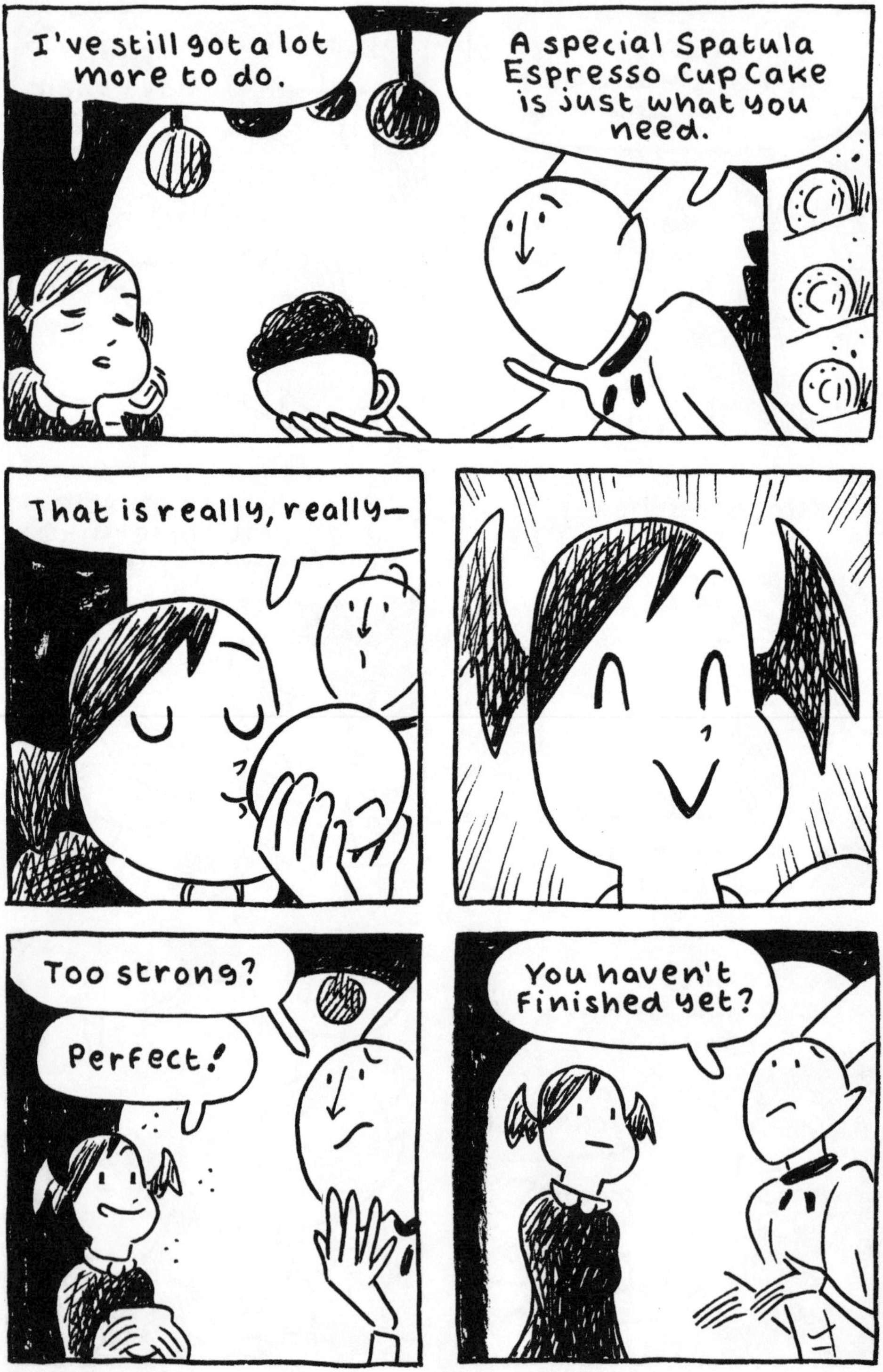
I've still got a lot more to do.
A special Spatula Espresso CupCake is just what you need.
That is really, really—
Too strong?
Perfect!
You haven't finished yet?

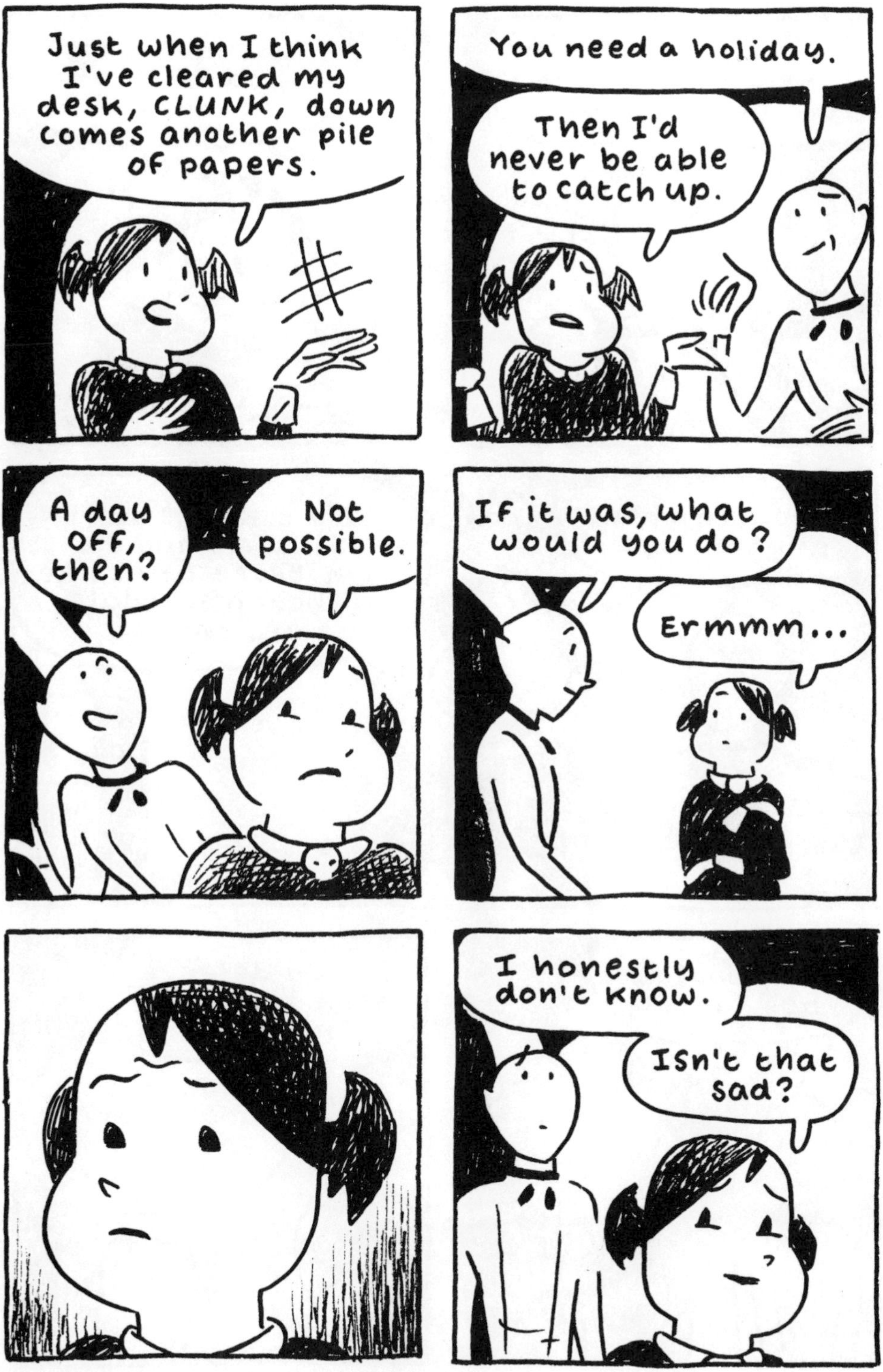
Just when I think I've cleared my desk, CLUNK, down comes another pile of papers.
You need a holiday.
Then I'd never be able to catch up.
A day off, then?
Not possible.
If it was, what would you do?
Ermmm...
I honestly don't know.
Isn't that sad?

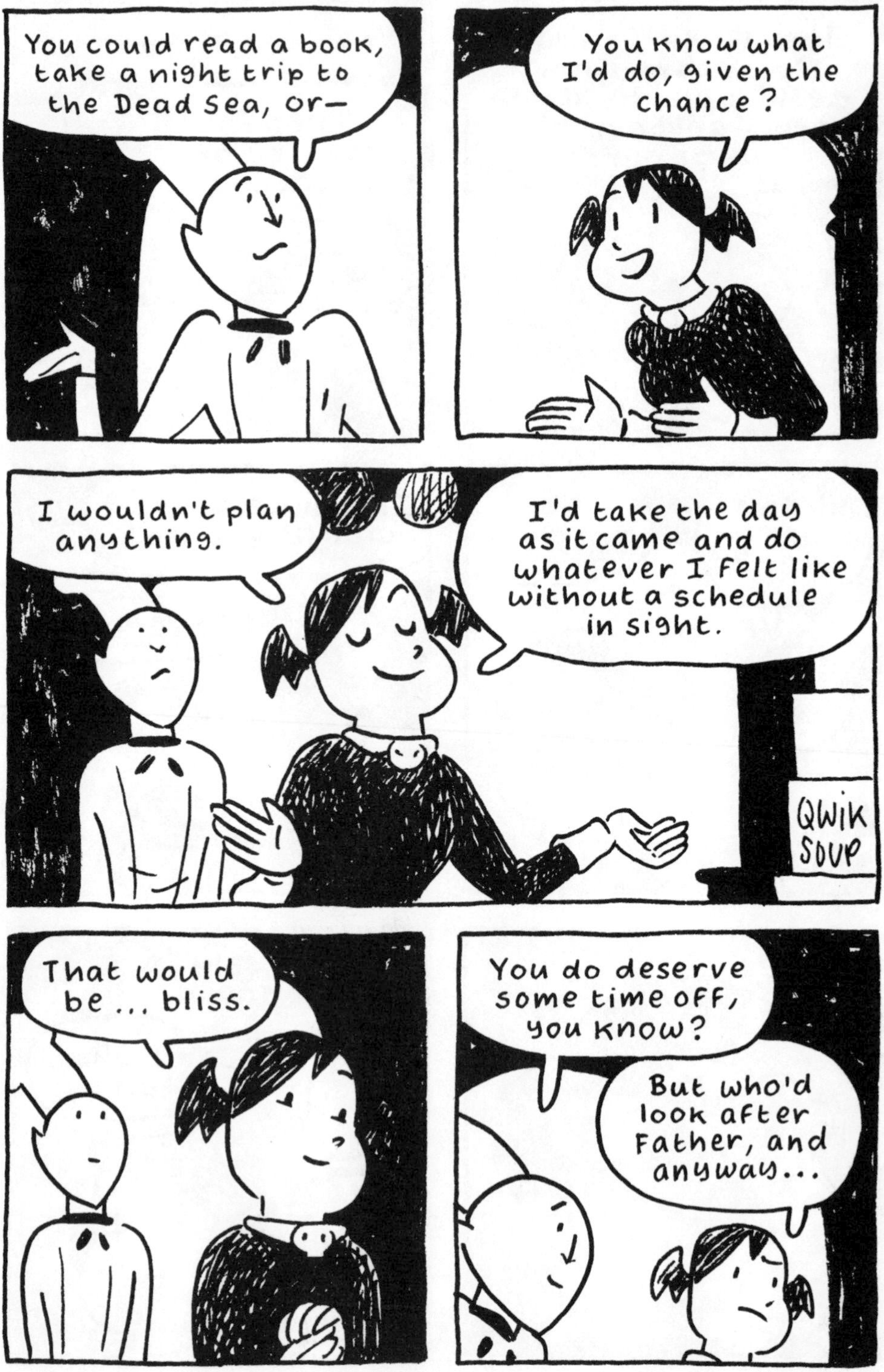
You could read a book, take a night trip to the Dead Sea, or—
You know what I'd do, given the chance?
I wouldn't plan anything.
I'd take the day as it came and do whatever I felt like without a schedule in sight.
QWIK SOUP
That would be ... bliss.
You do deserve some time off, you know?
But who'd look after Father, and anyway...

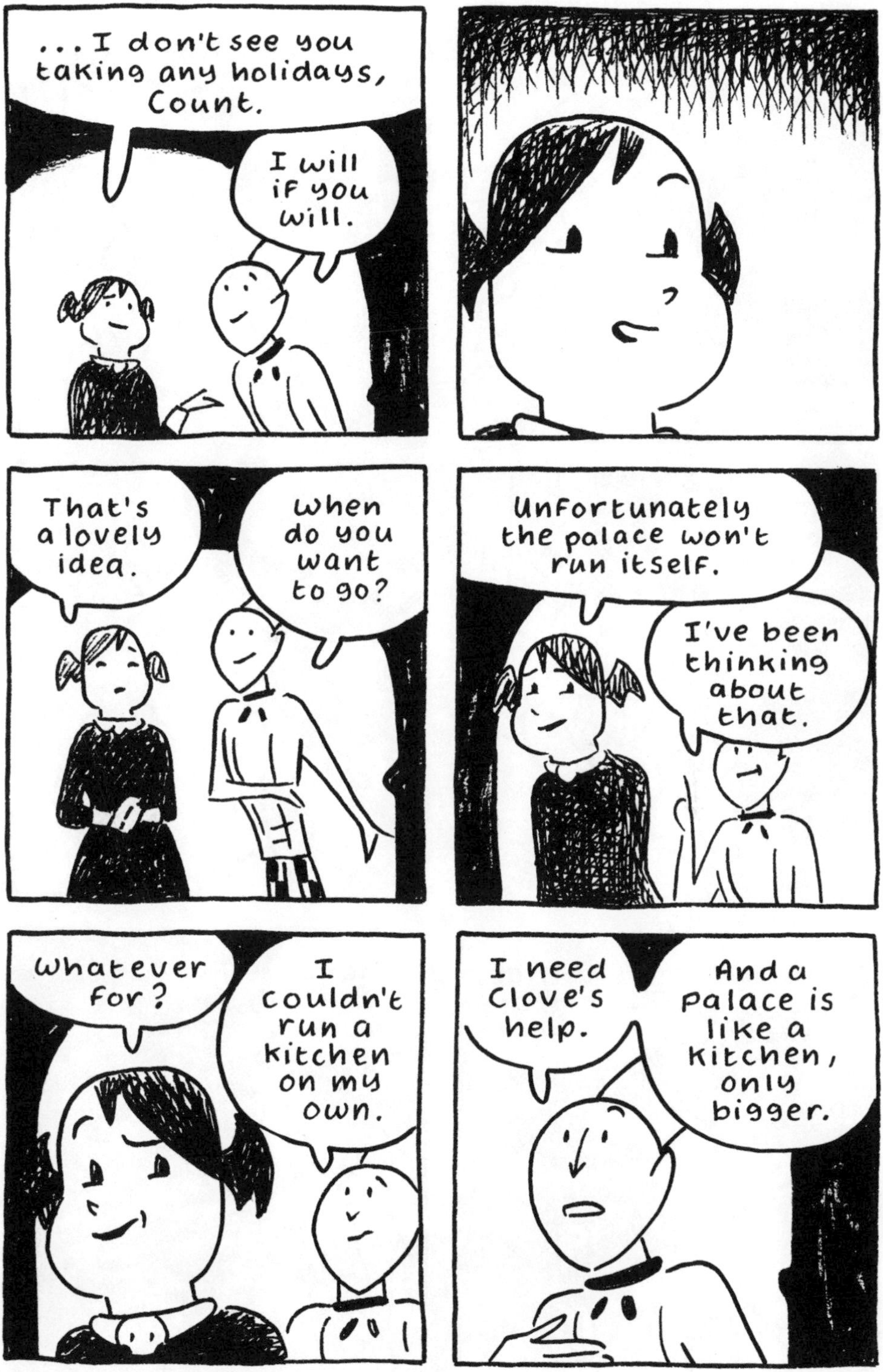
...I don't see you taking any holidays, Count.
I will if you will.
That's a lovely idea.
When do you want to go?
Unfortunately the palace won't run itself.
I've been thinking about that.
Whatever for?
I couldn't run a kitchen on my own.
I need Clove's help.
And a palace is like a kitchen, only bigger.

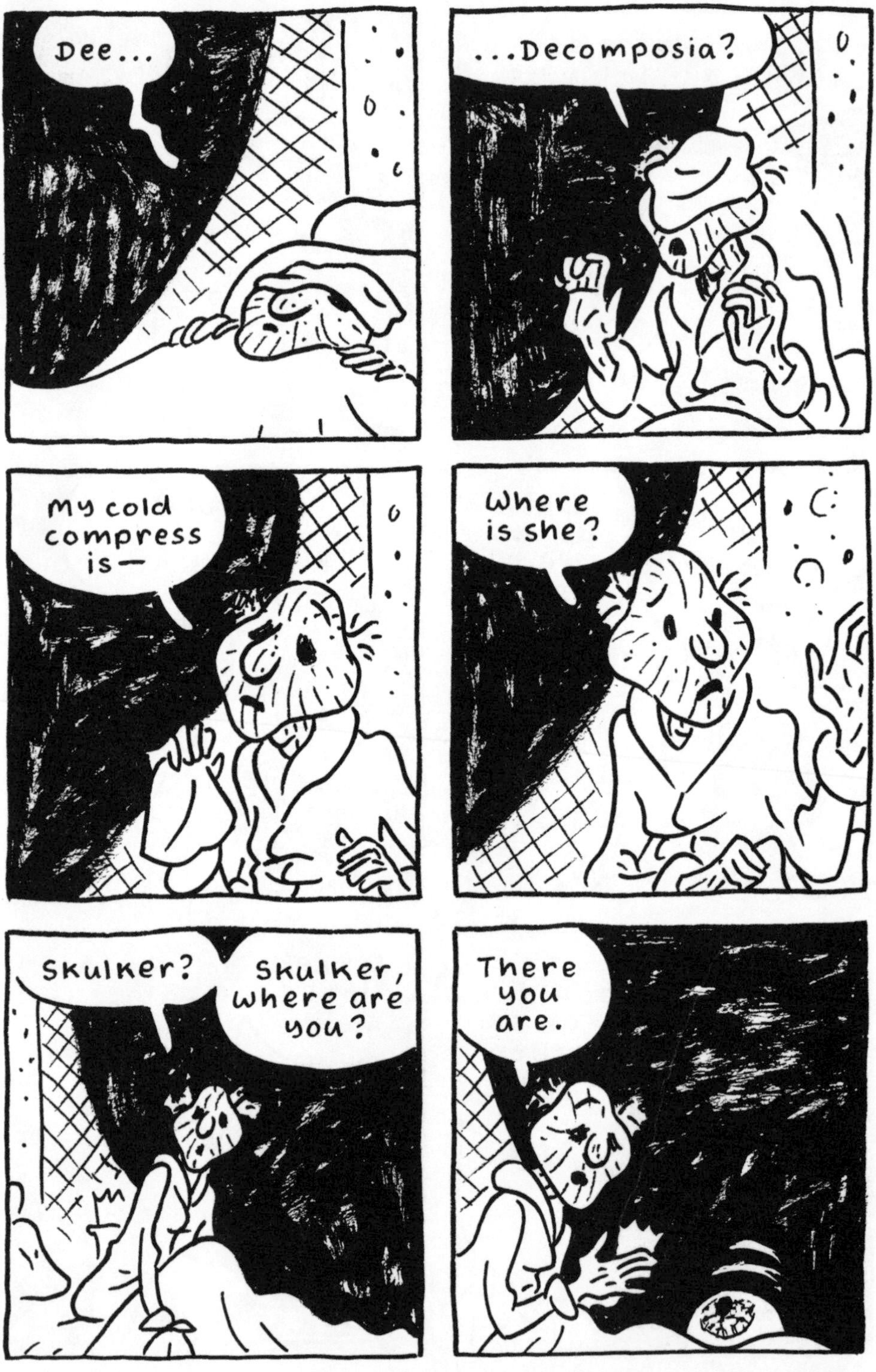
Dee...
...Decomposia?
My cold compress is—
Where is she?
Skulker?
Skulker, where are you?
There you are.

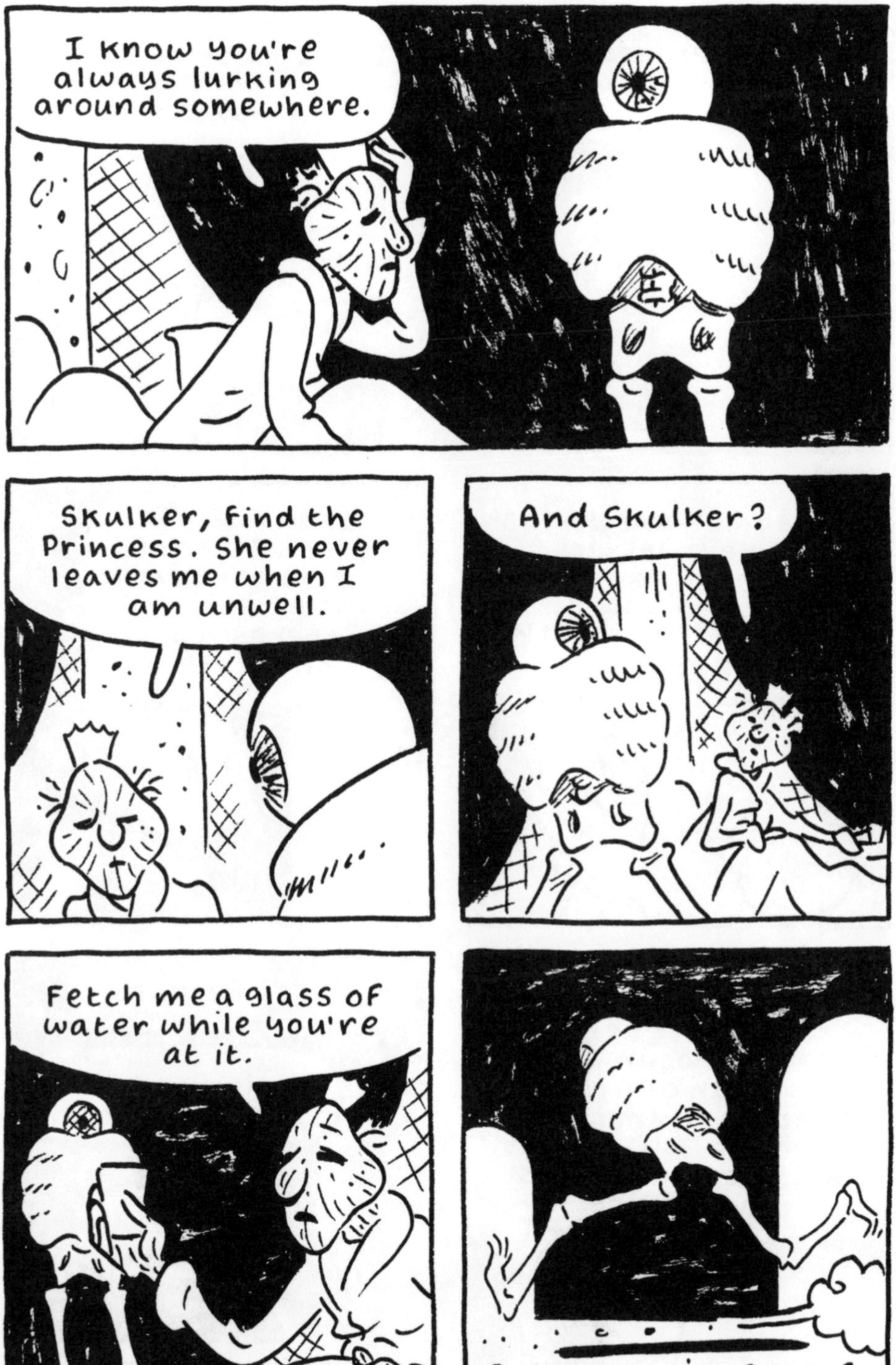
I know you're always lurking around somewhere.
Skulker, find the Princess. She never leaves me when I am unwell.
And Skulker?
Fetch me a glass of water while you're at it.

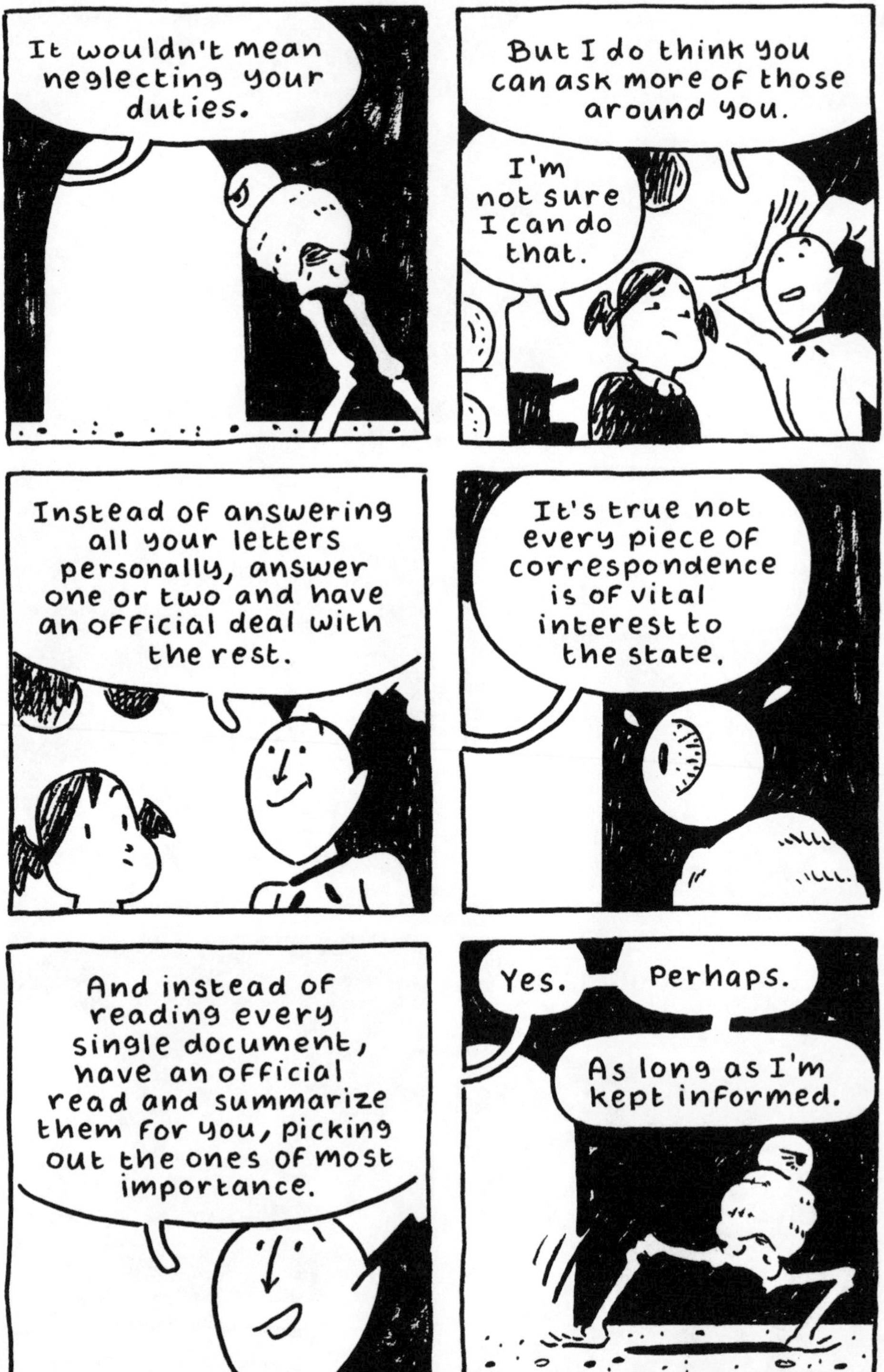
It wouldn't mean neglecting your duties.
But I do think you can ask more of those around you.
I'm not sure I can do that.
Instead of answering all your letters personally, answer one or two and have an official deal with the rest.
It's true not every piece of correspondence is of vital interest to the state.
And instead of reading every single document, have an official read and summarize them for you, picking out the ones of most importance.
Yes.
Perhaps.
As long as I'm kept informed.

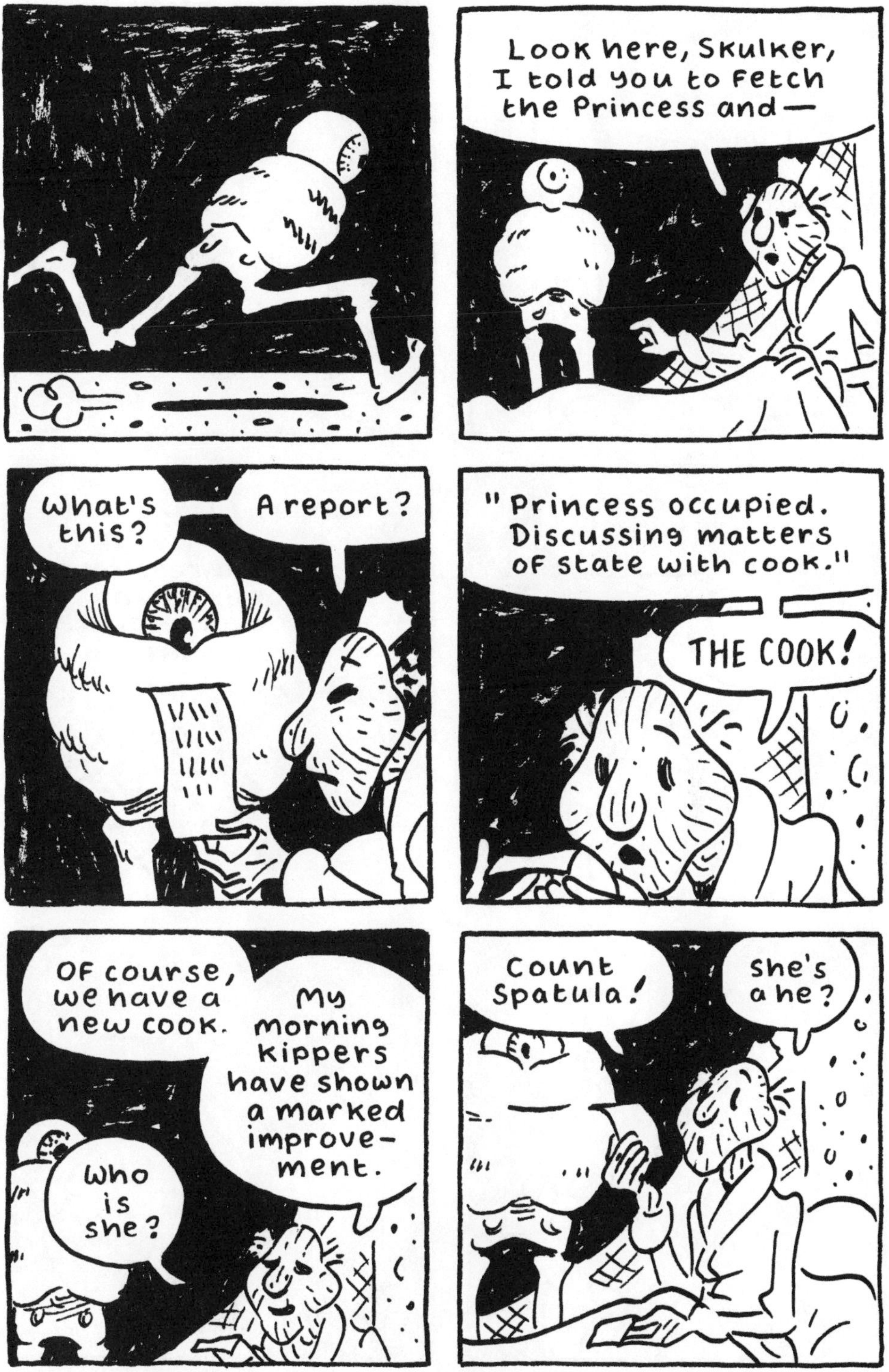
Look here, Skulker, I told you to fetch the Princess and—
What's this?
A report?
"Princess occupied. Discussing matters of state with cook."
THE COOK!
Of course, we have a new cook.
My morning kippers have shown a marked improvement.
Who is she?
Count Spatula!
She's a he?

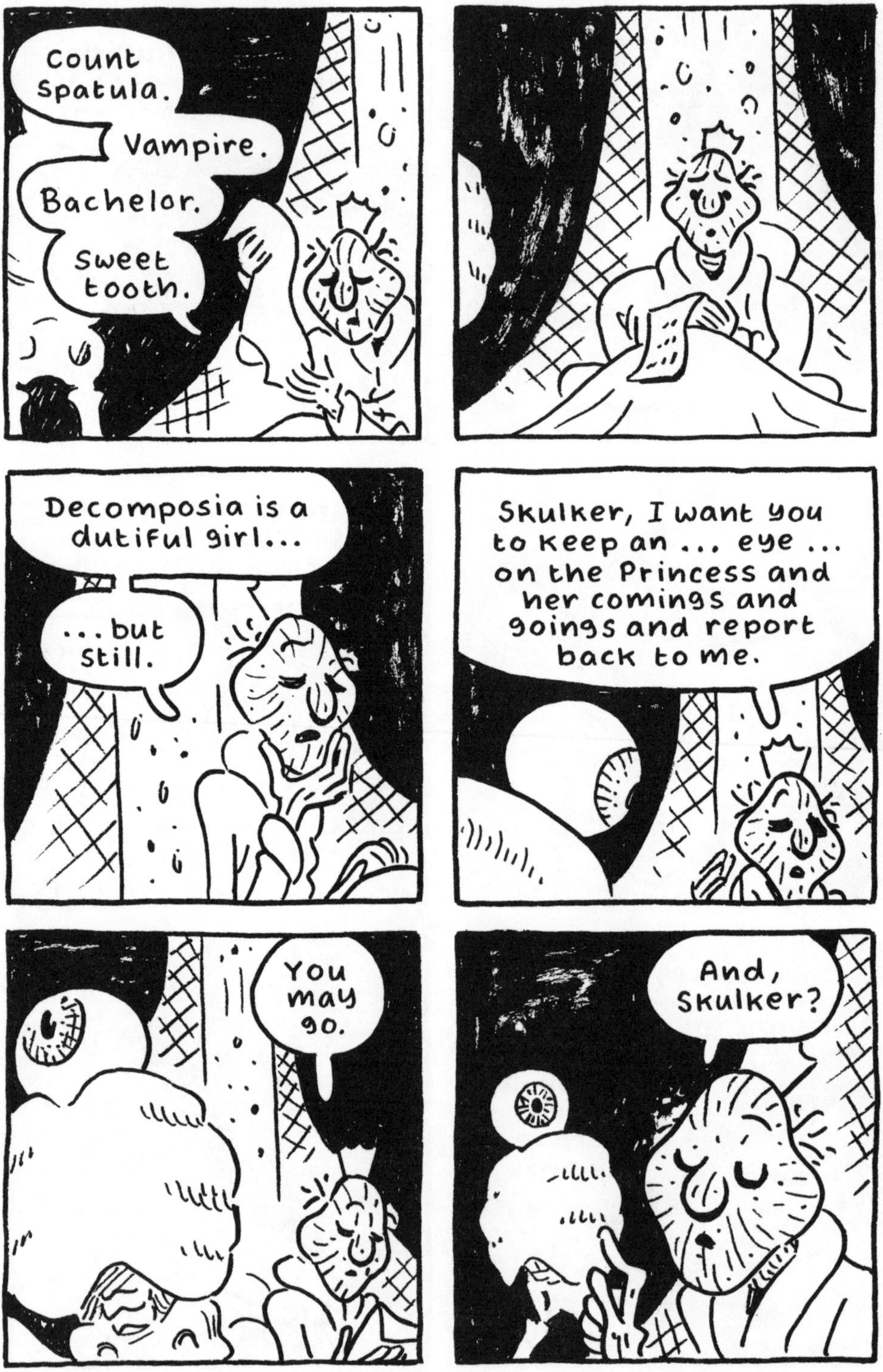
Count Spatula.
Vampire.
Bachelor.
Sweet tooth.
Decomposia is a dutiful girl...
...but still.
Skulker, I want you to keep an ... eye ... on the Princess and her comings and goings and report back to me.
You may go.
And, Skulker?

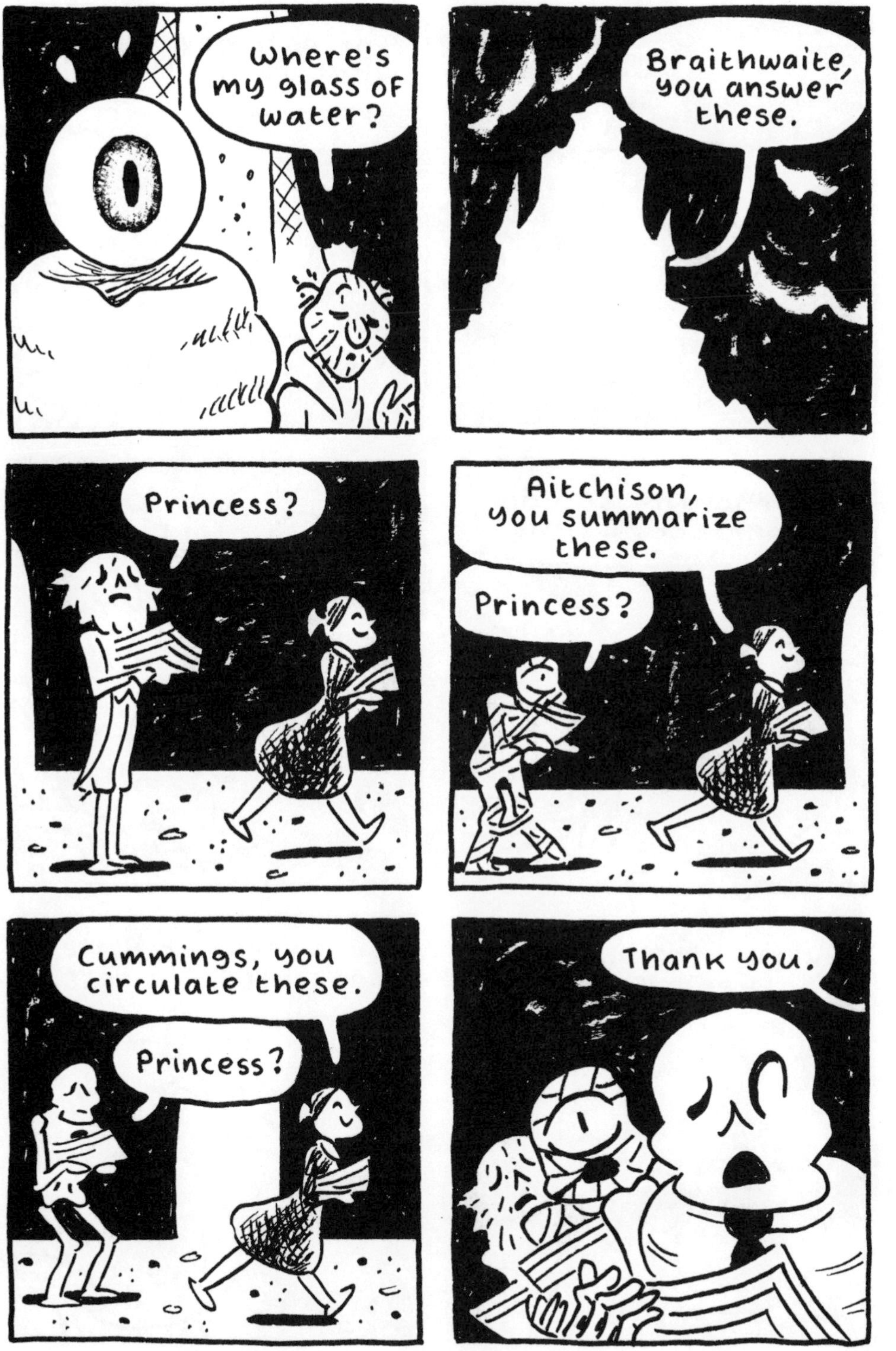
Where's my glass of water?
Braithwaite, you answer these.
Princess?
Aitchison, you summarize these.
Princess?
Cummings, you circulate these.
Princess?
Thank you.

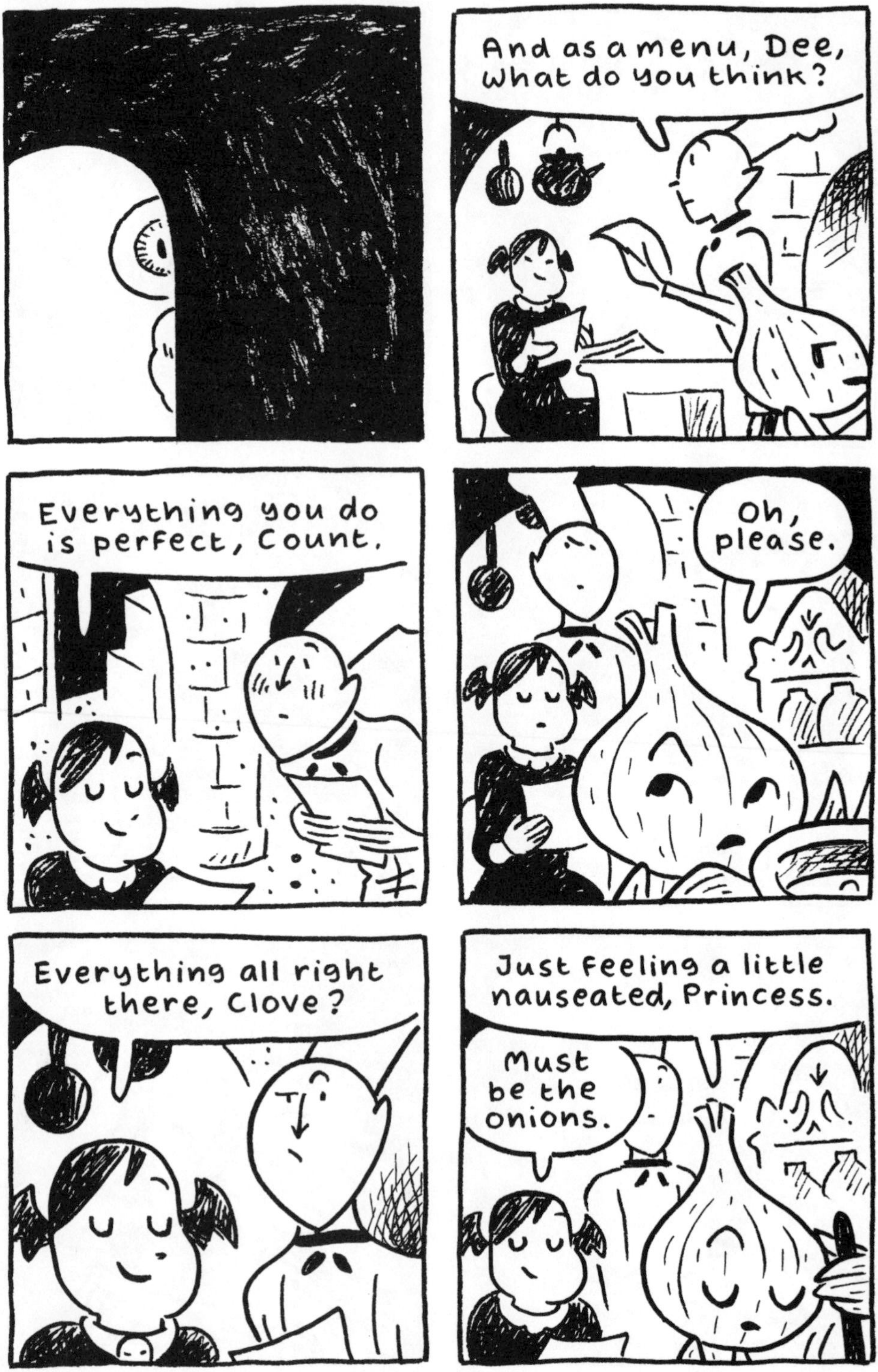
And as a menu, Dee, what do you think?
Everything you do is perfect, Count.
Oh, please.
Everything all right there, Clove?
Just feeling a little nauseated, Princess.
Must be the onions.

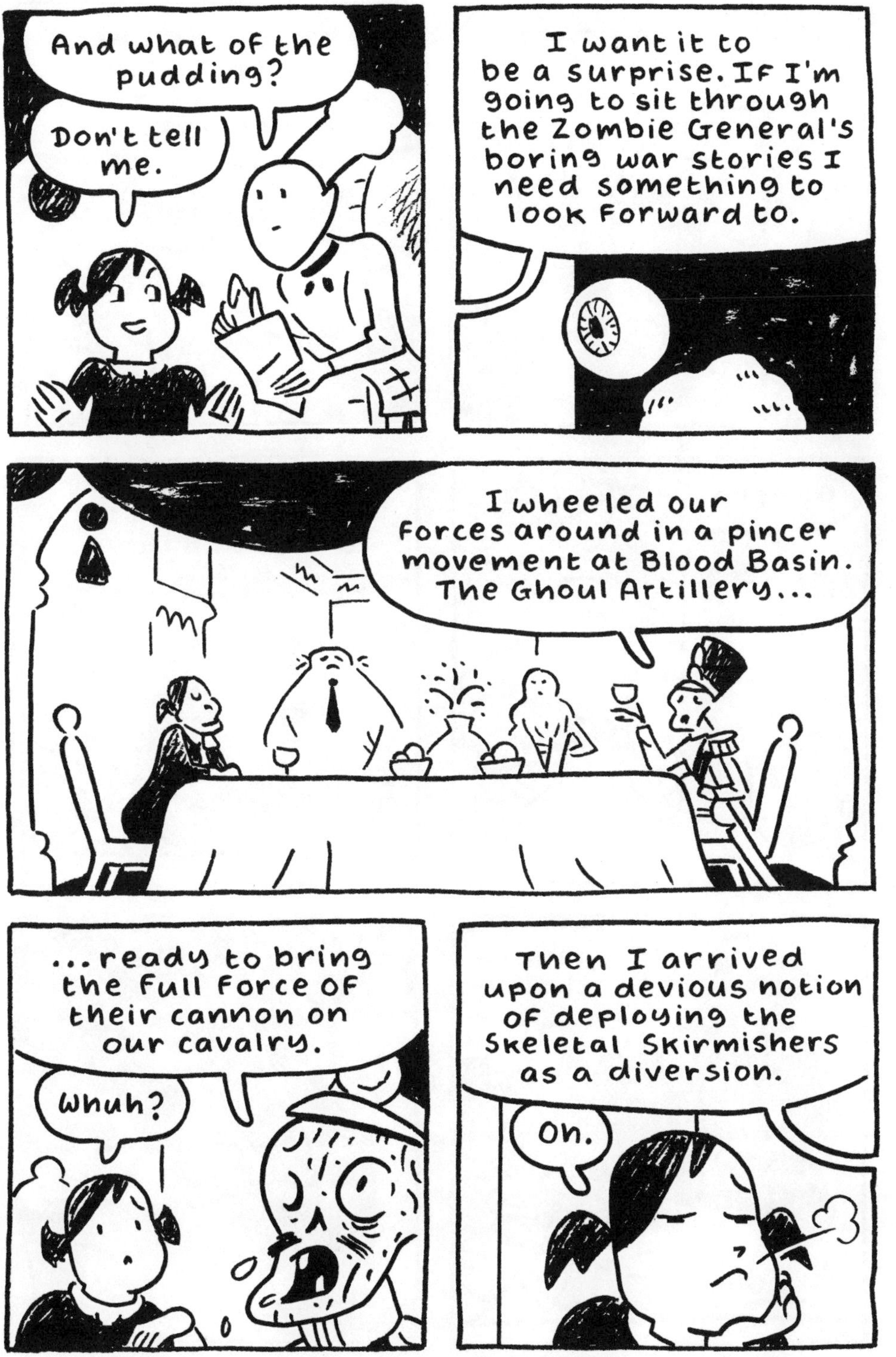
And what of the pudding?
Don't tell me.
I want it to be a surprise. If I'm going to sit through the Zombie General's boring war stories I need something to look forward to.
I wheeled our forces around in a pincer movement at Blood Basin. The Ghoul Artillery...
...ready to bring the full force of their cannon on our cavalry.
Whuh?
Then I arrived upon a devious notion of deploying the Skeletal Skirmishers as a diversion.
Oh.

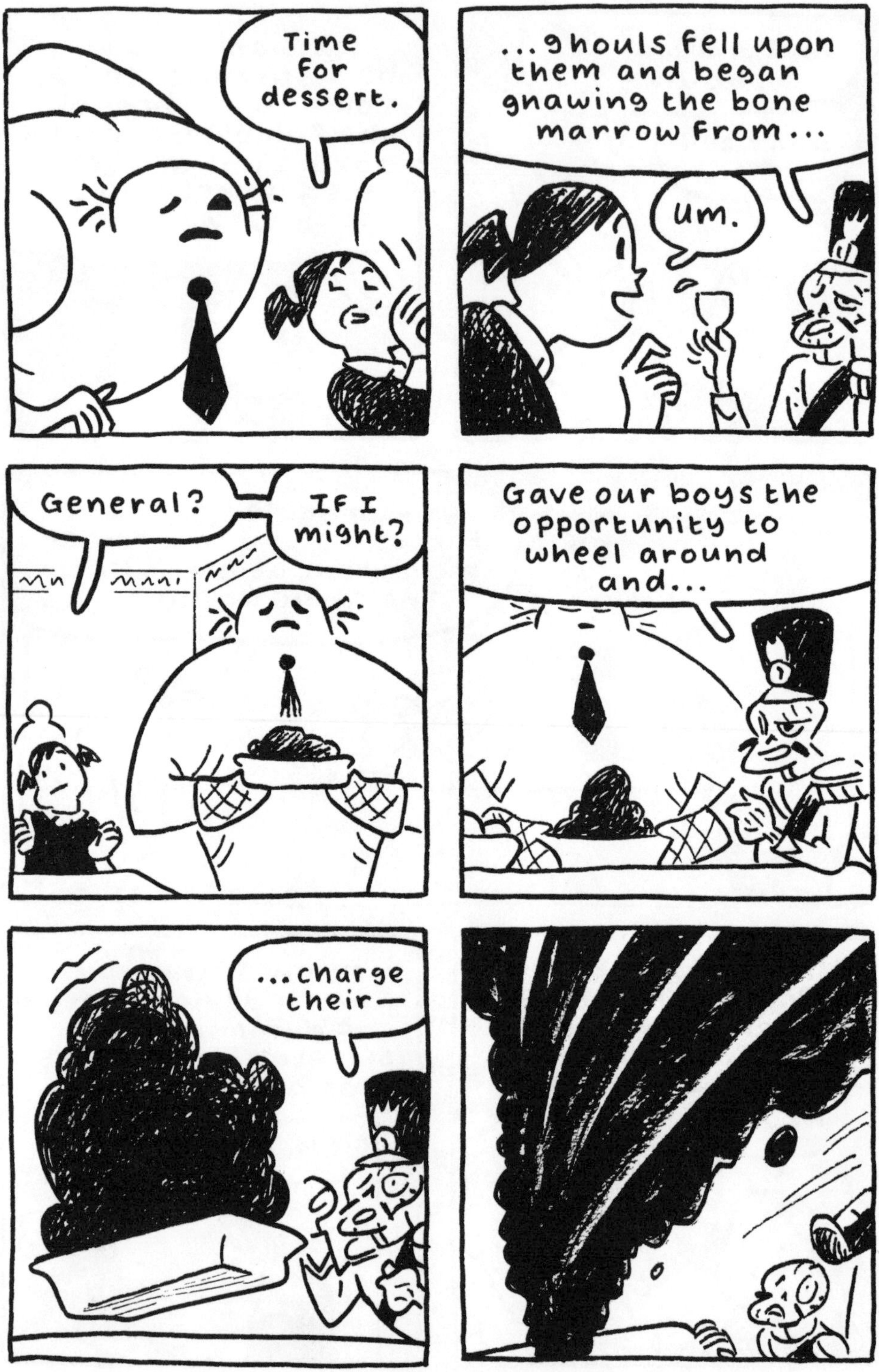
Time for dessert.
...ghouls fell upon them and began gnawing the bone marrow from...
Um.
General?
If I might?
Gave our boys the opportunity to wheel around and...
...charge their—

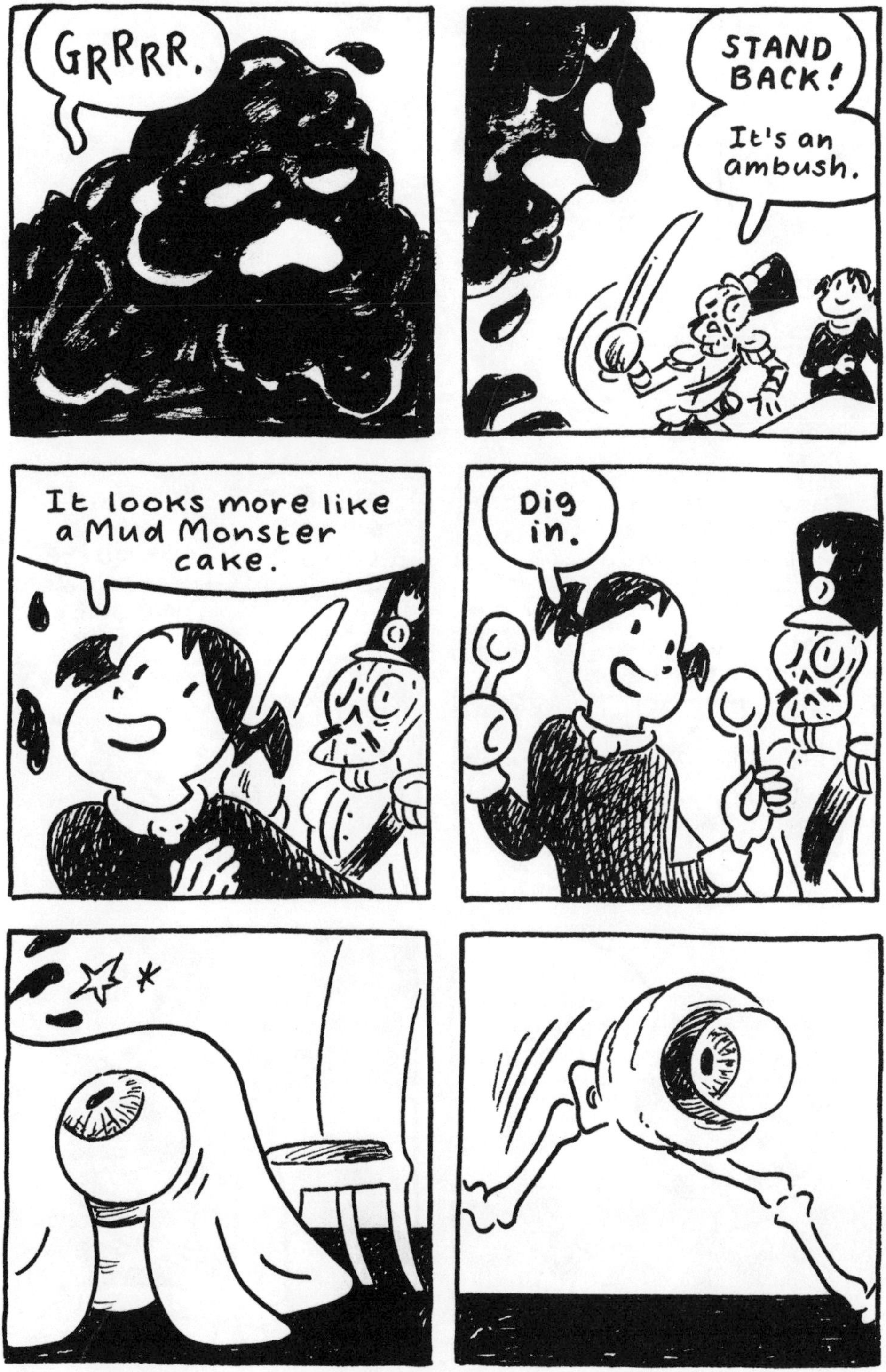
GRRRR.
STAND BACK! It's an ambush.
It looks more like a Mud Monster cake.
Dig in.

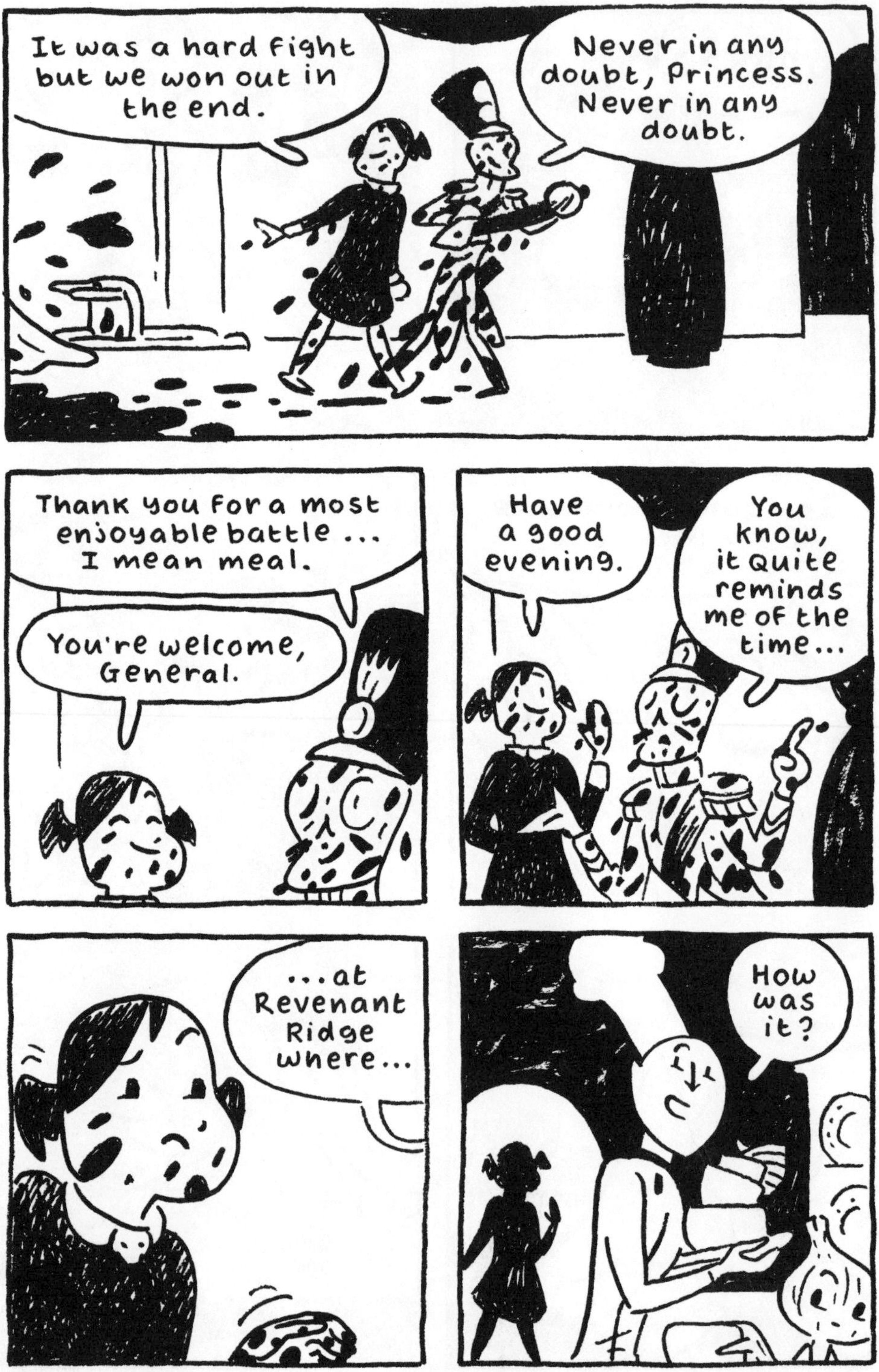
It was a hard fight but we won out in the end.
Never in any doubt, Princess. Never in any doubt.
Thank you for a most enjoyable battle ... I mean meal.
You're welcome, General.
Have a good evening.
You know, it quite reminds me of the time...
...at Revenant Ridge where...
How was it?

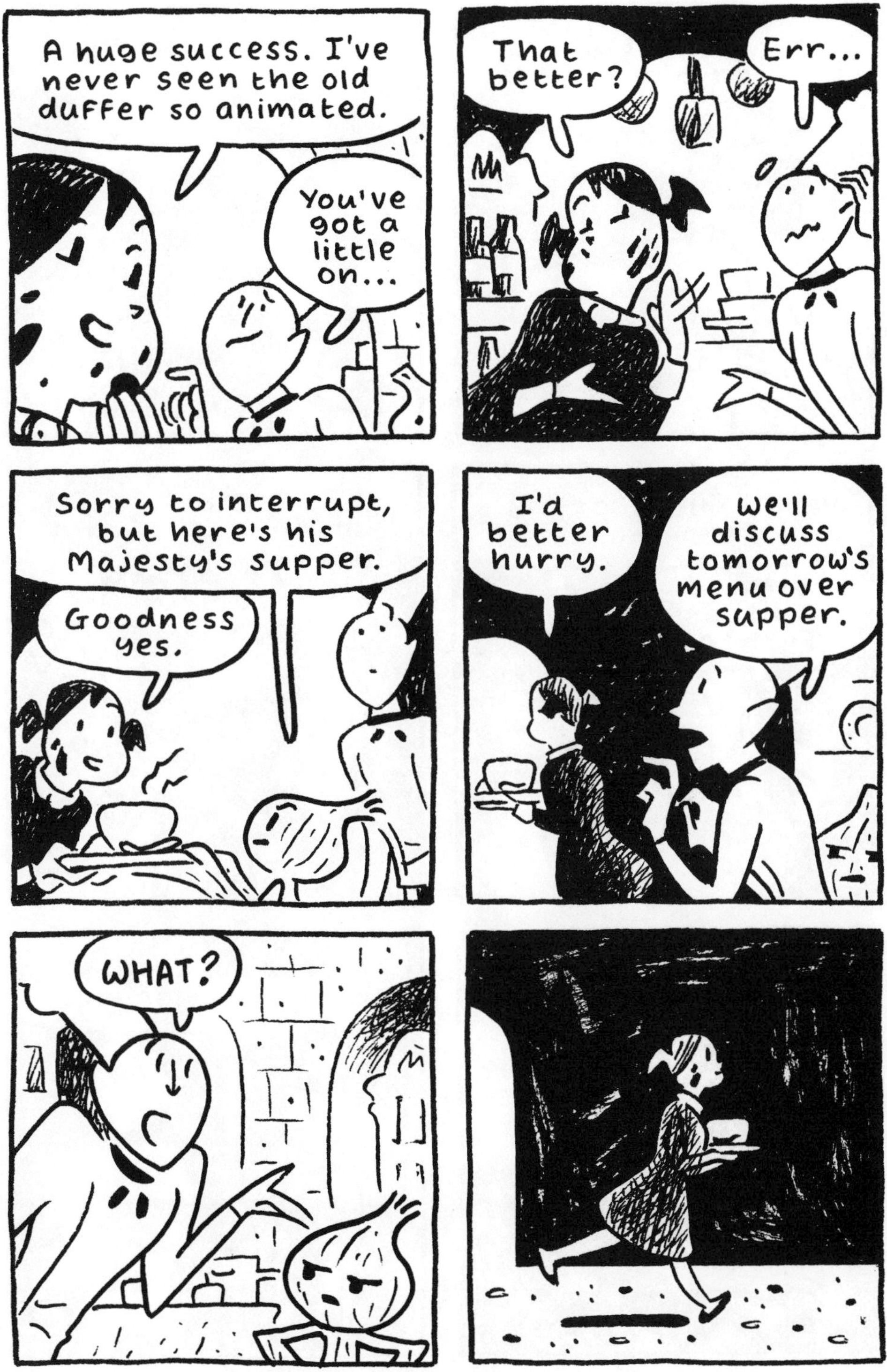

A huge success. I've never seen the old duffer so animated.
You've got a little on...
That better?
Err...
Sorry to interrupt, but here's his Majesty's supper.
Goodness yes.
I'd better hurry.
We'll discuss tomorrow's menu over supper.
WHAT?

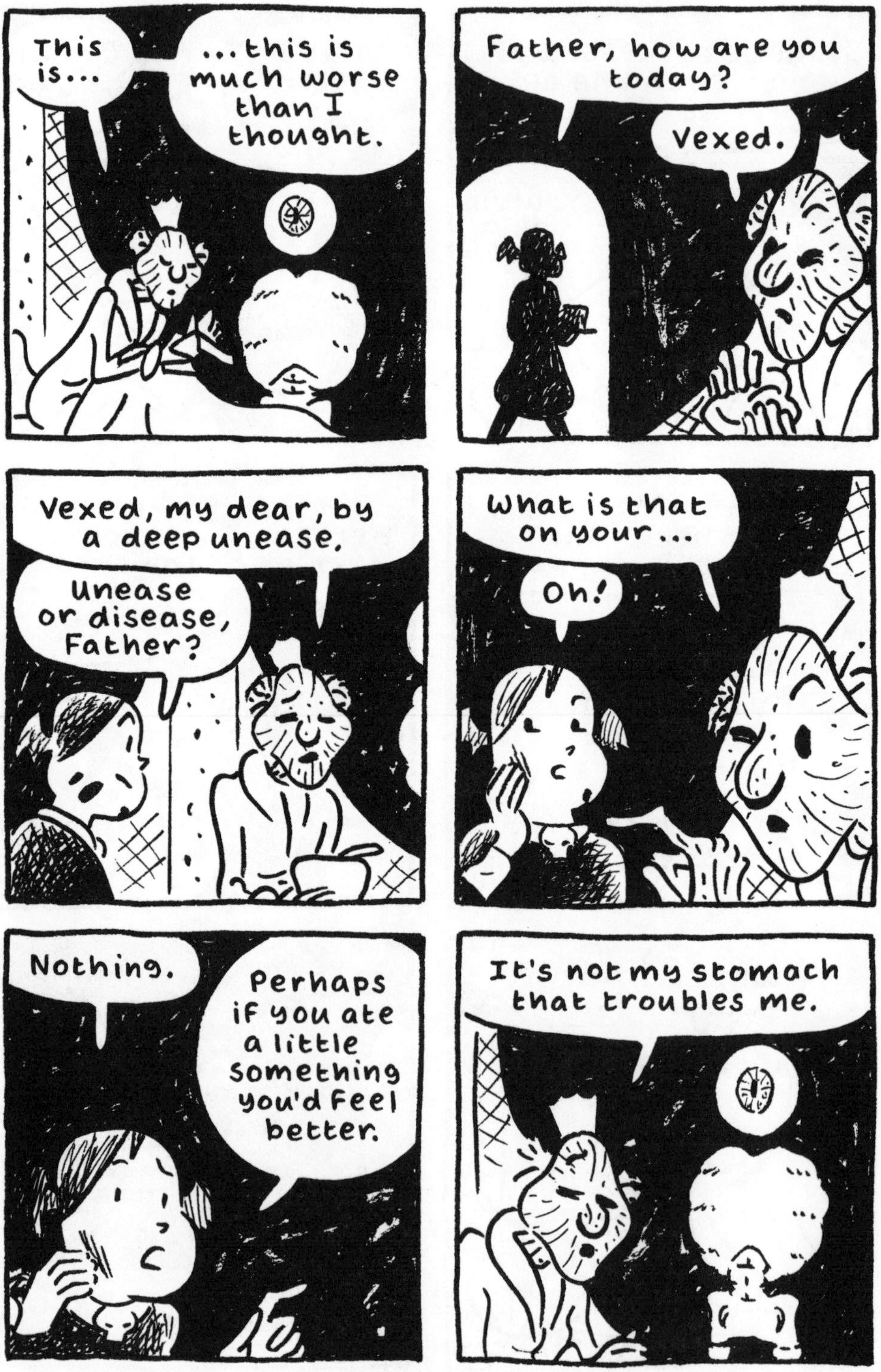
This is...
...this is much worse than I thought.
Father, how are you today?
Vexed.
Vexed, my dear, by a deep unease.
Unease or disease, Father?
What is that on your...
Oh!
Nothing.
Perhaps if you ate a little something you'd feel better.
It's not my stomach that troubles me.

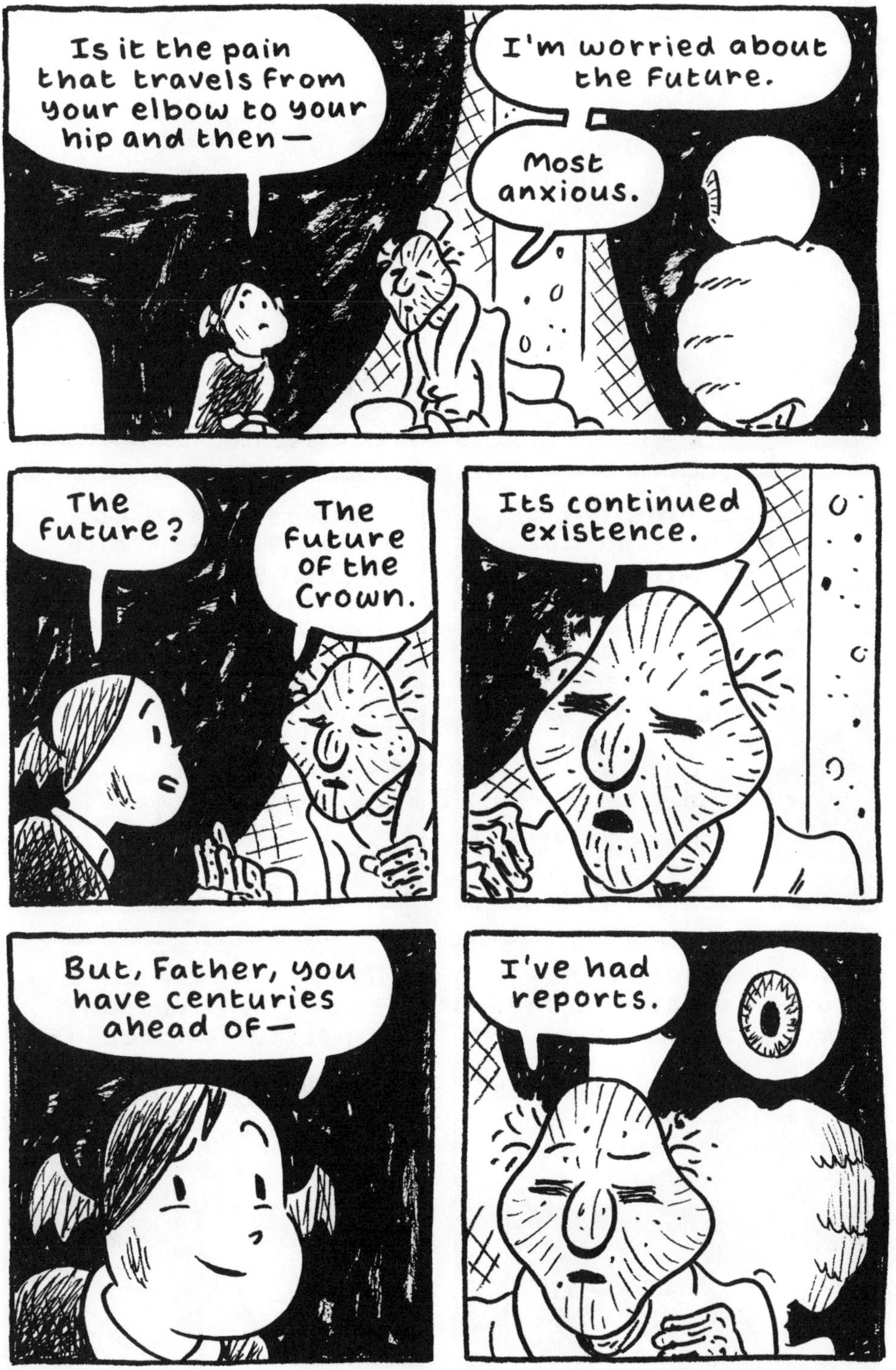
Is it the pain that travels from your elbow to your hip and then—
I'm worried about the future.
Most anxious.
The future?
The future of the Crown.
Its continued existence.
But, Father, you have centuries ahead of—
I've had reports.

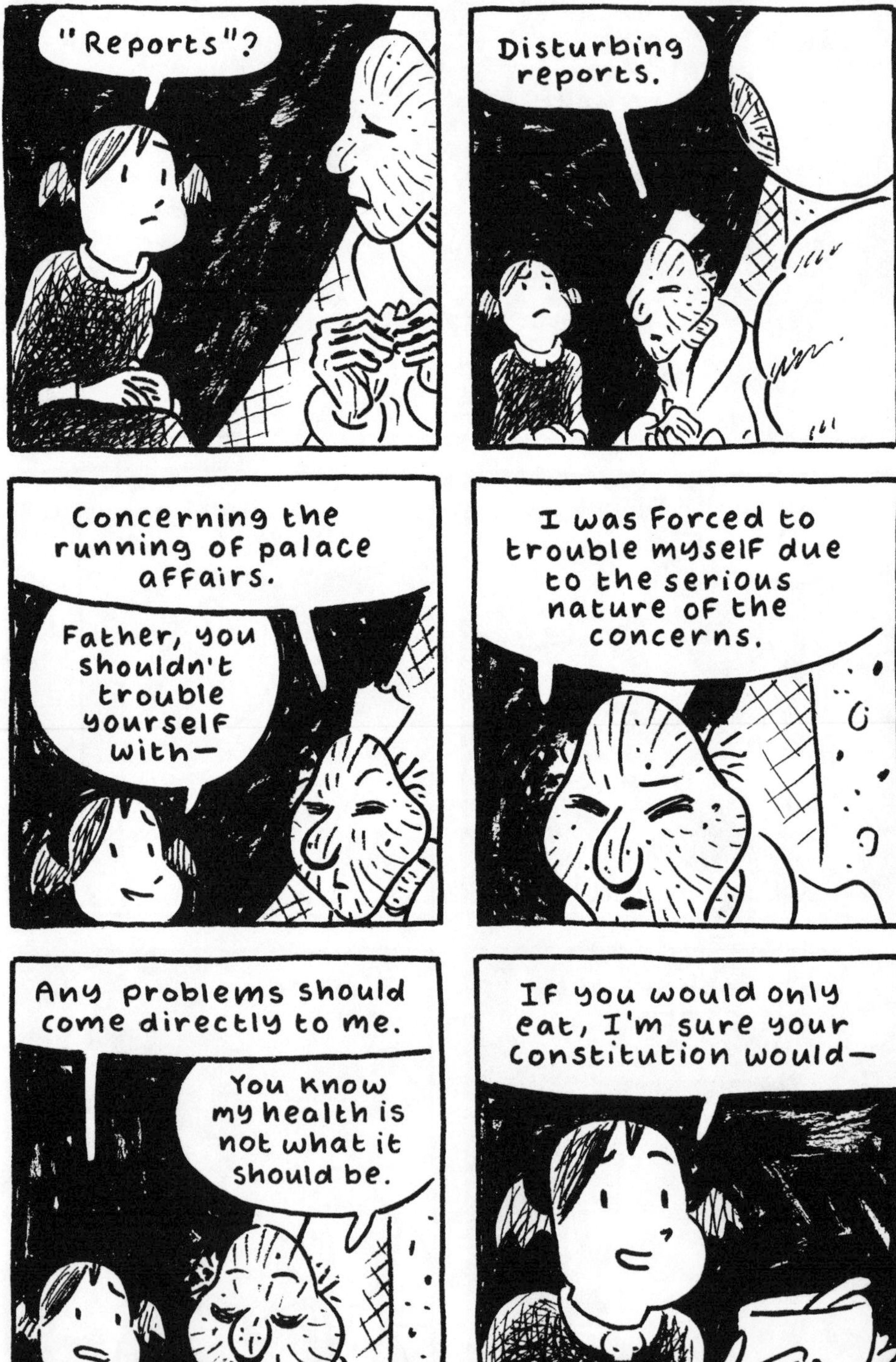
"Reports"?
Disturbing reports.
Concerning the running of palace affairs.
Father, you shouldn't trouble yourself with—
I was Forced to trouble myself due to the serious nature of the concerns.
Any problems should come directly to me.
You know my health is not what it should be.
If you would only eat, I'm sure your constitution would—

If you truly cared for my well-being you would not act in a way that causes me such distress.

Distress? Father, I would never do anything like that.

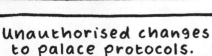

I don't know what these "reports" are but they're clearly untrue or... malicious.

I ... I honestly can't think of a single thing I've done that could possibly upset you.

Unauthorised changes to palace protocols.

I don't understand.

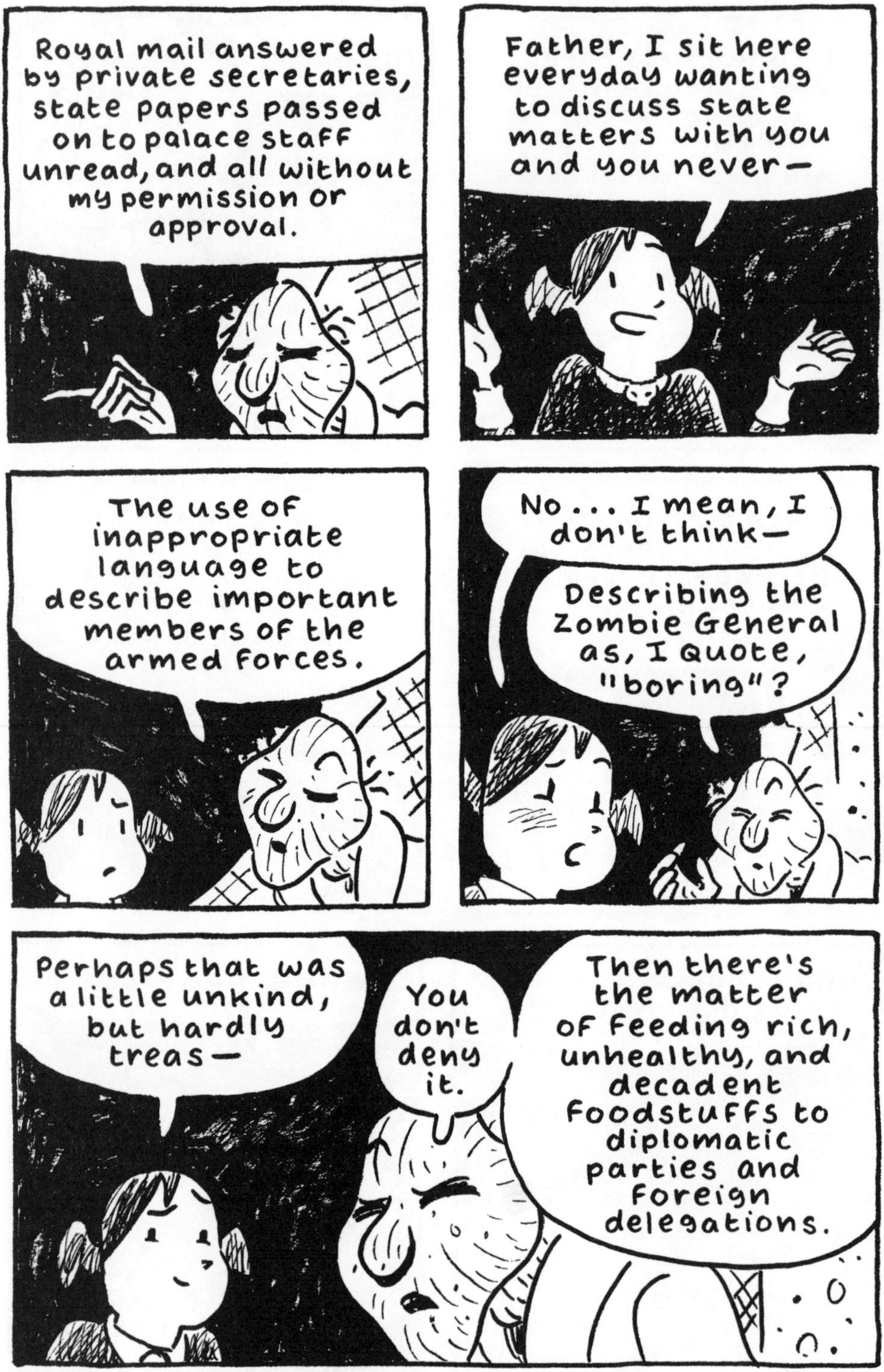
Royal mail answered by private secretaries, state papers passed on to palace staff unread, and all without my permission or approval.
Father, I sit here everyday wanting to discuss state matters with you and you never—
The use of inappropriate language to describe important members of the armed forces.
No... I mean, I don't think—
Describing the Zombie General as, I quote, "boring"?
Perhaps that was a little unkind, but hardly treas—
You don't deny it.
Then there's the matter of feeding rich, unhealthy, and decadent foodstuffs to diplomatic parties and foreign delegations.

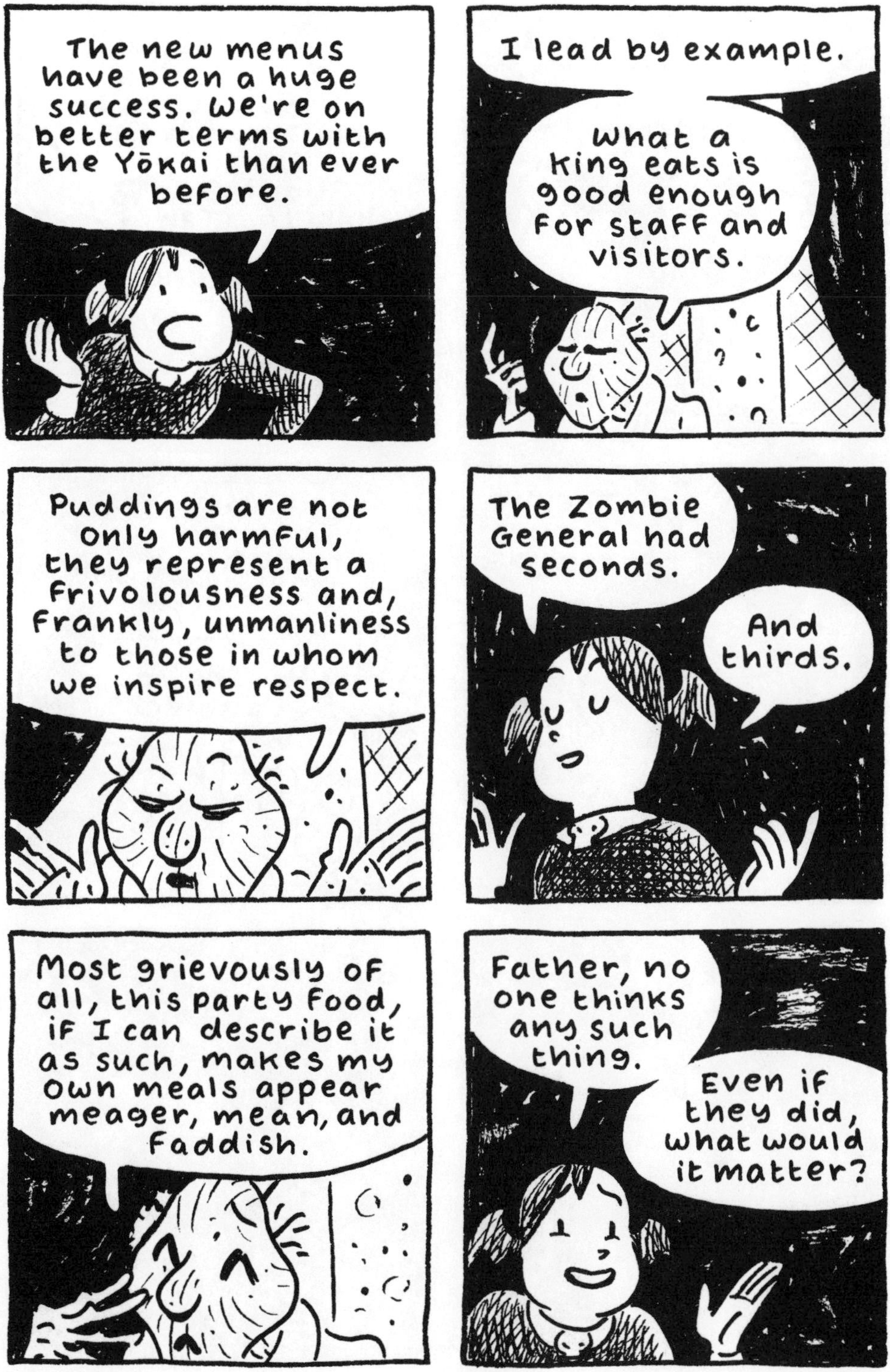
The new menus have been a huge success. We're on better terms with the Yōkai than ever before.
I lead by example.
What a king eats is good enough for staff and visitors.
Puddings are not only harmful, they represent a frivolousness and, frankly, unmanliness to those in whom we inspire respect.
The Zombie General had seconds.
And thirds.
Most grievously of all, this party food, if I can describe it as such, makes my own meals appear meager, mean, and faddish.
Father, no one thinks any such thing.
Even if they did, what would it matter?

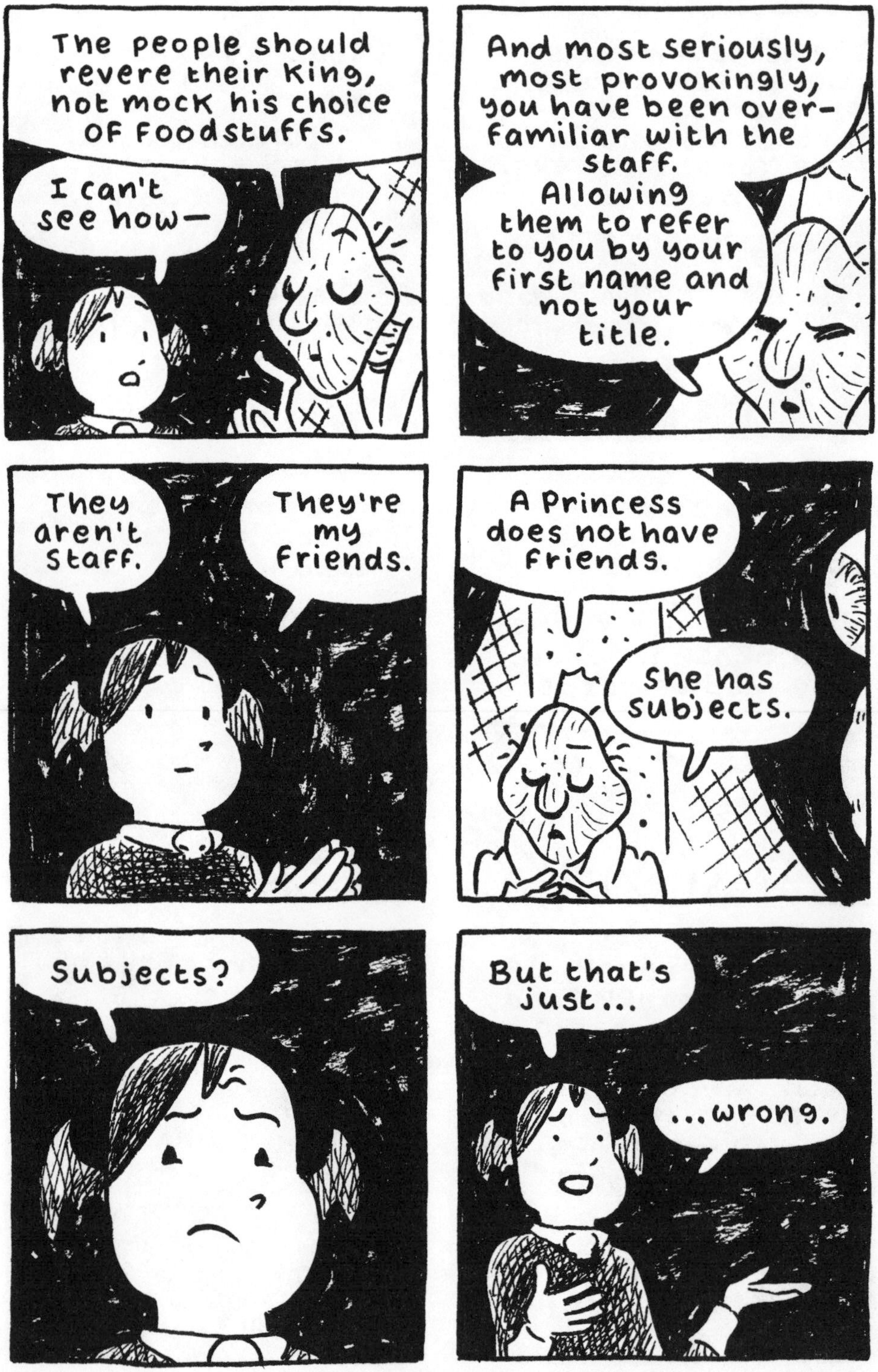
The people should revere their King, not mock his choice of foodstuffs.
I can't see how—
And most seriously, most provokingly, you have been over-familiar with the staff.
Allowing them to refer to you by your first name and not your title.
They aren't staff.
They're my friends.
A Princess does not have friends.
She has subjects.
Subjects?
But that's just...
...wrong.

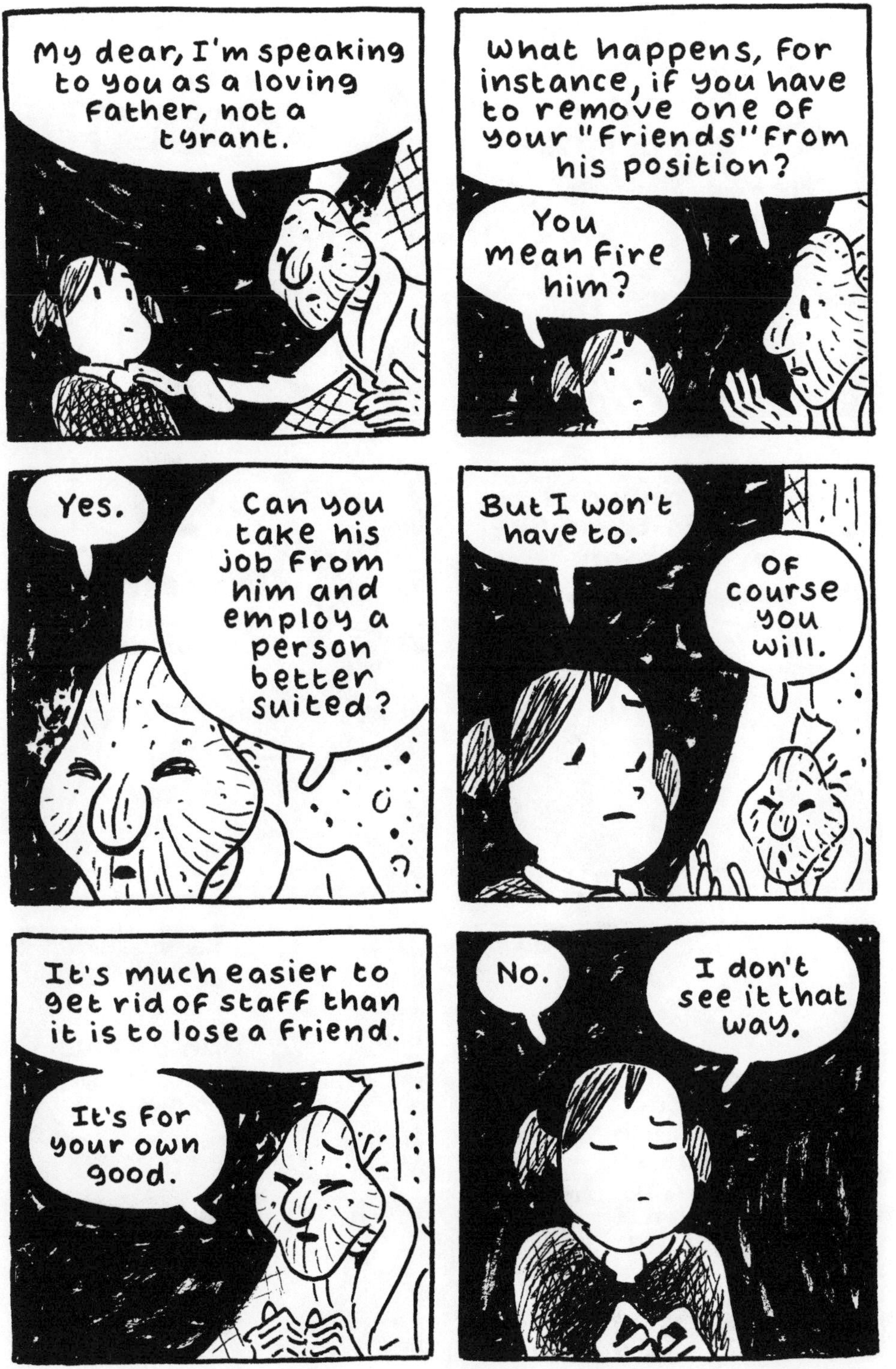
My dear, I'm speaking to you as a loving father, not a tyrant.
What happens, for instance, if you have to remove one of your "friends" from his position?
You mean fire him?
Yes.
Can you take his job from him and employ a person better suited?
But I won't have to.
Of course you will.
It's much easier to get rid of staff than it is to lose a friend.
It's for your own good.
No.
I don't see it that way.

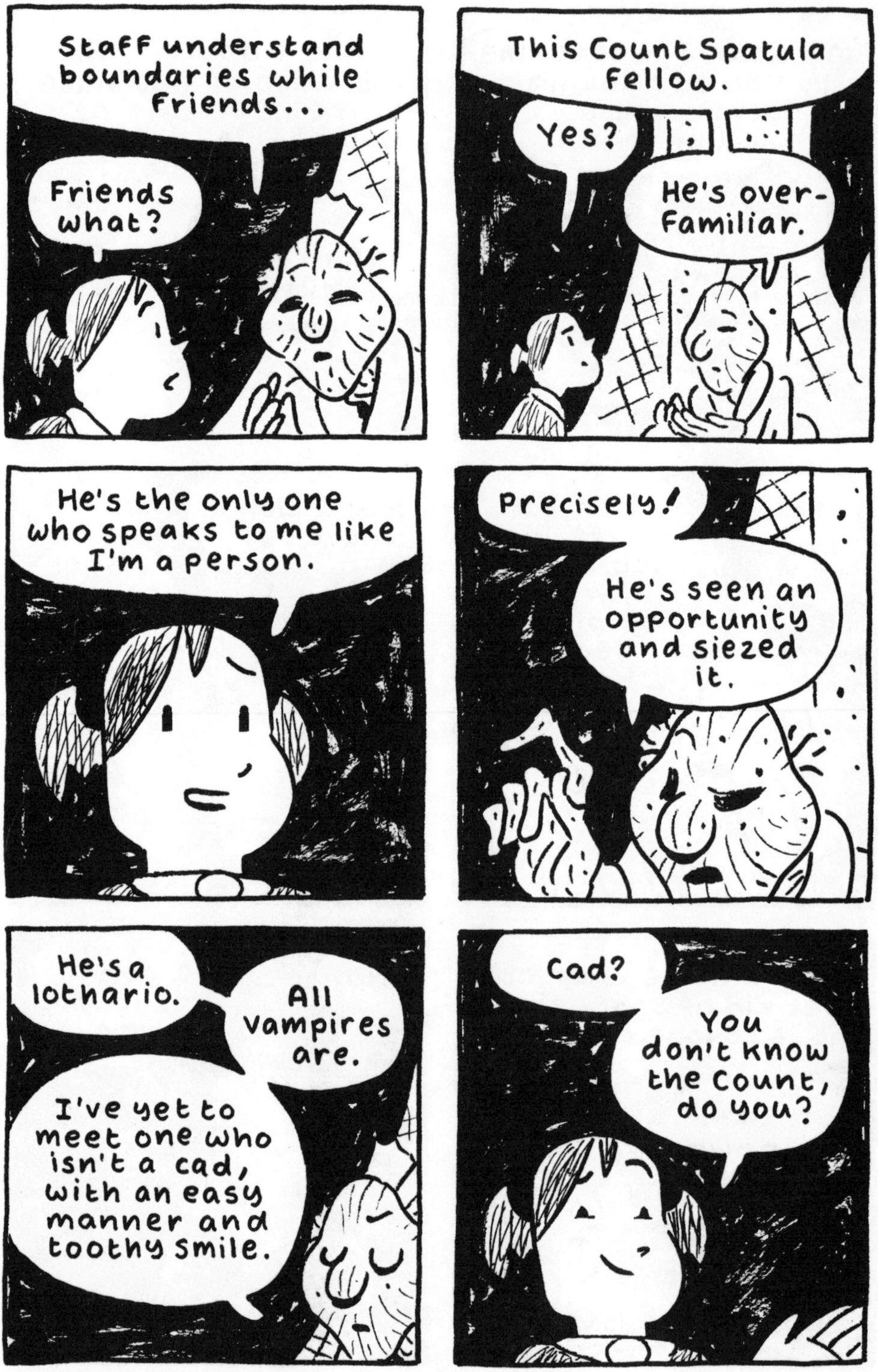
Staff understand boundaries while Friends...
Friends what?
This Count Spatula Fellow.
Yes?
He's over-familiar.
He's the only one who speaks to me like I'm a person.
Precisely!
He's seen an opportunity and siezed it.
He's a lothario.
All vampires are.
I've yet to meet one who isn't a cad, with an easy manner and toothy smile.
Cad?
You don't know the Count, do you?

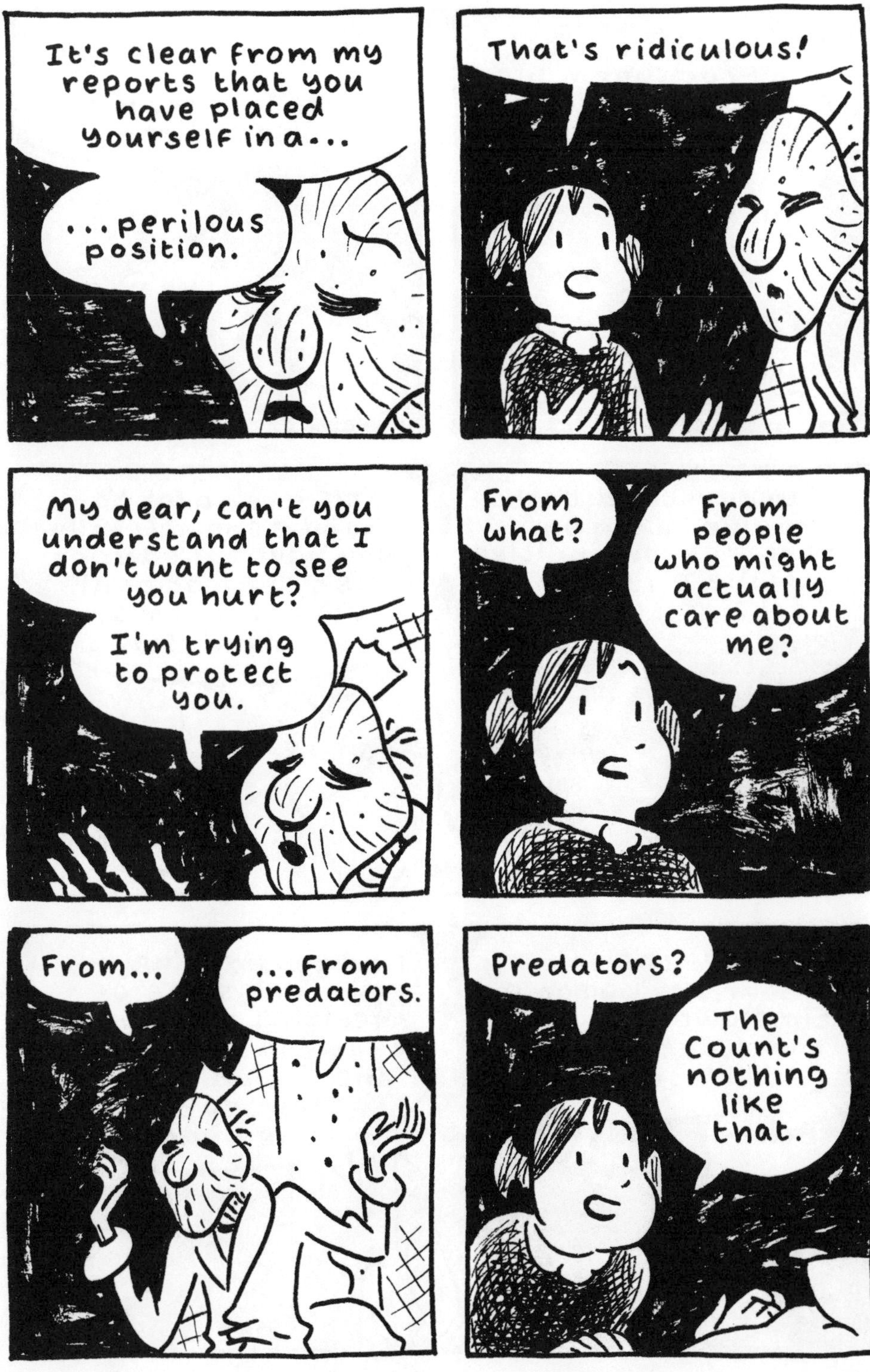
It's clear from my reports that you have placed yourself in a...
...perilous position.
That's ridiculous!
My dear, can't you understand that I don't want to see you hurt?
I'm trying to protect you.
From what?
From people who might actually care about me?
From...
...from predators.
Predators?
The Count's nothing like that.

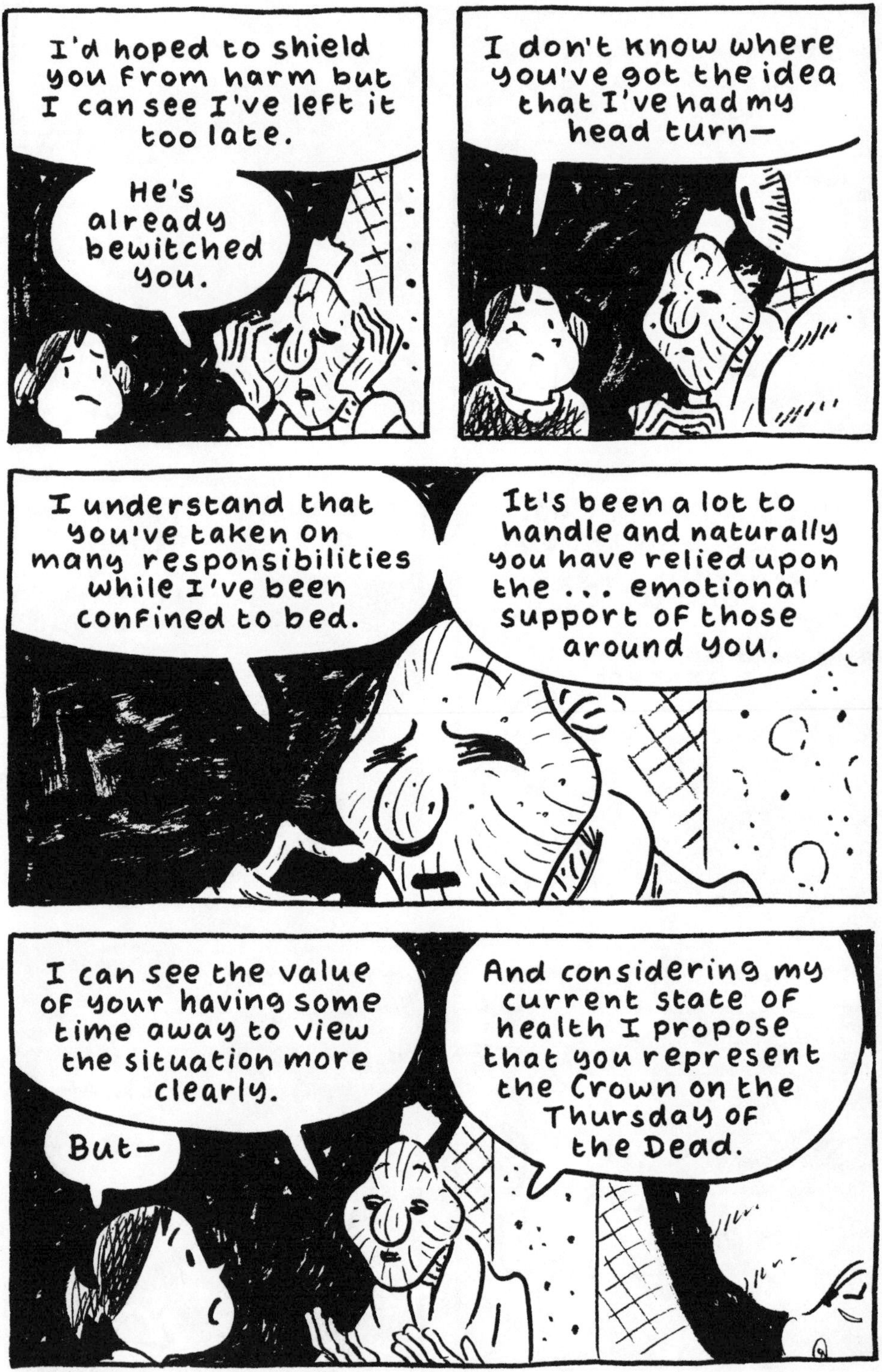
I'd hoped to shield you from harm but I can see I've left it too late.
He's already bewitched you.
I don't know where you've got the idea that I've had my head turn—
I understand that you've taken on many responsibilities while I've been confined to bed.
It's been a lot to handle and naturally you have relied upon the ... emotional support of those around you.
I can see the value of your having some time away to view the situation more clearly.
But—
And considering my current state of health I propose that you represent the Crown on the Thursday of the Dead.

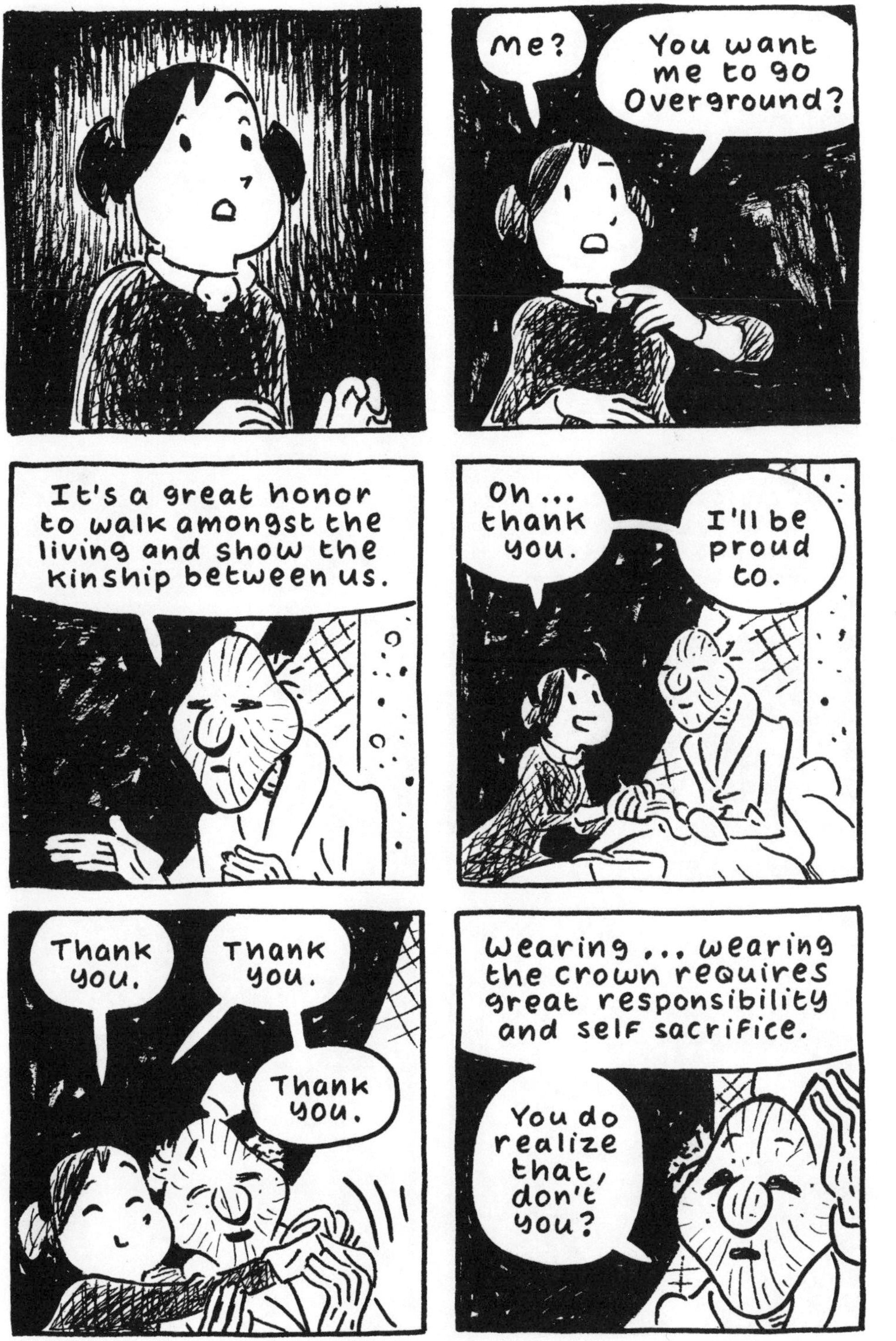
Me?
You want me to go Overground?
It's a great honor to walk amongst the living and show the kinship between us.
Oh ... thank you.
I'll be proud to.
Thank you.
Thank you.
Thank you.
Wearing ... wearing the crown requires great responsibility and self sacrifice.
You do realize that, don't you?

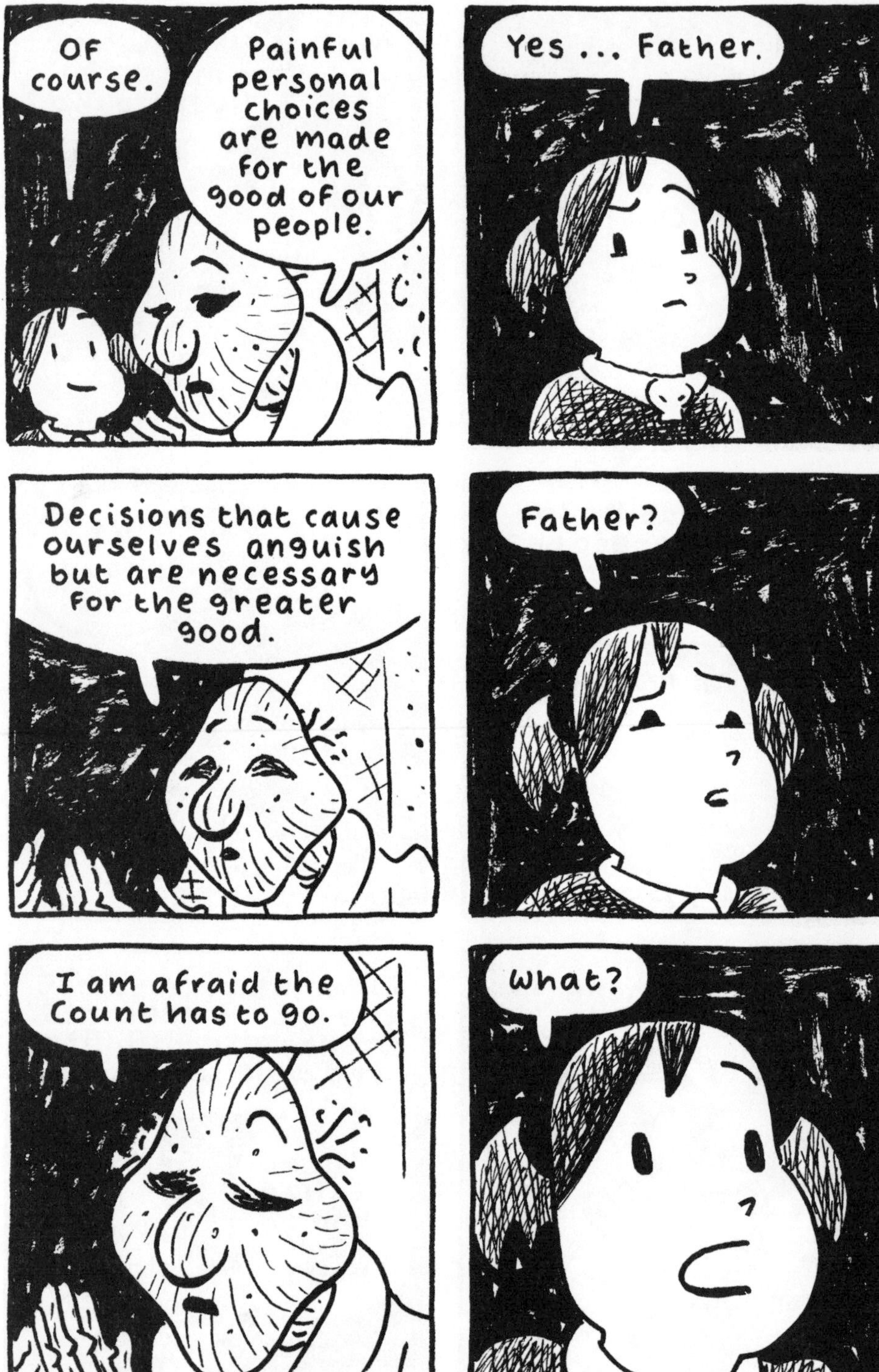
Of course.
Painful personal choices are made for the good of our people.
Yes ... Father.
Decisions that cause ourselves anguish but are necessary for the greater good.
Father?
I am afraid the Count has to go.
What?

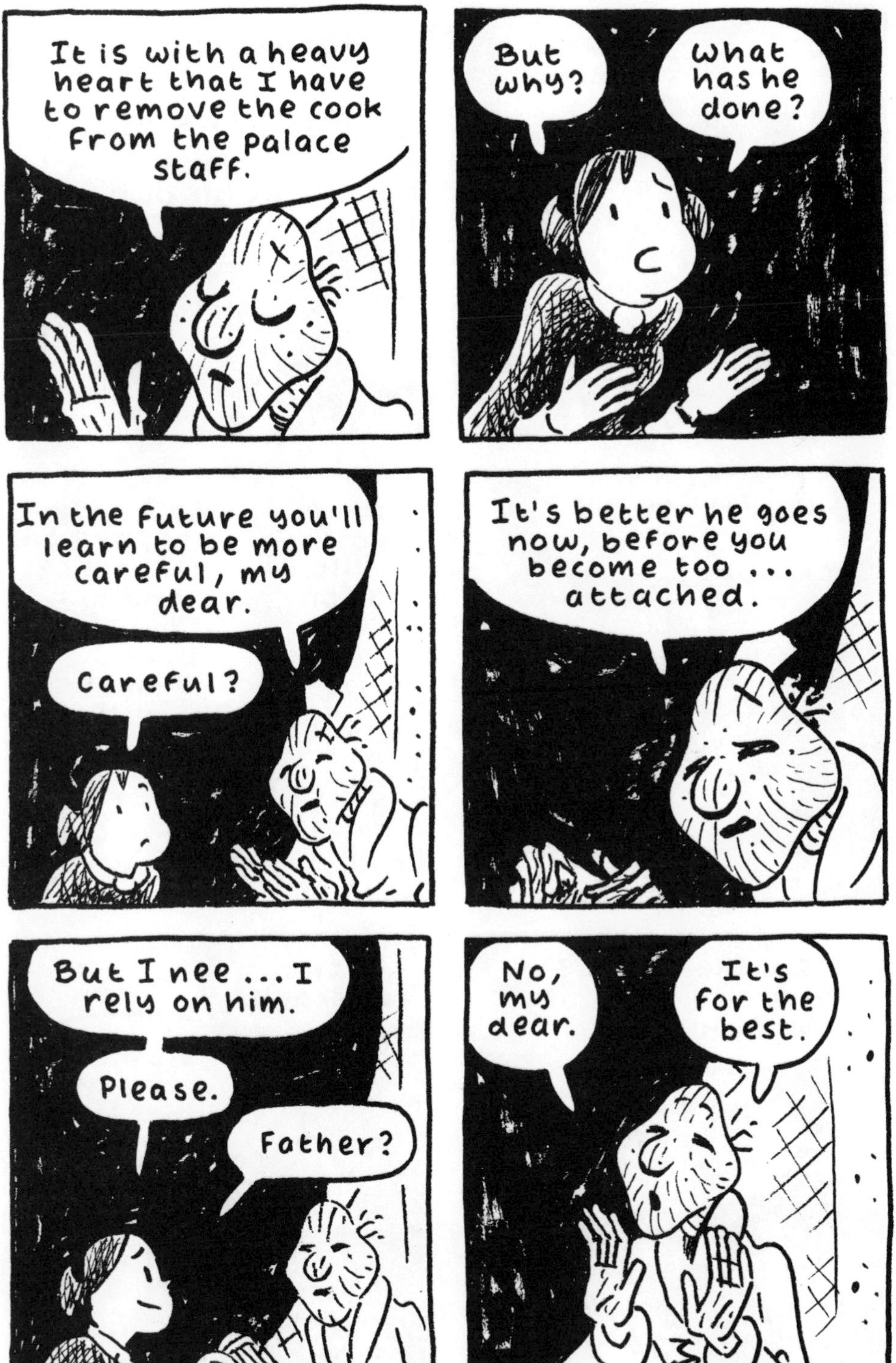
It is with a heavy heart that I have to remove the cook from the palace staff.
But why?
What has he done?
In the future you'll learn to be more careful, my dear.
Careful?
It's better he goes now, before you become too ... attached.
But I nee ... I rely on him.
Please.
Father?
No, my dear.
It's for the best.

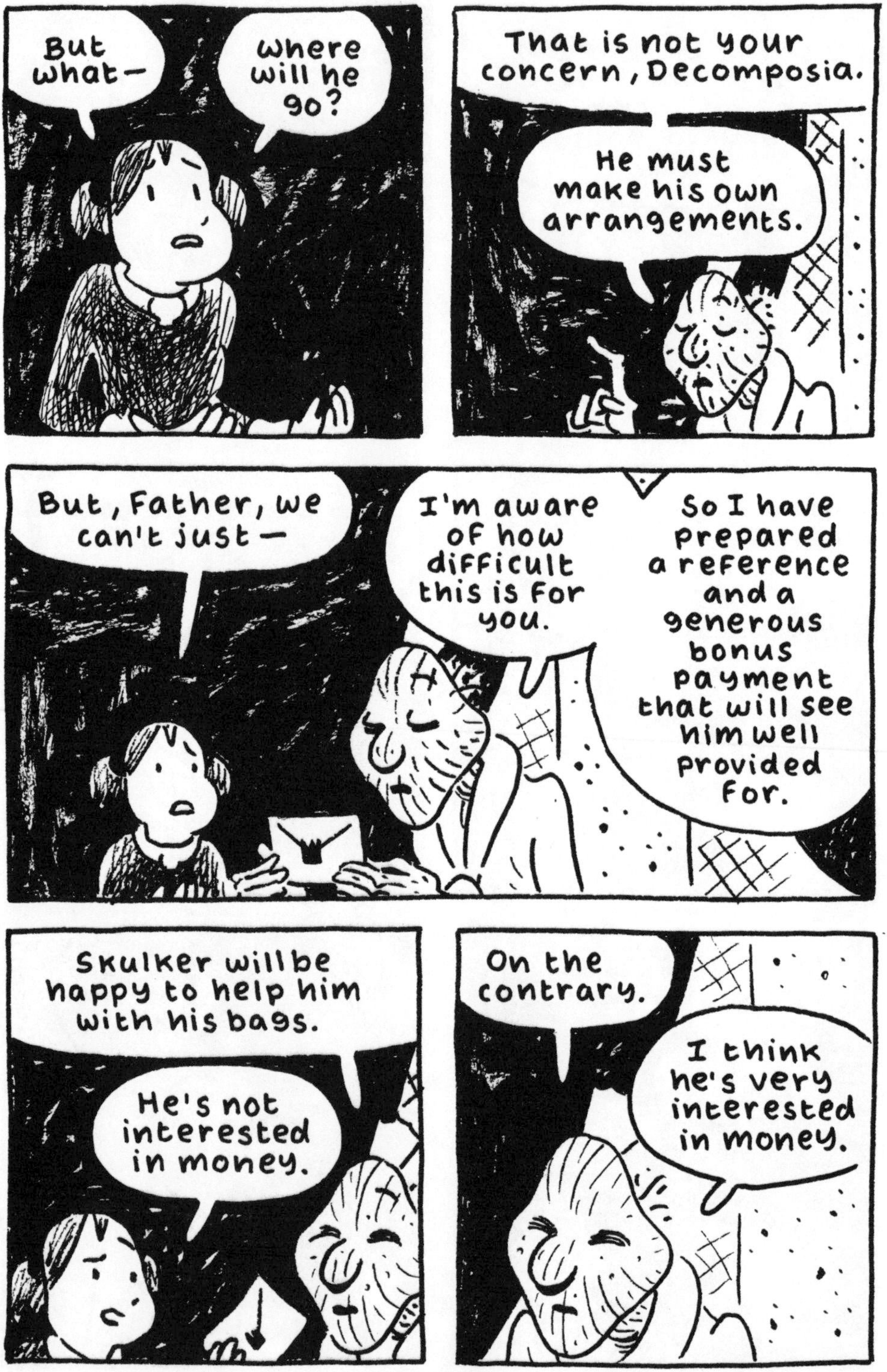
But what—
where will he go?
That is not your concern, Decomposia.
He must make his own arrangements.
But, Father, we can't just—
I'm aware of how difficult this is for you.
So I have prepared a reference and a generous bonus payment that will see him well provided for.
Skulker will be happy to help him with his bags.
He's not interested in money.
On the contrary.
I think he's very interested in money.

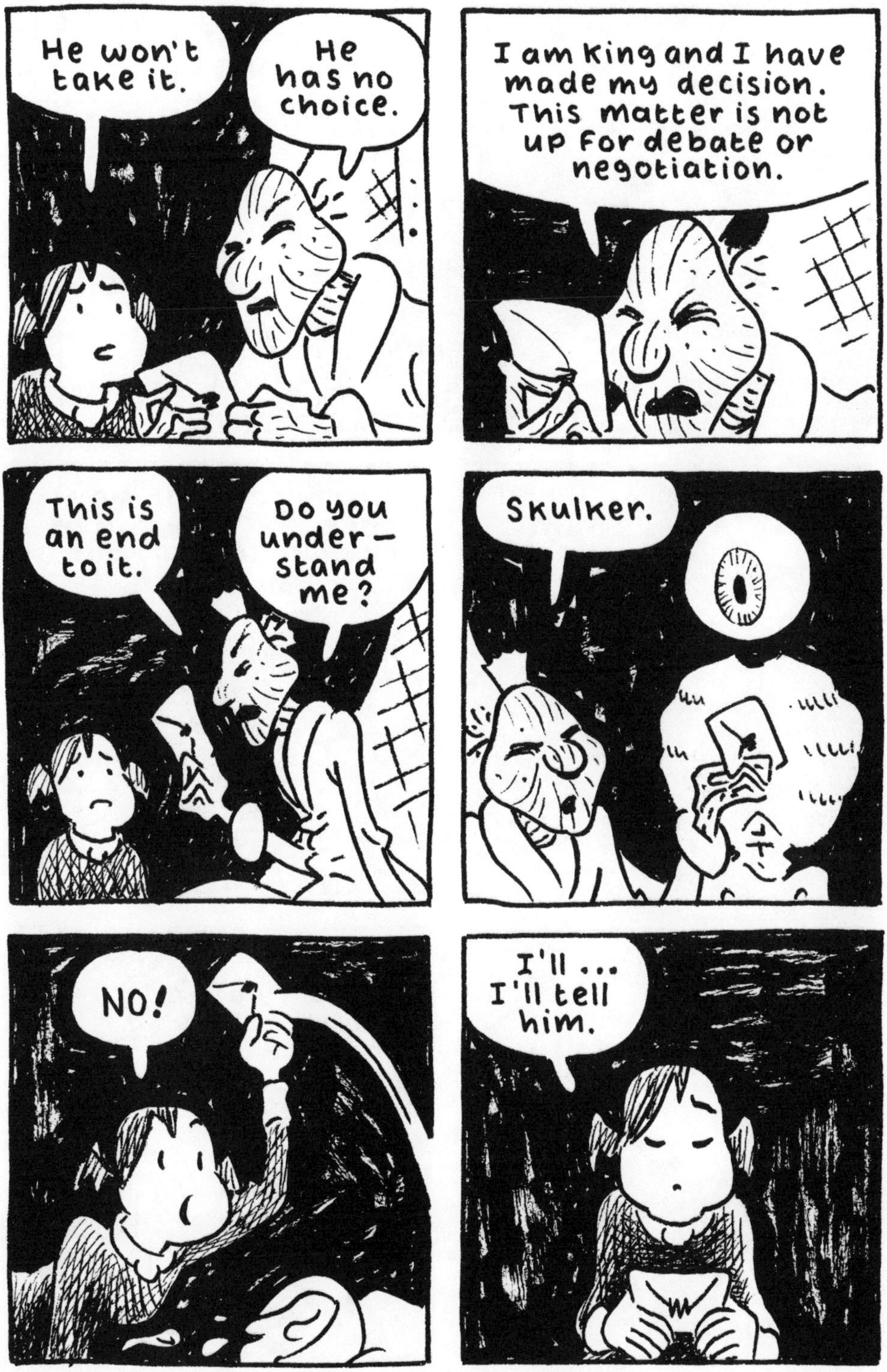
He won't take it.
He has no choice.
I am King and I have made my decision. This matter is not up for debate or negotiation.
This is an end to it.
Do you under-stand me?
Skulker.
NO!
I'll ... I'll tell him.

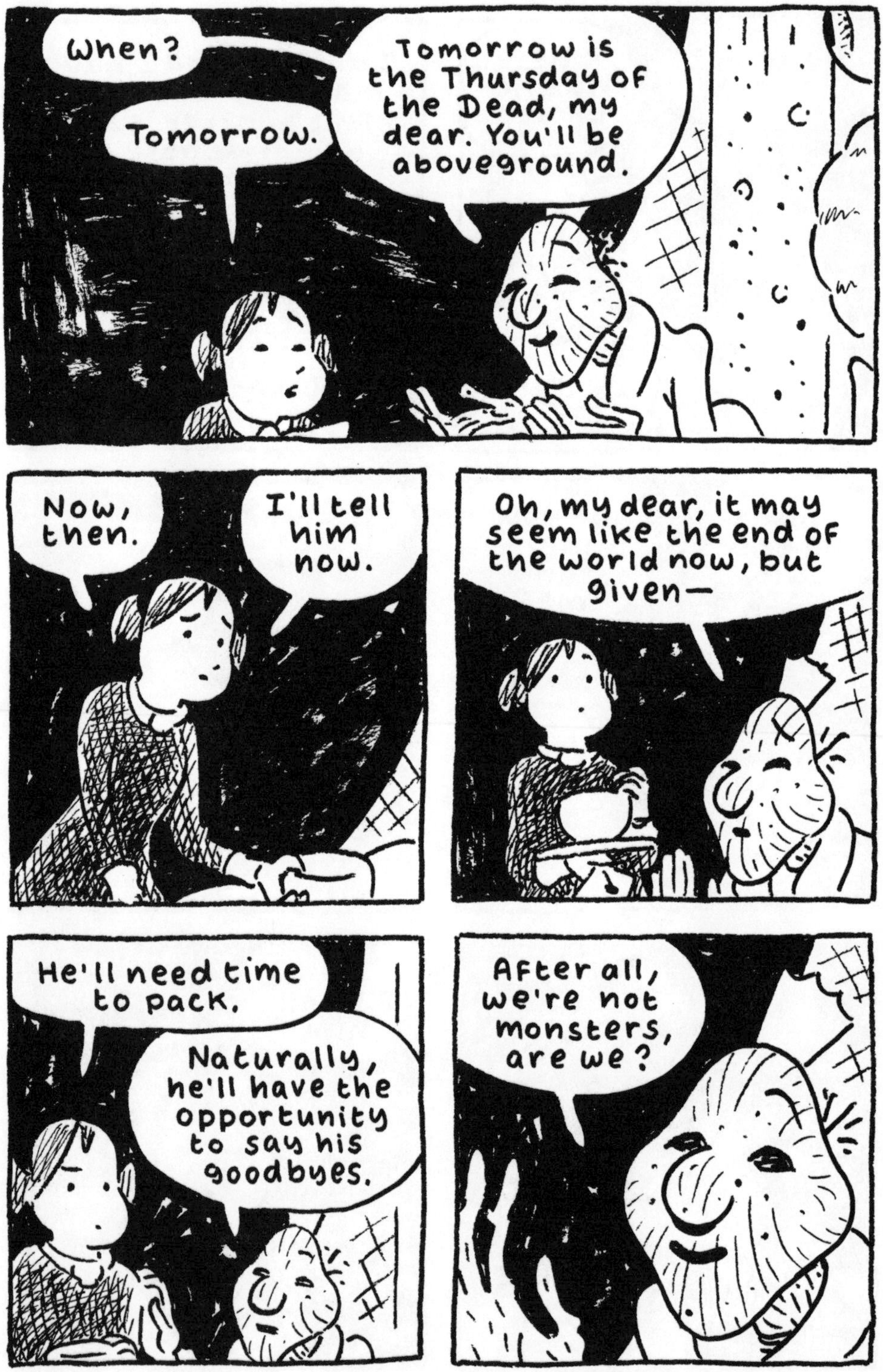
When?
Tomorrow.
Tomorrow is the Thursday of the Dead, my dear. You'll be aboveground.
Now, then.
I'll tell him now.
Oh, my dear, it may seem like the end of the world now, but given—
He'll need time to pack.
Naturally, he'll have the opportunity to say his goodbyes.
After all, we're not monsters, are we?

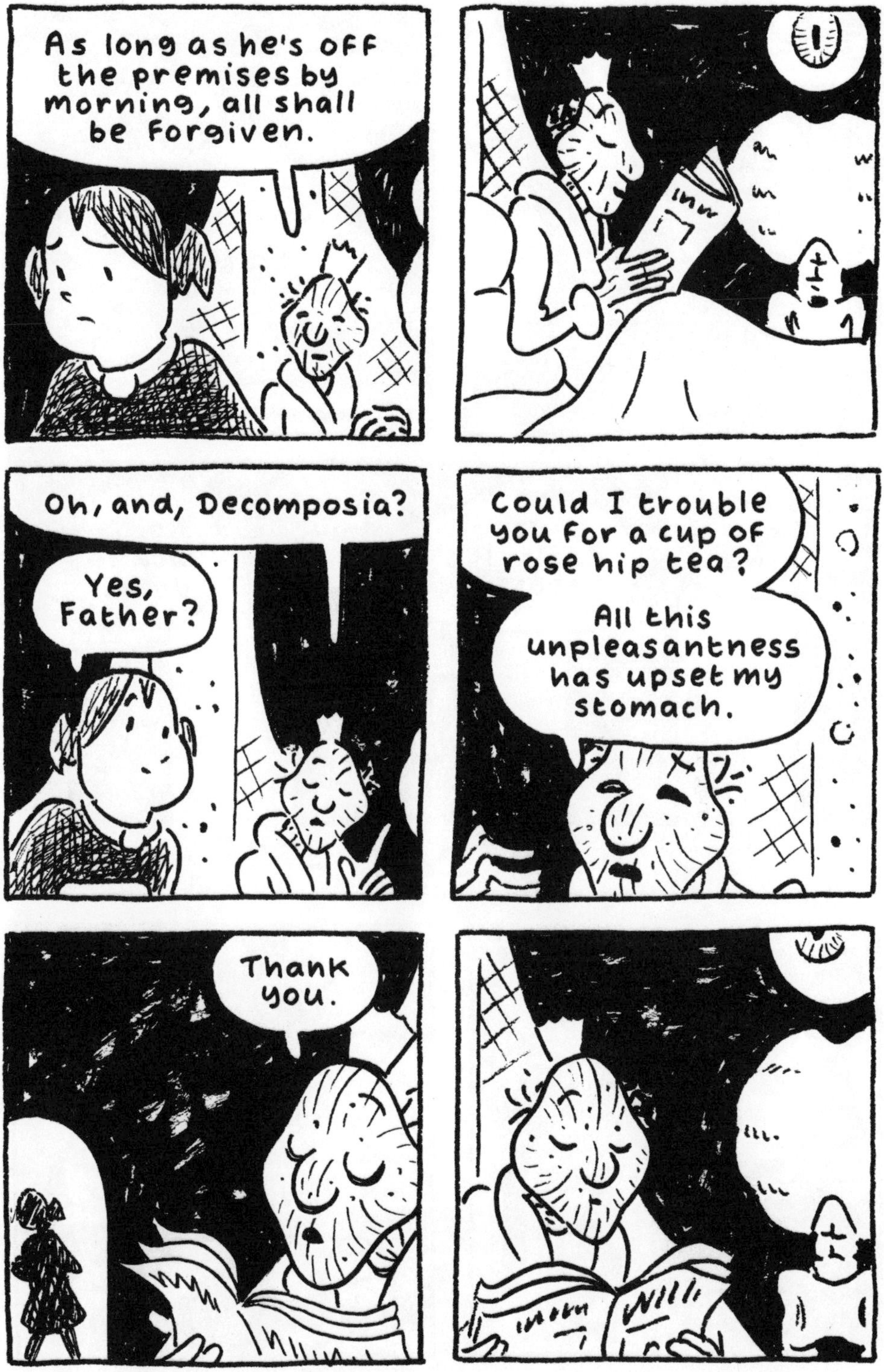
As long as he's off the premises by morning, all shall be forgiven.
Oh, and, Decomposia?
Yes, Father?
Could I trouble you for a cup of rose hip tea?
All this unpleasantness has upset my stomach.
Thank you.

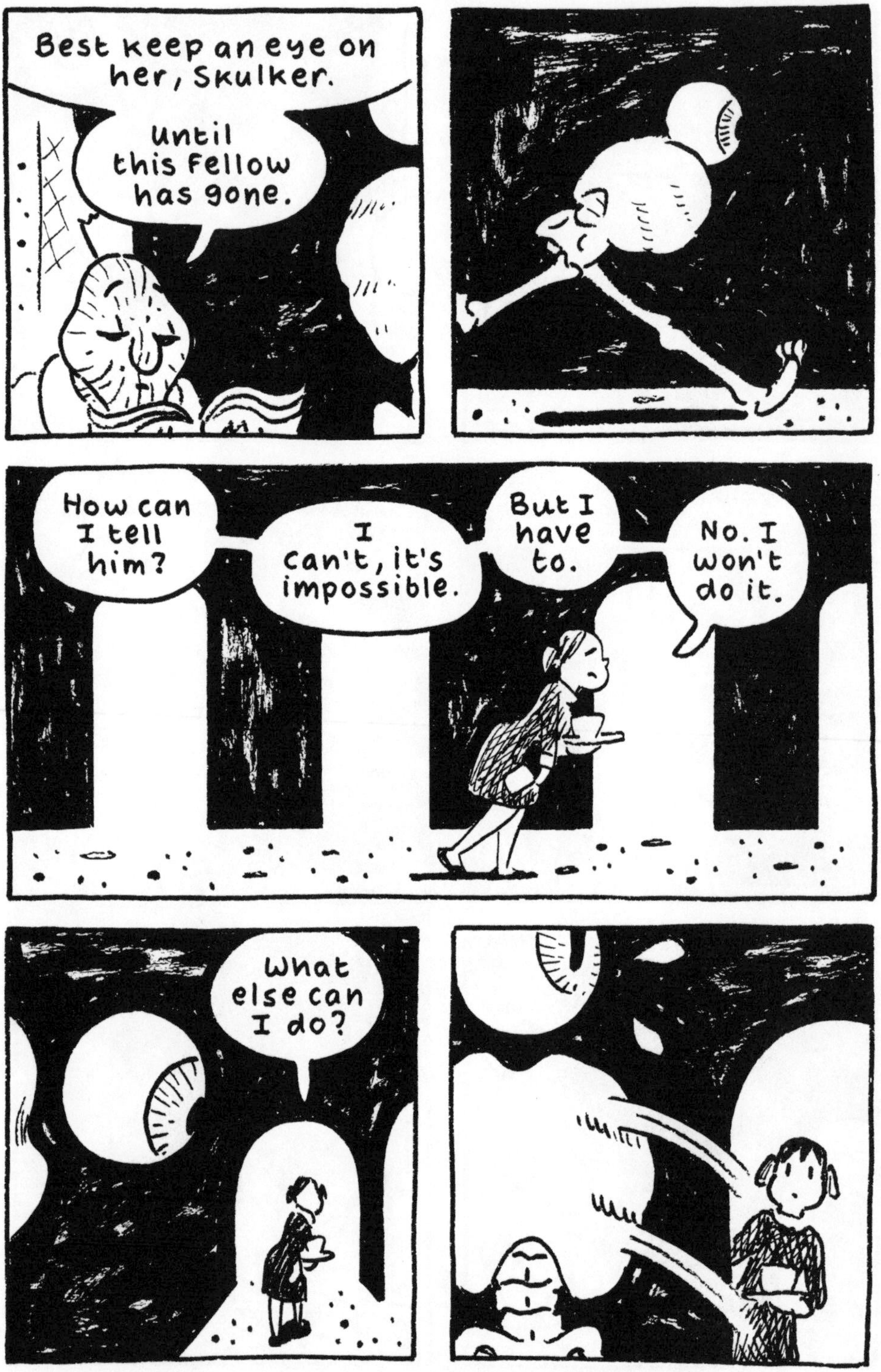
Best keep an eye on her, Skulker.
Until this fellow has gone.
How can I tell him?
I can't, it's impossible.
But I have to.
No. I won't do it.
What else can I do?

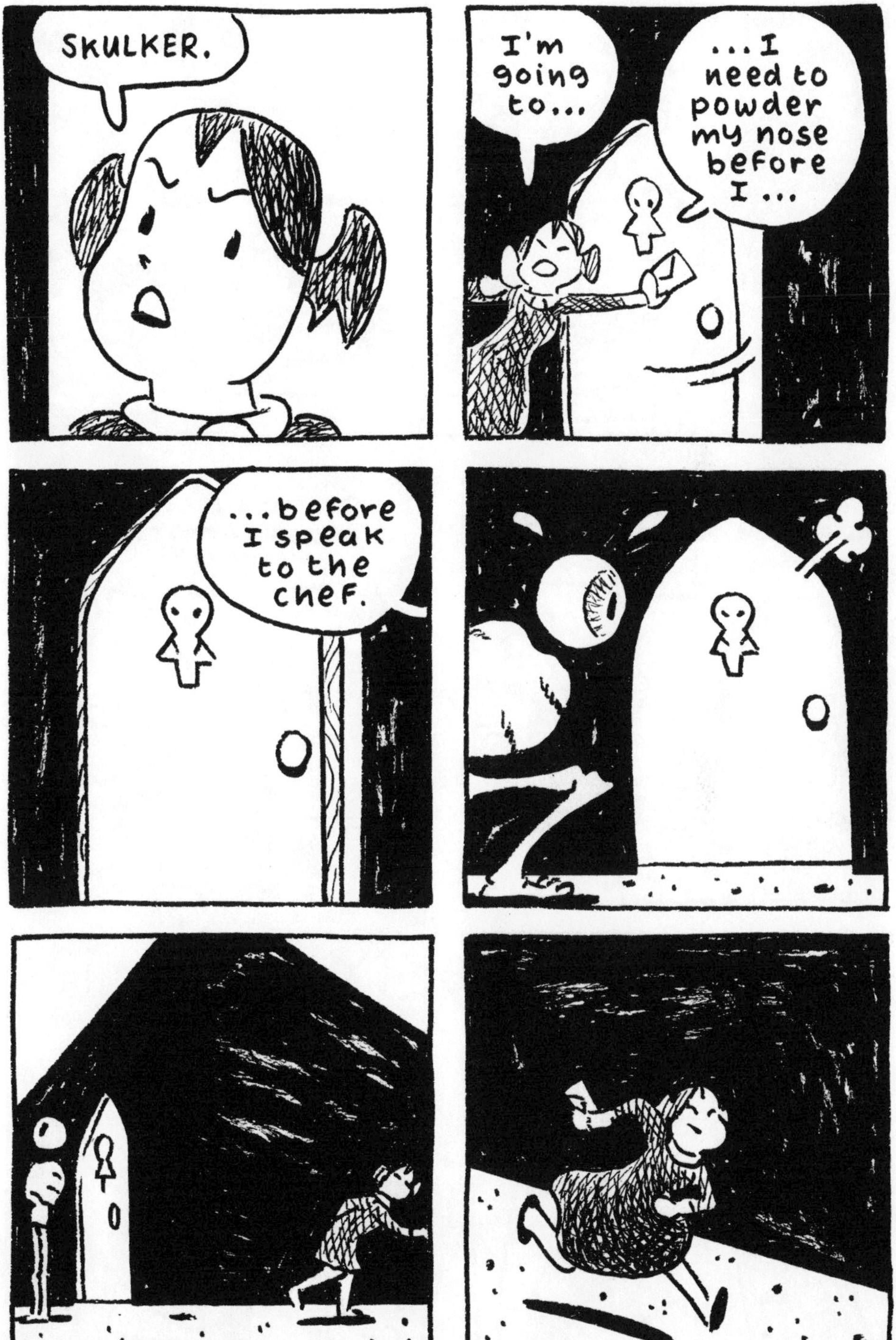
SKULKER.
I'm going to...
...I need to powder my nose before I...
...before I speak to the chef.

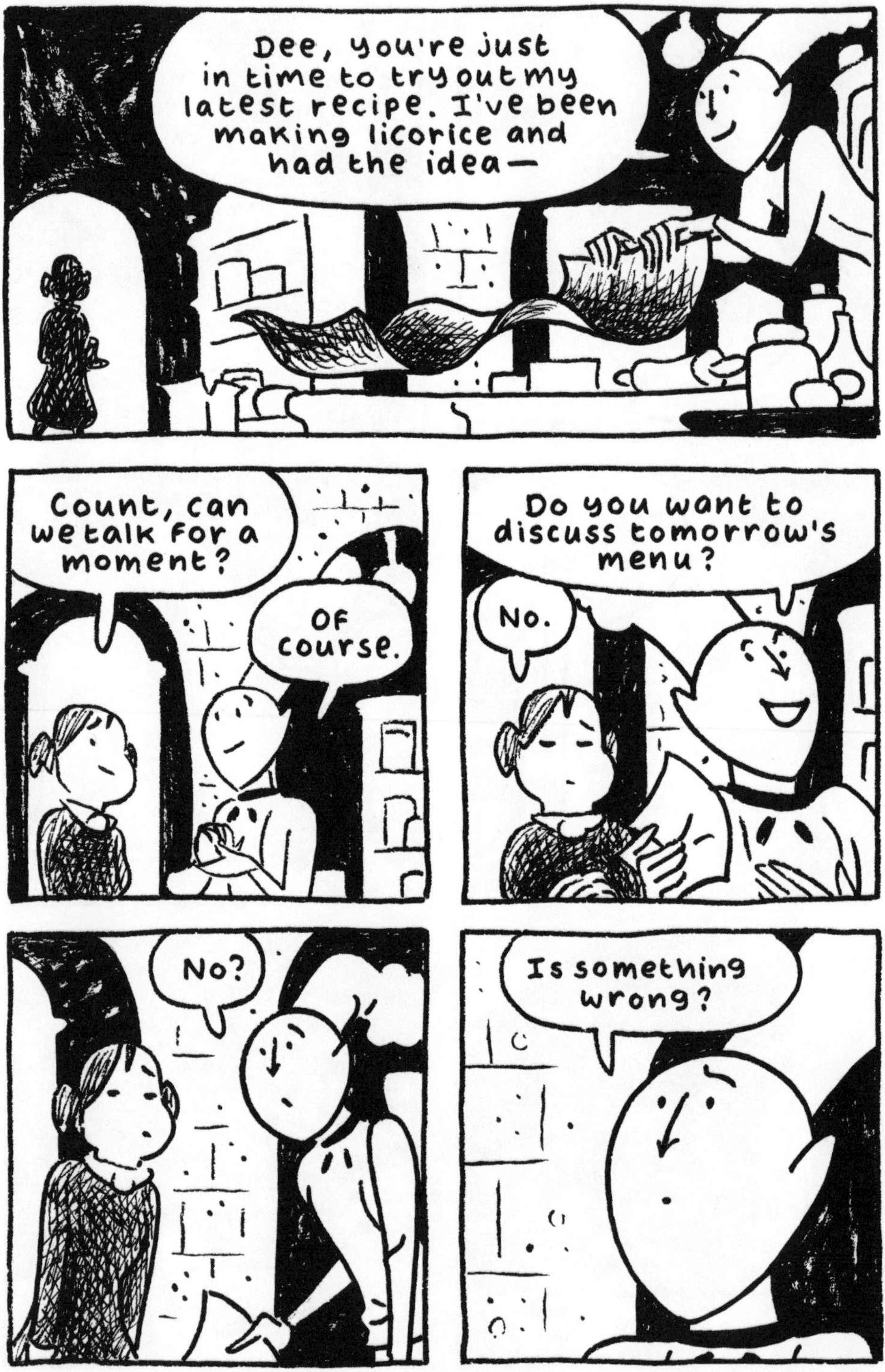
Dee, you're just in time to try out my latest recipe. I've been making licorice and had the idea—
Count, can we talk for a moment?
Of course.
Do you want to discuss tomorrow's menu?
No.
No?
Is something wrong?

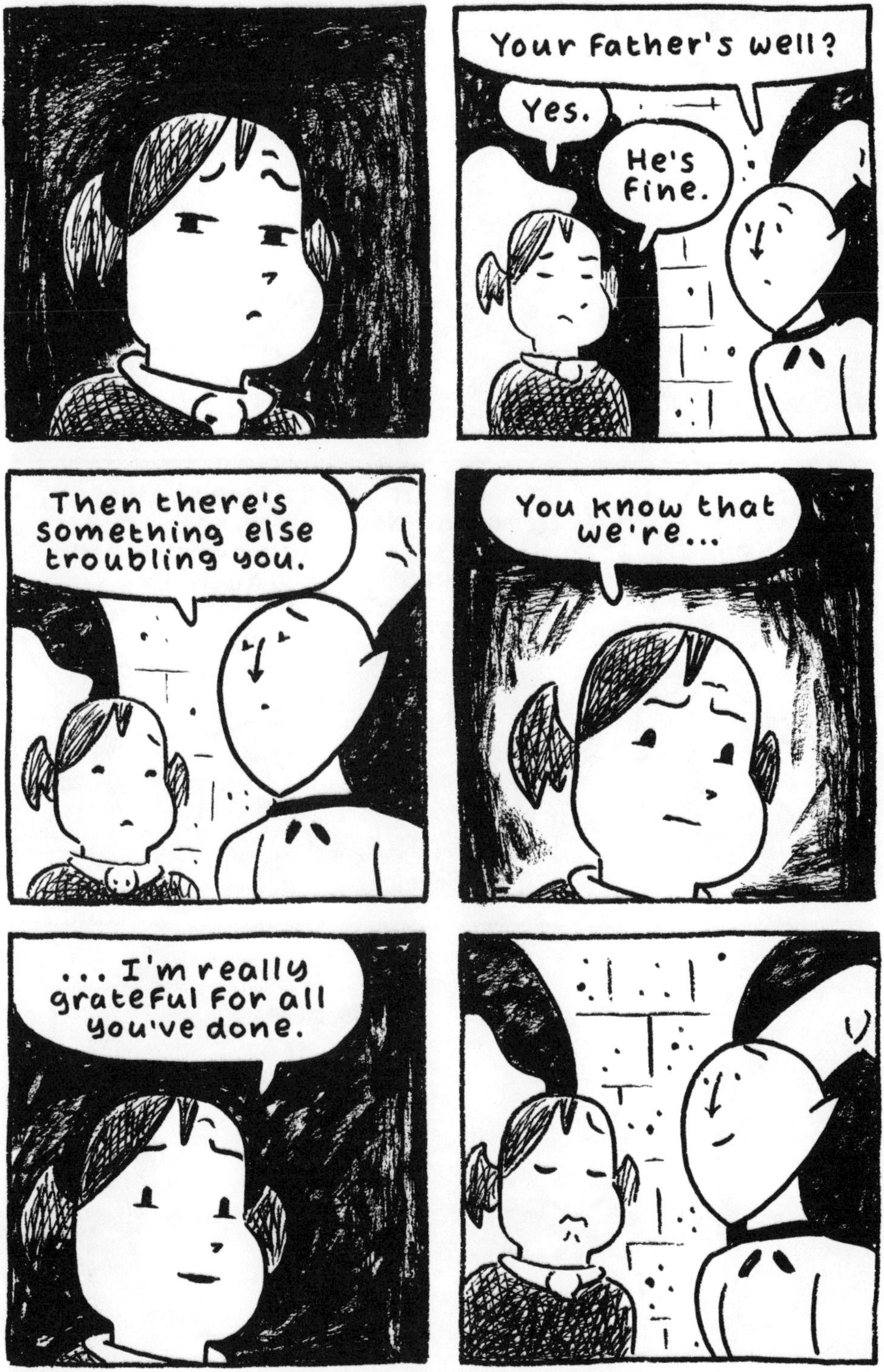
Your father's well?
Yes.
He's fine.
Then there's something else troubling you.
You know that we're...
... I'm really grateful for all you've done.

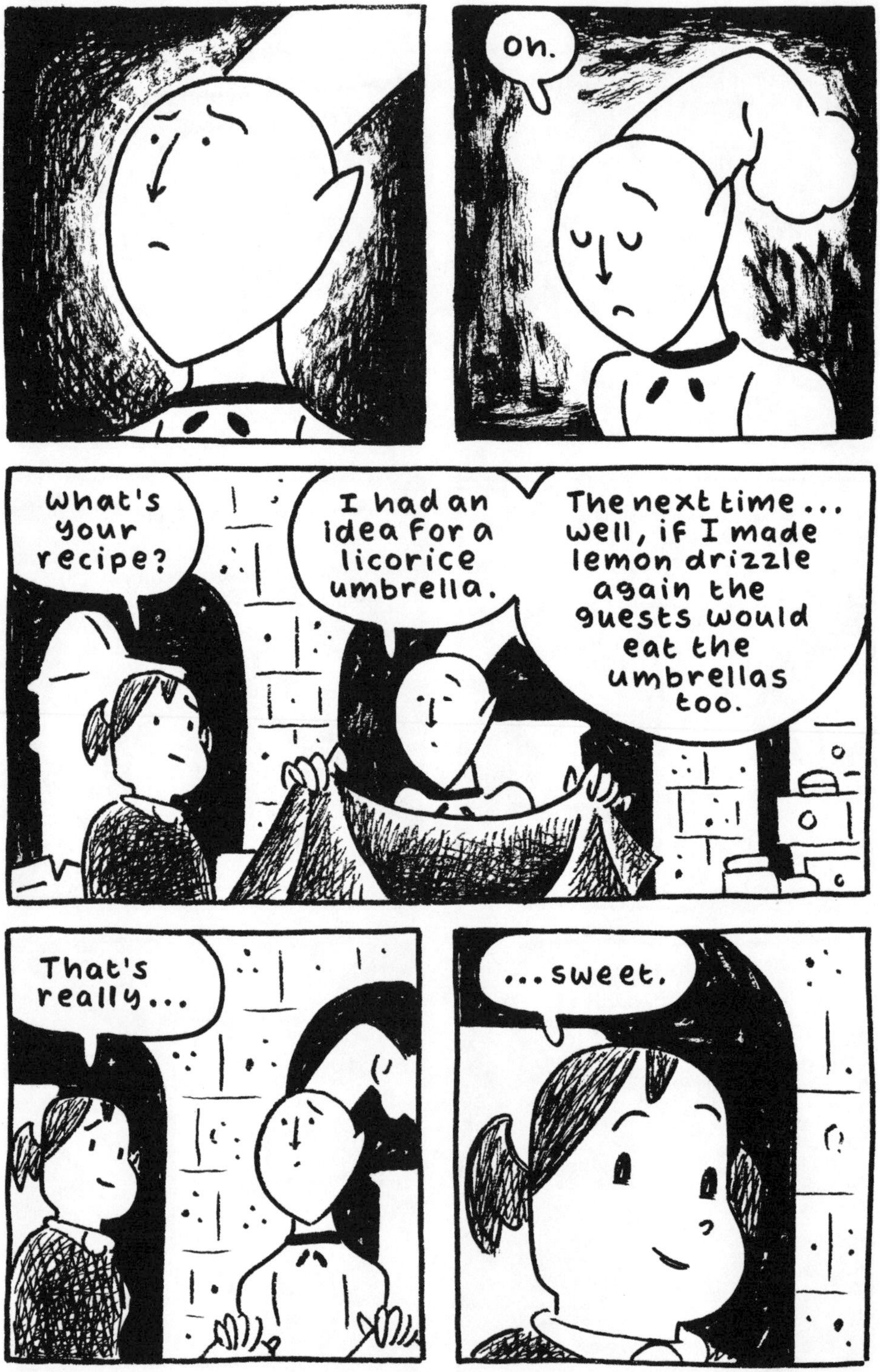

Oh.
What's your recipe?
I had an idea for a licorice umbrella.
The next time... well, if I made lemon drizzle again the guests would eat the umbrellas too.
That's really...
...sweet.

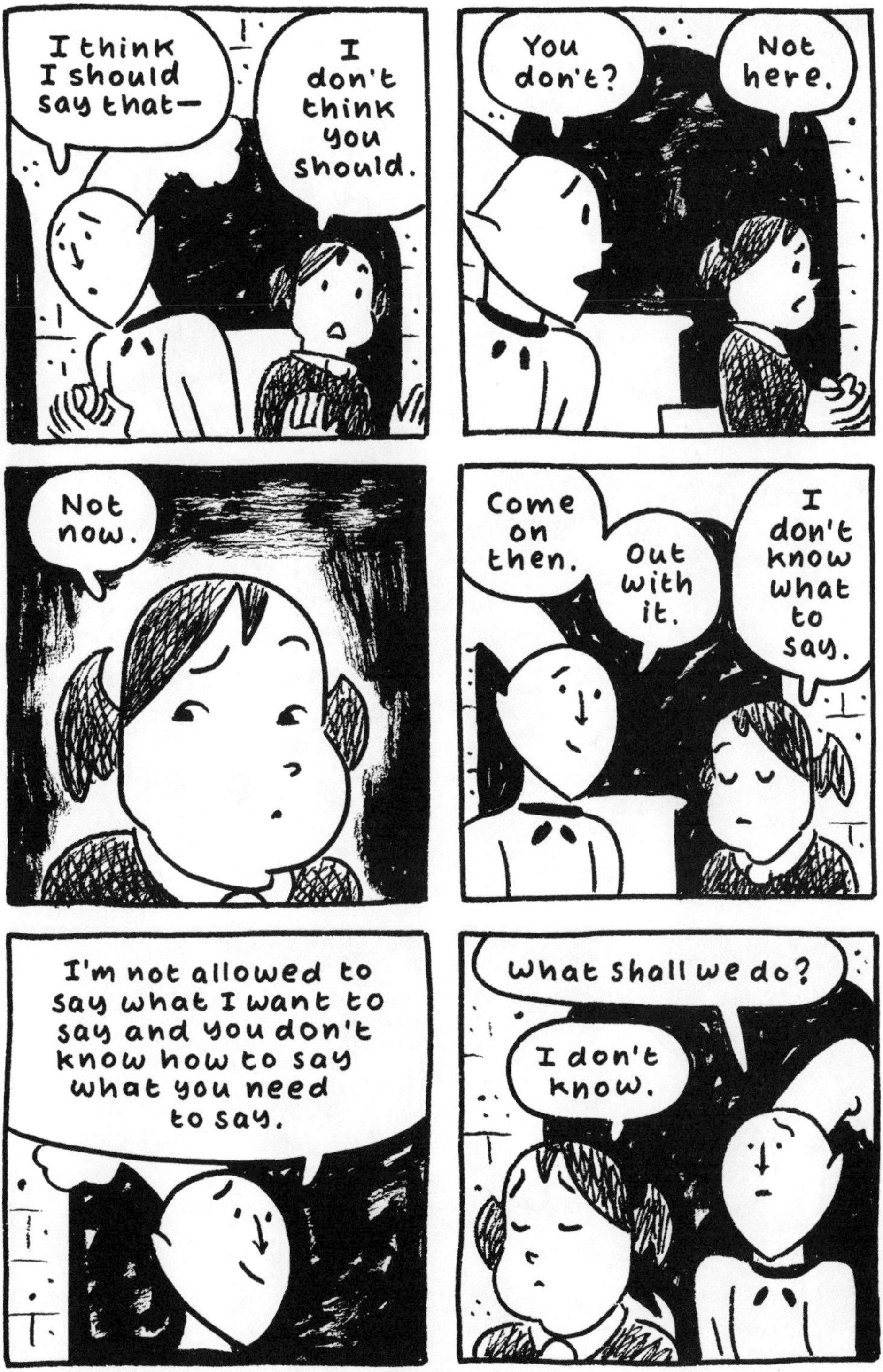
I think I should say that—
I don't think you should.
You don't?
Not here.
Not now.
Come on then.
Out with it.
I don't know what to say.
I'm not allowed to say what I want to say and you don't know how to say what you need to say.
What shall we do?
I don't know.

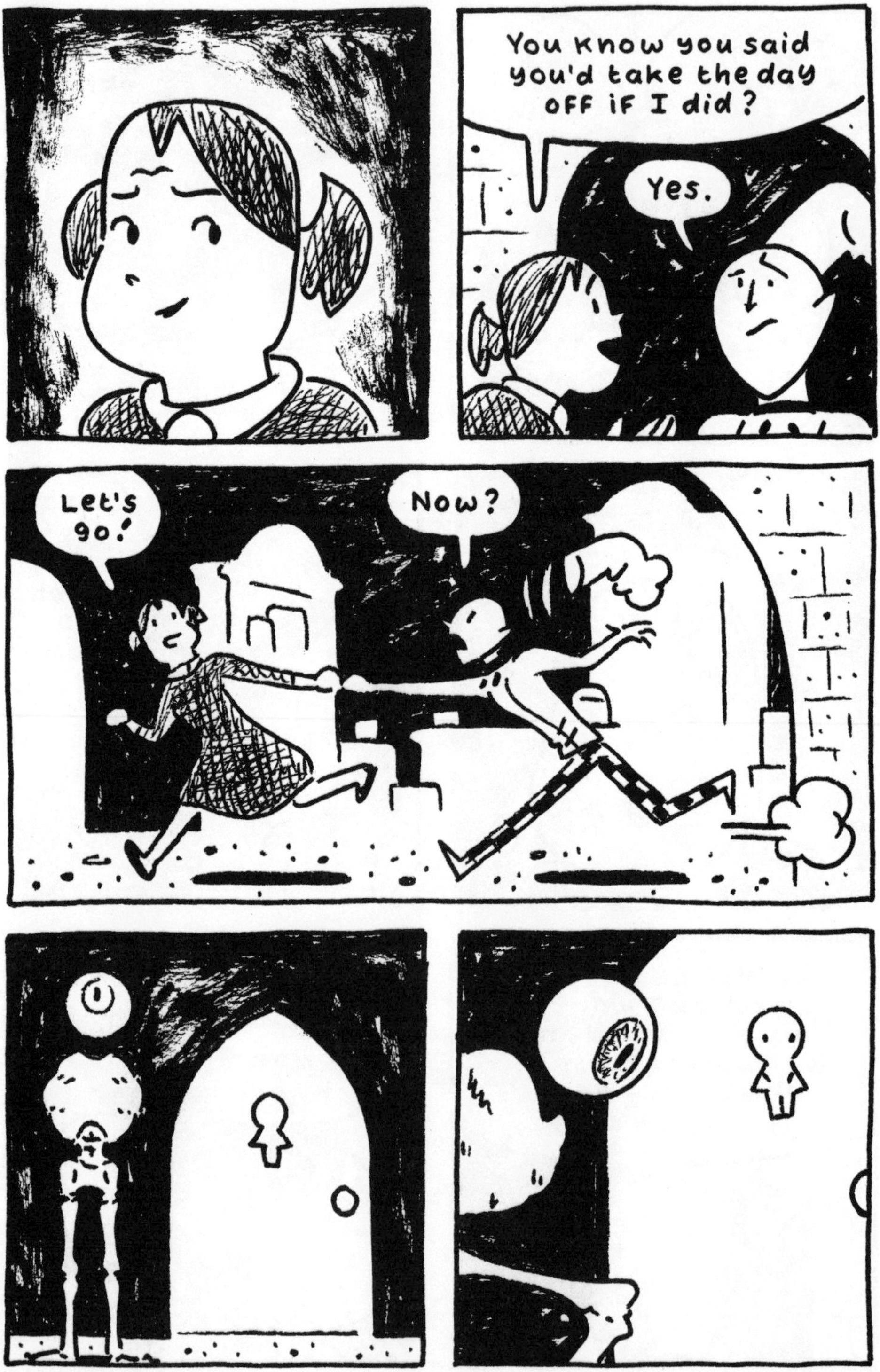
You know you said you'd take the day off if I did?
Yes.
Let's go!
Now?

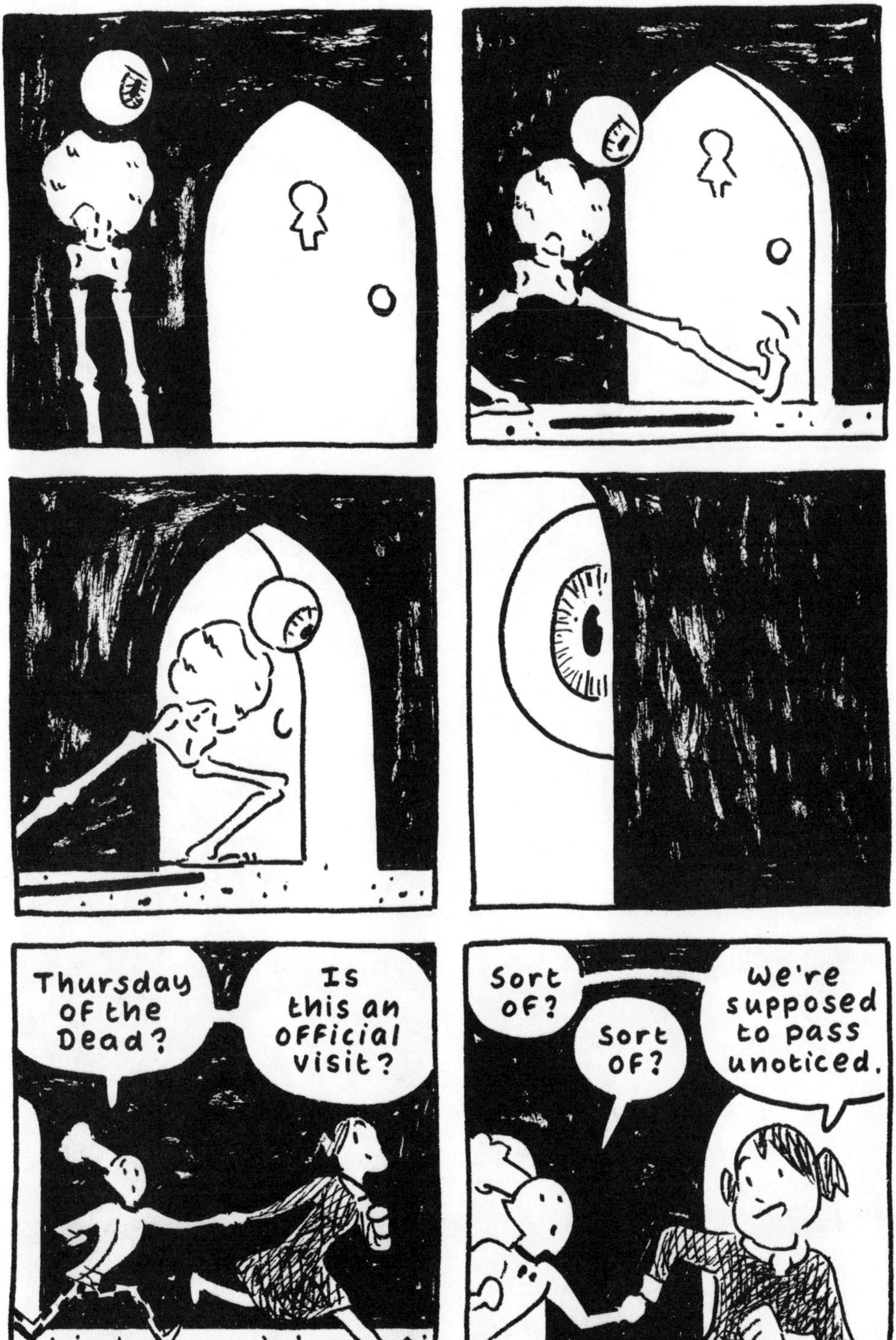

Thursday of the Dead?
Is this an official visit?
Sort of?
Sort of?
We're supposed to pass unoticed.

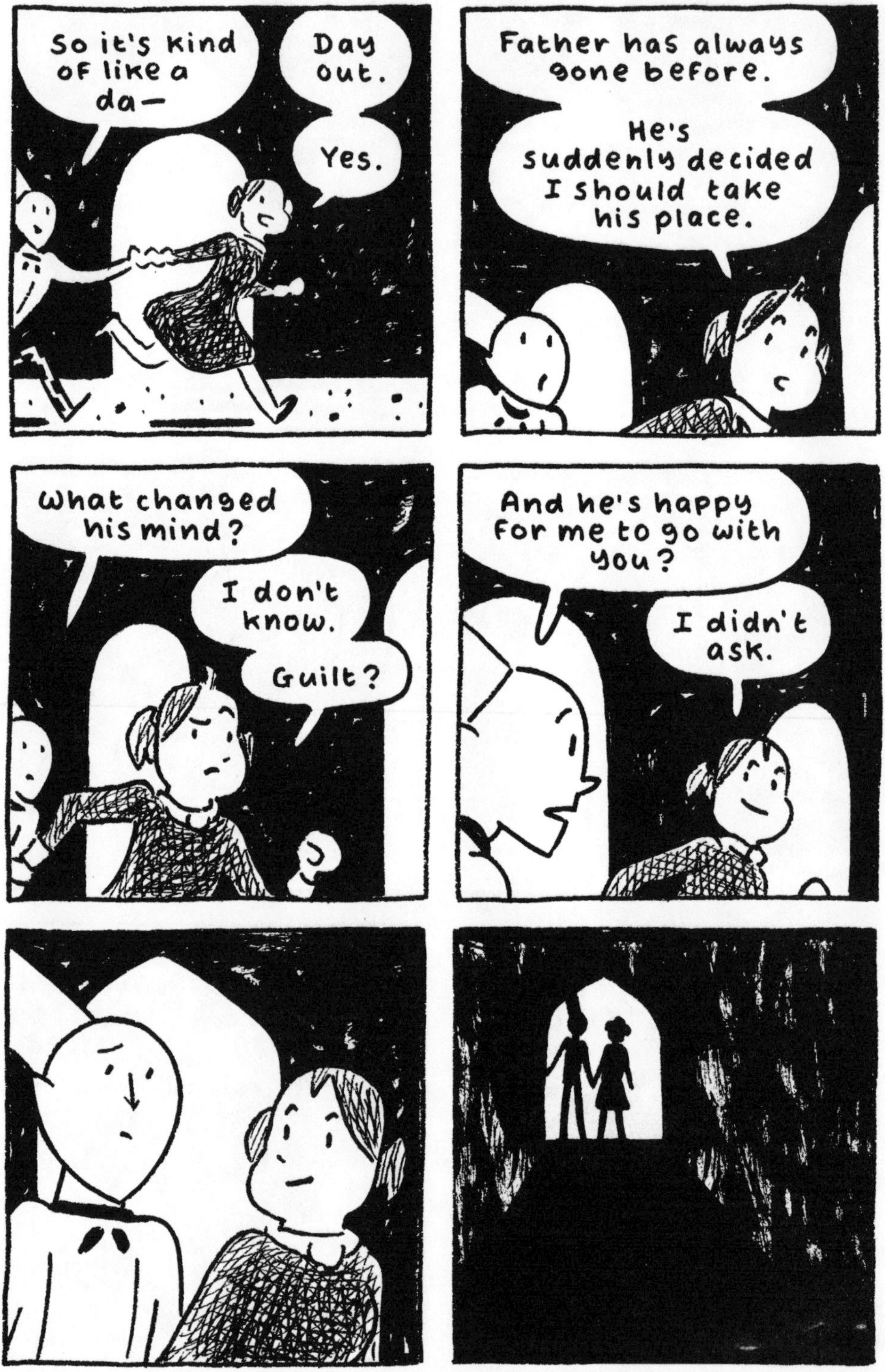
So it's kind of like a da—
Day out.
Yes.
Father has always gone before.
He's suddenly decided I should take his place.
What changed his mind?
I don't know.
Guilt?
And he's happy for me to go with you?
I didn't ask.

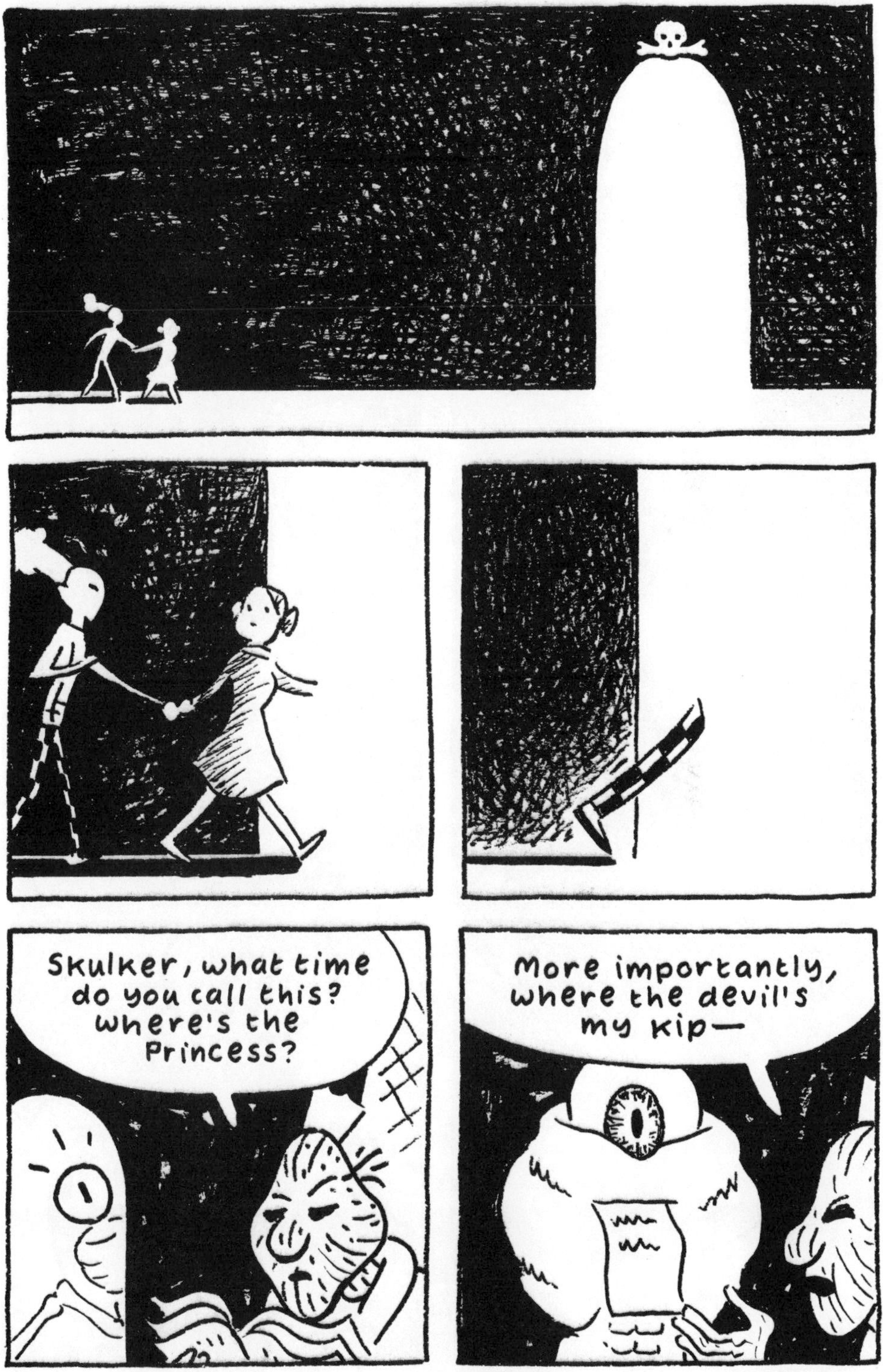
Skulker, what time do you call this? where's the Princess?
More importantly, where the devil's my kip—

What do you mean, she's gone? Princesses do not disappear, certainly not before breakfast.
And what about the cook, has he packed and gone yet?
WHAT!
Bright, isn't it?

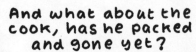

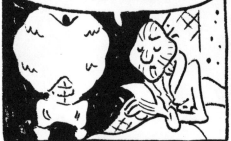

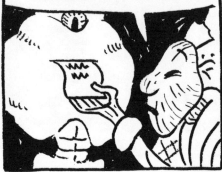

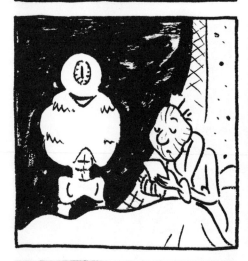

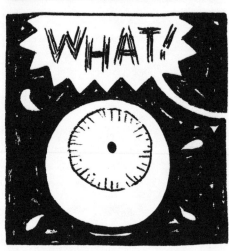

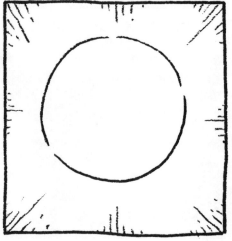

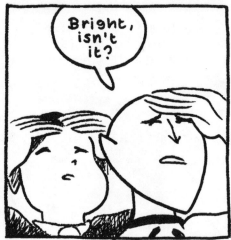

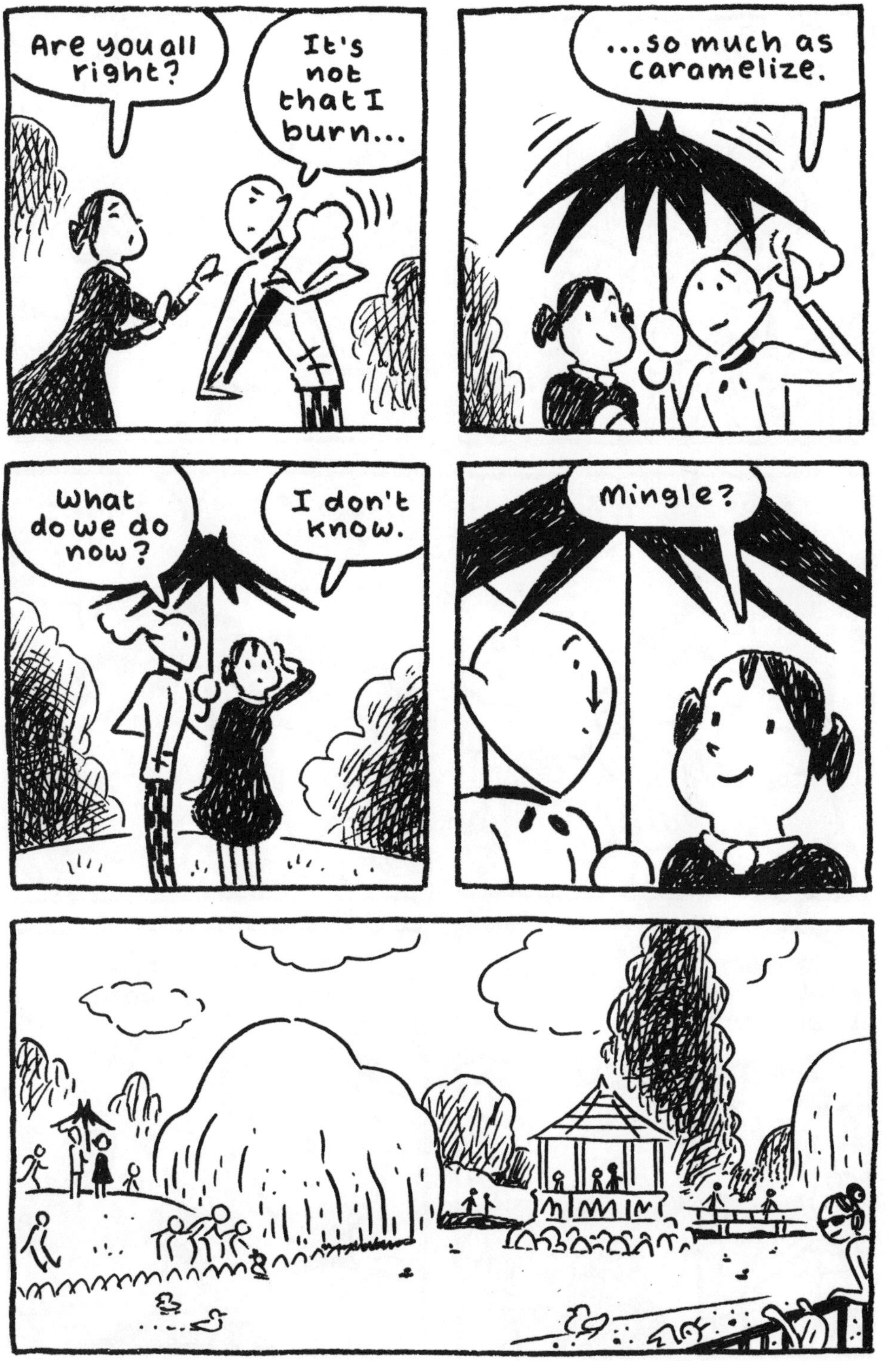
Are you all right?
It's not that I burn...
...so much as caramelize.
What do we do now?
I don't know.
Mingle?

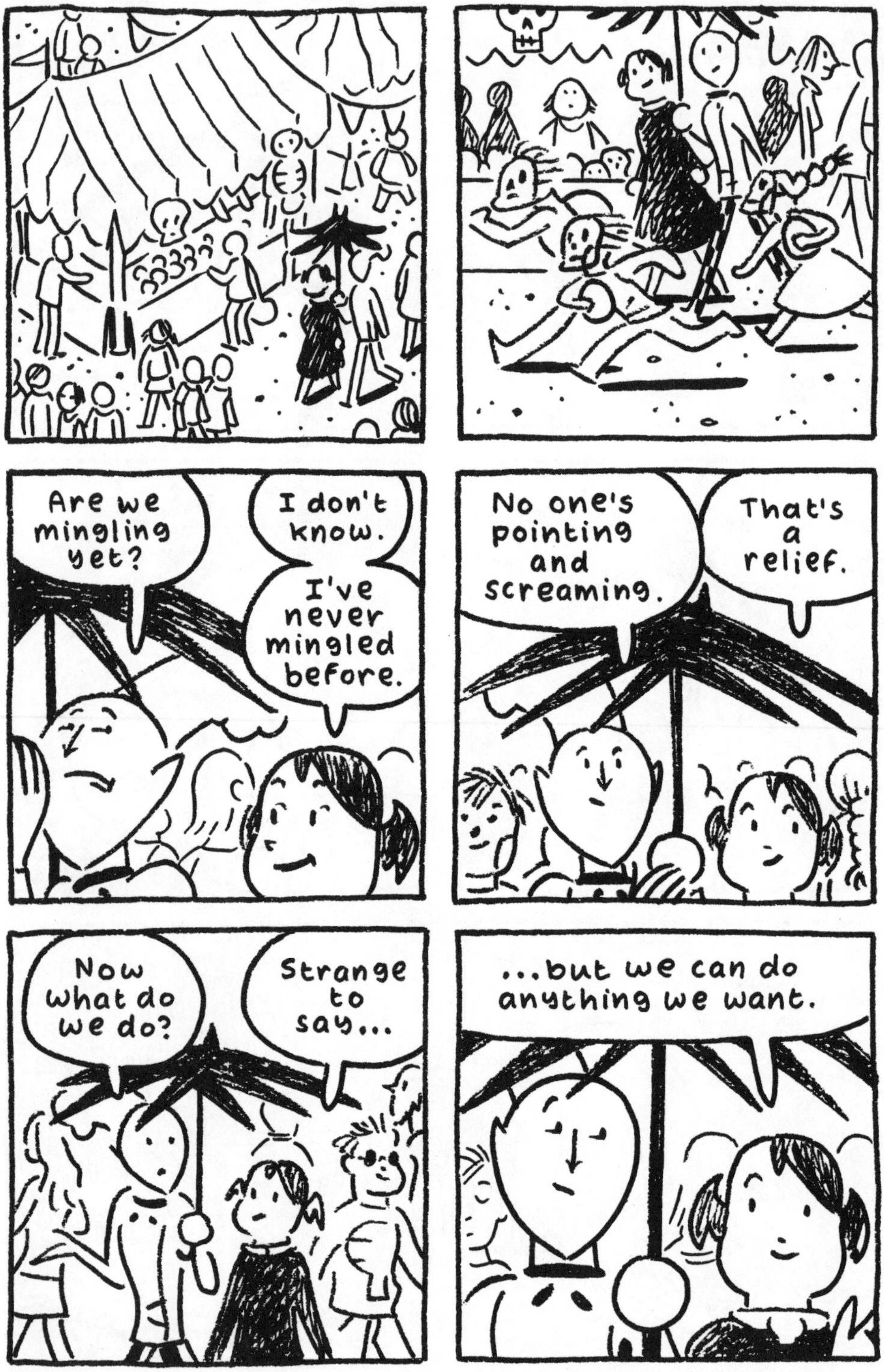
Are we mingling yet?
I don't know.
I've never mingled before.
No one's pointing and screaming.
That's a relief.
Now what do we do?
Strange to say...
...but we can do anything we want.

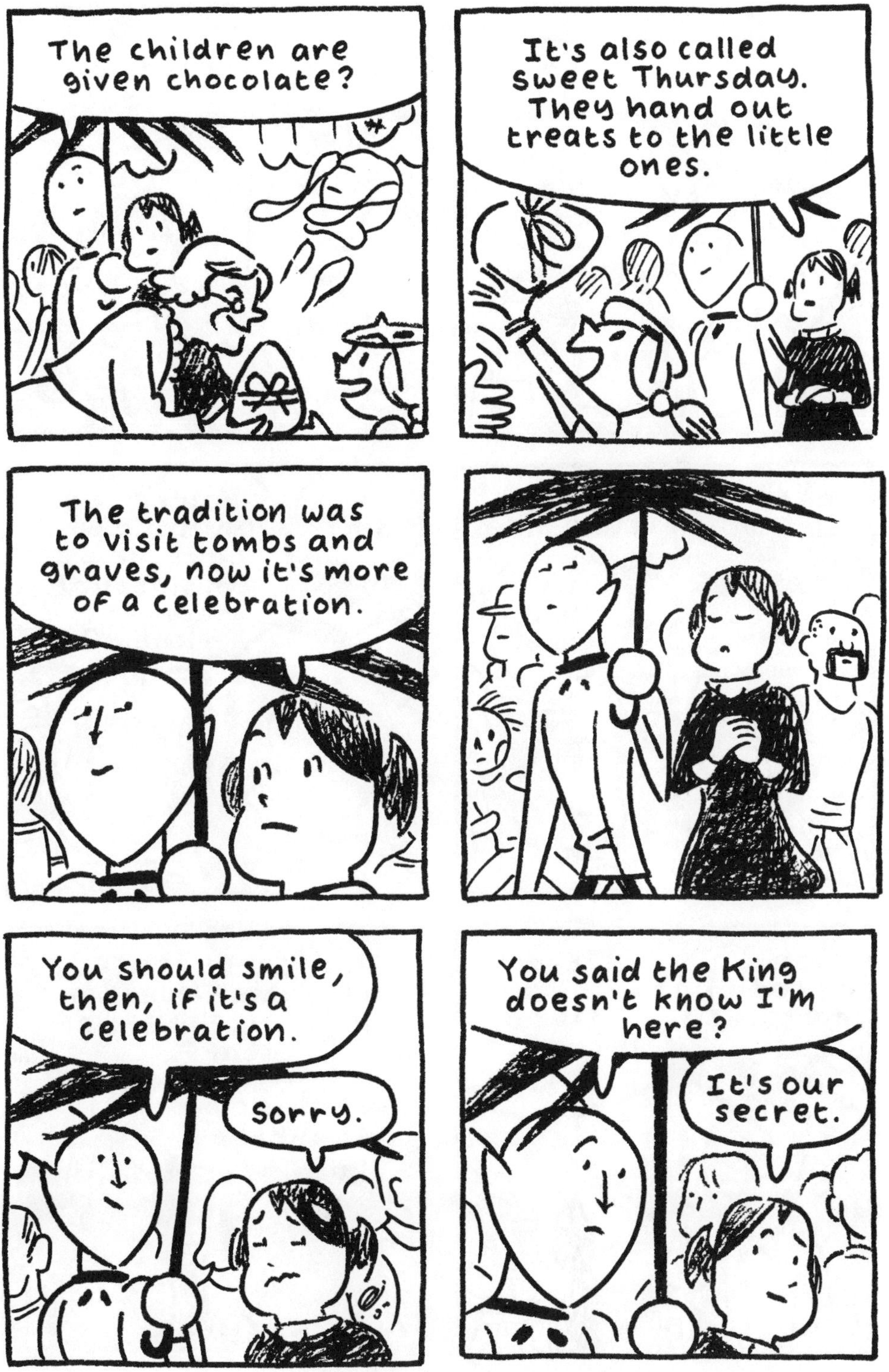
The children are given chocolate?
It's also called sweet Thursday. They hand out treats to the little ones.
The tradition was to visit tombs and graves, now it's more of a celebration.
You should smile, then, if it's a celebration.
Sorry.
You said the King doesn't know I'm here?
It's our secret.

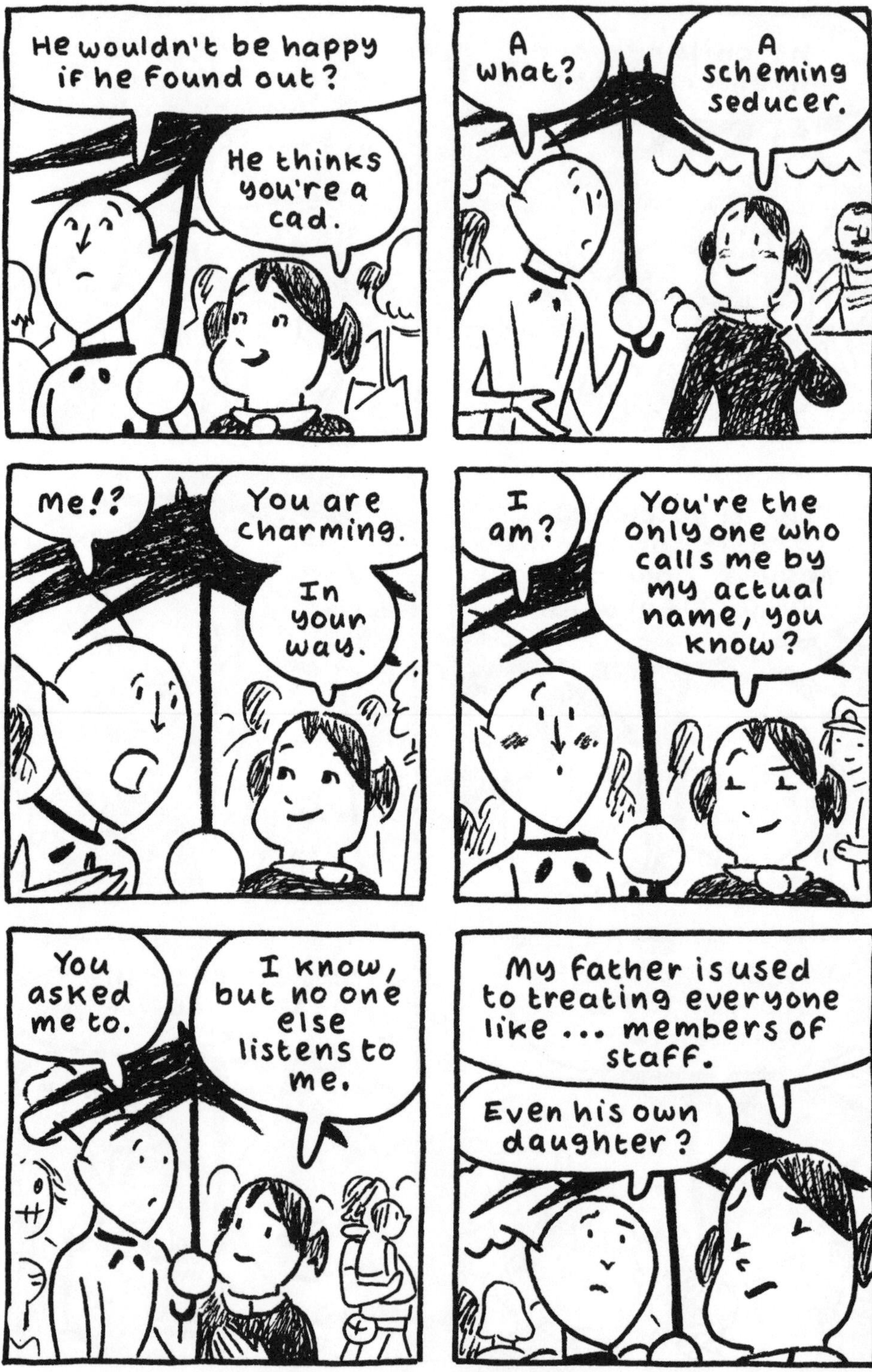
He wouldn't be happy if he found out?
He thinks you're a cad.
A what?
A scheming seducer.
Me!?
You are charming.
In your way.
I am?
You're the only one who calls me by my actual name, you know?
You asked me to.
I know, but no one else listens to me.
My father is used to treating everyone like ... members of staff.
Even his own daughter?

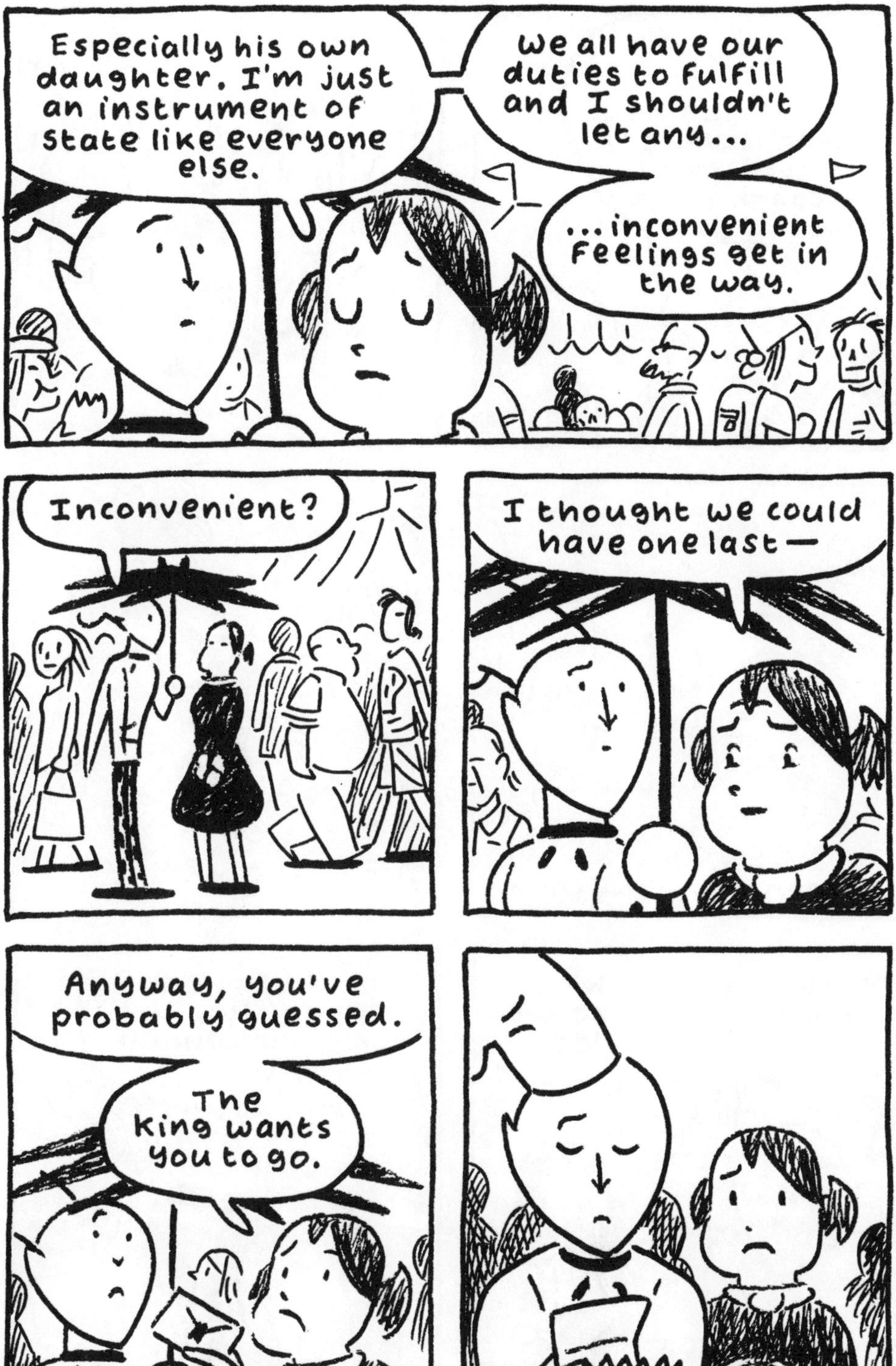

Especially his own daughter. I'm just an instrument of state like everyone else.
We all have our duties to fulfill and I shouldn't let any...
...inconvenient feelings get in the way.
Inconvenient?
I thought we could have one last—
Anyway, you've probably guessed.
The King wants you to go.

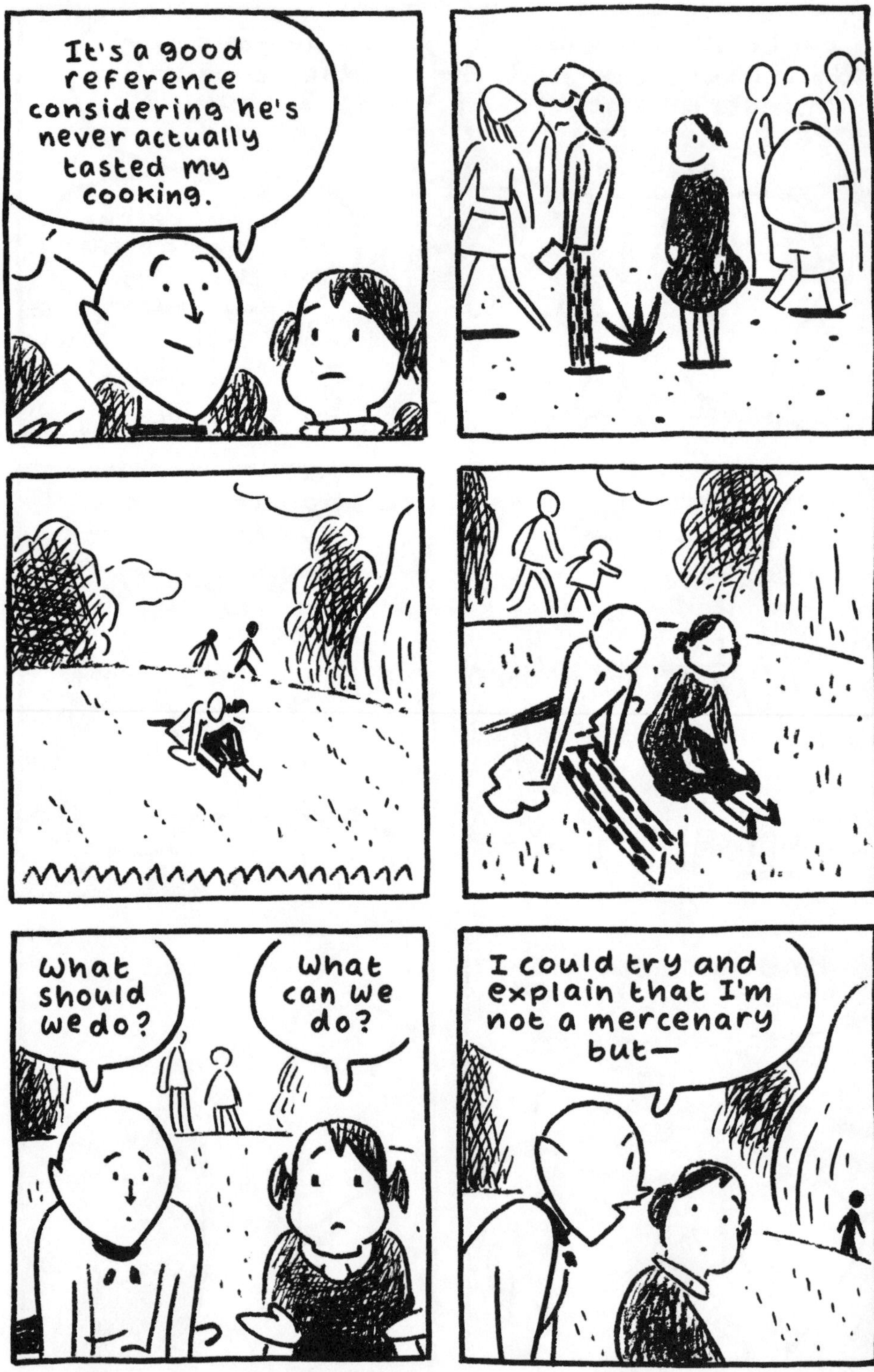
It's a good reference considering he's never actually tasted my cooking.
What should we do?
What can we do?
I could try and explain that I'm not a mercenary but—

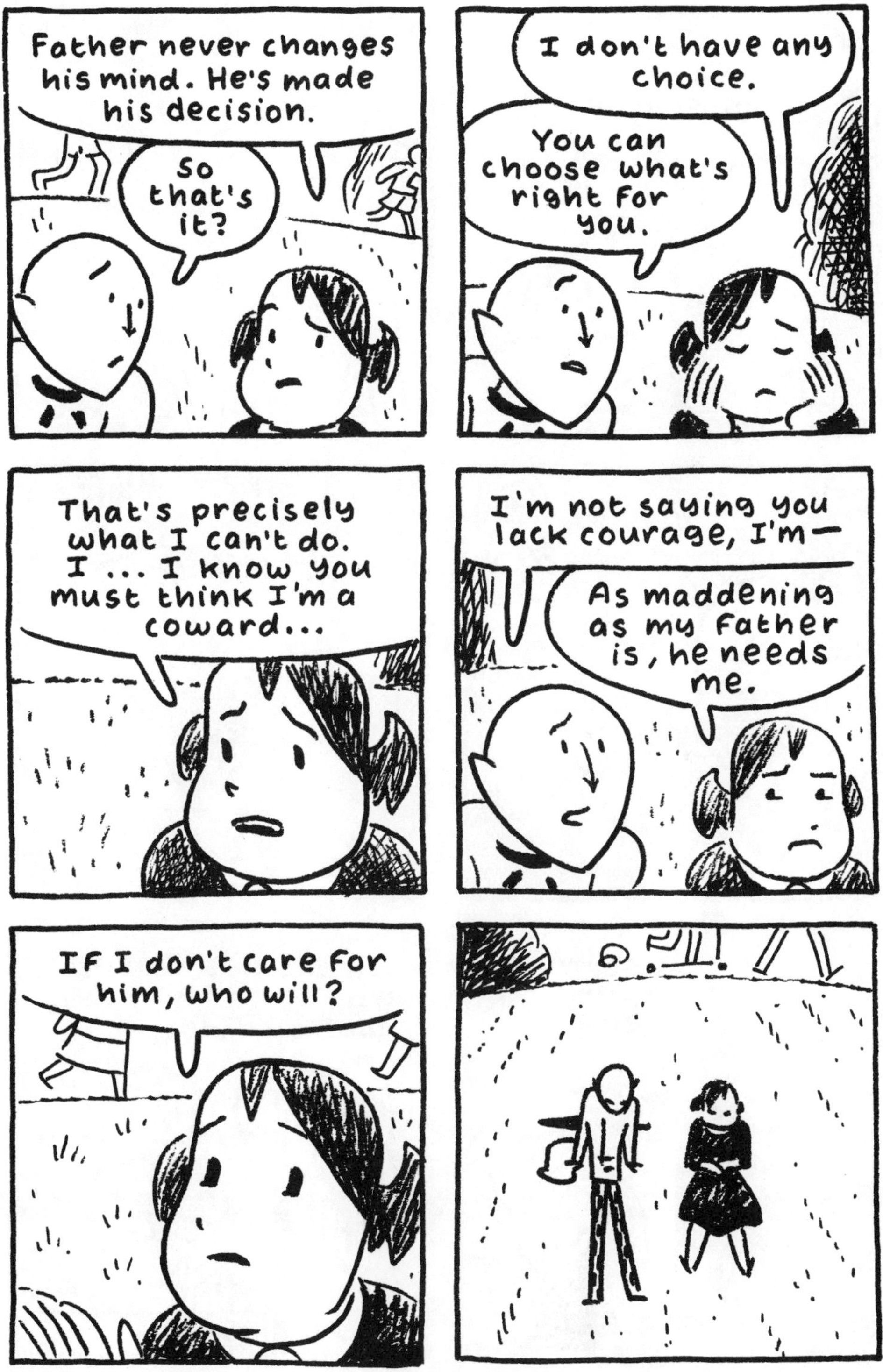
Father never changes his mind. He's made his decision.
So that's it?
I don't have any choice.
You can choose what's right for you.
That's precisely what I can't do. I ... I know you must think I'm a coward...
I'm not saying you lack courage, I'm—
As maddening as my father is, he needs me.
If I don't care for him, who will?

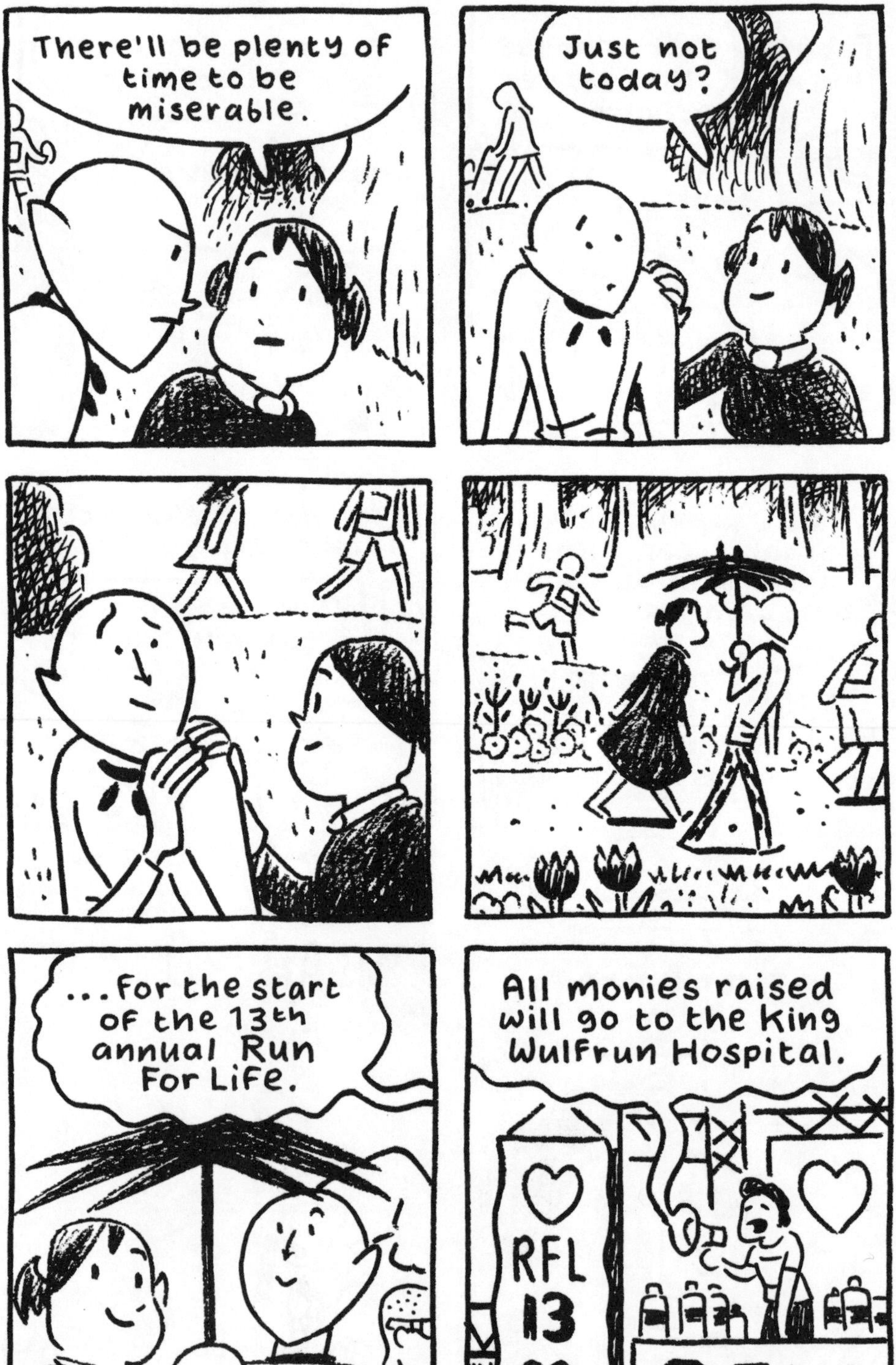
There'll be plenty of time to be miserable.
Just not today?
...For the start of the 13th annual Run For Life.
All monies raised will go to the King Wulfrun Hospital.
RFL 13

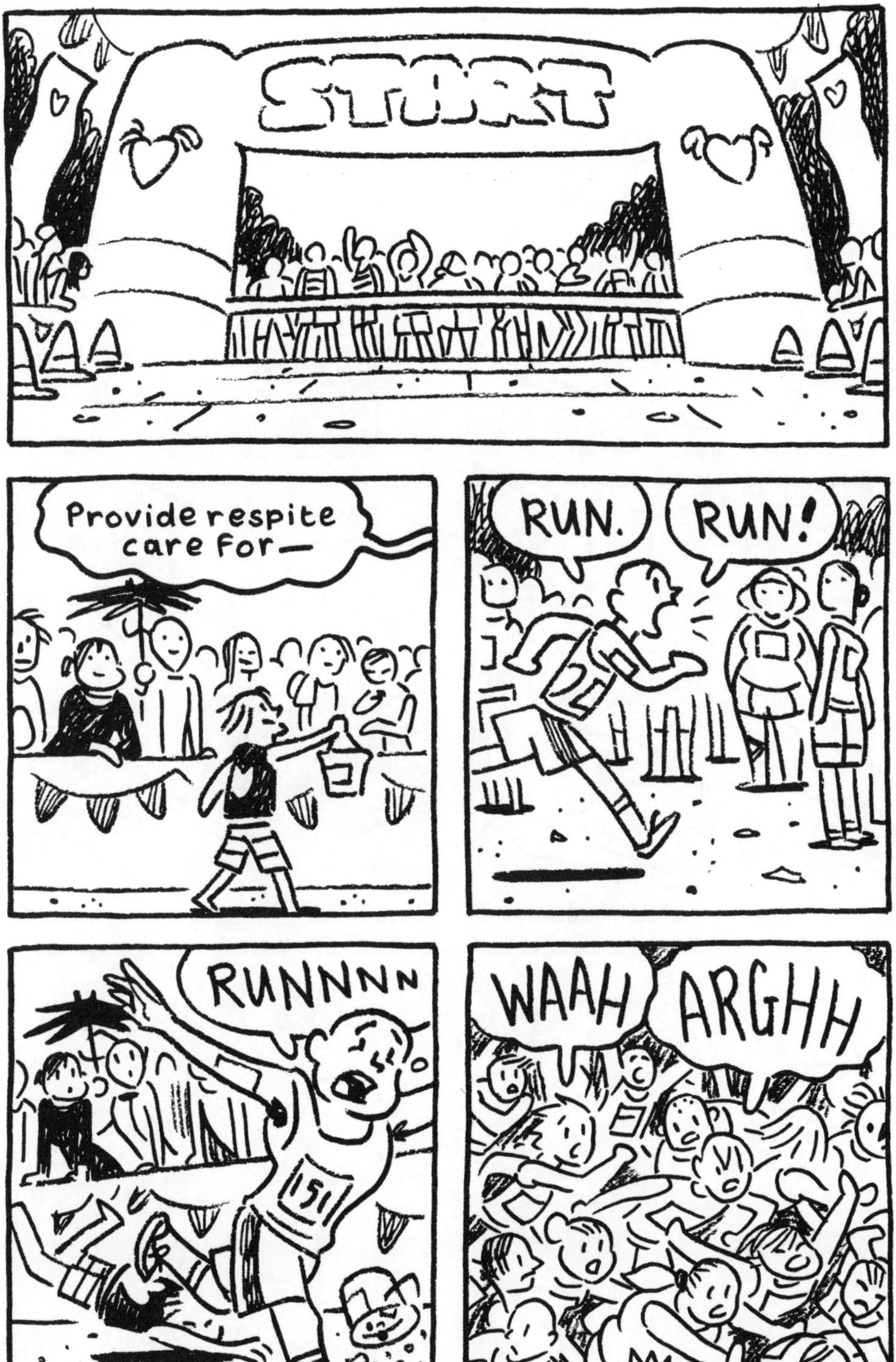
START
Provide respite care for—
RUN.
RUN!
RUNNNN
WAAH
ARGHH

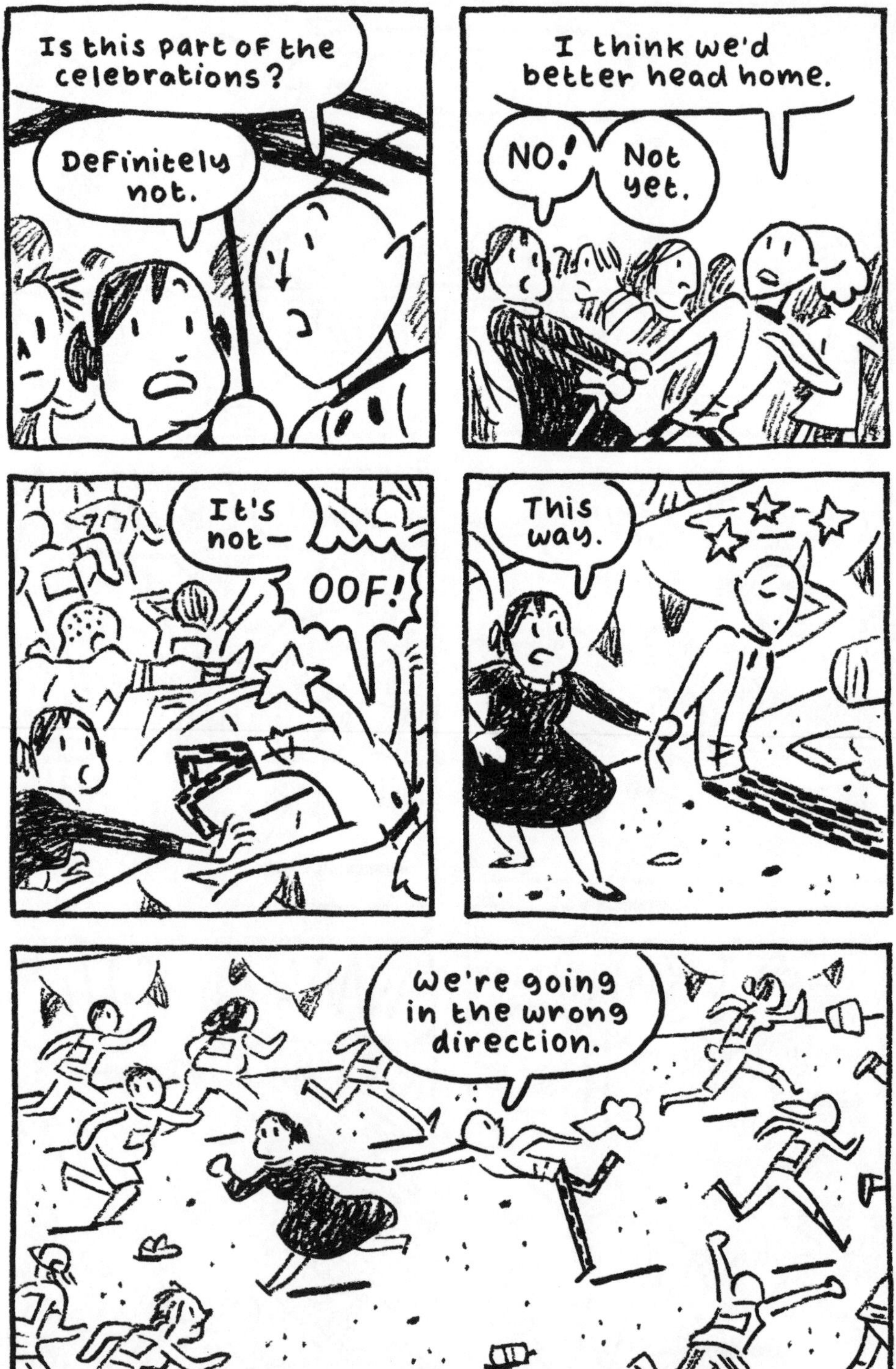
Is this part of the celebrations?
Definitely not.
I think we'd better head home.
NO!
Not yet.
It's not—
OOF!
This way.
We're going in the wrong direction.

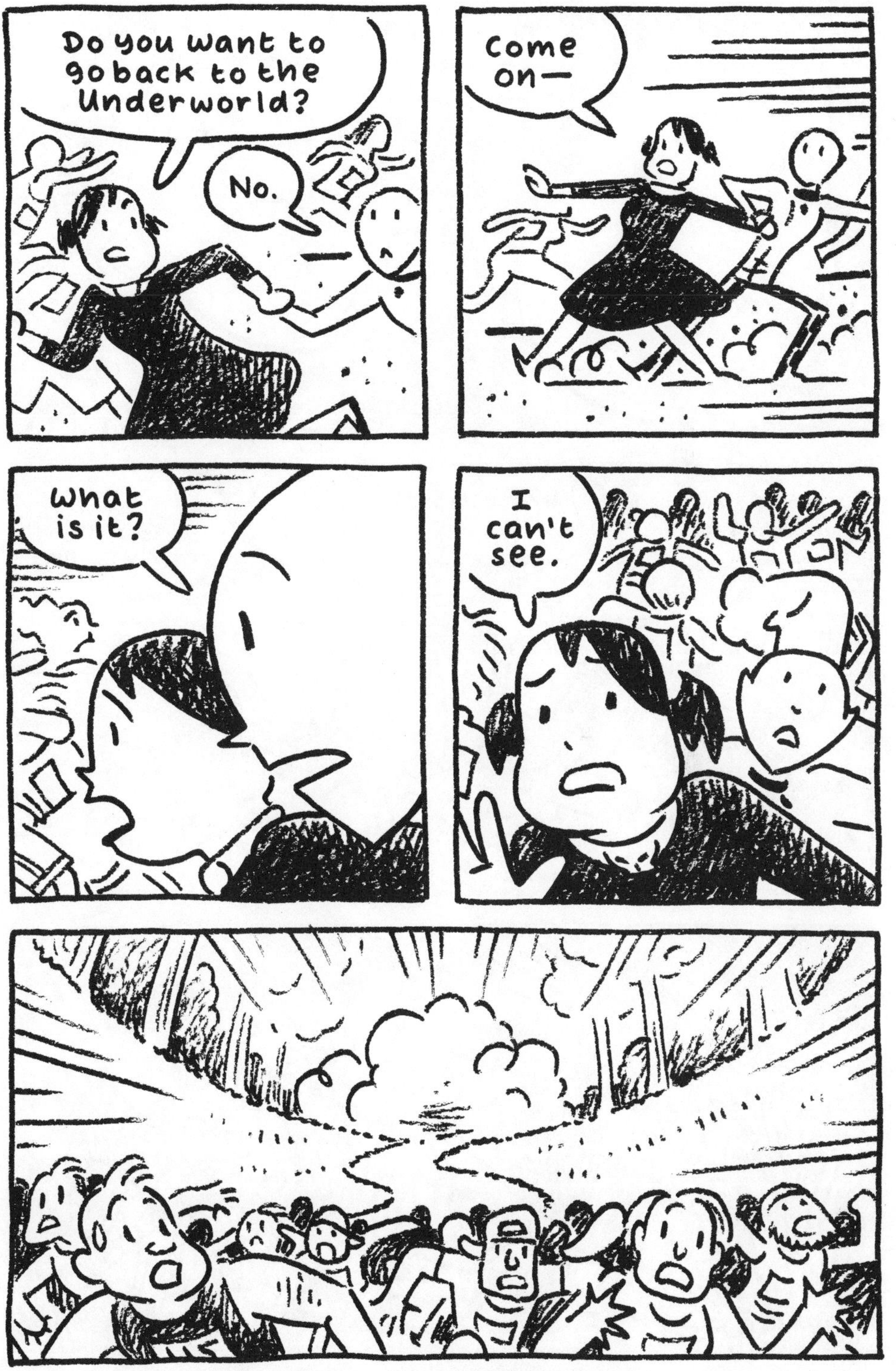
Do you want to go back to the Underworld?
No.
Come on—
What is it?
I can't see.

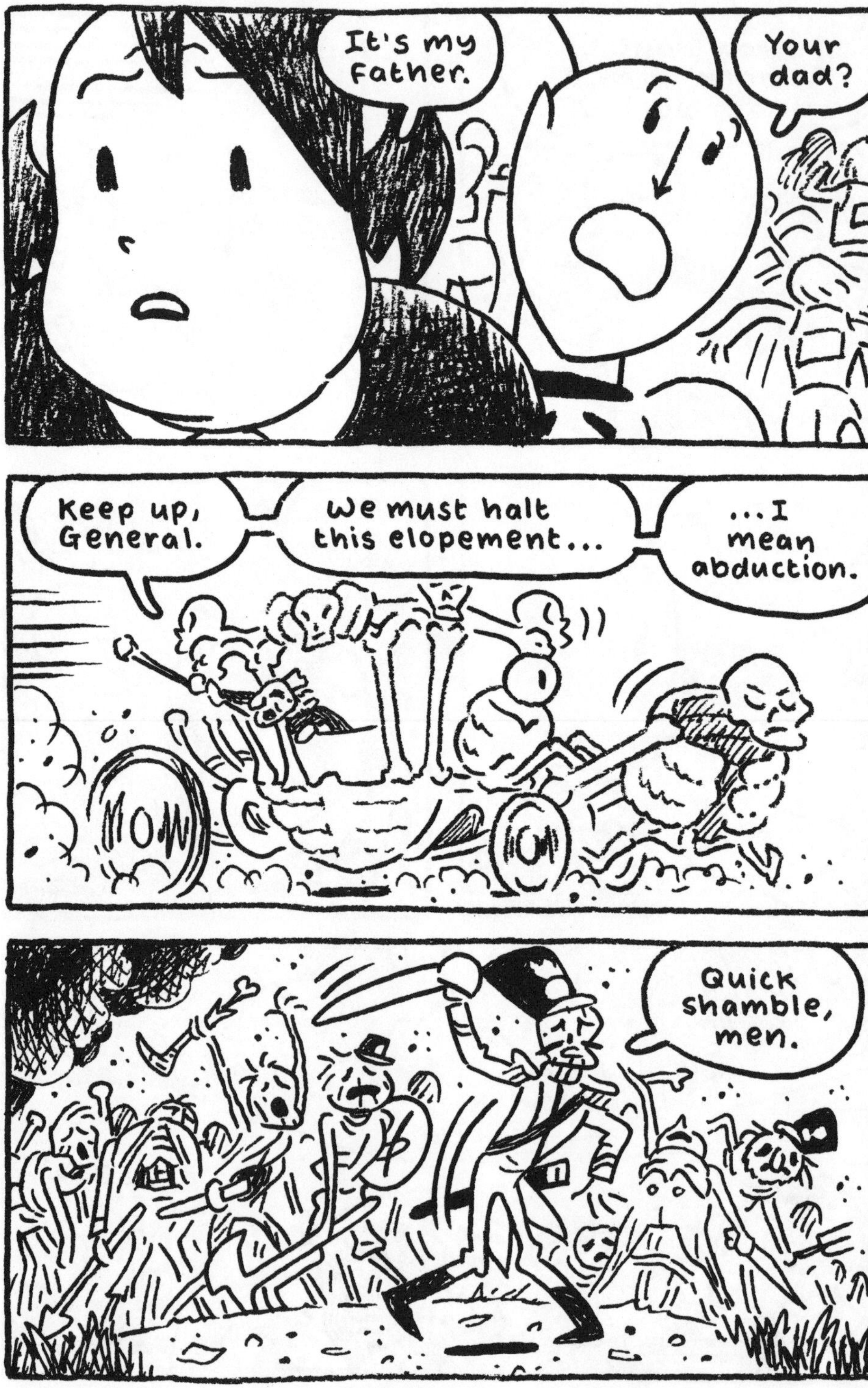
It's my Father.
Your dad?
Keep up, General.
We must halt this elopement...
...I mean abduction.
WOW
Quick shamble, men.

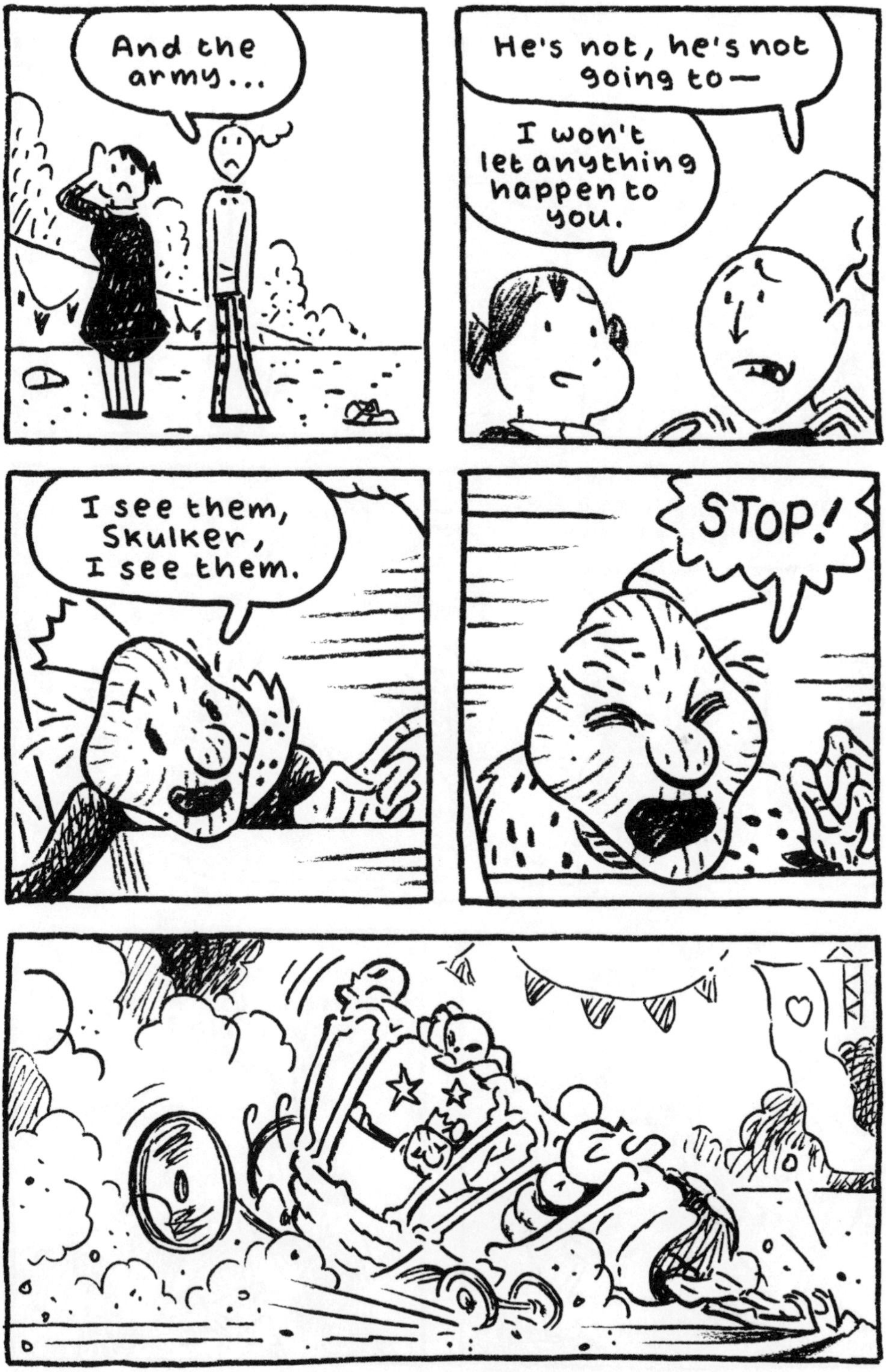
And the army...
He's not, he's not going to—
I won't let anything happen to you.
I see them, Skulker, I see them.
STOP!

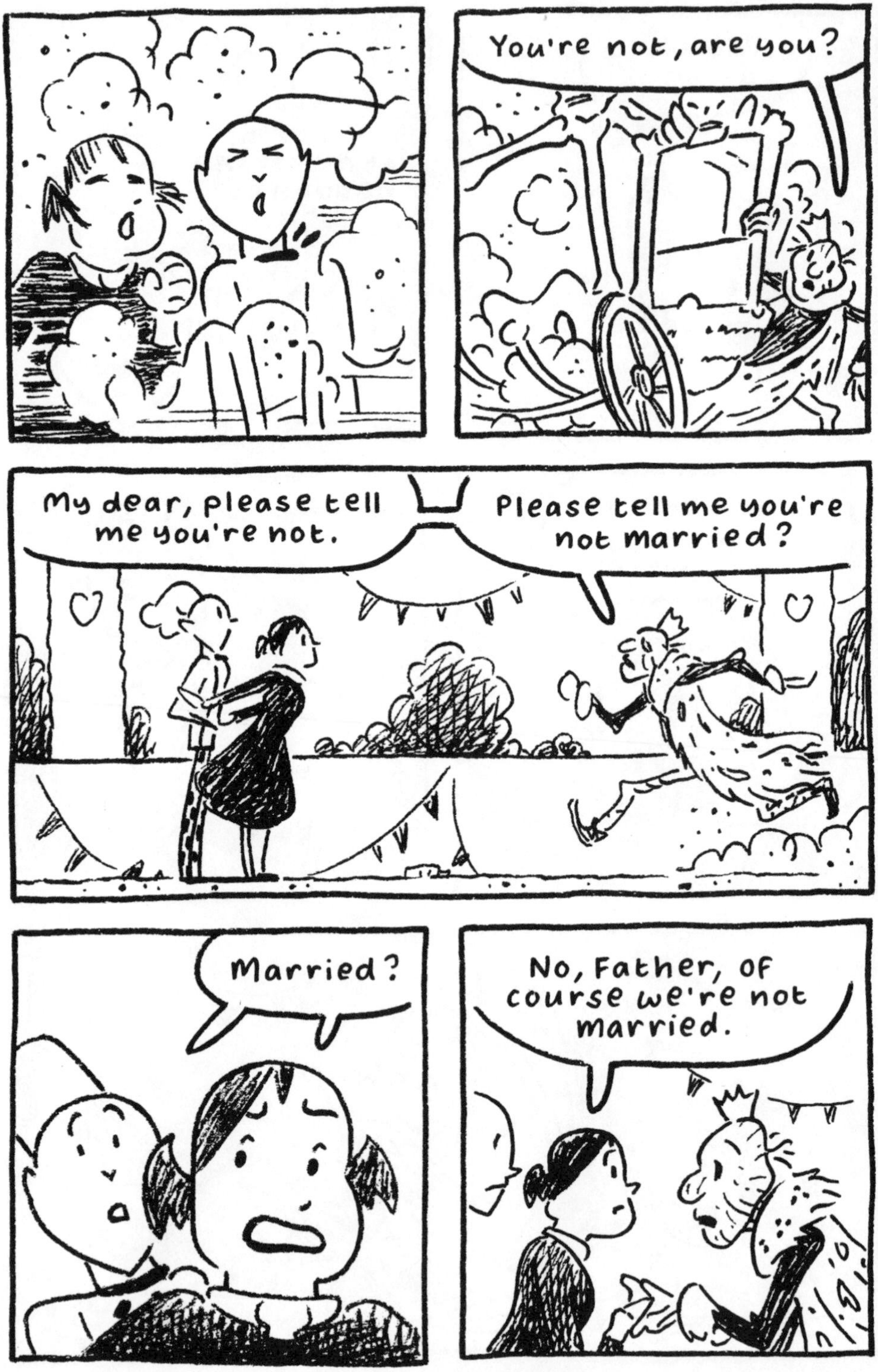
You're not, are you?
My dear, please tell me you're not.
Please tell me you're not married?
Married?
No, Father, of course we're not married.

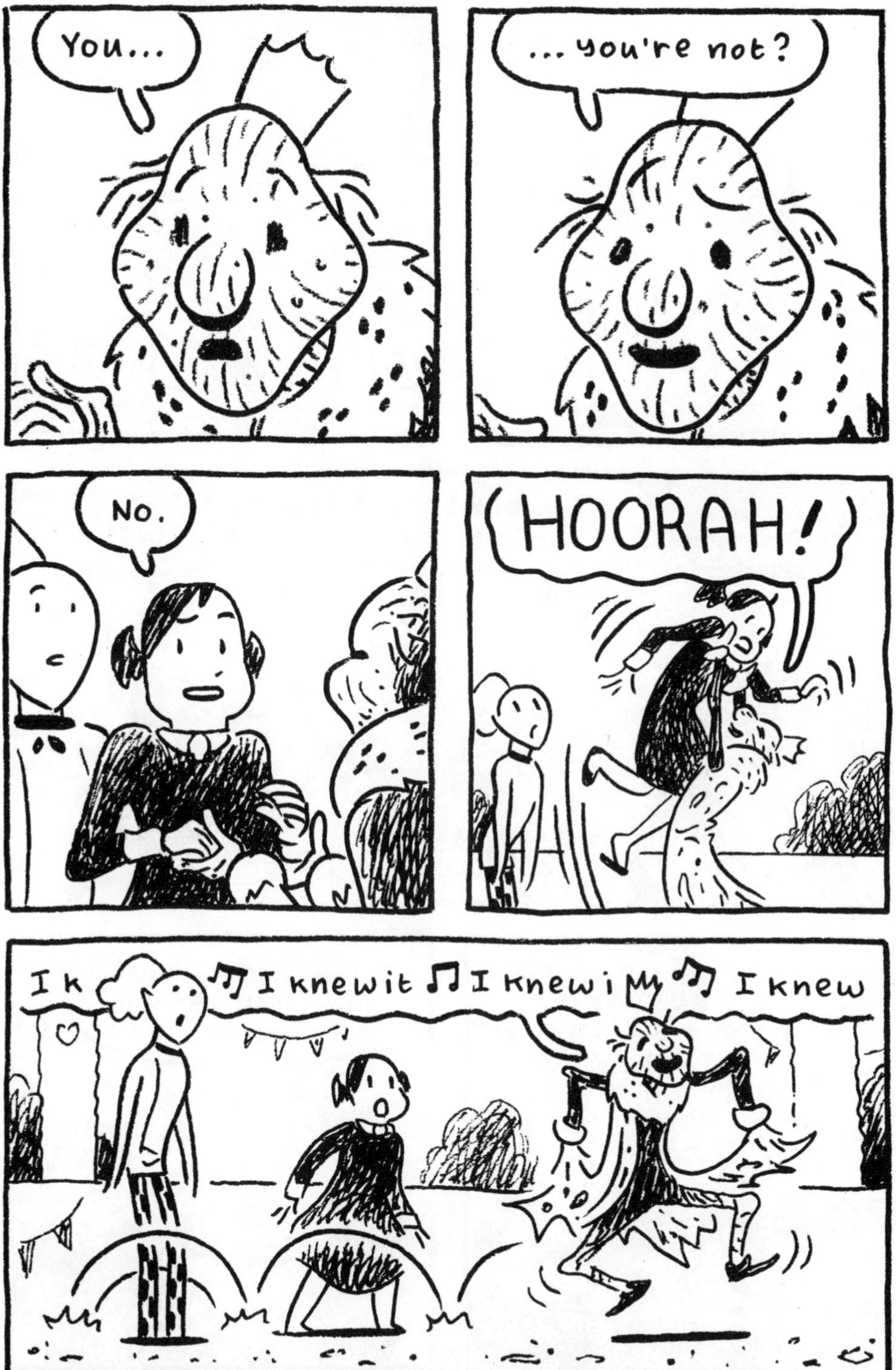
You...
...you're not?
No.
HOORAH!
I k ♫ I knew it ♫ I knew i ♫ I knew

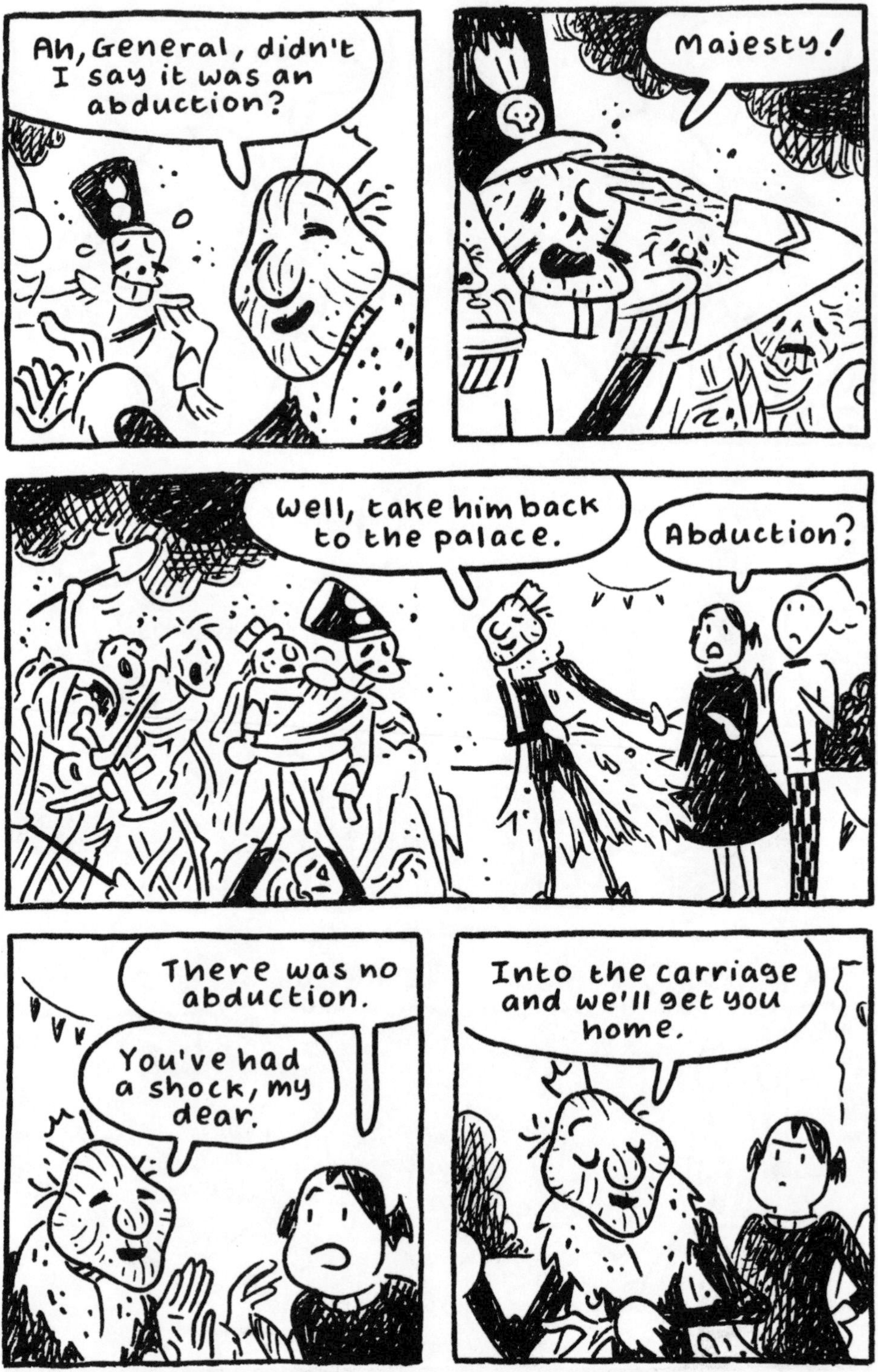
Ah, General, didn't I say it was an abduction?
Majesty!
Well, take him back to the palace.
Abduction?
There was no abduction.
You've had a shock, my dear.
Into the carriage and we'll get you home.

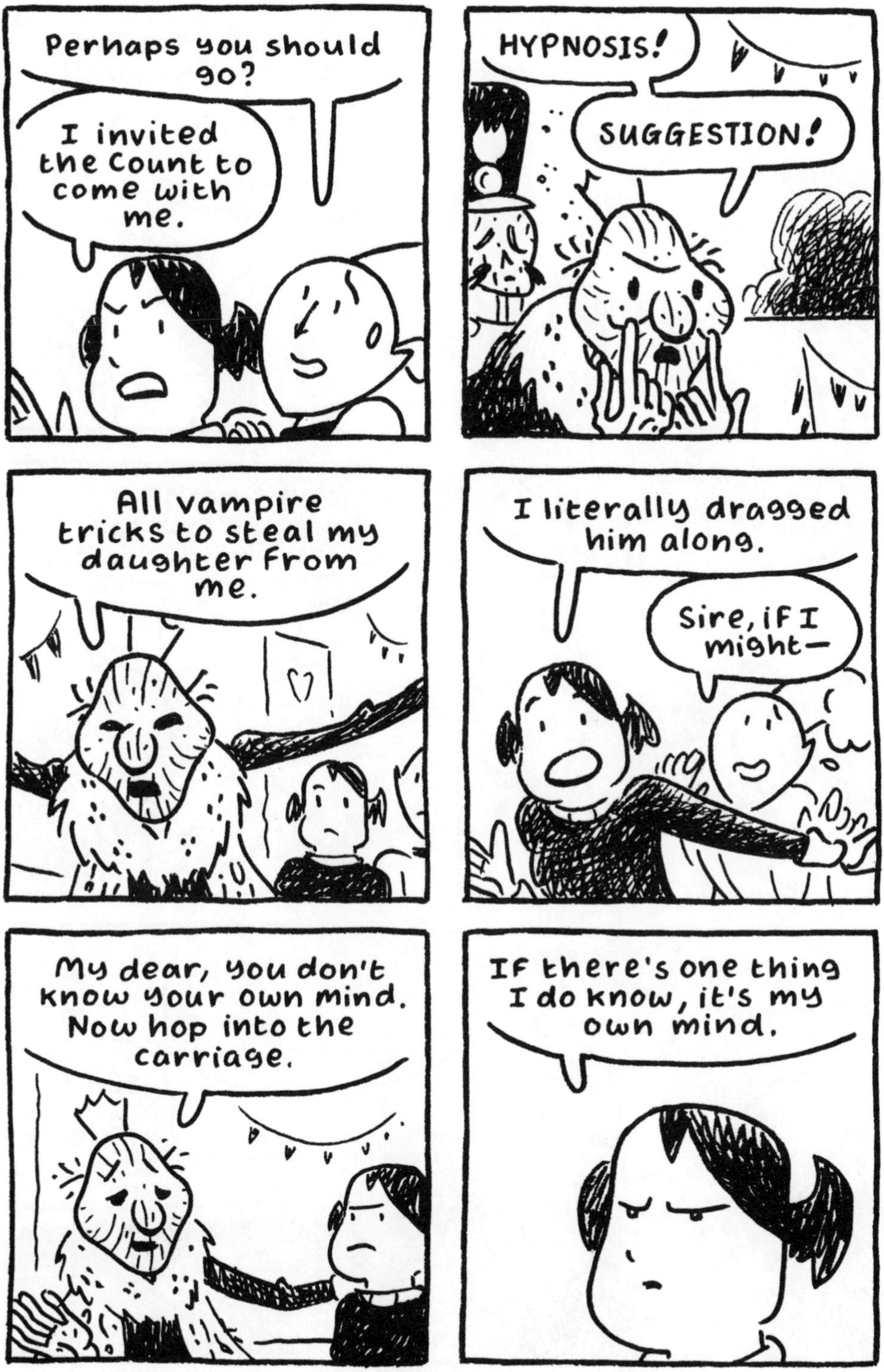
Perhaps you should go?
I invited the Count to come with me.
HYPNOSIS!
SUGGESTION!
All vampire tricks to steal my daughter from me.
I literally dragged him along.
Sire, if I might—
My dear, you don't know your own mind. Now hop into the carriage.
If there's one thing I do know, it's my own mind.

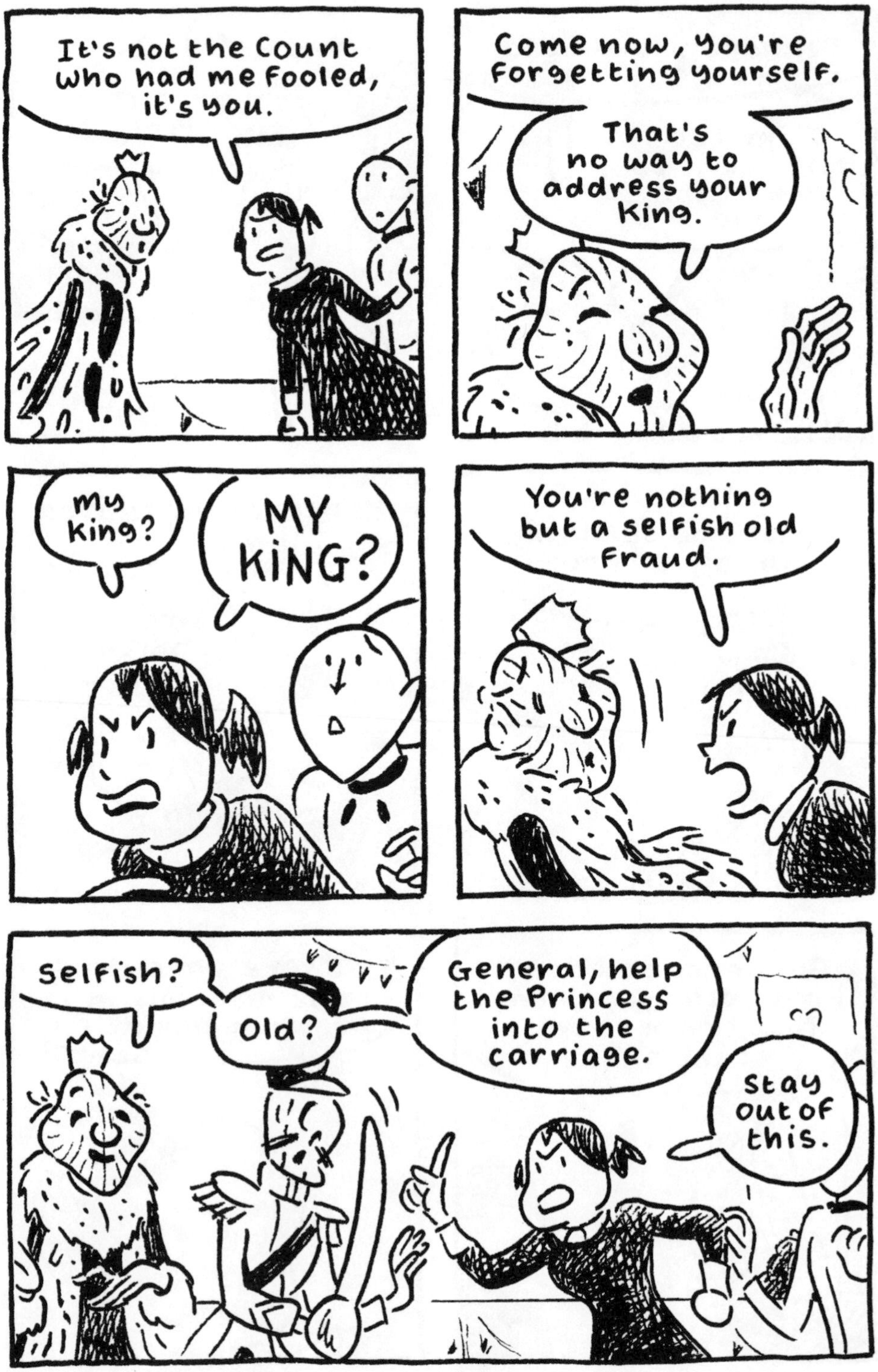
It's not the Count who had me fooled, it's you.
Come now, you're forgetting yourself.
That's no way to address your King.
My King?
MY KING?
You're nothing but a selfish old fraud.
Selfish?
Old?
General, help the Princess into the carriage.
Stay out of this.

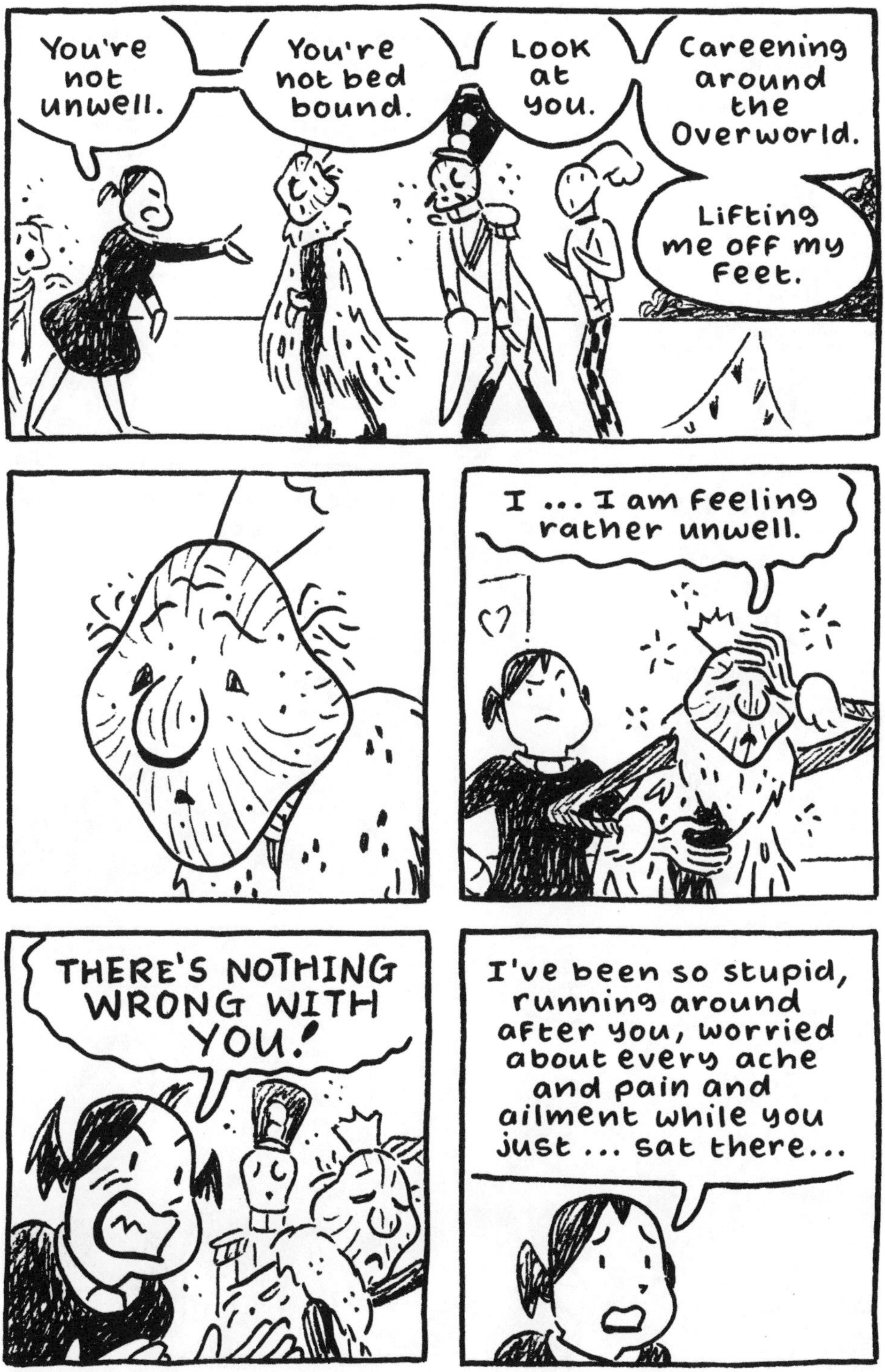
You're not unwell.
You're not bed bound.
Look at you.
Careening around the Overworld.
Lifting me off my feet.
I ... I am feeling rather unwell.
THERE'S NOTHING WRONG WITH YOU!
I've been so stupid, running around after you, worried about every ache and pain and ailment while you just ... sat there...

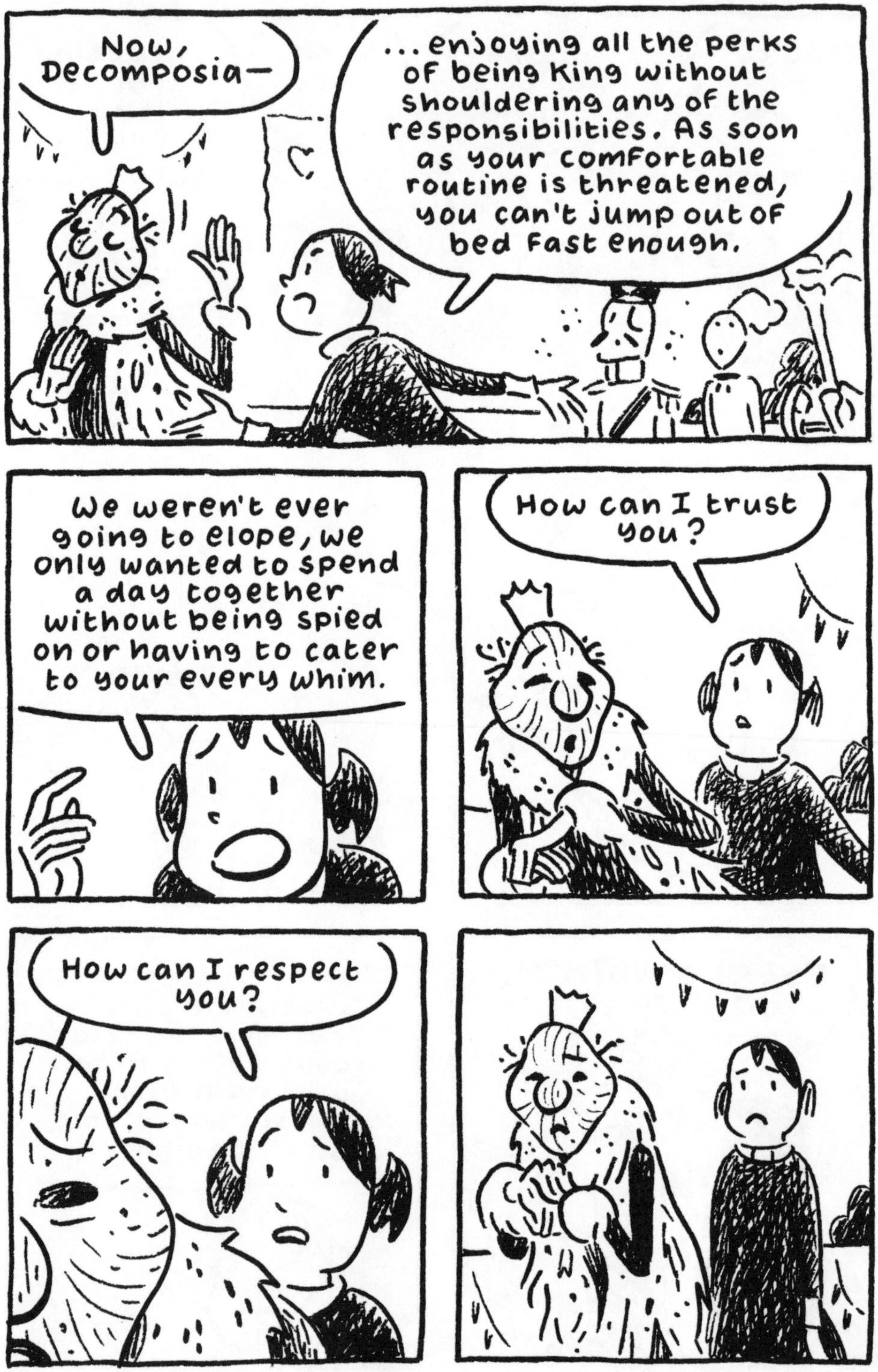

Now, Decomposia—
...enjoying all the perks of being king without shouldering any of the responsibilities. As soon as your comfortable routine is threatened, you can't jump out of bed fast enough.
We weren't ever going to elope, we only wanted to spend a day together without being spied on or having to cater to your every whim.
How can I trust you?
How can I respect you?

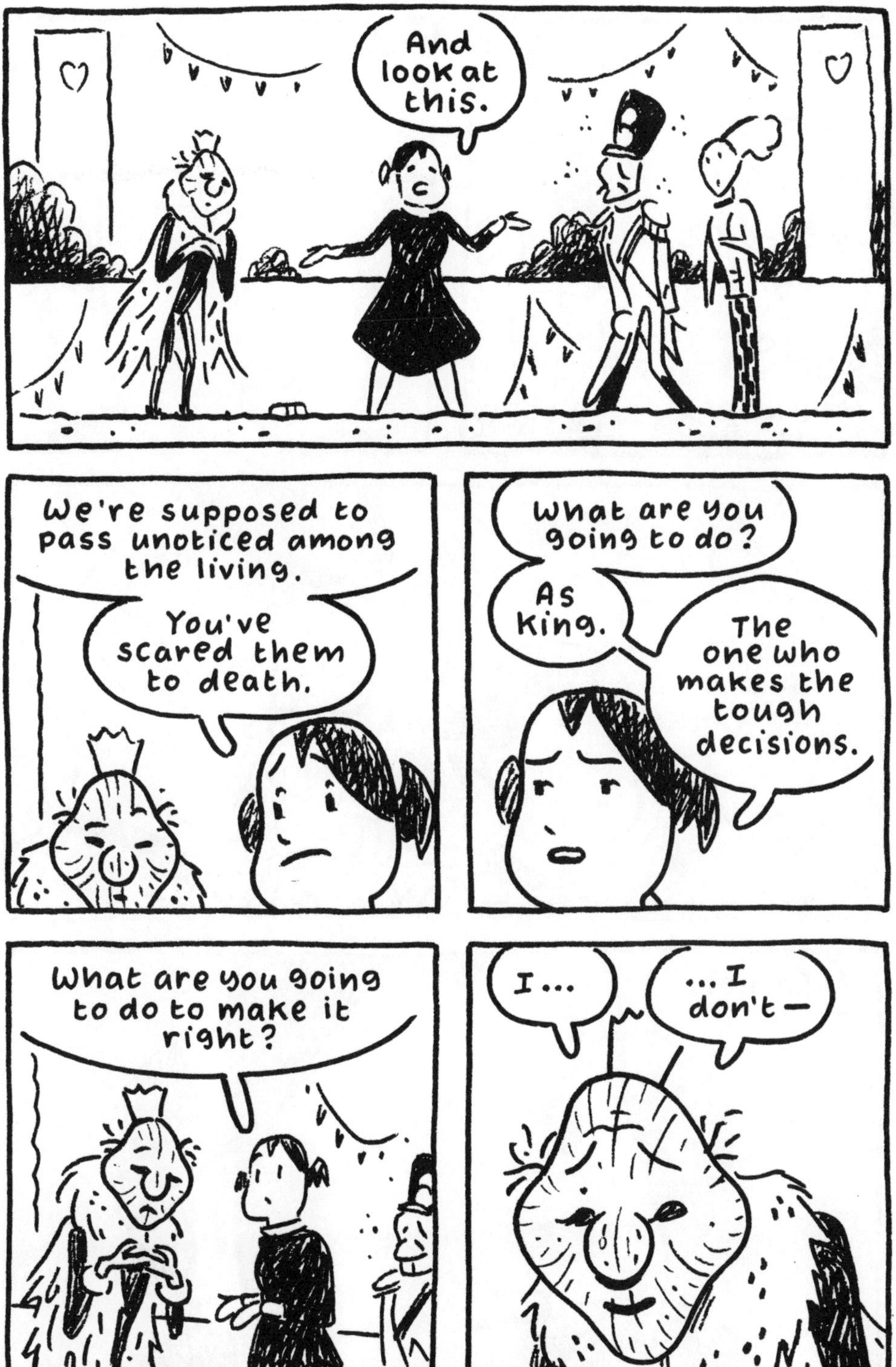
And look at this.
We're supposed to pass unoticed among the living.
You've scared them to death.
What are you going to do?
As King.
The one who makes the tough decisions.
What are you going to do to make it right?
I...
...I don't—

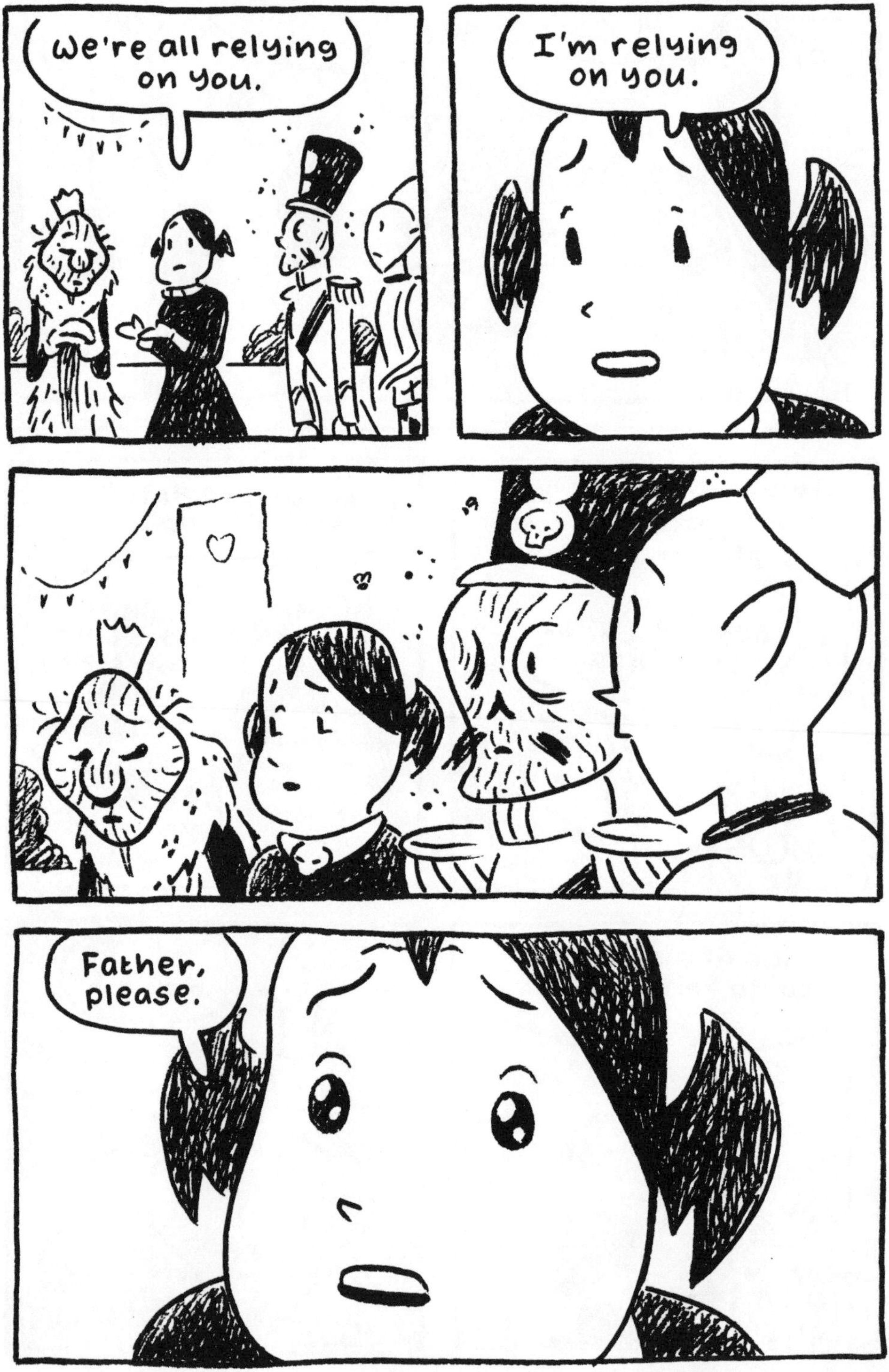
We're all relying on you.
I'm relying on you.
Father, please.

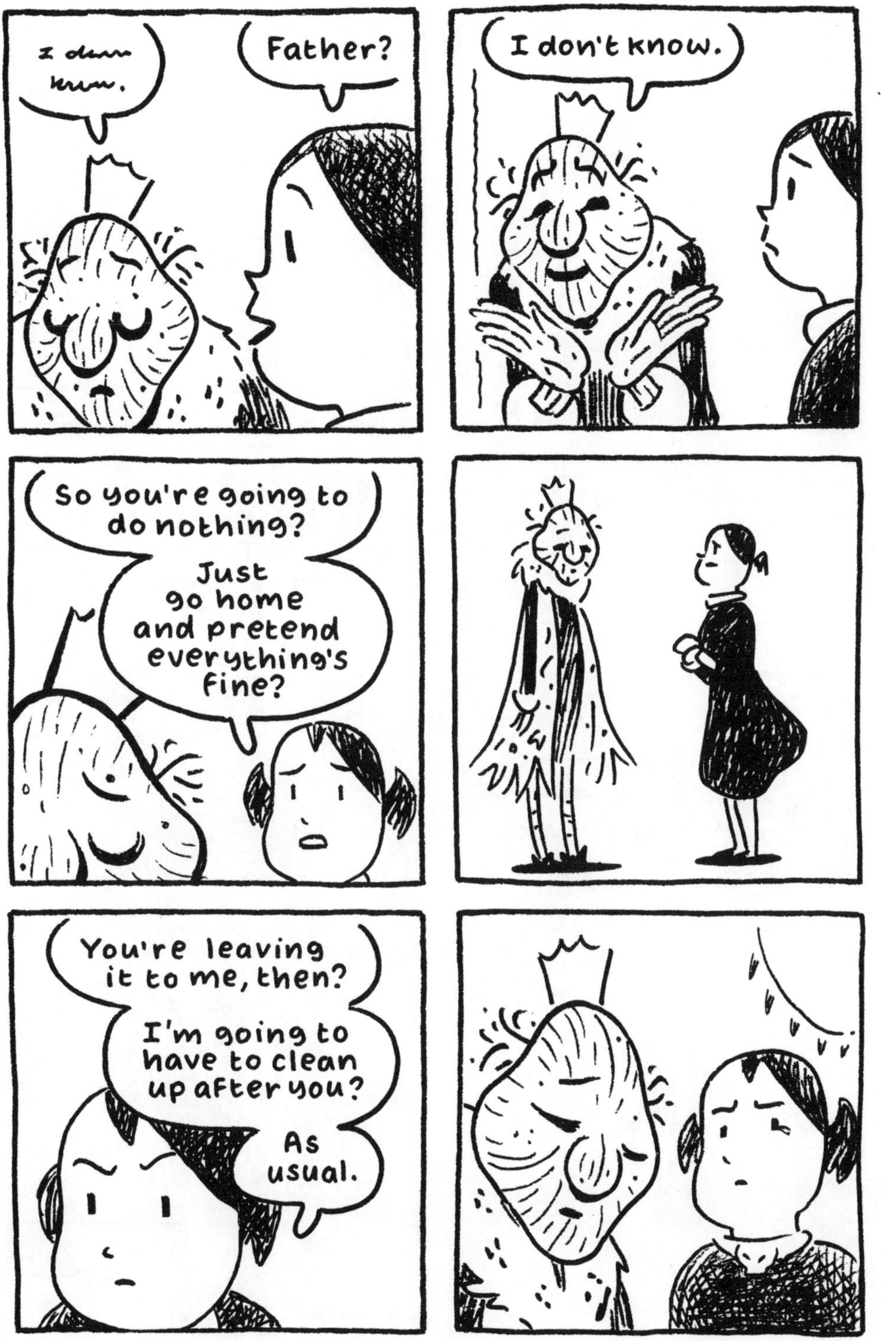
Father?
I don't know.
So you're going to do nothing?
Just go home and pretend everything's fine?
You're leaving it to me, then?
I'm going to have to clean up after you?
As usual.

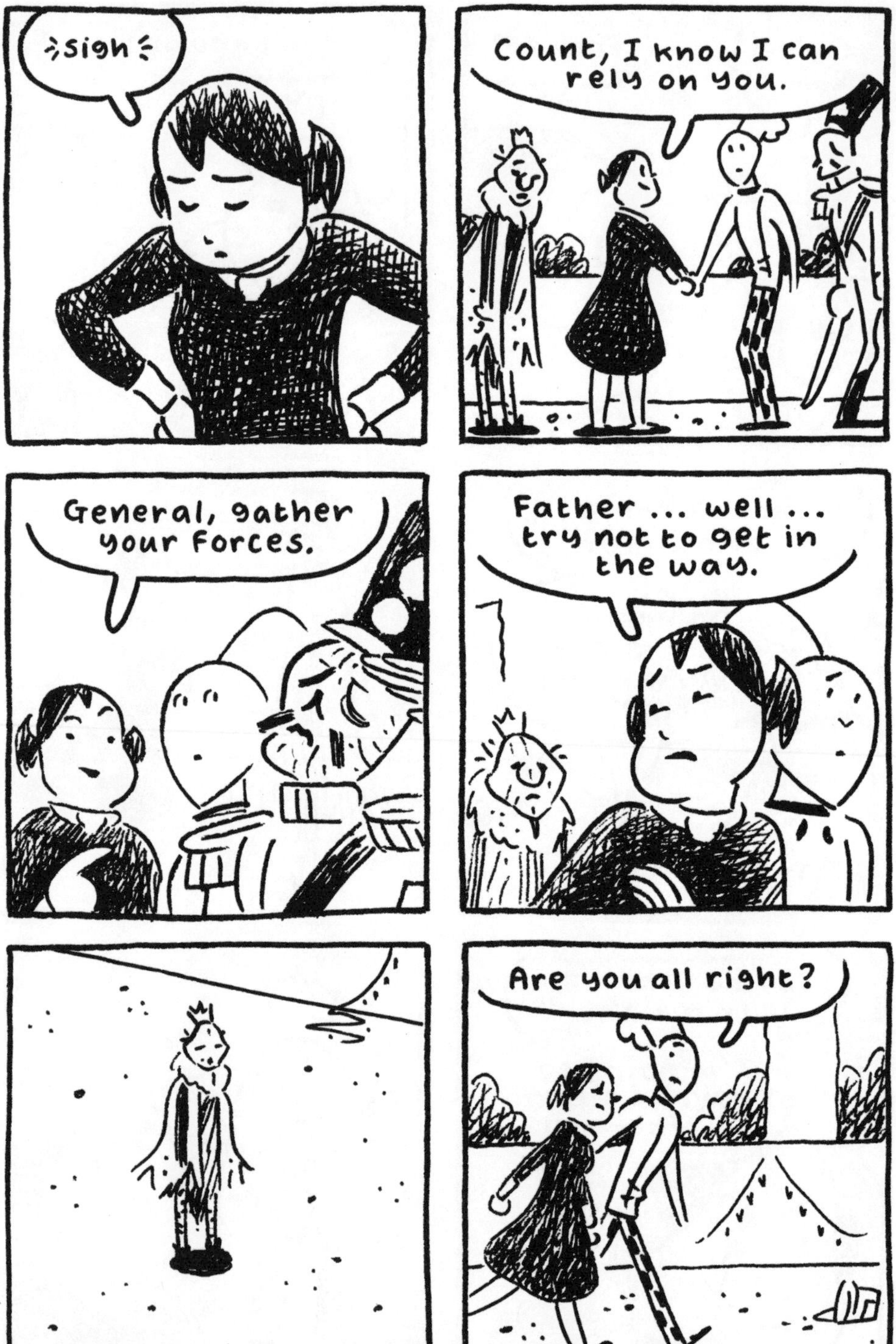

sigh
Count, I know I can rely on you.
General, gather your forces.
Father ... well ... try not to get in the way.
Are you all right?

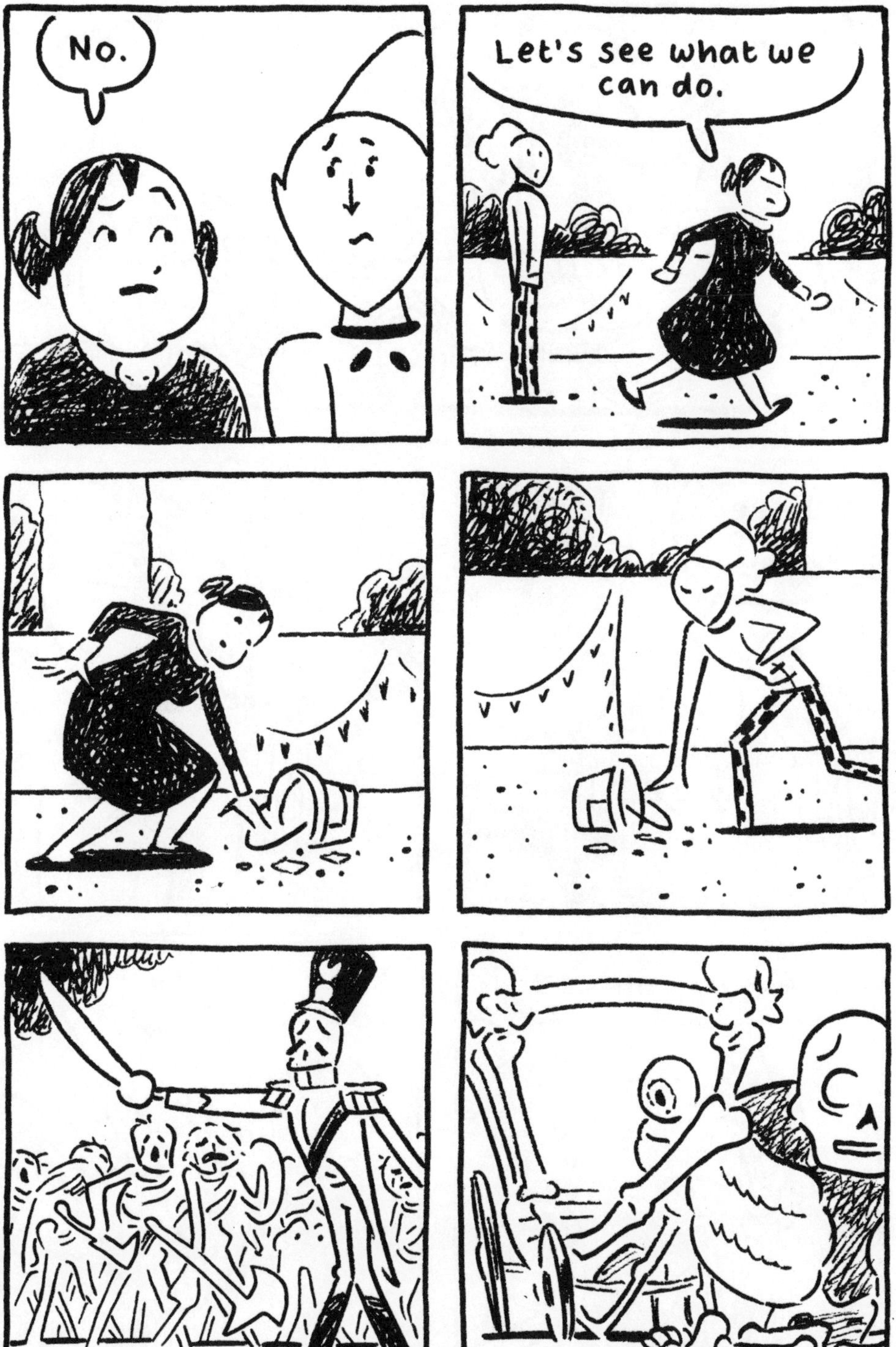
No.
Let's see what we can do.

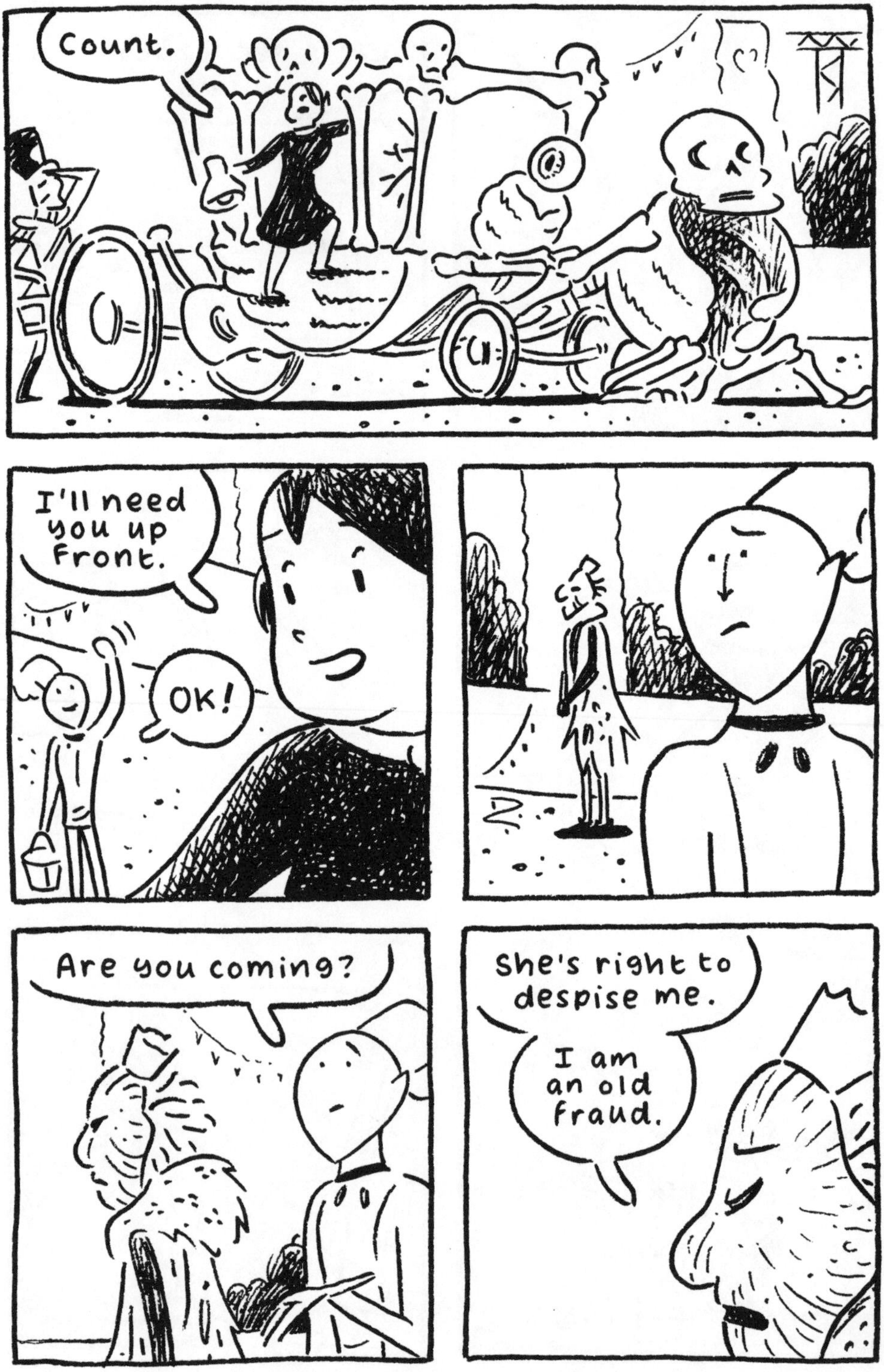
Count.
I'll need you up front.
OK!
Are you coming?
She's right to despise me.
I am an old fraud.

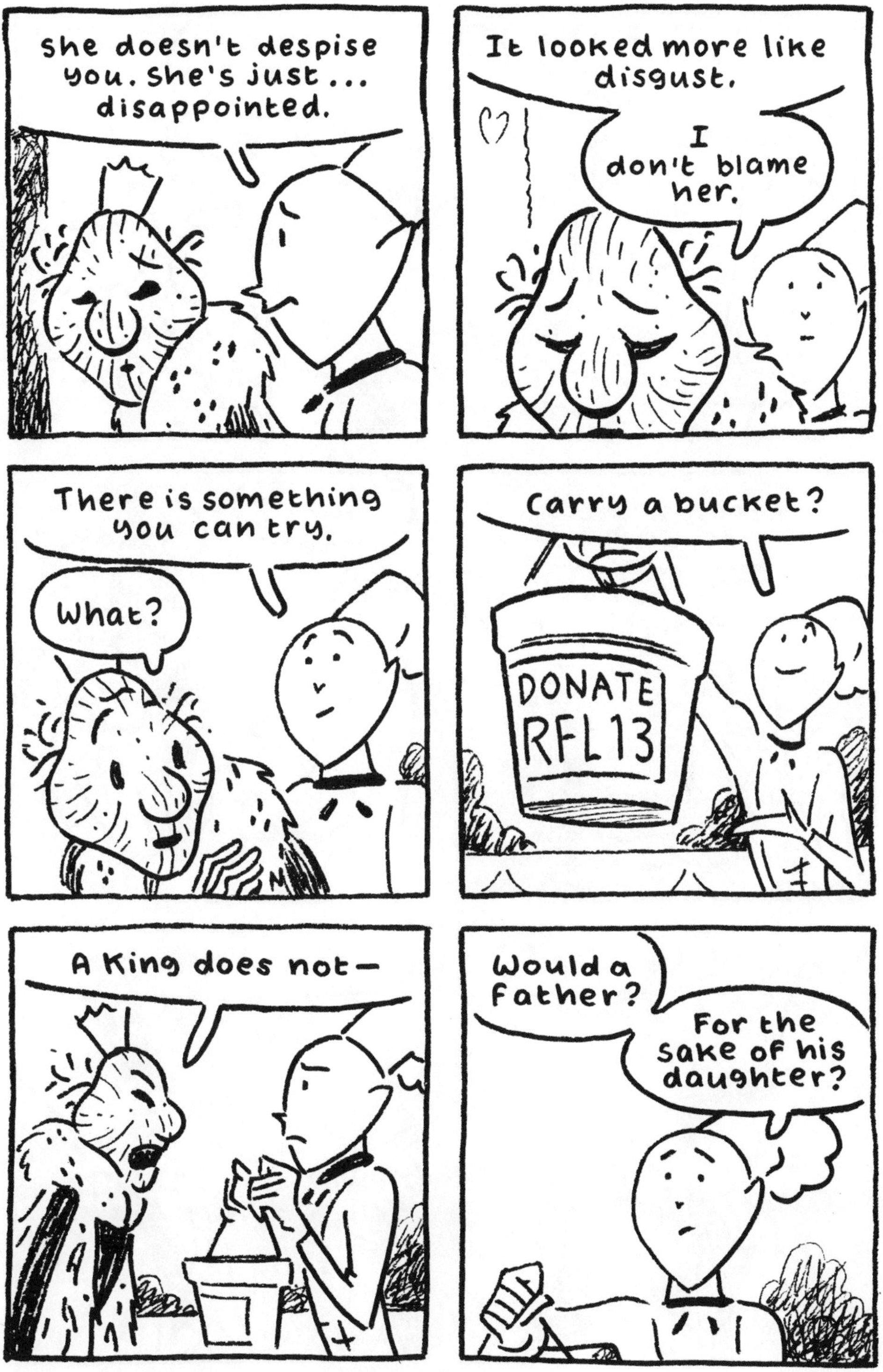
She doesn't despise you. She's just... disappointed.
It looked more like disgust.
I don't blame her.
There is something you can try.
What?
Carry a bucket?
DONATE RFL13
A King does not—
Would a father?
For the sake of his daughter?

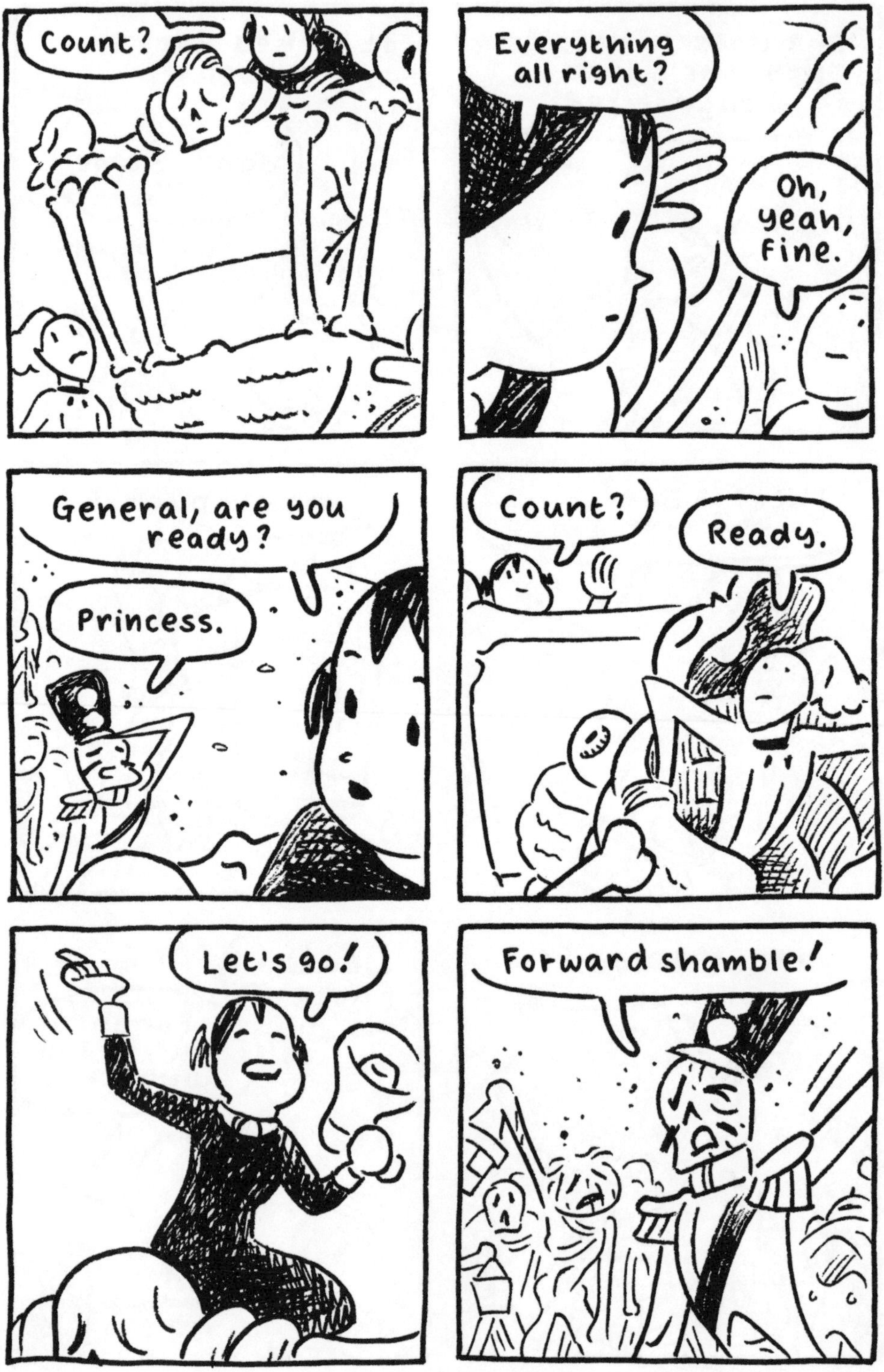
Count?
Everything all right?
Oh, yeah, fine.
General, are you ready?
Princess.
Count?
Ready.
Let's go!
Forward shamble!

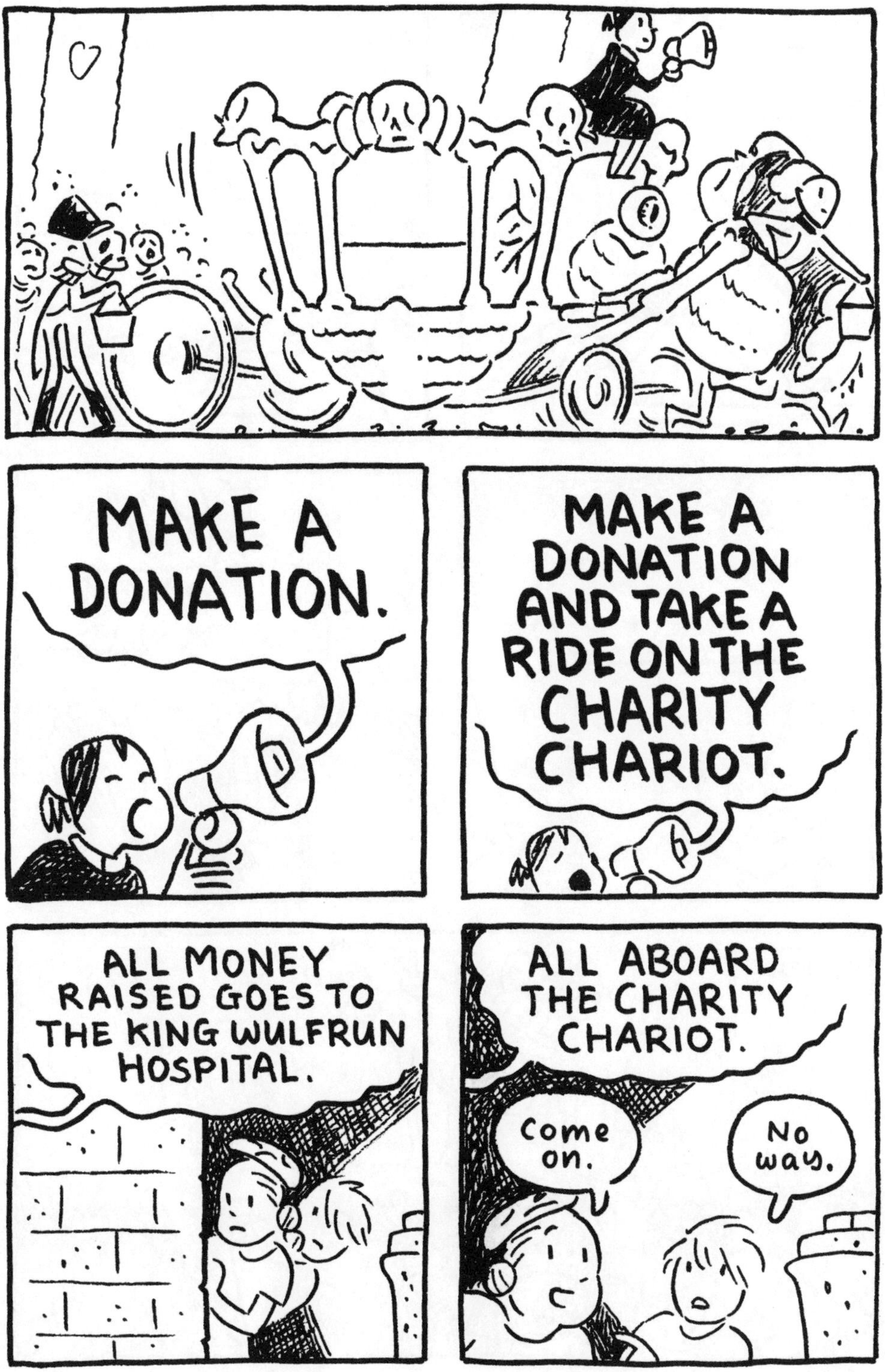
MAKE A DONATION.
MAKE A DONATION AND TAKE A RIDE ON THE CHARITY CHARIOT.
ALL MONEY RAISED GOES TO THE KING WULFRUN HOSPITAL.
ALL ABOARD THE CHARITY CHARIOT.
Come on.
No way.

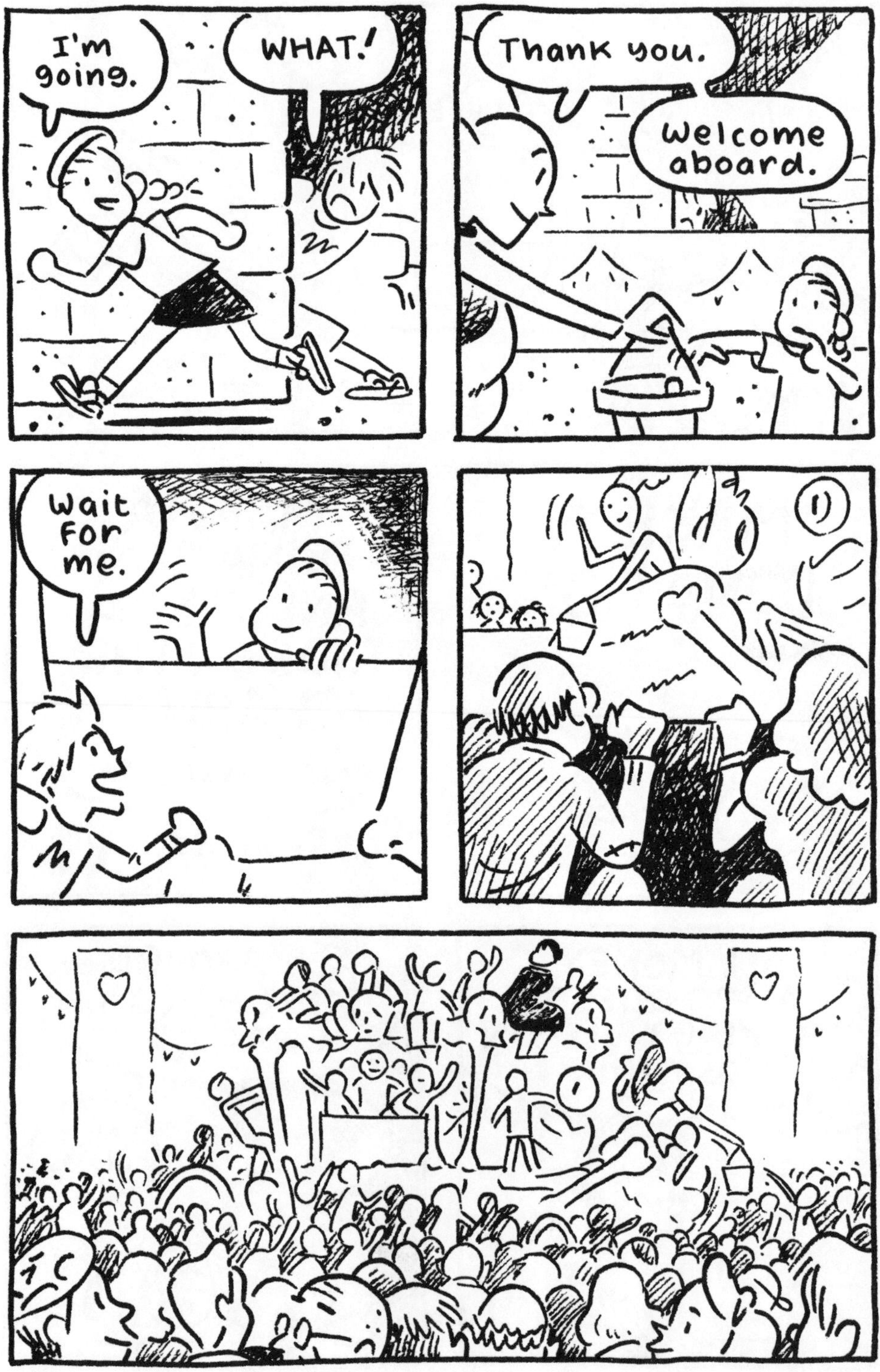
I'm going.
WHAT!
Thank you.
Welcome aboard.
Wait for me.

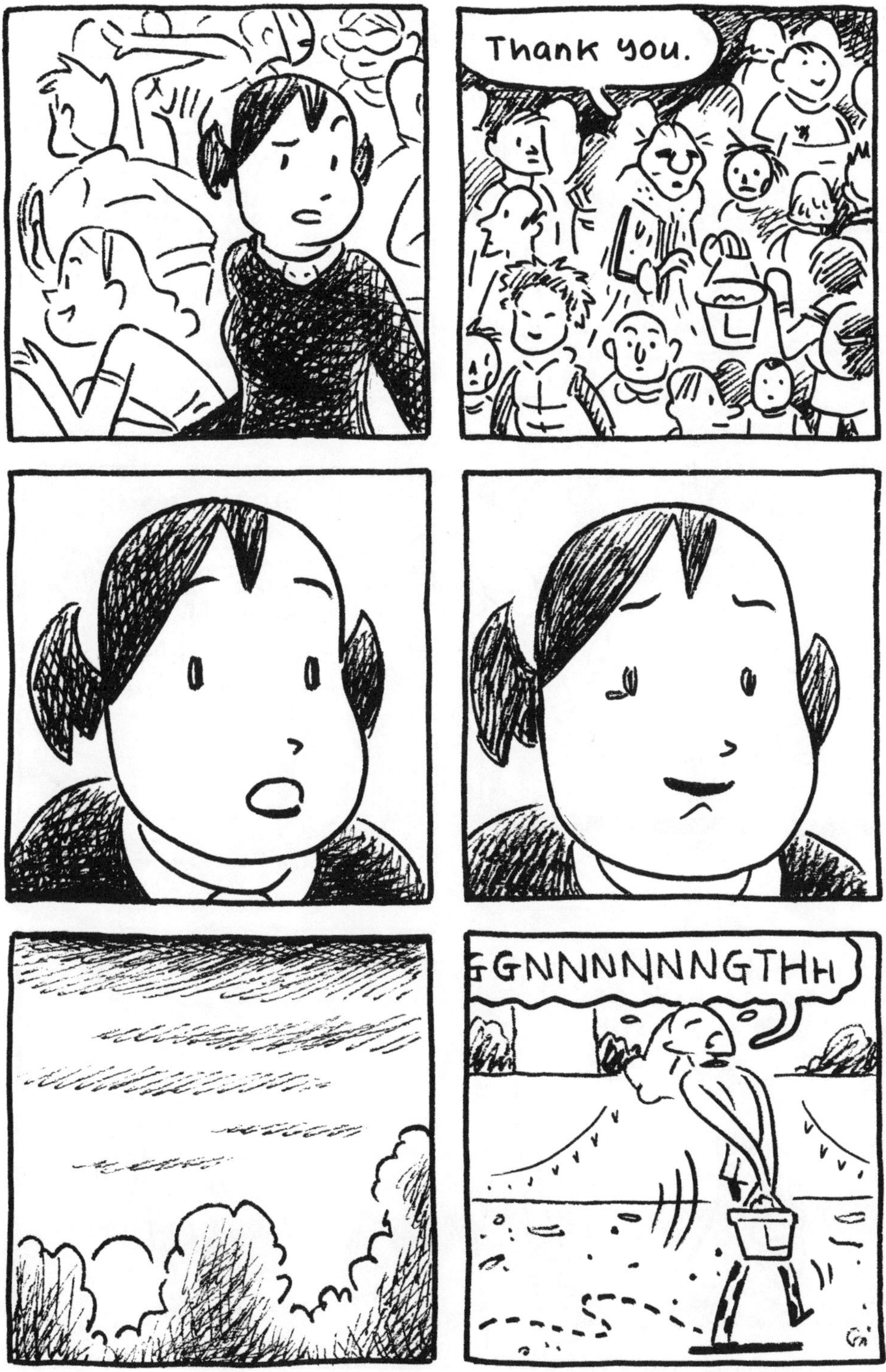
Thank you.
GNNNNNNGTHH

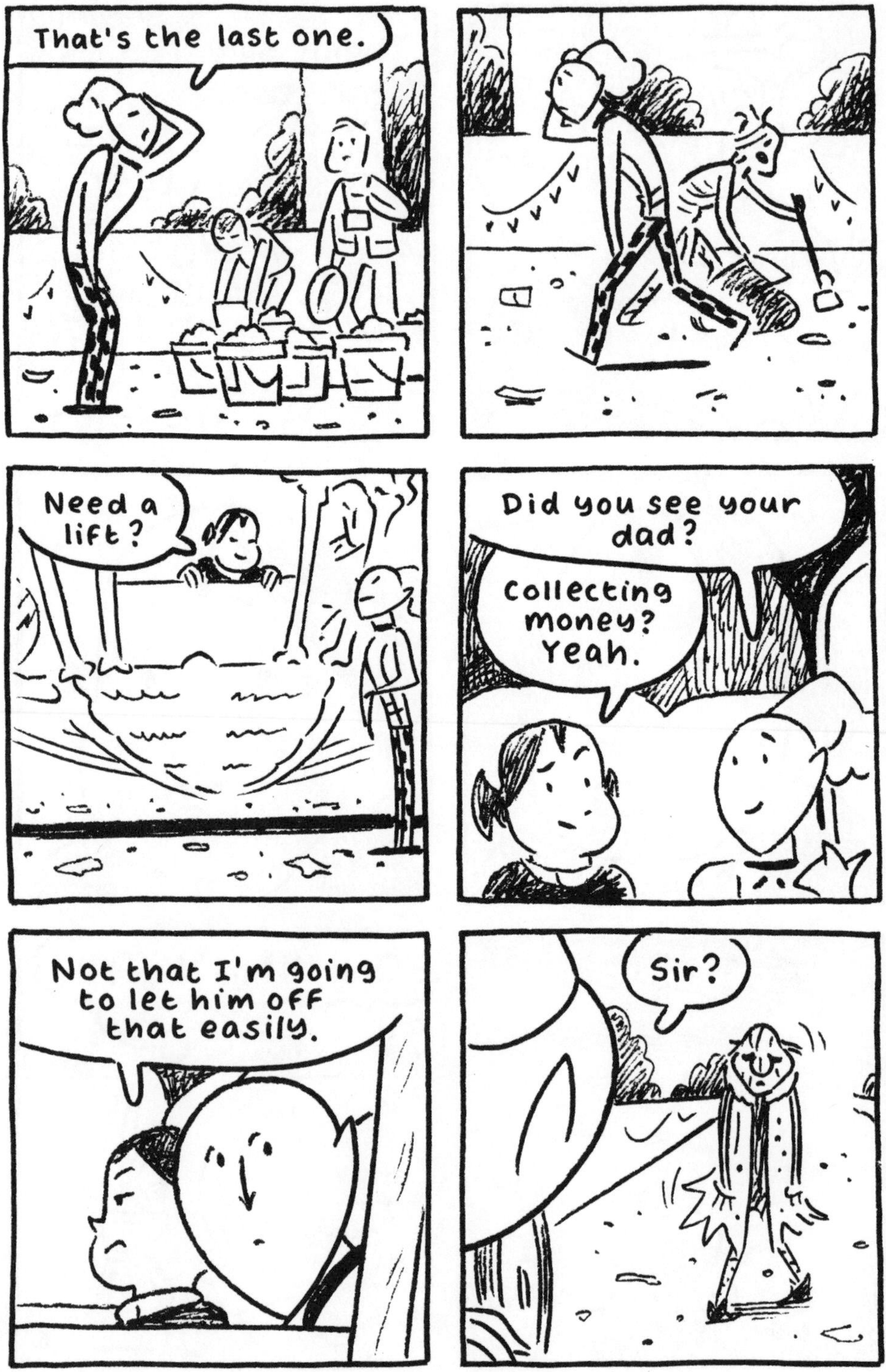
That's the last one.
Need a lift?
Did you see your dad?
Collecting money? Yeah.
Not that I'm going to let him off that easily.
Sir?

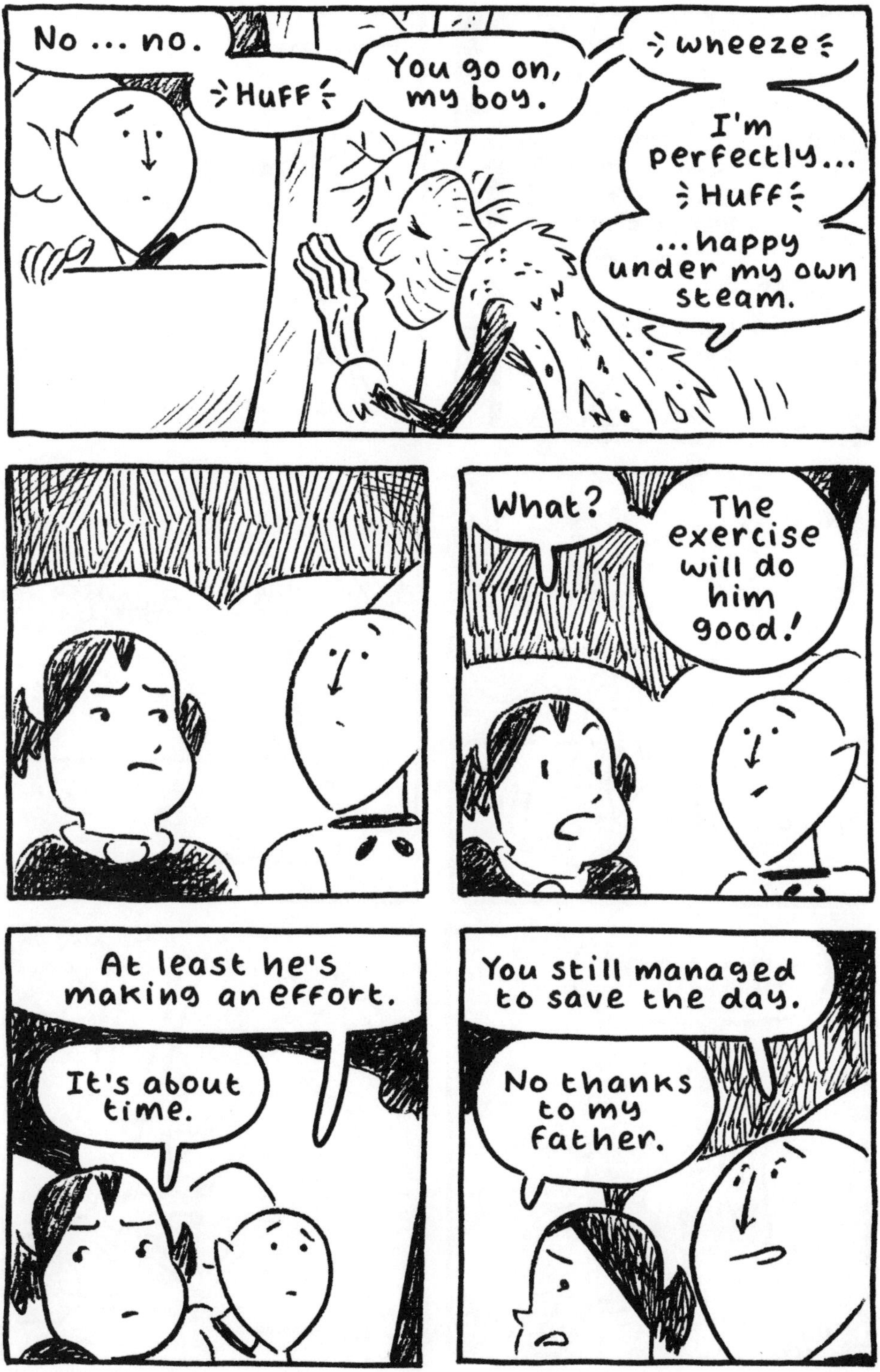
No ... no.
HUFF
You go on, my boy.
wheeze
I'm perfectly...
HUFF
...happy under my own steam.
What?
The exercise will do him good!
At least he's making an effort.
It's about time.
You still managed to save the day.
No thanks to my father.

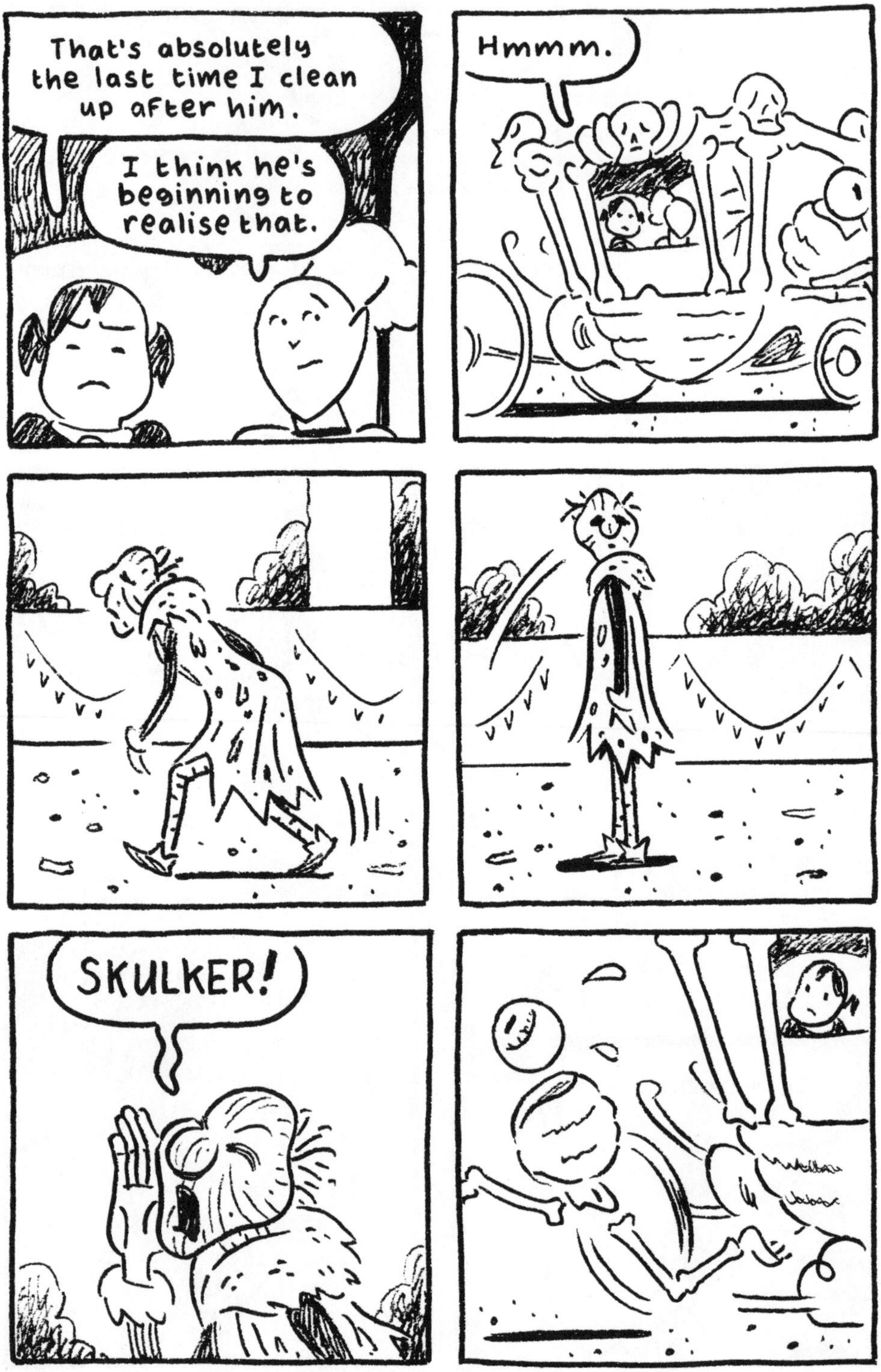
That's absolutely the last time I clean up after him.
I think he's beginning to realise that.
Hmmm.
SKULKER!

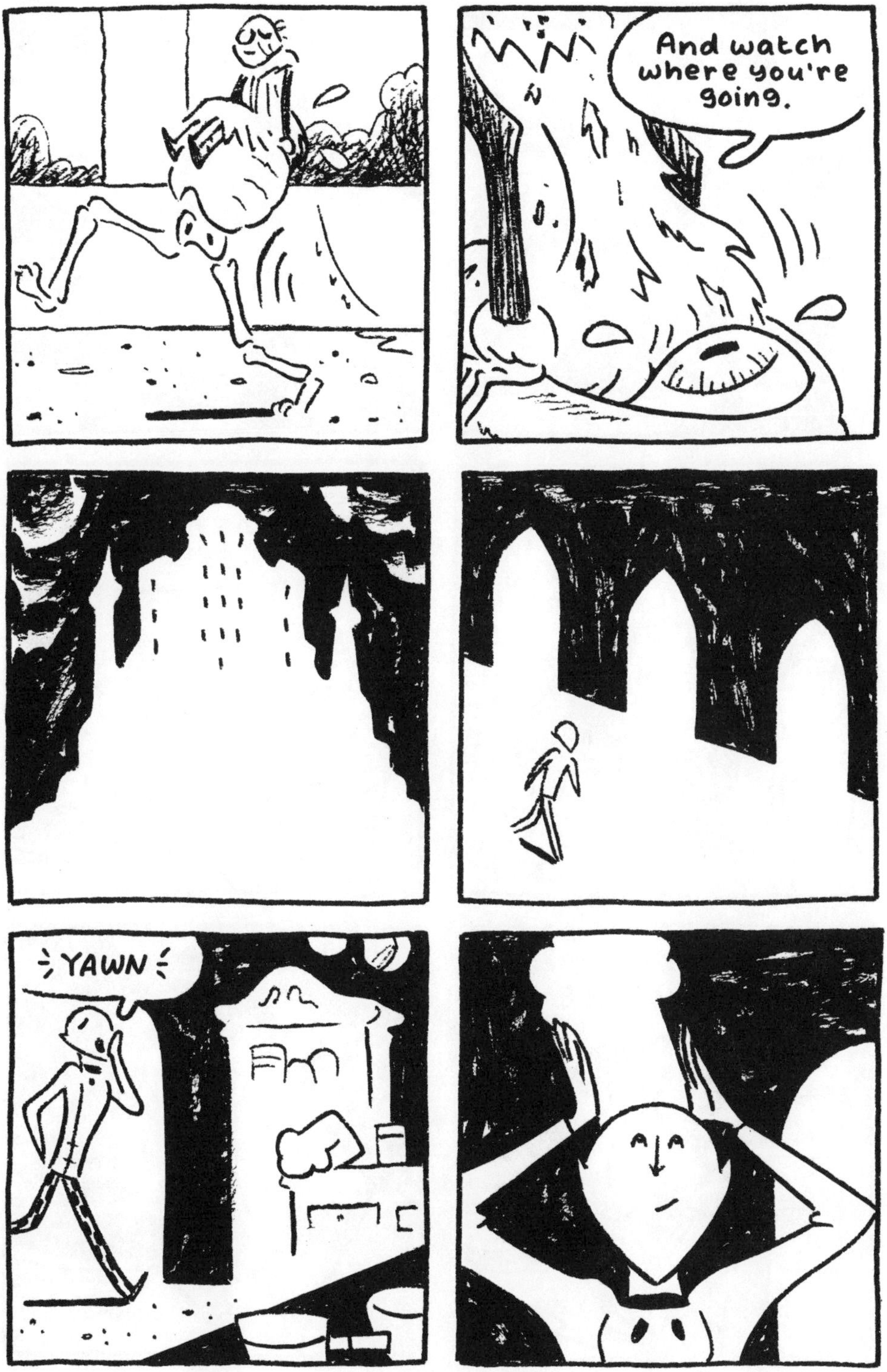
And watch where you're going.
YAWN

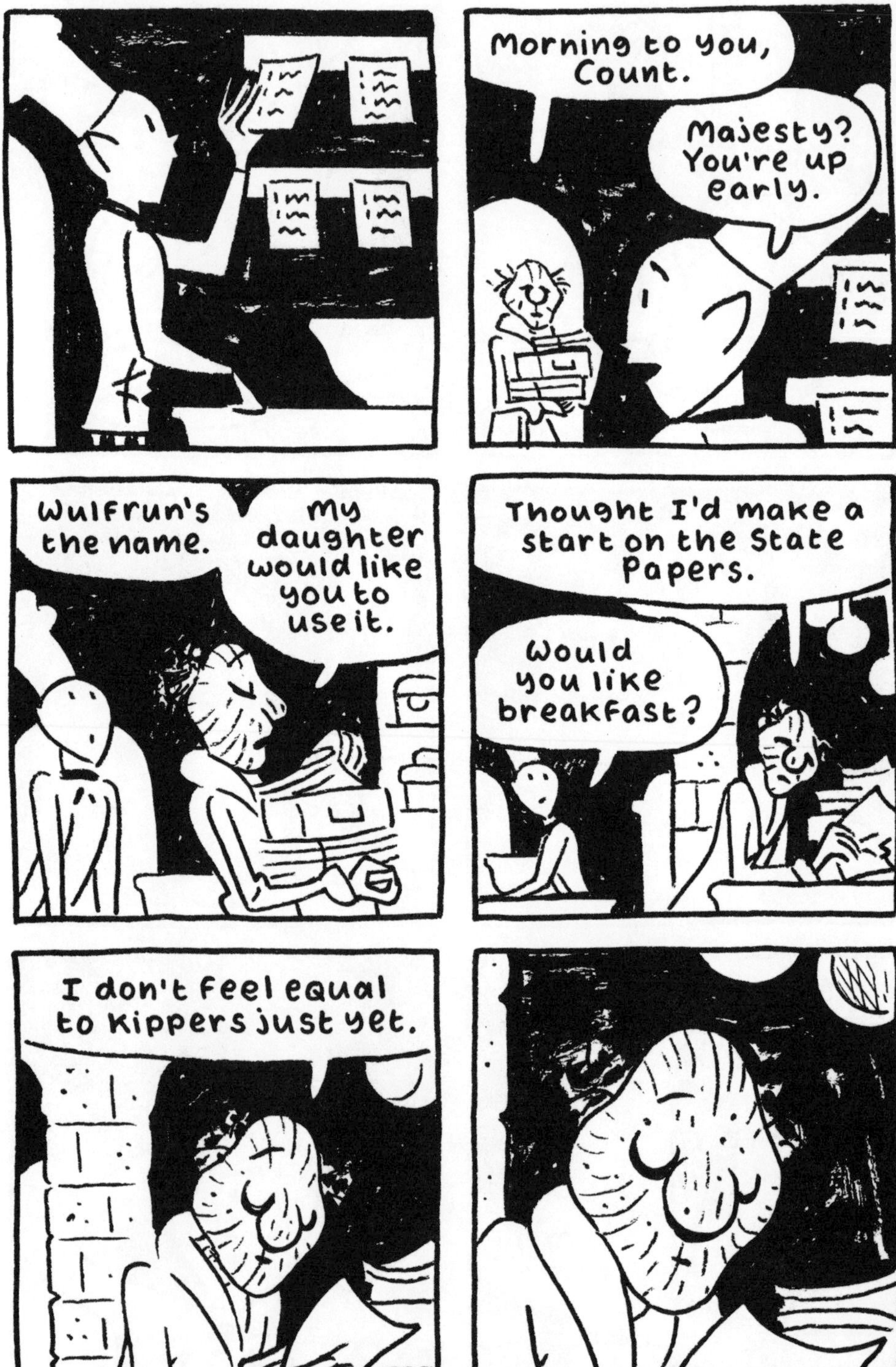
Morning to you, Count.
Majesty? You're up early.
Wulfrun's the name.
My daughter would like you to use it.
Thought I'd make a start on the State Papers.
Would you like breakfast?
I don't feel equal to kippers just yet.

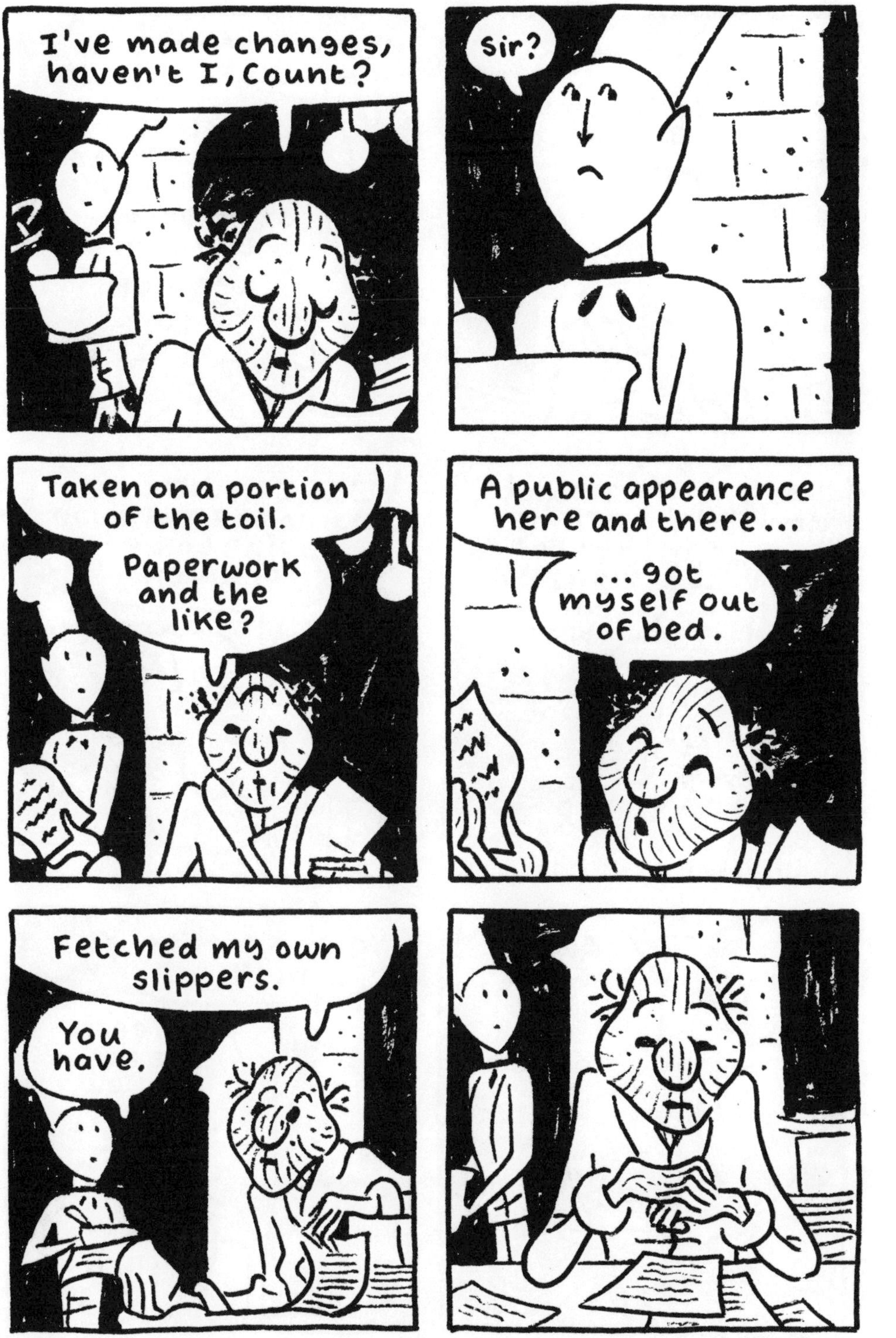
I've made changes, haven't I, Count?
Sir?
Taken on a portion of the toil.
Paperwork and the like?
A public appearance here and there...
...got myself out of bed.
Fetched my own slippers.
You have.

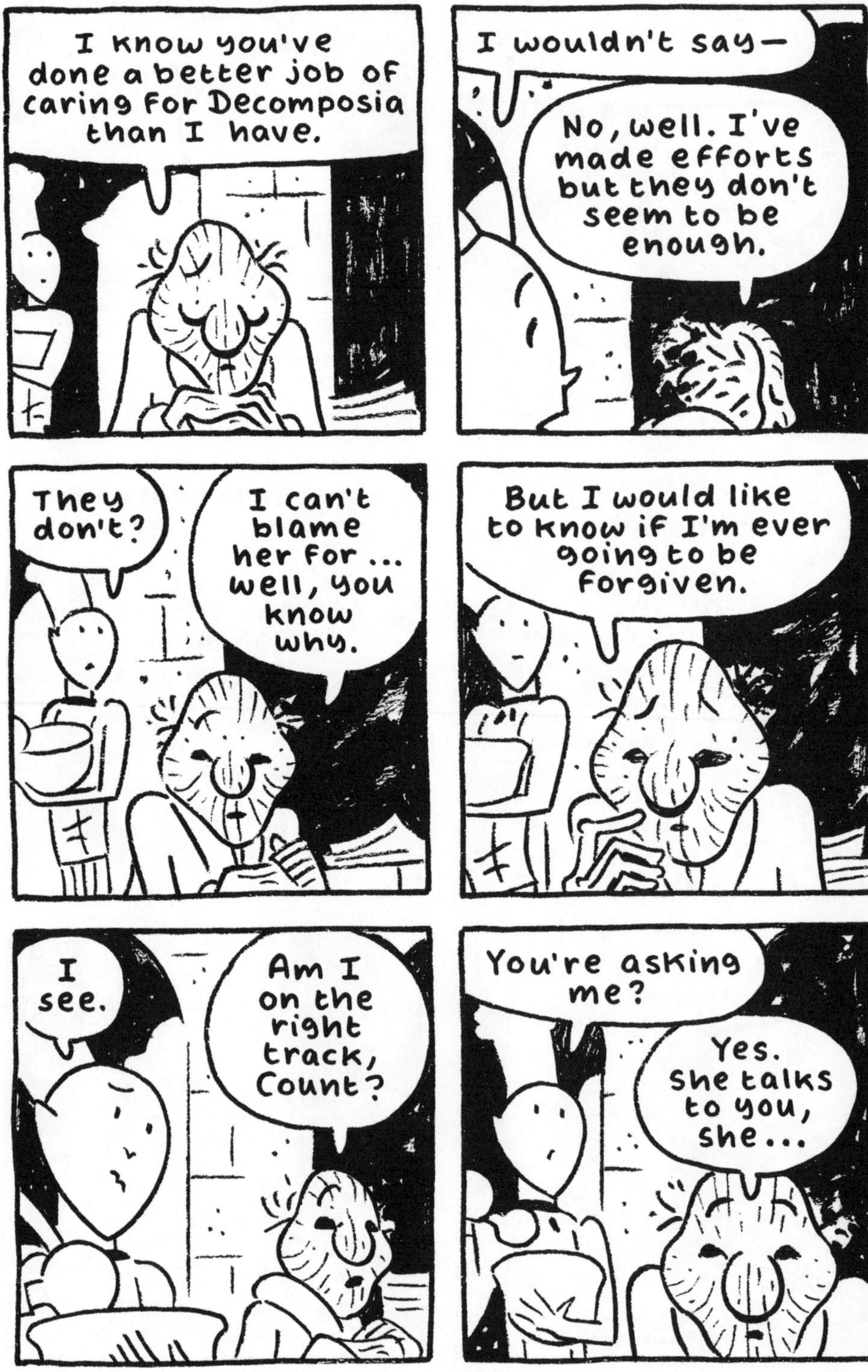
I know you've done a better job of caring for Decomposia than I have.
I wouldn't say—
No, well. I've made efforts but they don't seem to be enough.
They don't?
I can't blame her for ... well, you know why.
But I would like to know if I'm ever going to be forgiven.
I see.
Am I on the right track, Count?
You're asking me?
Yes. She talks to you, she...

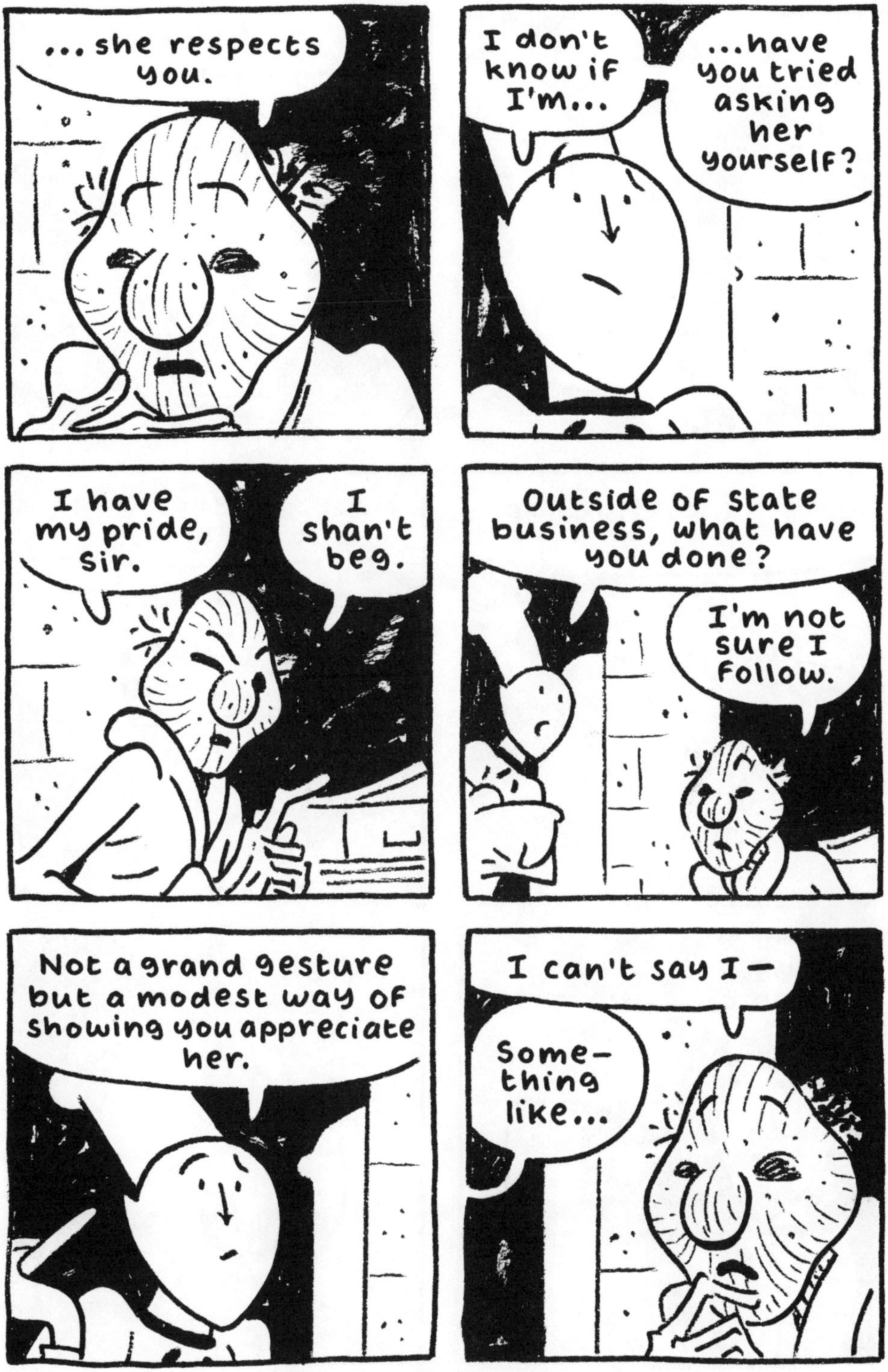
...she respects you.
I don't know if I'm...
...have you tried asking her yourself?
I have my pride, sir.
I shan't beg.
Outside of state business, what have you done?
I'm not sure I follow.
Not a grand gesture but a modest way of showing you appreciate her.
I can't say I—
Something like...

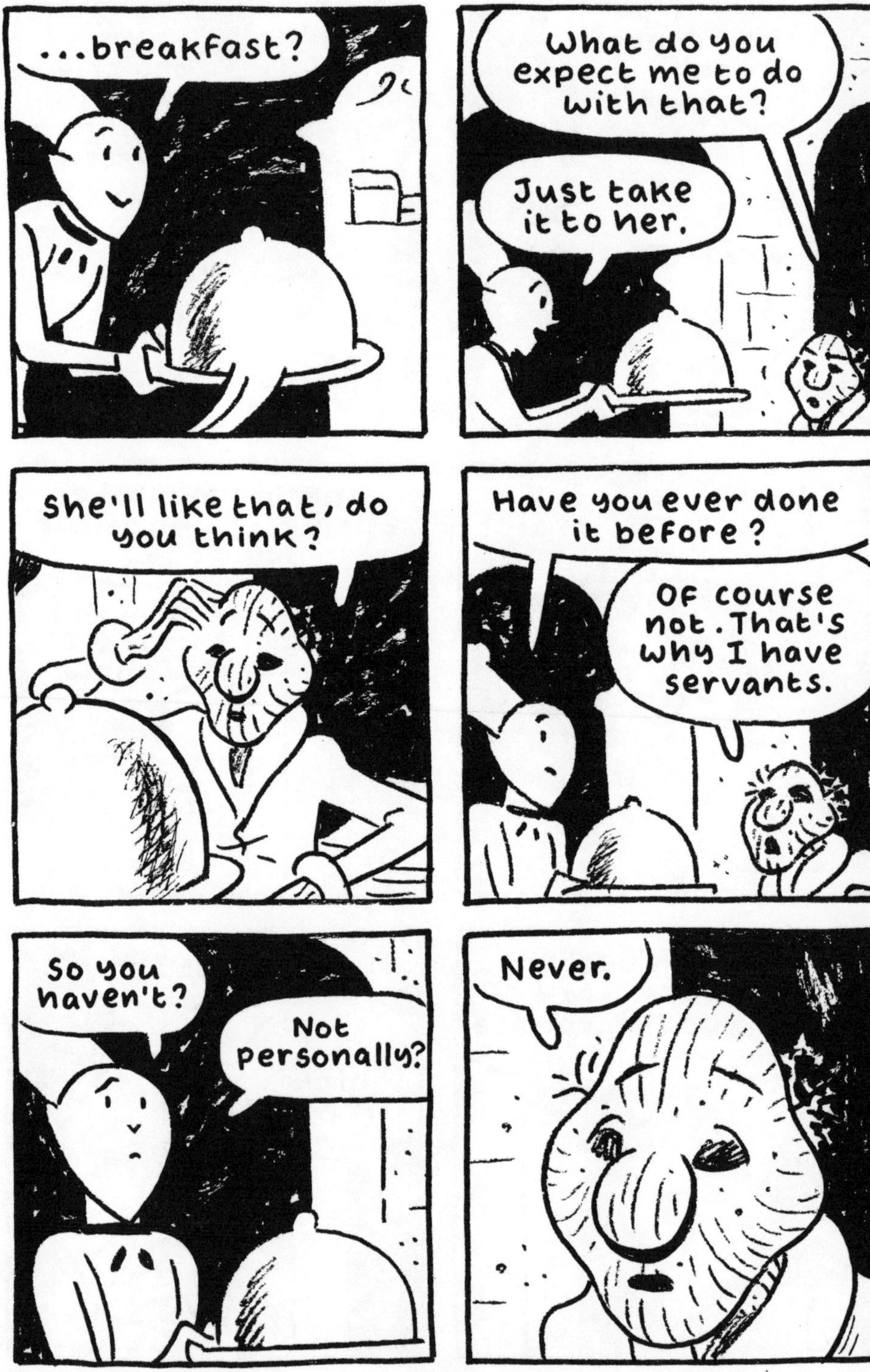
...breakfast?
What do you expect me to do with that?
Just take it to her.
She'll like that, do you think?
Have you ever done it before?
Of course not. That's why I have servants.
So you haven't?
Not personally?
Never.

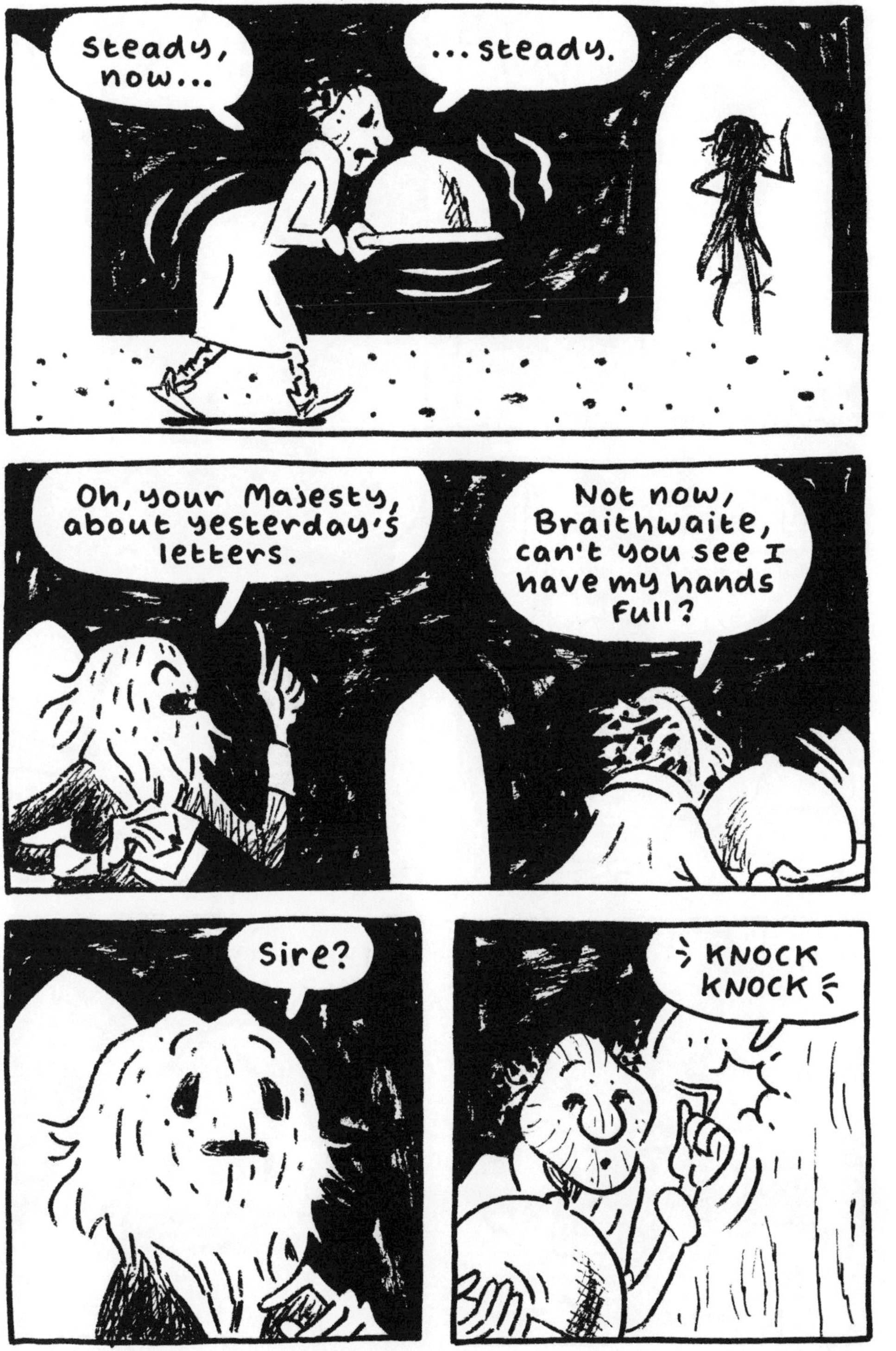
Steady, now...
...steady.
Oh, your Majesty, about yesterday's letters.
Not now, Braithwaite, can't you see I have my hands full?
Sire?
KNOCK KNOCK

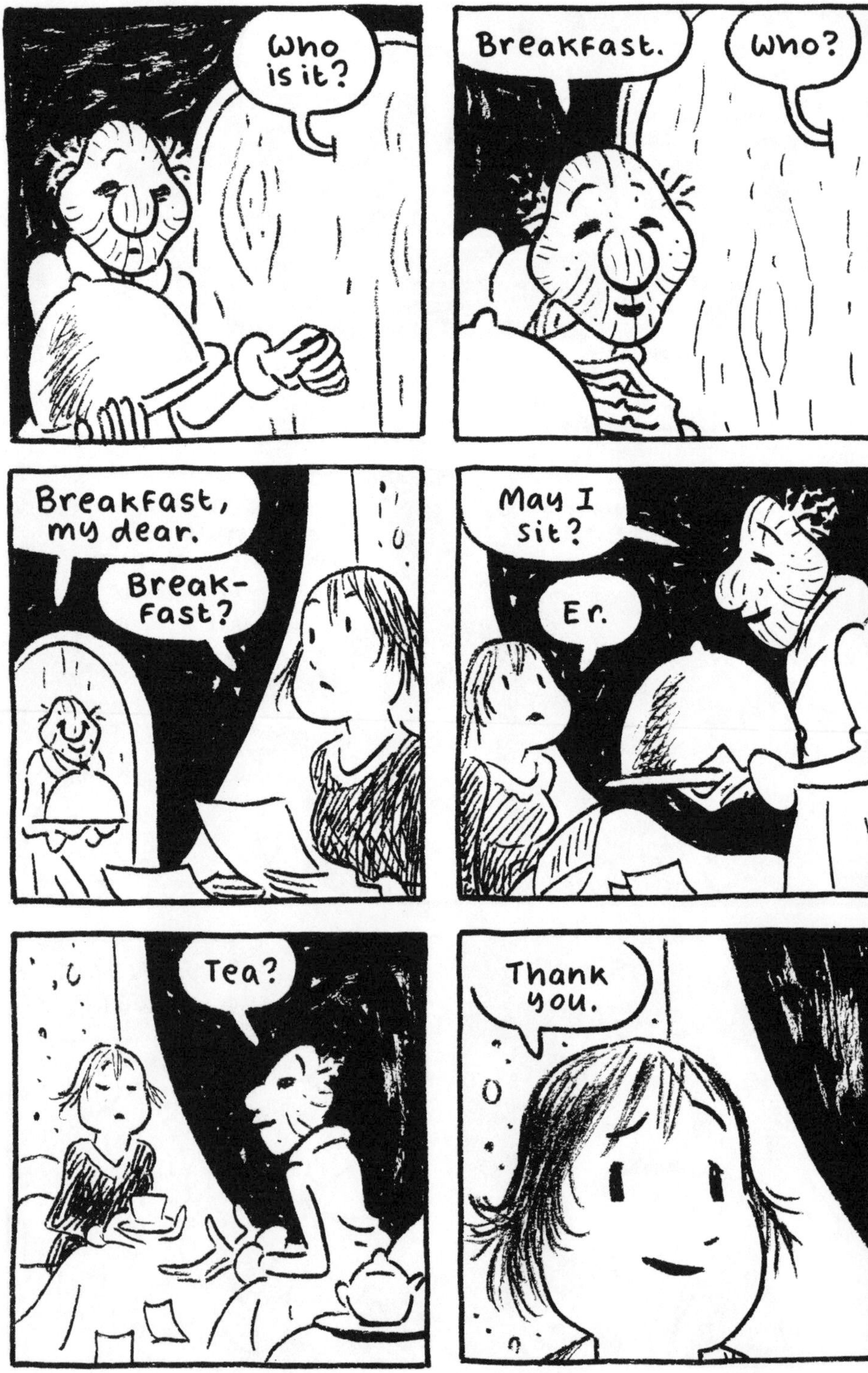
Who is it?
Breakfast.
Who?
Breakfast, my dear.
Break-fast?
May I sit?
Er.
Tea?
Thank you.

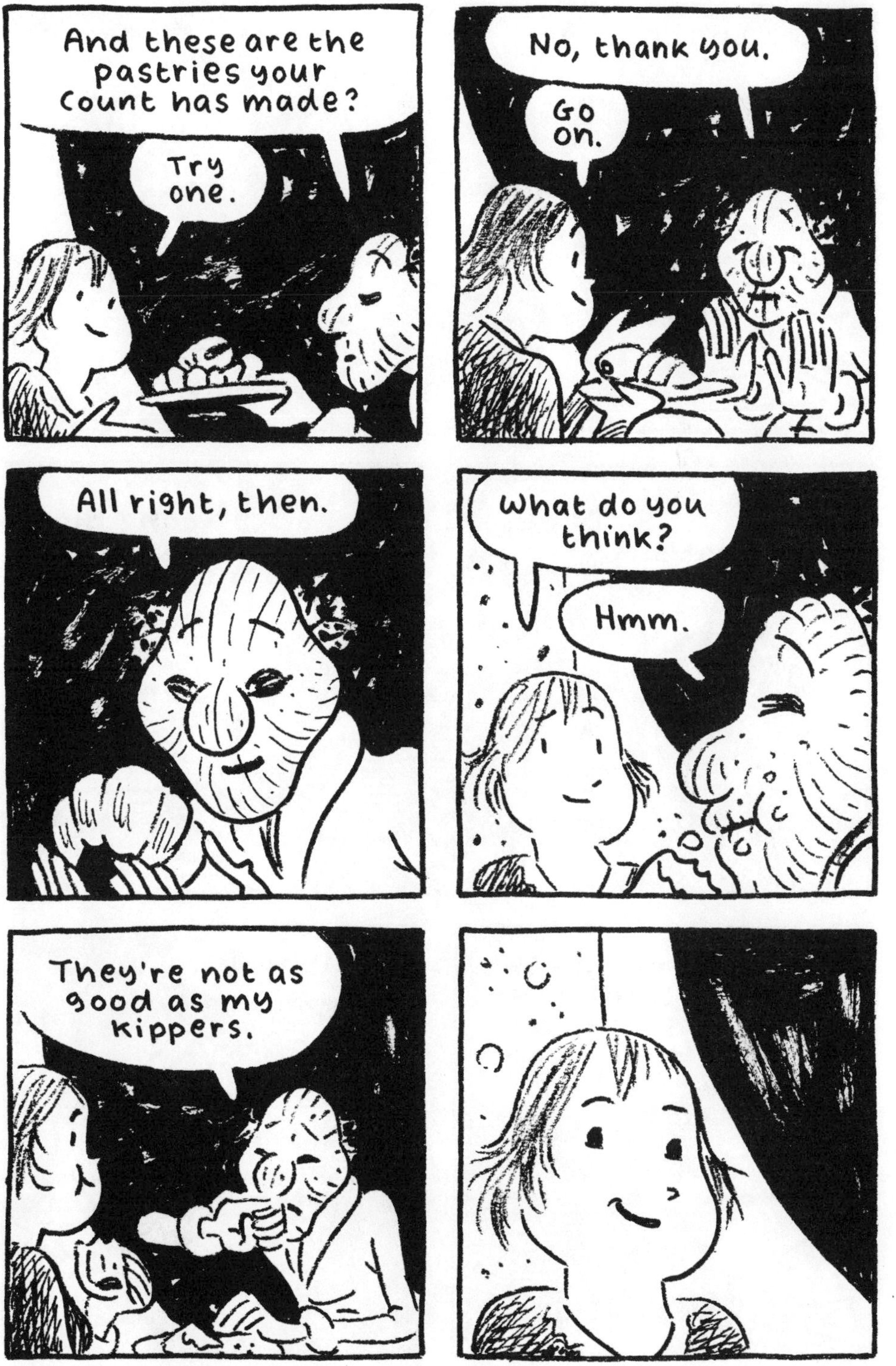
And these are the pastries your count has made?
Try one.
No, thank you.
Go on.
All right, then.
What do you think?
Hmm.
They're not as good as my kippers.

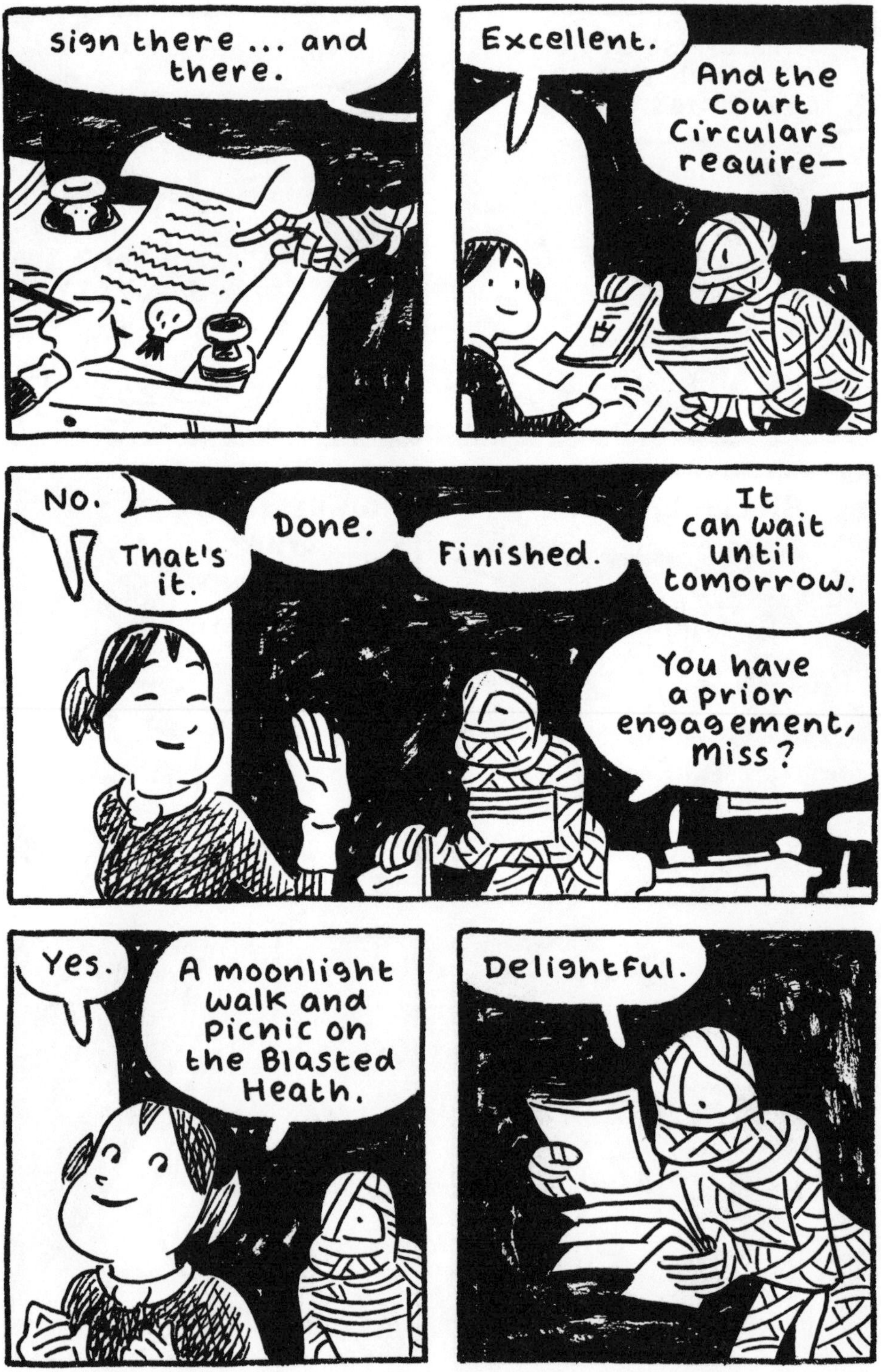
Sign there ... and there.
Excellent.
And the Court Circulars require—
No.
That's it.
Done.
Finished.
It can wait until tomorrow.
You have a prior engagement, Miss?
Yes.
A moonlight walk and picnic on the Blasted Heath.
Delightful.

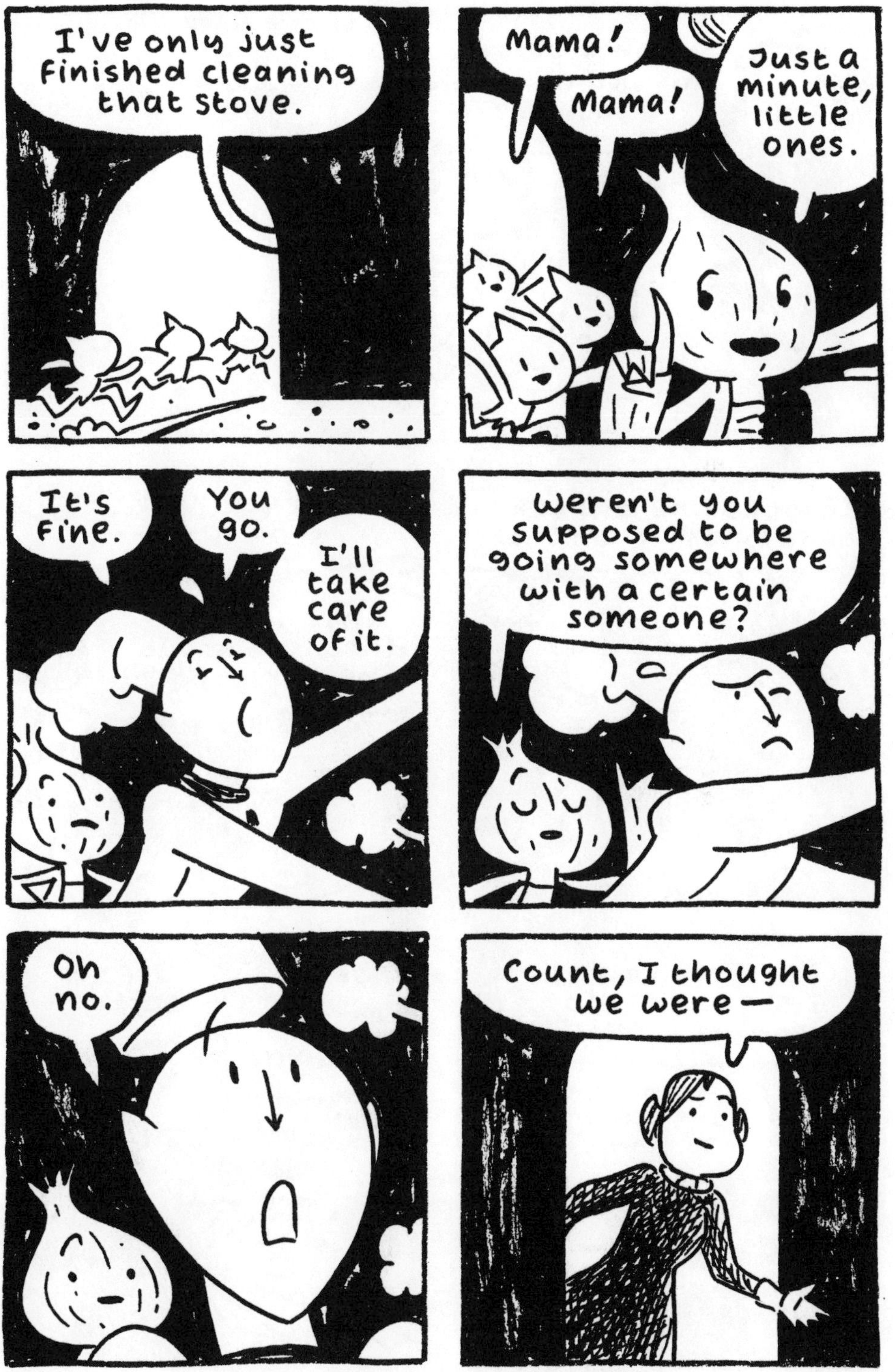
I've only just finished cleaning that stove.
Mama!
Mama!
Just a minute, little ones.
It's fine.
You go.
I'll take care of it.
Weren't you supposed to be going somewhere with a certain someone?
Oh no.
Count, I thought we were—

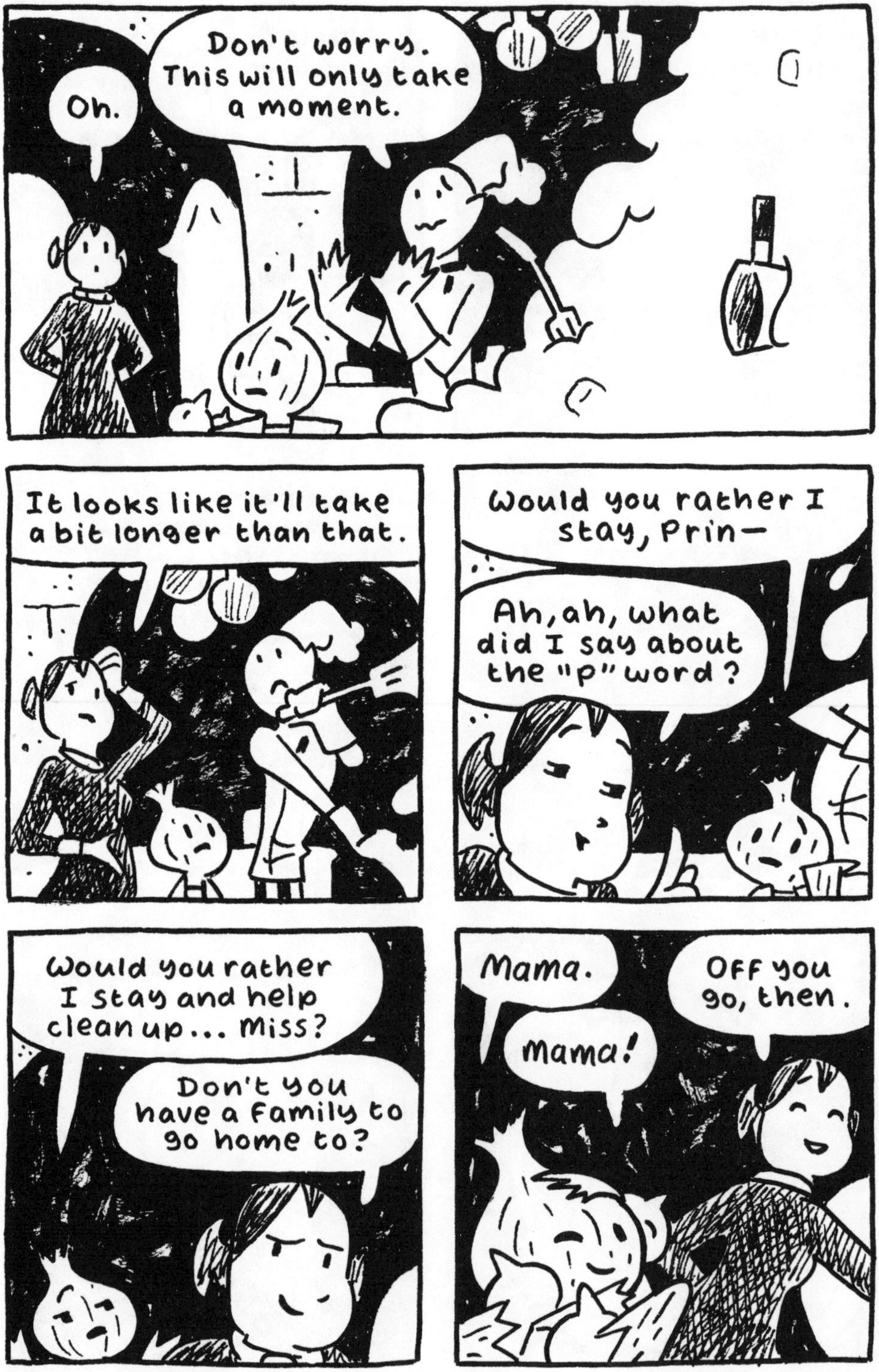
Oh.
Don't worry. This will only take a moment.
It looks like it'll take a bit longer than that.
Would you rather I stay, Prin—
Ah, ah, what did I say about the "p" word?
Would you rather I stay and help clean up... Miss?
Don't you have a family to go home to?
Mama.
Mama!
Off you go, then.

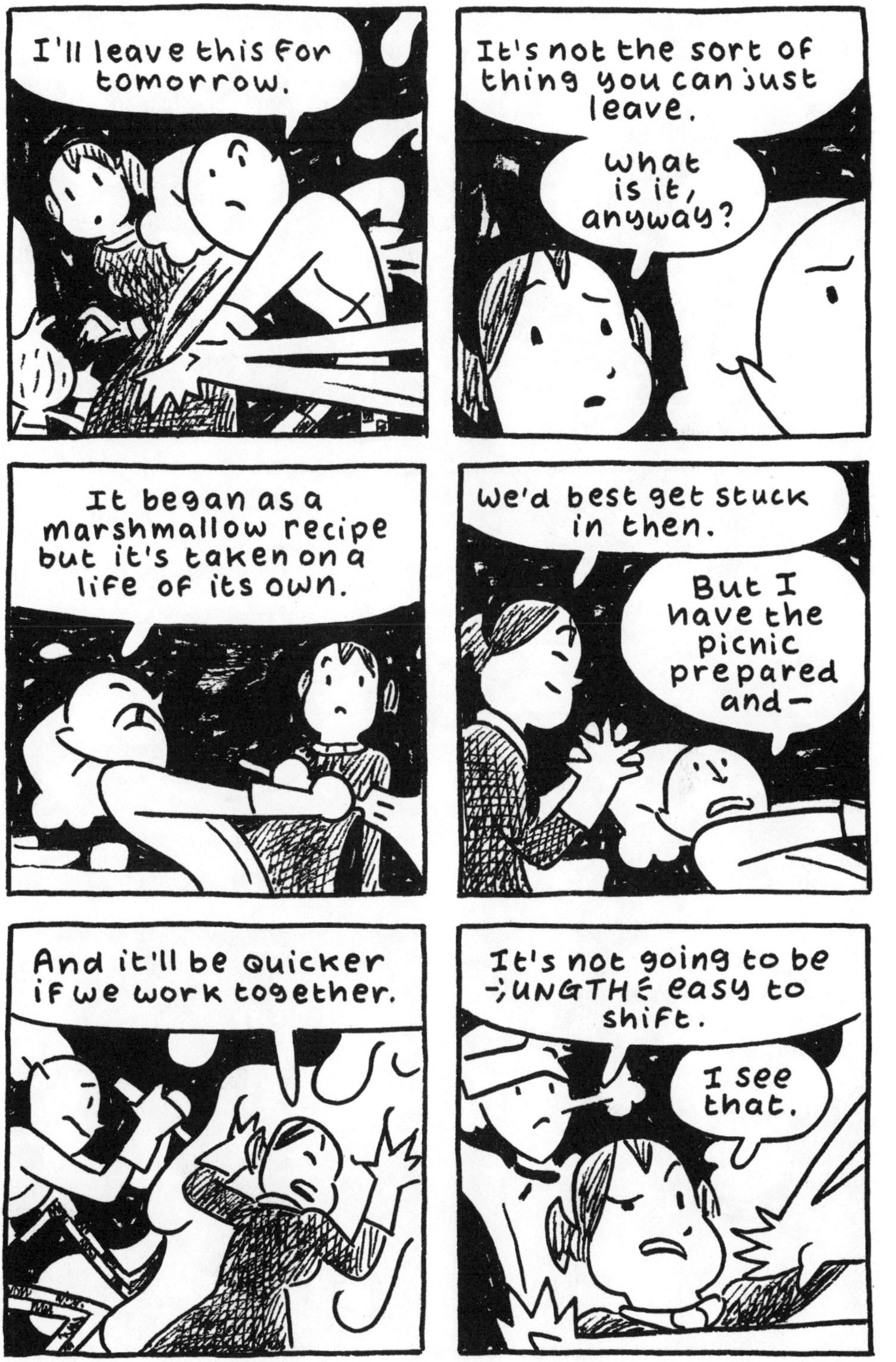
I'll leave this for tomorrow.
It's not the sort of thing you can just leave.
What is it, anyway?
It began as a marshmallow recipe but it's taken on a life of its own.
We'd best get stuck in then.
But I have the picnic prepared and—
And it'll be quicker if we work together.
It's not going to be UNGTH easy to shift.
I see that.

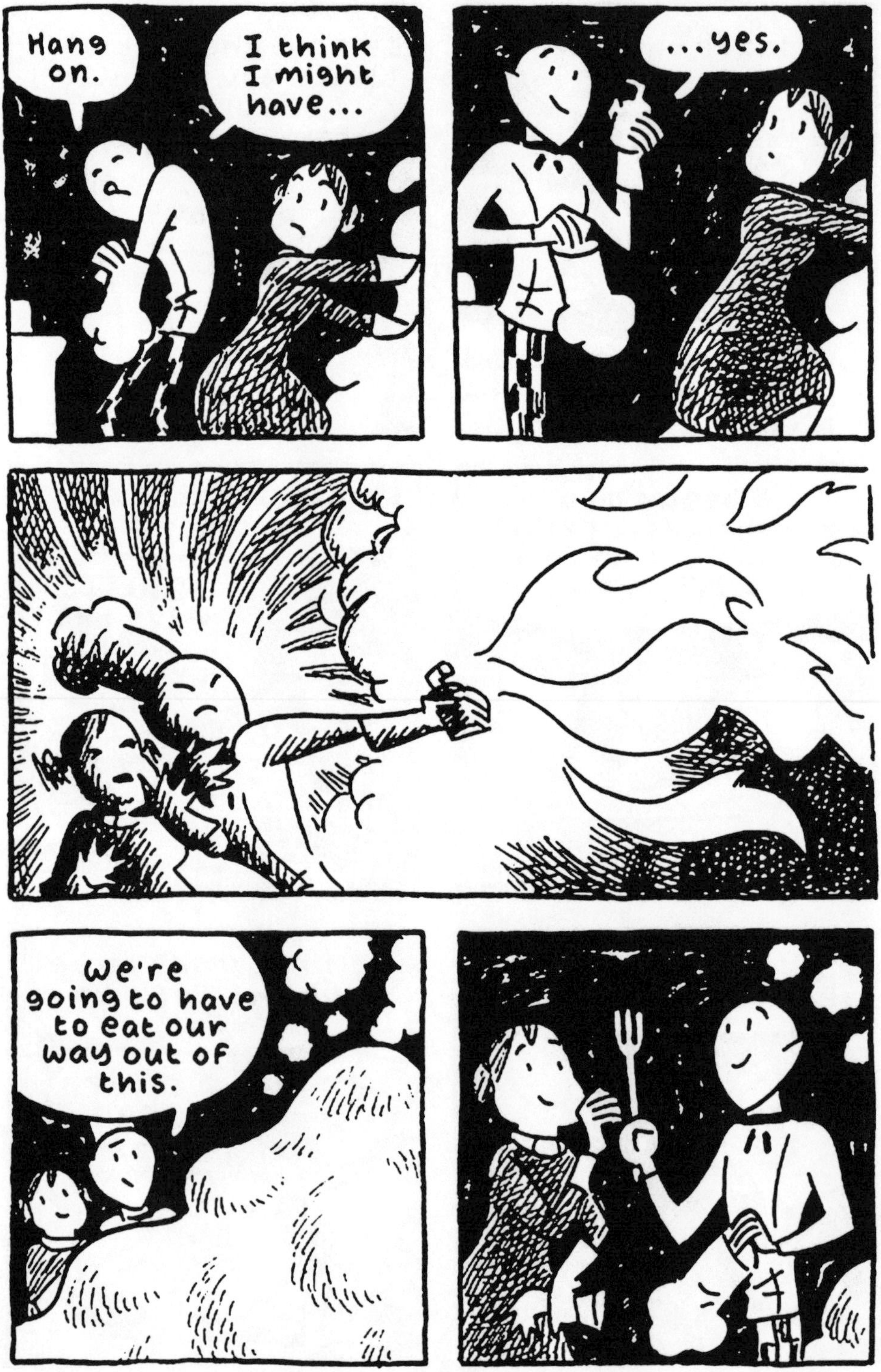
Hang on.
I think I might have...
...yes.
We're going to have to eat our way out of this.

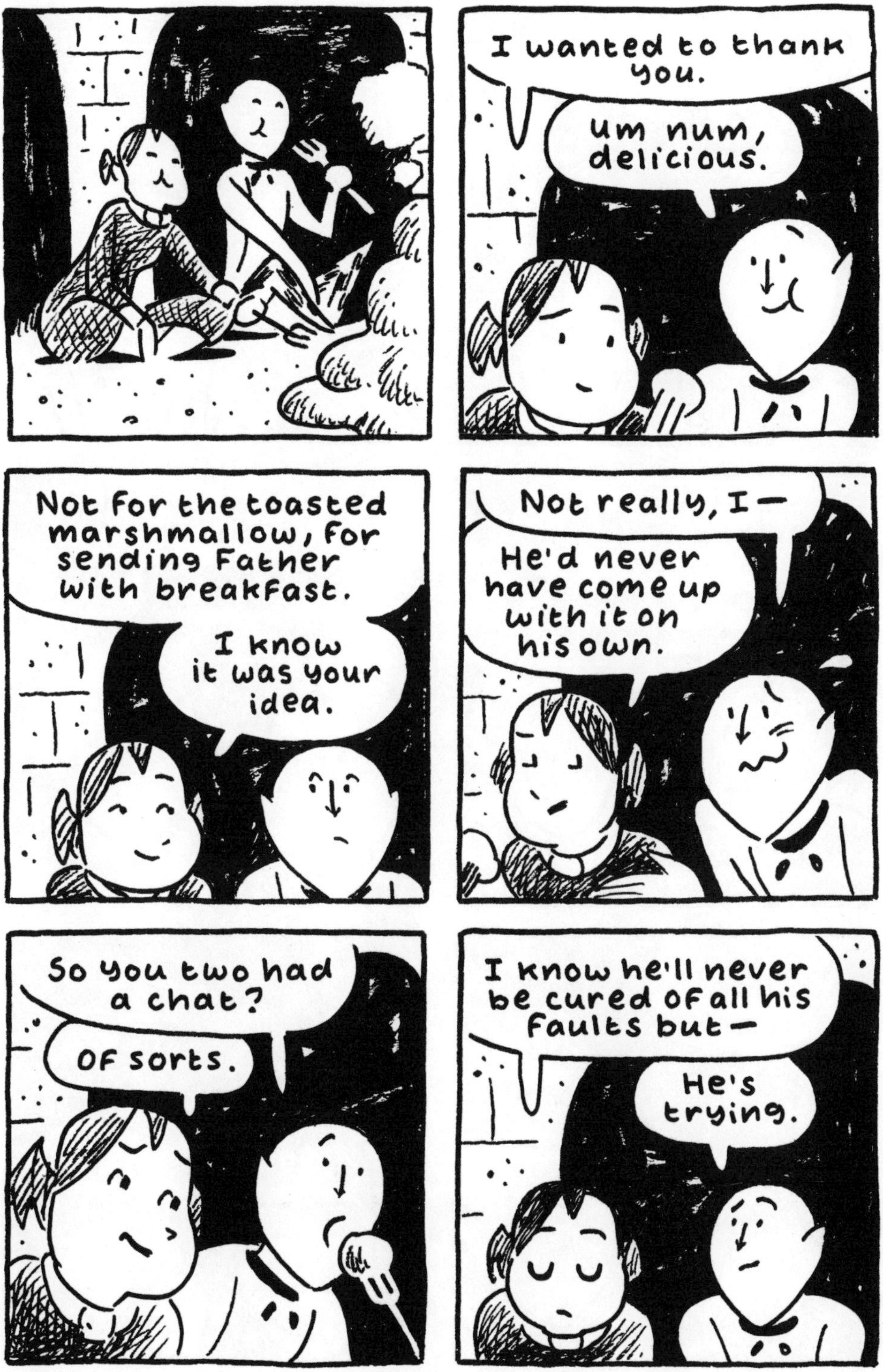
I wanted to thank you.
um num, delicious.
Not for the toasted marshmallow, for sending Father with breakfast.
I know it was your idea.
Not really, I—
He'd never have come up with it on his own.
So you two had a chat?
Of sorts.
I know he'll never be cured of all his faults but—
He's trying.

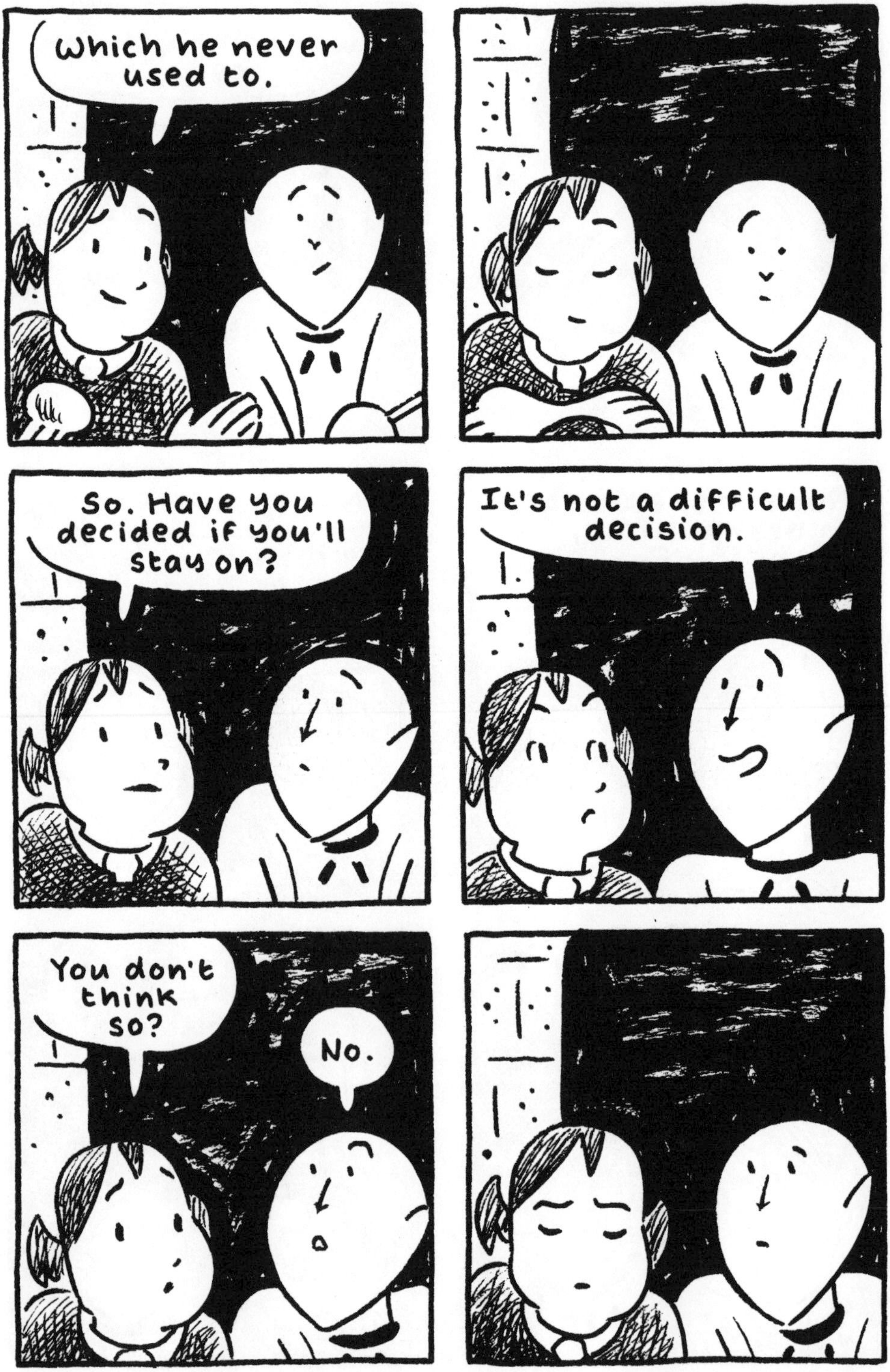
Which he never used to.
So. Have you decided if you'll stay on?
It's not a difficult decision.
You don't think so?
No.

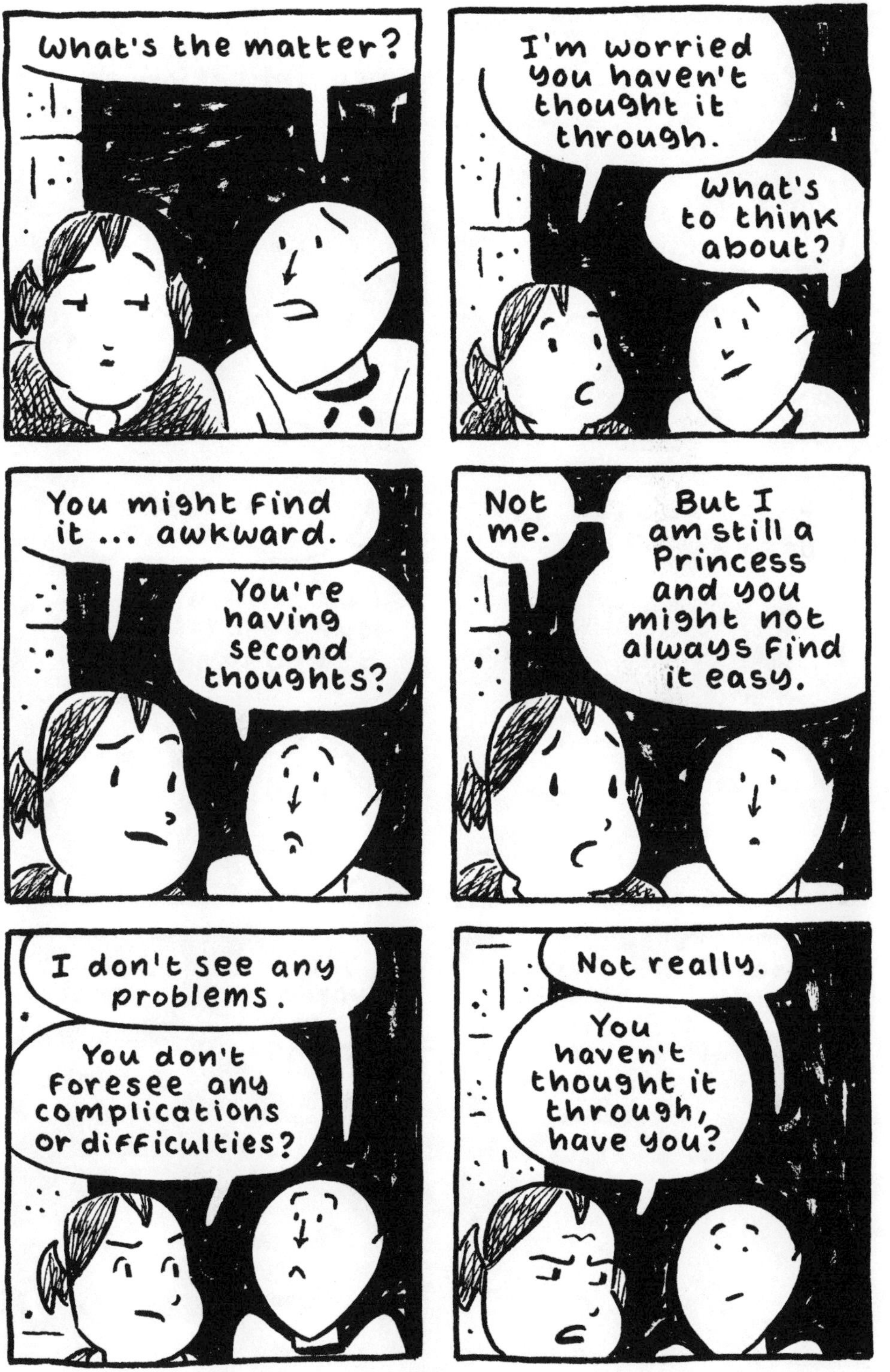
What's the matter?
I'm worried you haven't thought it through.
What's to think about?
You might find it ... awkward.
You're having second thoughts?
Not me.
But I am still a Princess and you might not always find it easy.
I don't see any problems.
You don't foresee any complications or difficulties?
Not really.
You haven't thought it through, have you?

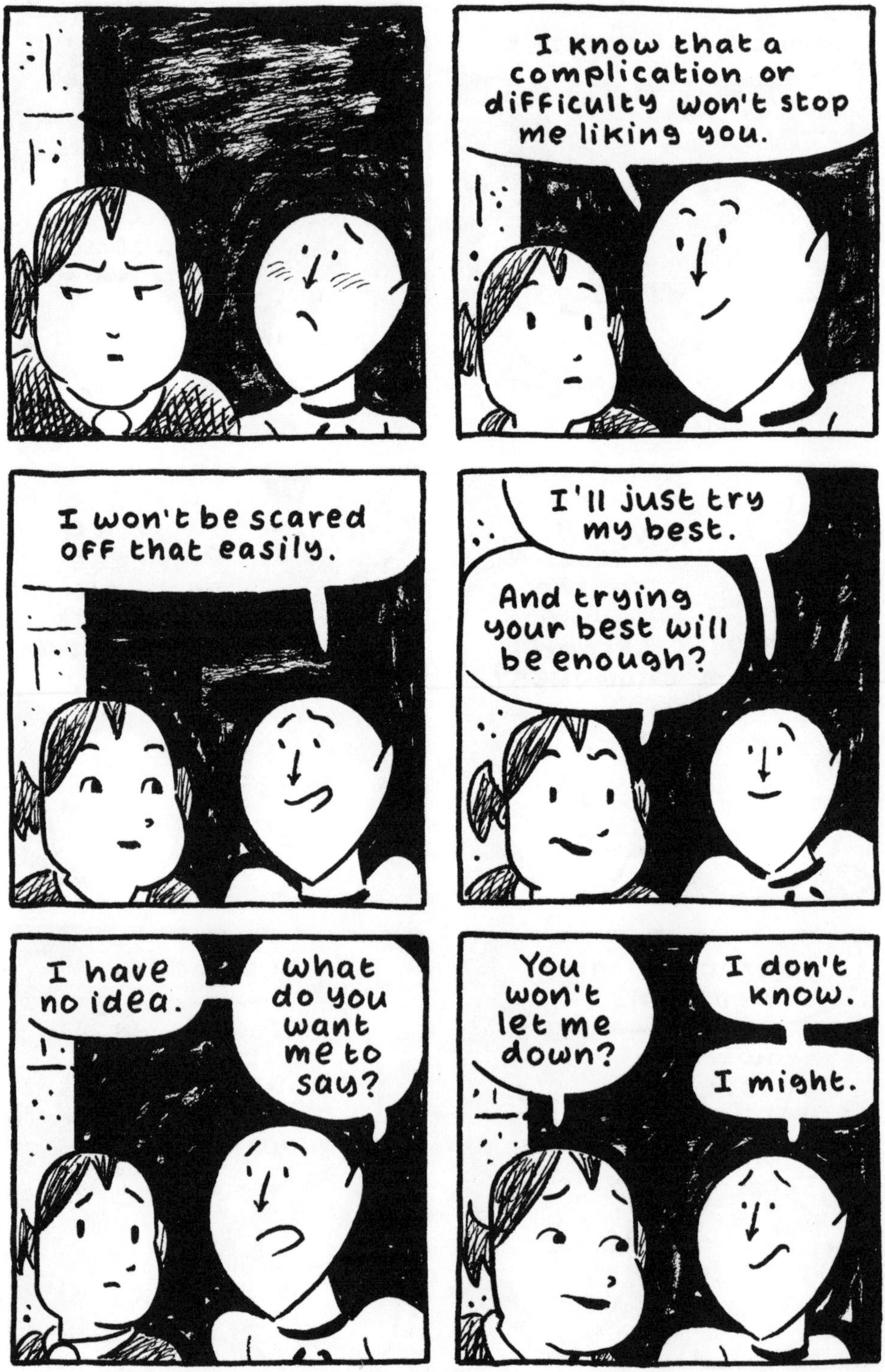
I know that a complication or difficulty won't stop me liking you.
I won't be scared off that easily.
I'll just try my best.
And trying your best will be enough?
I have no idea.
What do you want me to say?
You won't let me down?
I don't know.
I might.

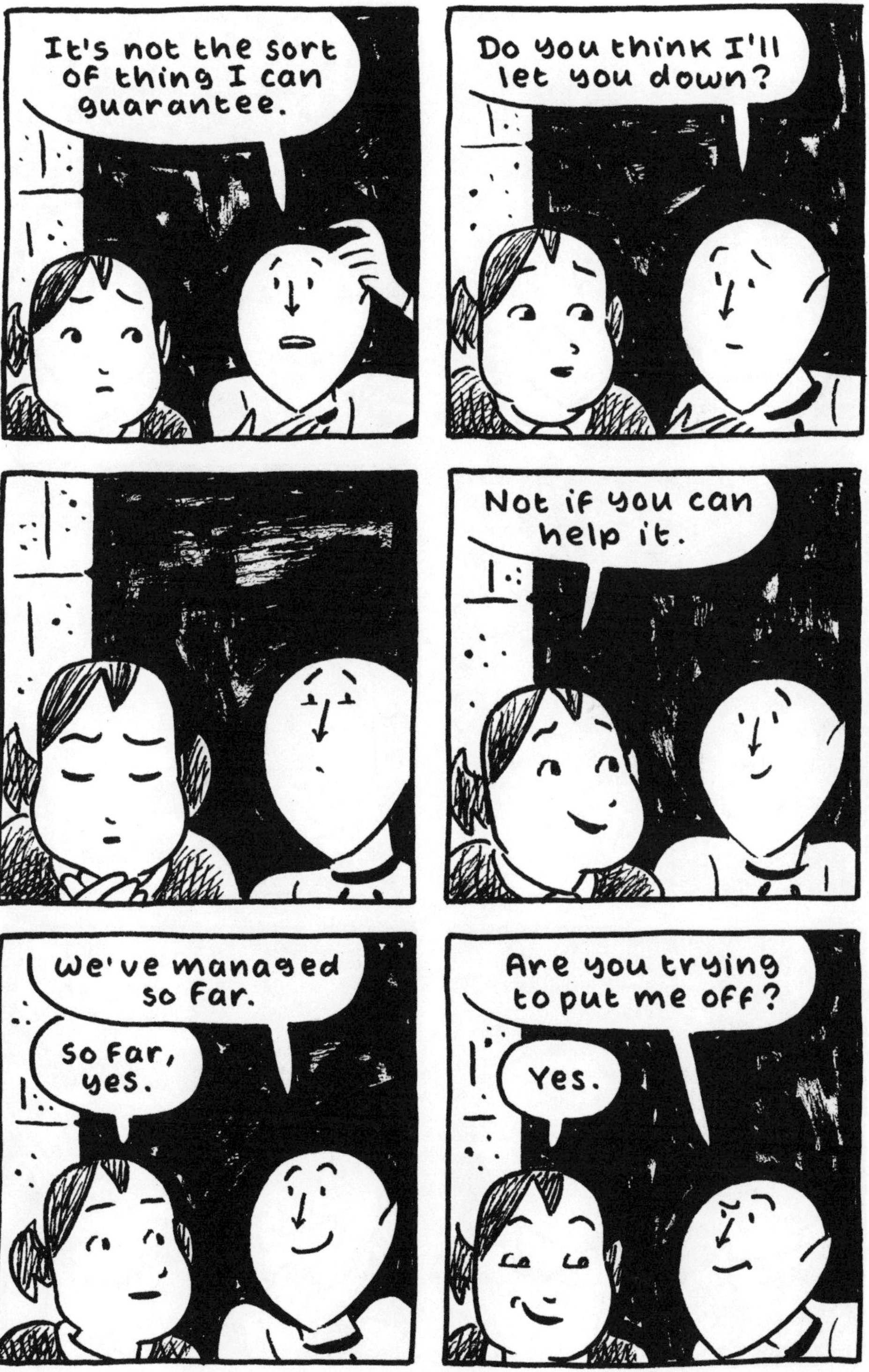
It's not the sort of thing I can guarantee.
Do you think I'll let you down?
Not if you can help it.
We've managed so far.
So far, yes.
Are you trying to put me off?
Yes.

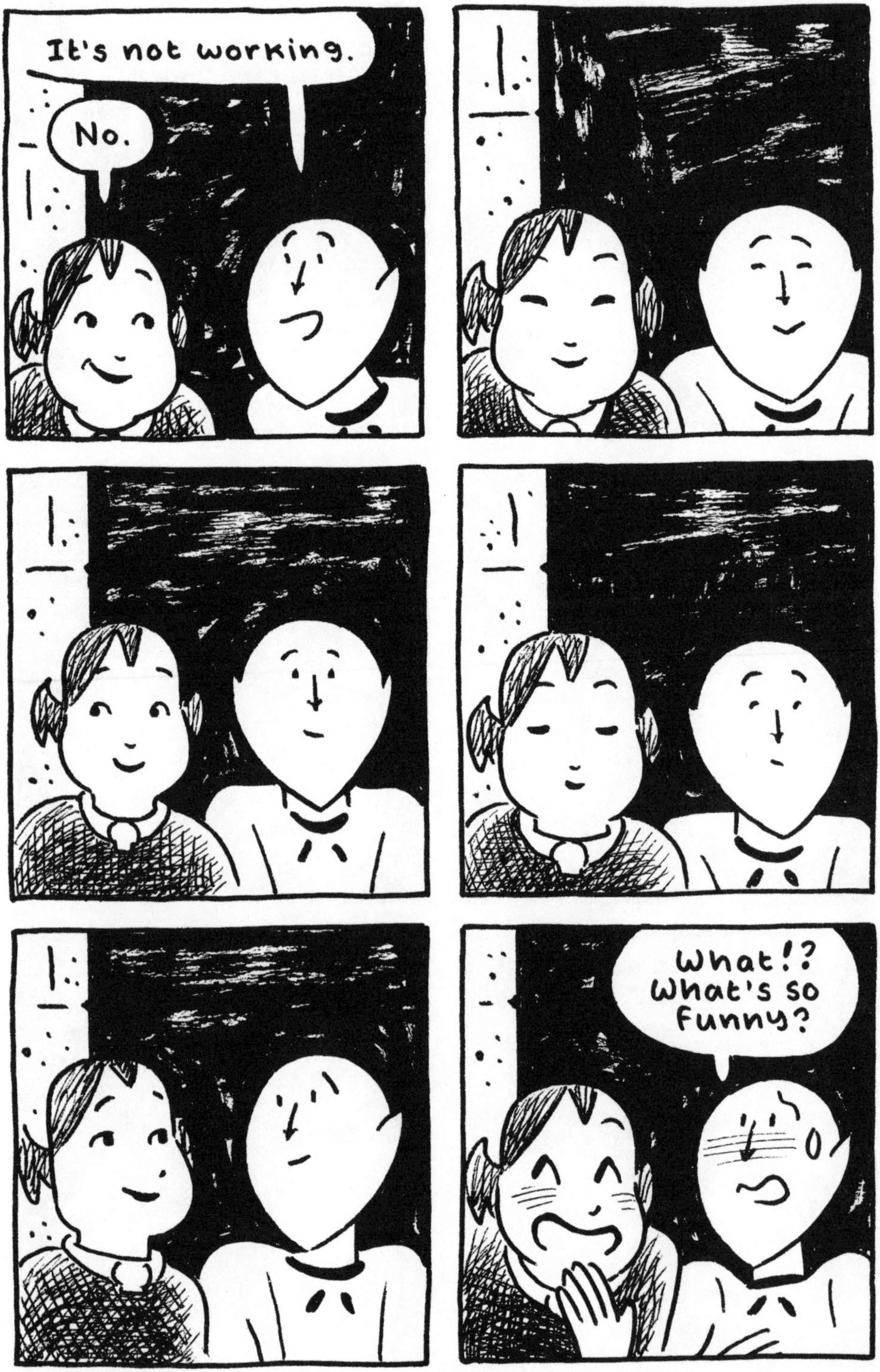
It's not working.
No.
What!? What's so funny?

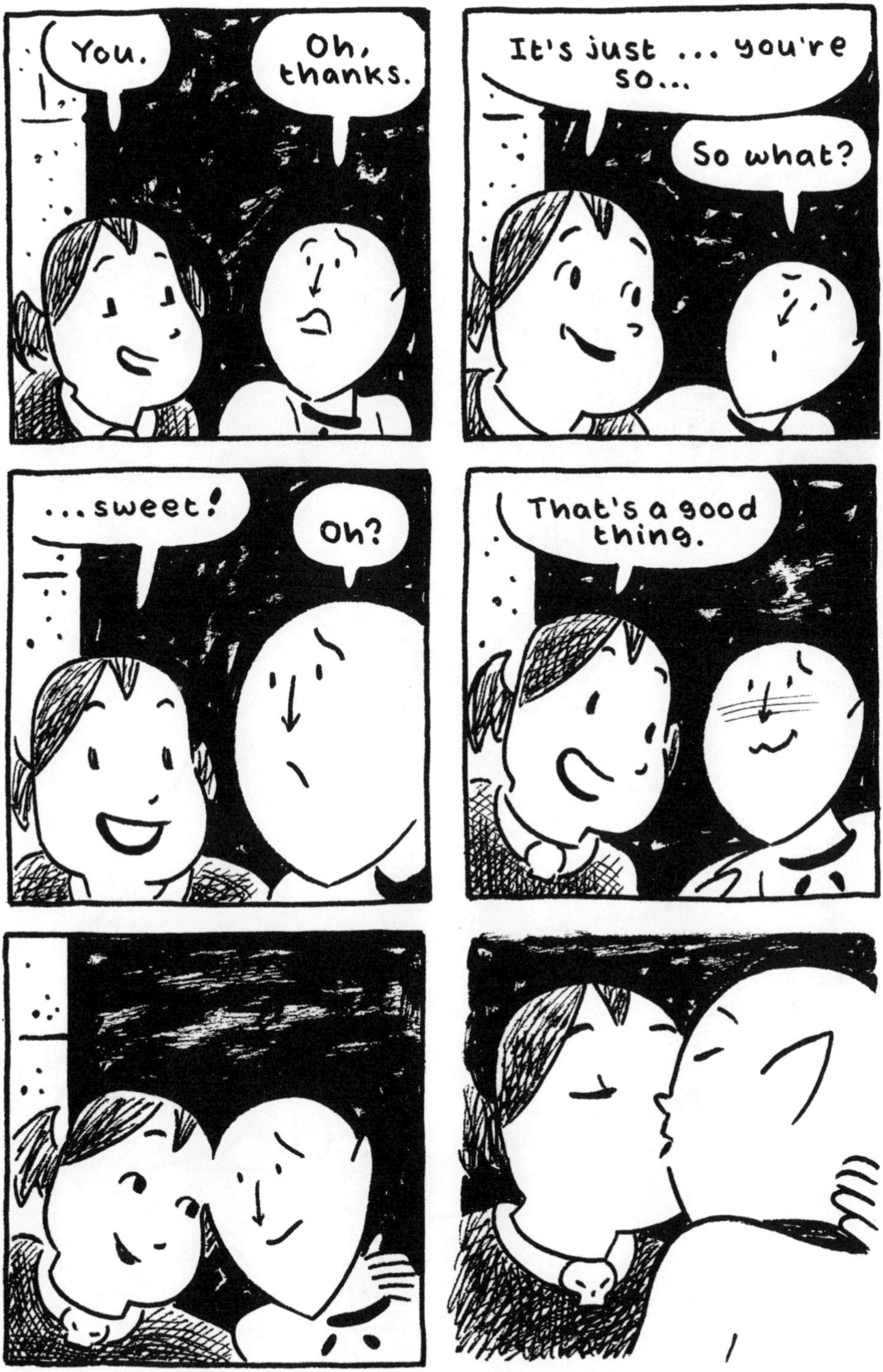
You.
Oh, thanks.
It's just ... you're so...
So what?
...sweet!
Oh?
That's a good thing.

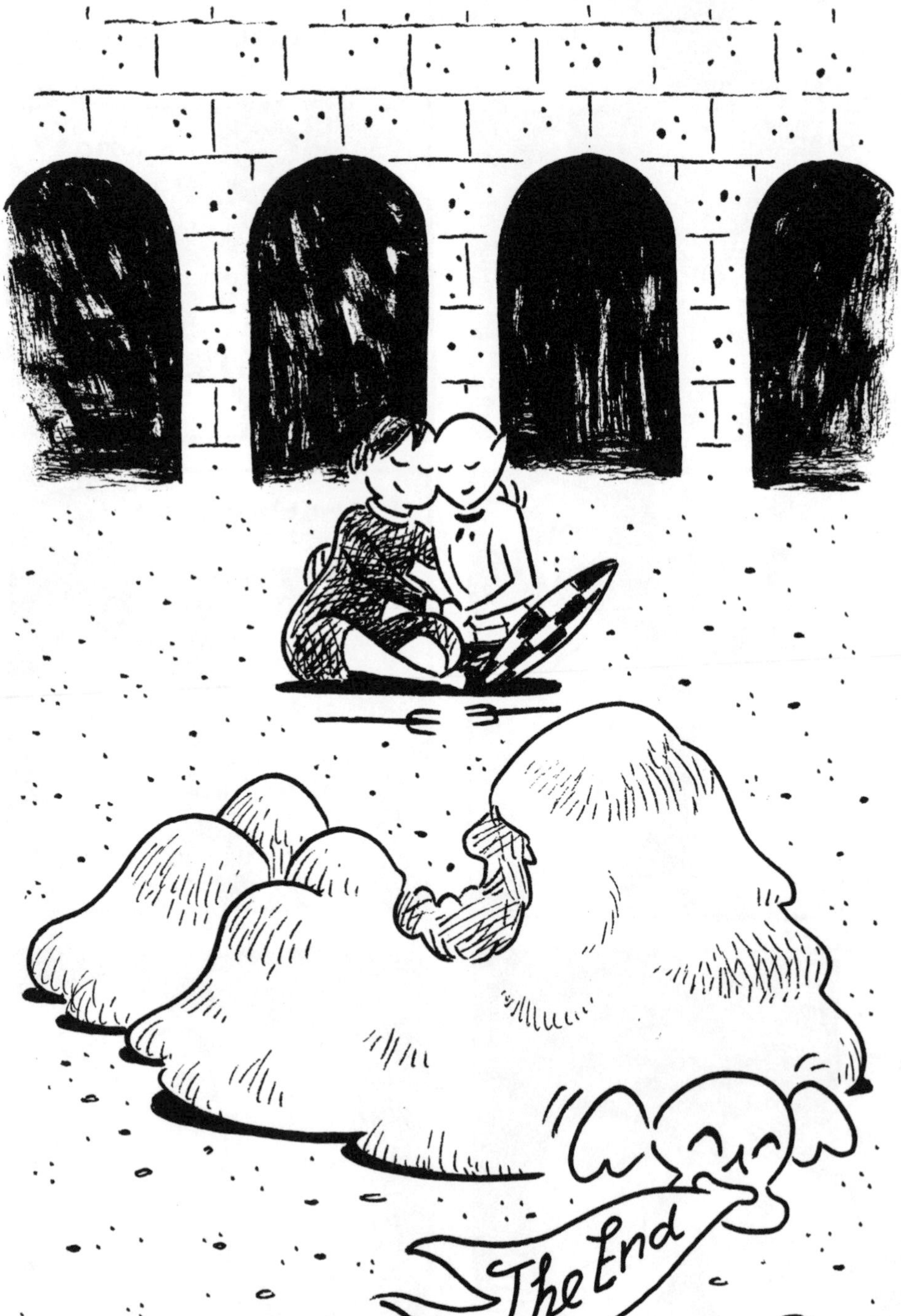
The End

# Sketches

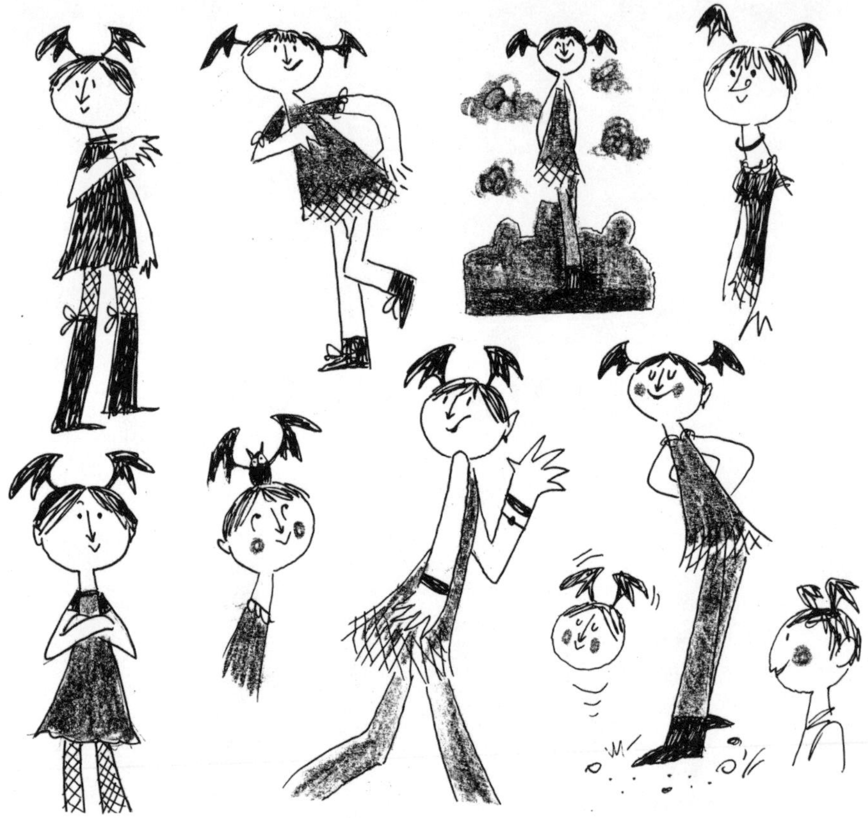

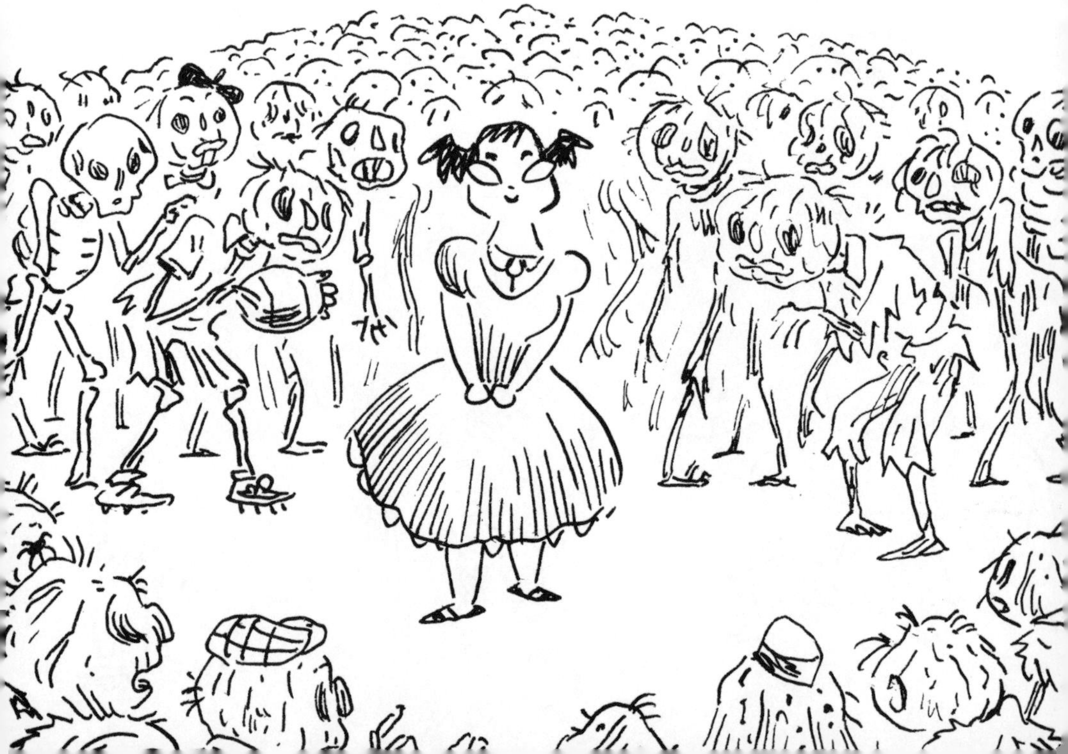

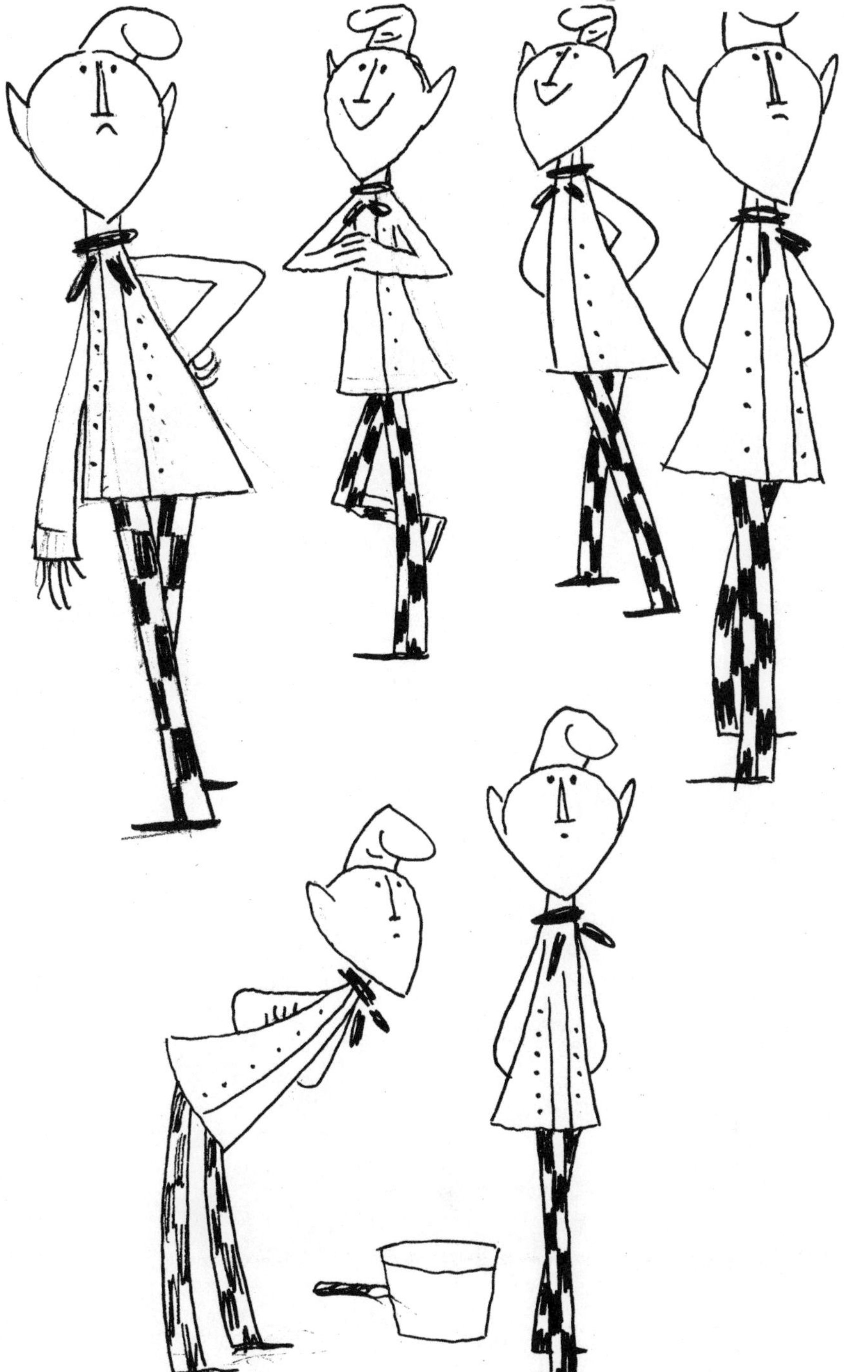

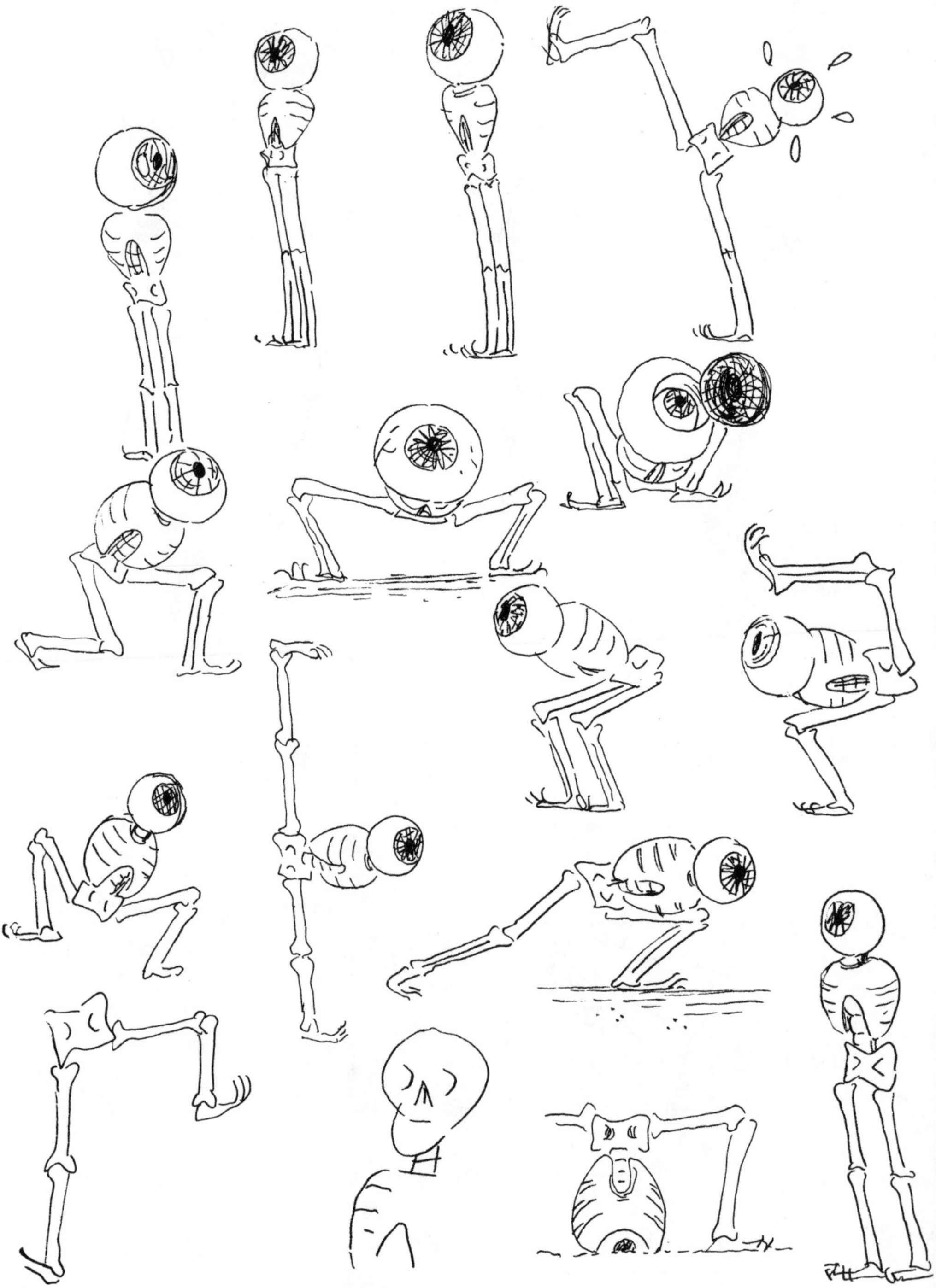

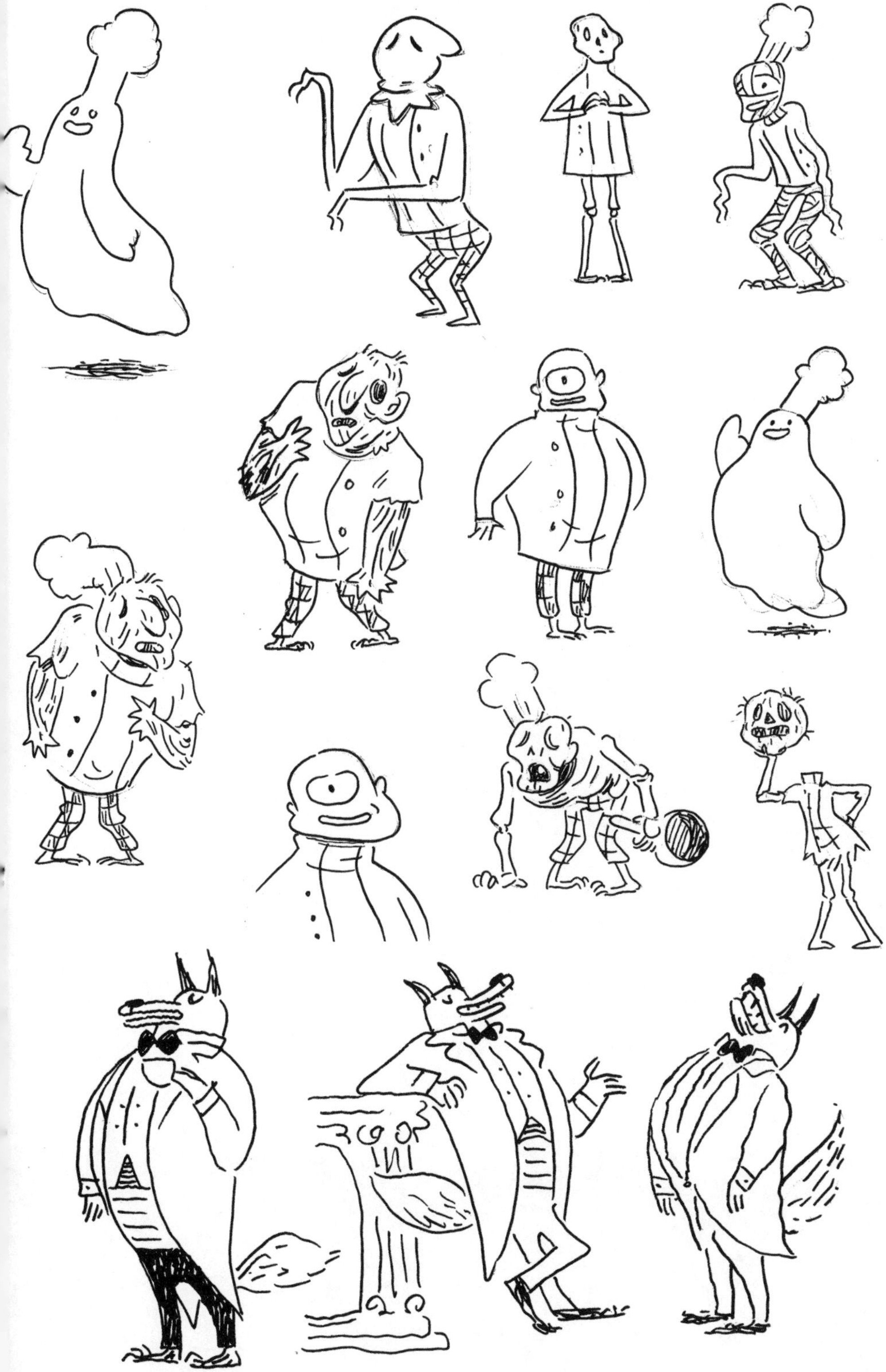

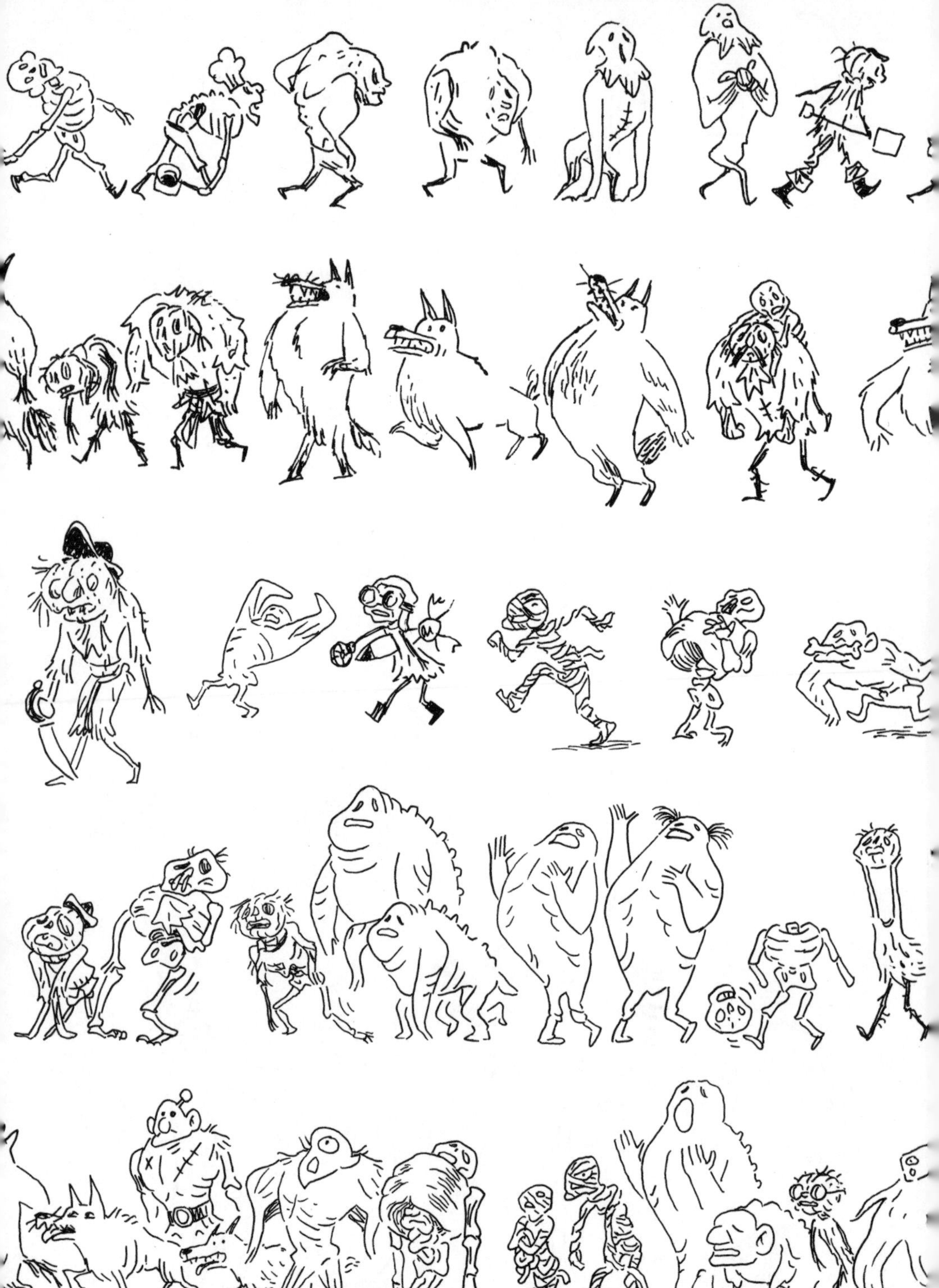